Praise for Larissa Reinhart's Cherry Tucker Mysteries

DEATH IN PERSPECTIVE (#4)

"*Death in Perspective* is one fasten-your-seatbelt, pedal-to-the-metal mystery, and Cherry Tucker is the perfect sleuth to have behind the wheel. Smart, feisty, as tough as she is tender, Cherry's got justice in her crosshairs, and *Death in Perspective* is an accomplished addition to this winning series."
– Tina Whittle,
Author of the Tai Randolph Mysteries

"Loved it! I feel I might have dated Cherry Tucker once, she's that real; she's also funny, tough, and brilliant. Now she's even involved in theatre—maybe that's where we met."
– Phillip DePoy,
Edgar Award Winning Author

"Reinhart succeeds in mixing laughter with the serious topic of cyber-bully through blogs and texts, all the while developing a chemistry between Cherry and Luke that absolutely sizzles."
– *Kings River Life Magazine*

"Cherry is a quirky spitfire that lights the match that sets her little town on fire. With a laugh here and a laugh there, I enjoyed this whodunit and I'm eager to see what happens next in the adventures of Cherry Tucker."
– *Dru's Book Musings*

"Artist and accidental detective Cherry Tucker goes back to high school and finds plenty of trouble and skeletons...Reinhart's charming, sweet-tea flavored series keeps getting better!"
– Gretchen Archer,
USA Today Bestselling Author of the Davis Way Crime Caper Series

D1562669

HIJACK IN ABSTRACT (#3)

"The fast-paced plot careens through small-town politics and deadly rivalries, with zany side trips through art-world shenanigans and romantic hijinx. Like front-porch lemonade, Reinhart's cast of characters offer a perfect balance of tart and sweet."

– Sophie Littlefield,
Bestselling Author of *A Bad Day for Sorry*

"Cherry is back–tart-tongued and full of sass. With her paint-stained fingers in every pie, she's in for a truckload of trouble."

– J.J. Murphy,
Author of the Algonquin Round Table Mysteries

"Bless her heart. Artist Cherry Tucker just can't help chasing after justice, even when it lands her up to her eyeballs in Russian gangsters, sexy exes, and treacherous truckers. A rambunctious mystery as Southern as chess pie and every bit as delectable."

– Jane Sevier,
Author of the Psychic Socialite 1930s Memphis Mysteries

"A true work of art...I didn't want this book to end! I was so caught up in Cherry's crazy life, I wanted to just keep reading."

– Gayle Trent,
Author of *Battered to Death*

"Reinhart manages to braid a complicated plot into a tight and funny tale...Cozy fans will love this latest Cherry Tucker mystery."

– Mary Marks,
New York Journal of Books

"Cherry Tucker's got an artist's palette of problems, but she handles them better than da Vinci on a deadline. Bust out your gesso and get primed for humor, hijackings, and a handful of hunks!"

– Diane Vallere,
Author of the Style & Error and Mad for Mod Mystery Series

STILL LIFE IN BRUNSWICK STEW (#2)

"Reinhart's country-fried mystery is as much fun as a ride on the Tilt-a-Whirl at a state fair. Her sleuth wields a paintbrush and unravels clues with equal skill and flair. Readers who like a little small-town charm with their mysteries will enjoy Reinhart's series."

— Denise Swanson,
New York Times Bestselling Author of the Scumble River and Devereaux's Dime Store Mysteries

"*Still Life in Brunswick Stew* proves beyond doubt that Larissa Reinhart and her delightful amateur sleuth Cherry Tucker will be around to entertain us for many books to come."

— Lois Winston,
Author of the Anastasia Pollack Crafting Mystery series

"Cherry Tucker finds trouble without even looking for it, and plenty of it finds her in *Still Life in Brunswick Stew*...this mystery keeps you laughing and guessing from the first page to the last. A whole-hearted five stars."

— Denise Grover Swank,
New York Times and *USA Today* Bestselling Author

"Reinhart lined up suspects like a pinsetter in a bowling alley, and darned if I could figure out which ones to knock down...Can't wait to see what Cherry paints herself into next."

— Donnell Ann Bell,
Bestselling Author of *The Past Came Hunting*

"The hilariously droll Larissa Reinhart cooks up a quirky and entertaining page-turner! This charming mystery is delightfully Southern, surprisingly edgy, and deliciously unpredictable."

— Hank Phillippi Ryan,
Agatha, Anthony and Macavity Award-Winning Author

PORTRAIT OF A DEAD GUY (#1)

"*Portrait of a Dead Guy* is an entertaining mystery full of quirky characters and solid plotting...Highly recommended for anyone who likes their mysteries strong and their mint juleps stronger!"

— Jennie Bentley,
New York Times Bestselling Author of *Flipped Out*

"Reinhart is a truly talented author and this book was one of the best cozy mysteries we reviewed this year...We highly recommend this book to all lovers of mystery books. Our Rating: 4.5 Stars."

— *Mystery Tribune*

"The tone of this marvelously cracked book is not unlike Sophie Littlefield's brilliant *A Bad Day for Sorry*, as author Reinhart dishes out shovelfuls of ribald humor and mayhem."

— Betty Webb,
Mystery Scene Magazine

"Larissa Reinhart's masterfully crafted whodunit, *Portrait of a Dead Guy*, provides high-octane action with quirky, down-home characters and a trouble-magnet heroine who'll steal readers' hearts."

—Debby Giusti,
Author of *The Captain's Mission* and *The Colonel's Daughter*

"A fun, fast-paced read and a rollicking start to her Cherry Tucker Mystery Series. If you like your stories southern-fried with a side of romance, this book's for you!"

— Leslie Tentler,
Author of *Midnight Caller*

DEATH IN PERSPECTIVE

**The Cherry Tucker Mystery Series
by Larissa Reinhart**

Novels

PORTRAIT OF A DEAD GUY (#1)
STILL LIFE IN BRUNSWICK STEW (#2)
HIJACK IN ABSTRACT (#3)
DEATH IN PERSPECTIVE (#4)

Novellas

QUICK SKETCH (prequel to PORTRAIT)
(in HEARTACHE MOTEL)

DEATH IN PERSPECTIVE

A Cherry Tucker Mystery

LARISSA REINHART

HENERY PRESS

DEATH IN PERSPECTIVE
A Cherry Tucker Mystery
Part of the Henery Press Mystery Collection

First Edition
Trade paperback edition | June 2014

Henery Press
www.henerypress.com

Copyright © 2014 by Larissa Hoffman
Author photograph by Scott Asano

ISBN-13: 978-1-940976-18-1

Printed in the United States of America

To Trey, Sophie, and Luci.
You are my greatest blessing.

ACKNOWLEDGMENTS

A huge thank you to Diana Concepcion, Noel Holland, and Phillip Depoy for your advice and expertise. Also to my fellow hens Gretchen Archer, Terri L. Austin, and LynDee Walker for their friendship and input. Gina Neibrugge and Sally Reinhart for helping me to plot over margaritas. To all the Mystery Minions for their friendship and support. Love you guys! To Dru Ann Love for the cover release opportunities and encouragement. To Ann Charles for reading while writing and preparing for a move. Tina Whittle for reading and recommending Tai's doppleganger to your fans. Trey and the girls for putting up with a wife/mother with W.S.B.S. (writer's scattered brain syndrome). And to everyone at Henery Press who puts Cherry Tucker in readers' hands, especially my incredibly talented and indefatigable editor, Kendel Flaum, who has taken a fledgling press and given it giant raptor wings.

ONE

Someone should have told me Maranda Pringle was dead. For the past twenty minutes, I'd been sitting in her office, picking at my Toulouse La'Lilac painted nails and wondering where in the hell Miss Pringle could be. Hindsight later taught me she'd be found somewhere in that mystical realm between the Peerless Day Academy and the Great Beyond, but currently, it ticked me off that Miss Pringle had clearly forgotten I had a twelve o'clock appointment with Principal Cleveland. I had spent plenty of time waiting on principals in my previous life as a high school troublemaker, so waiting on one now had brought back feelings of anxiety.

Which was why my nails appeared so spotty.

Before I had the nerve to leave Miss Pringle's small antechamber and knock on Principal Cleveland's door, another woman entered Miss Pringle's room and proceeded to stare at me for a long five seconds before finding her voice. Her blunt blonde bob, expensive blue suit, and no-nonsense designer pumps gave her a look of authority, but a snazzy, silk scarf knotted around her neck said, "I'm also fashionable."

"Who are you?" she asked. "Why are you in Miss Pringle's office?"

"I'm Cherry Tucker. I'm waiting for Principal Cleveland to discuss my clearance for working with the drama department on the backdrop and props for *Romeo and Juliet*."

My fingers flew to smooth my cornsilk blonde strands and straighten my belted Bert and Ernie t-shirt dress. I had figured school personnel would appreciate *Sesame Street* characters as educational innovators. And as most teachers I knew wore khakis and polo shirts and I owned neither a khaki nor a polo, retrofitted *Sesame Street* attire from the Big Boys department would have to do for an interview.

"I am the assistant principal, Brenda Cooke. Why would the drama department need help with the stage art? We have a fully equipped art department."

I waited a moment to see if the question was rhetorical. Then I remembered this was a school and teachers expected answers. "I got a call from a Mr. Tinsley needing an artist to help with 'original art pieces' for his 'avant-garde' musical production of *Romeo and Juliet*. Why he doesn't ask the art teacher, I haven't the faintest. But here I am."

When she didn't respond, I added, "I'm an artist. Portrait artist by trade, but classically trained at Savannah College of Art and Design in a number of genres. I'm also a graduate of Halo High School, and although I know your school is located near Line Creek, I figure you don't have the animosity toward Halo's Fighting Angels that Line Creek Legions does. As you're a private school and all."

"I'm not sure about this," said Ms. Cooke. "I can get you the background check paperwork, though. At the moment, I need you to leave this office. Why don't you leave your card with me and Principal Cleveland or I will get back with you."

I knew what that meant. I stuck my proverbial foot in the metaphorical door. "How about I swing by later today? Your drama teacher wanted me to start as soon as possible."

"Today is not a good day." Ms. Cooke's shoulders sagged, and she dropped her principal swagger. "Actually, we just learned we lost Miss Pringle this past weekend. Principal Cleveland is at her home right now and this afternoon we're having an emergency staff meeting."

"Bless your heart. I'm sorry to hear that. I had no idea." My cheeks reddened at my hustle to gain a job when the school had just lost their secretary.

"I'm sorry I wasn't aware of your appointment." She offered a faint smile and took my business card. "After the staff meeting, I'll talk to Mr. Tinsley, our drama teacher, and find out what's going on. He has his own budget and tends to make unilateral decisions. I didn't realize he had spoken to Mr. Cleveland about hiring you."

"No problem." I smiled. "I'm very sorry to hear about Miss Pringle, though. Was she sick?"

"It was unexpected."

I reached for Ms. Cooke's hands and squeezed. "That's just horrible."

Ms. Cooke nodded. "Thank you. It's tragic, but I'm worried about the school. I don't want to see our students suffer from this loss."

"Of course." I dropped her hands and turned to pick up my portfolio bag.

"I'll get you the fingerprint cards and forms for the background check. Drop them off at your convenience." She moved to stoop behind Miss Pringle's desk, thumbed through her file drawer, and returned with the forms.

I slipped them into my satchel. "Thank you, ma'am. Sorry again to hear about poor Miss Pringle."

I left Ms. Cooke in the small office and walked into the large reception area. Students chatted in small groups and harried teachers trotted through, clutching reams of copies in their arms. At the front desk, I eyed the woman who had sent me to poor Miss Pringle's office and wondered why no one had told her Miss Pringle would no longer take visitors. The brunette did not have the khakis look. She had the sleek haircut, chunky jewelry, and tasteful yet cleavage-baring top of someone who had never considered pursuing the not-for-profit world of teaching.

I stopped at the front desk and leaned a hip against the counter.

Mrs. Brunette raised a freshly waxed eyebrow and ran her eyes over Bert and Ernie. "Can I help you? Why aren't you in uniform? Are you new?"

"I'm not a student. I'm Cherry Tucker, the artist. You just sent me to Mr. Cleveland's office."

Mrs. Brunette turned slightly in her chair, enough to deliver the message that she didn't want to talk to me. "Right, I forgot. Did you need directions somewhere?"

"No, there's something you need to know. It's about sending folks into Miss Pringle's office."

Mrs. Brunette sighed. "Yes?"

"Don't do it anymore today."

"Thank you," she wiggled French manicured fingers in dismissal.

"Don't you want to know why?" The funny thing about dismissing me, it makes me want to stay. "Are you on staff here? You don't look like a teacher."

"Good Lord, no. I'm a parent. We're required to volunteer and this is one of my days." She readjusted so I could get the full frontal. Her cleavage showed a lift and separate appropriate for packaging bowling balls. Except she didn't need a bra. "I'm Pamela Hargraves. We live in Ballantyne."

Ballantyne Estates was an exclusive, gated community in Aureate County. Ballantyne culled folks who liked horse stables and golf course views with their country living. That and easy interstate access to Atlanta. Although inside Forks County, Peerless Day Academy hovered near the border of neighboring Aureate County because of a strange bite chomped out of Forks County's northwestern corner. A nibble almost taken from the township of Line Creek, which ticked those city officials off to no end.

"I suppose a lot of students come from Ballantyne. Y'all aren't too far from here. Like a twenty minute drive?"

"Yes. There's a bus, but my Kadence refuses to take it."

"Of course she does."

"We gave her a Volvo. Totally safe, but she's not allowed to drive it until she's sixteen."

"I know how frustrating that is. I started driving my Grandpa Ed's tractor when I was twelve. I learned how to drive the Jeep at fourteen. Stick shift, too. Used to take it out to the back forty to bring in the cows. Seemed ridiculous I wasn't allowed on the roads for another two years."

Pamela cocked her head, unsure if I was serious. "Anyway, what did you need?"

"It's Miss Pringle. She passed yesterday. So don't send anyone to her room today."

Pamela leaned forward, gripping my arm with her multi-ringed fingers. "No. Way. That bitch is dead?"

I cleared my throat and gave her the stare my now deceased Grandma Jo had used when I forgot my manners. "Yes, ma'am. Poor Miss Pringle."

"Have you met Miss Pringle?" Pamela wrinkled her nose.

"No, but I know enough not to speak ill of the dead."

"I should be sorry, but that woman made Kadence's life miserable."

I know this is where a better person should not give in to the call of gossip, particularly since Pamela Hargraves didn't seem to have a remorseful bone in her toned and botoxed body, but sometimes I'm just not a better person. Instead, I grabbed a nearby chair and scooted in next to her.

"What did Miss Pringle do to Kadence? I just assumed she was some kind of spinster with love in her heart for children. I also figured her for the house full of cats type."

In my imagination, Miss Pringle secretly gave butterscotch candies to the troublemakers leaving the principal's office. She knew the troublemaker didn't mean to bust Elvira Jenkins' nose. Fists tended to fly when Elvira made comments about the troublemaker's mother and fatherless state.

"Spinster with love in her heart for children? Ha. Maranda Pringle never met a child she liked," said Pamela. "And I guess you could call her a spinster, but that's by choice. Her legs have trouble closing. Ask Principal Cleveland. And Coach Newcomb. Actually, may as well ask some Peerless fathers, too."

"Whoa. I guess she didn't have a house full of cats either."

Pamela turned in her chair. "Chantelle, can you grab me a yearbook?" She waited for a young girl to flit to another part of the room, bring back the thick book, and return to the corner where the girl and her friends loitered in matching gray plaid uniforms.

Flipping through the yearbook, Pamela stopped on the administration page and tapped on a picture. "That is Maranda Pringle."

The color photo showed a platinum blonde thirty-something with green eyes, an impish smile, and gleaming white teeth.

"Not the Miss Pringle I had imagined," I said.

"That woman made Kadence miserable. Those girls, too." Pamela jerked her head to the huddle of seventeen-year-olds in the corner. "They're office helpers. Part of a work experience class run by Mrs. Overmeyer. It's hard for her to find students to work in the office."

"What did Miss Pringle do to the girls?"

"She's plain ol' mean. Snarky. Gives them crap jobs. Poor Kadence. One of her teachers sent her to Principal Cleveland's office. Said Kade talked too much in class and didn't pay attention or some nonsense. Miss Pringle had her in tears by the time Kadence had to go in to speak to Cleveland."

"What happened?"

"It's not what Maranda Pringle said, it's how she said it. The words didn't matter. Something about being pretty and popular and boys. Things that should be a compliment, but when Maranda Pringle says them, they sound like a knife to the heart. Kadence wanted me to take her out of Peerless and put her in public school. Can you imagine?"

Considering I had graduated from public school, I could not imagine. But I could understand how pretty words could get twisted to sound ugly.

"Poor Kadence," I said. "Why would the school keep Miss Pringle if she was so horrible to the students?"

"Well, she had Principal Cleveland eating out of her hand for one thing. And two, she's really good at her job. God, that cyberbullying thing last year really could have blown up on them if it wasn't for Maranda Pringle's quick thinking."

Pamela thumbed through the yearbook to the sophomore section and her finger landed on another photo, this time a young girl. "This poor thing committed suicide last year. We had a rough year, but Maranda Pringle saved the school."

"I had no idea," I said. "I vaguely remember hearing about a teen suicide, but I figured she was a victim of depression or something."

"Thanks to Miss Pringle, the news didn't get much coverage and her parents were too grief-stricken to care. I would have yelled my head off if that had happened to Kadence, but Ellis Madsen's parents moved away instead."

"Poor things."

Pamela sniffed. "Raise your kids to be strong. When Miss Pringle made Kadence cry, I told Kade she should not give a flying flip what some secretary thinks. These students have to build a strong backbone for today's world. Teens will always play head games, but now they take that crap online."

"Dang," I said. "That reminds me of something. I have my own Miss Pringle to deal with and I never thought about what could be happening online. My recent financial situation has limited my Internet options. I haven't checked my website or media pages in a long time."

"Don't you have an app on your phone?" Pamela pulled out her bejeweled phone and slid her finger across the screen. It brightened, and she tapped on a gleaming box. "I'll friend you, and we'll see what's on your wall."

I spelled as Pamela thumbed my name into the question mark box, then peered over her shoulder to view my page. "I have some messages from college friends. That's nice."

"You've also been tagged in a bunch of photos with this guy and girl. Aren't they a cute couple?" Pamela held the phone closer to her face, squinting. "Hang on, I want to make the pictures bigger. Wow, he's a looker."

My stomach landed somewhere near my toes. "Dark curly hair, gray eyes, and dimples? Body of a Greek God? Square jaw and chiseled cheekbones?"

"Oh yeah, although I can't see the dimples." Pamela enlarged the screen.

"Who tagged me?"

"A Shawna Branson. But you're not in any of these pictures. Looks like the girl is Tara Mayfield, but the guy doesn't have an account. Wait, Shawna's written his name in the comments."

"Luke Harper."

"Yes. And the comment says, 'Congratulations, Tara. You and Luke Harper are the perfect couple. Don't worry about that crazy ex-girlfriend, Cherry Tucker.'"

I chewed the inside of my cheek instead of saying what wasn't appropriate for a school.

"There are more pictures. Do you want to see them?" Pamela held out her phone.

"Not really. I'll see you later, Miss Pamela. I've got to scoot."

"Come talk to me next time you're at Peerless. Wait." She held up her hand to stop me, then glanced at her phone and back to me. "You're this Cherry Tucker?"

"Yep, the crazy ex-girlfriend. Nice to meet you, ma'am."

I pushed out of my chair, waved to the girls hiding from the deceased Miss Pringle, and walked out of the office. Knowing how schools felt about running in halls, I kept my boots moving at a fast pace through the foyer until they reached the front door. Banging through, I hit top speed in the parking lot, charging toward my yellow Datsun pickup waiting in the visitor's spot.

I needed to speak to Luke Harper. About his step-cousin, Shawna Branson. And his crazy ex-girlfriend. Who was not one Cherry Tucker.

TWO

Knowing I could find Deputy Luke Harper at the Forks County Sheriff's Office meant I could also get my fingerprint and background whatnot completed. As I enjoyed killing multiple fowl with single stones, I pointed my pickup toward Line Creek. The county highways I traveled from Peerless Day Academy to the Sheriff's Department were much like the path I had been on with Luke. Lots of meandering roads that dead ended, forcing you to stop and wait for someone to pass before you could turn. Sharp, blind curves in the hillier terrain that can be unnerving. A lot of travel without getting very far.

I had a million excuses as to why I should pass by Luke Harper Boulevard. He could act the scoundrel. Sometimes unsympathetic. Easy to irritate. In other words, a real man. But all that went away when his gray eyes—actually ultramarine mixed with Prussian blue, a teeny Mars Black, and a daub of titanium white—fell upon mine.

For now, I proposed friendship while we waited out several roadblocks. Such as one Tara Mayfield, who didn't want to add the prefix ex to girlfriend. Luke also needed to prove to my family that not all Bransons were untrustworthy swindlers and snobs. Besides, Luke's stepfamily didn't feel much better about me.

Long ago, someone decided the Ballards and Bransons twain should never meet. Which apparently included my Tucker and his Harper.

Nevertheless, Luke had fixed on pursuing me. Most recently, he sought me out at Red's County Line Tap's annual Halloween party. Surrounded by Halo's hardest partiers dressed as pimps and ho's, I had donned more creative costume attire. Painted a Renaissance landscape backdrop in ochres and siennas, cut a big hole in the canvas, inserted my head, and went as the *Mona Lisa*. Luke wore a dusty pair of Wranglers, boots, and a western shirt. The ever-present Tara dressed in her high school cheer duds, but everyone forgave her because she is so damned cute.

In the crowded bar, Luke's cowboy had found my *Mona Lisa* smile and pulled me into the gents' bathroom before our friends and family could notice.

"I screwed up." Beneath the shadow of his white cowboy hat, his eyes had appeared charcoal. "And I mean to make it up to you."

"You step out with me and we're going to get smacked from flying horse hockey on all sides," I said.

"Those are their issues. Not ours," he said. "Just let me know I have a chance. Just one kiss. A kiss to hold us until some of this blows over."

And that's when Nik had kicked in the bathroom door. Unfortunately, my sister's newly wedded husband had been fed only the ugly version of my romance with Luke.

His kick alerted my brother, Cody. Who, misinterpreting our bathroom cluster, threatened to kill Luke.

Which led to my sister, Casey, pitching a fit for all to hear.

And then Red booted us all from the party.

Luke paid for the broken door.

Which I appreciated since Nik didn't have a job.

Did I mention which side of the tracks my family lived on in comparison to Luke's?

By the time my rusty, yellow Datsun pickup chugged into the parking lot of Forks County Sheriff's Department, I had mellowed from Shawna's slight and determined to return to Peerless Day Academy with my background check before their staff meeting. I also thought this fingerprinting trip might provide me with an opportunity to ask Uncle Will a few questions that had been bugging me as of late. I hopped from the truck, sped up the sidewalk, and into the cool blast of air currently conditioning the lobby of the sheriff's offices.

Behind a shatterproof, bulletproof, Plexiglass window, sat Tamara Riggs. The black, white, and red beads of Tamara's cornrow braided ponytail clicked as she lifted her chin to address me with don't-give-me-no-lip eyes. Tamara backed the Georgia Bulldogs with a ferocity that insisted on Dawg colors on every part of her person, including her hair and nails.

"Wha'cha need, Cherry?" asked Tamara. "I hope you're not hunting for Deputy Harper. I'm tired of shooing away his badge bunnies."

"Don't you lump me in with those women. I'm here on official business. Need to get fingerprinted for a background check. And if the sheriff is free, I'll take a word with him as well."

Tamara picked up the phone without dropping her stare. "We'll see who's around to do your fingerprints. The sheriff is in, but I don't know if he's available."

"Thank you, Miss Tamara."

She spoke into the phone, set the receiver down, and crooked a finger. "Come over here, hon'. I've got some words for you."

I strolled to the window and stopped spitting distance away. Tamara scared me a teeny bit. The rest of the force not so much, but Tamara's nature matched her favorite mascot. Her bulldog intensity made the rest of the deputies seem like pug puppies.

"Ma'am?"

"You know that sweet Tara Mayfield?" She waited for my acknowledgement and set her glare to high beam. "Not only did that little girl make Deputy Harper homemade lunches, she packed a meal for the whole station. Brought us pies. And did you know she visits the women's wing over at the jail? Bringing the Word of our Lord to those ingrates. That child is full of goodness and light."

"She's something special, all right," I muttered. I'd been hearing about the wondrous Tara Mayfield for weeks now, such as life was in small towns where folks loved minding other folks' business. Not many knew about my previous dealings (emphasis on the plurality of that relationship) with Luke Harper, but instinct guided them to point out Tara's catch.

"I've seen you and Harper eyeing each other." Tamara arched a brow. "Don't give me that look, like you don't know what I'm talking about. I've watched y'all act like a pair of horny squirrels, just flying around each other in circles. Now I know he says he doesn't want to see Tara Mayfield no more, but I'm hoping that will change. Don't go messing with him."

I sucked in the frosty air and blew out my heat. "Miss Tamara, it's not me. I'm not the horny squirrel. Luke and I are friends, that's all."

"You best be telling the truth, because the boys and women in back, they like that Tara Mayfield. And her cooking. And with your history of messing around in police business that ain't your business, you need the backing of these boys in brown."

"I get it," I said. "And I don't mean to mess with police business. I just get pulled into it through association."

"I know the sheriff may as well be your daddy, but I'm just trying to help you. I like you, Cherry, but I don't trust you. You're a wild one and in my line of work, I don't trust wild children."

"Thank you, Miss Tamara. As I'm twenty-six, I think you can stop calling me a wild child. I have a business—"

"That's not making you any money."

"And a house—"

"That belongs to your granddaddy. You are a wild child, Cherry Tucker, and at twenty-six, it's time to settle yourself down and behave. Go find yourself a real job and another man and leave Deputy Harper and the Sheriff's Office alone."

"Lord have mercy, Miss Tamara." I stomped toward the door to wait out her buzz. "Is this because I don't bring you food? Next time I need fingerprinting done, I'll bring you a pie."

The heavy door swung open, framing the mighty figure of Sheriff Will Thompson. Thirty years ago, his height and build got him a position as defensive tackle for the Bulldogs. Today, the linebacker appetite remained, but his bulk had gravitated toward the south end of his torso. However, the man could still hustle. I'd seen him chase down and tackle a kid who had graffitied the side of a barn.

Of course, that'd been a while. The kid was me at age ten.

"Hey, Uncle Will." I hopped on my toes to give him a quick hug before I squeezed past his bulk and into the hallway. "Can you print me?"

"Sure thing, sugar." His chocolate brown eyes twinkled. "I'm glad to hear you're getting a job at Peerless Day. Are you going to be teaching art?"

"No, sir." I felt a bit flummoxed by everyone's inclination for me to find a steady paycheck. "I don't have teaching training. The drama teacher needs help with some artwork for the stage. They're doing *Romeo and Juliet*."

"When I was a boy, the students had to paint the scenery. Things sure have changed." He shook his head, pointed toward a door at the end of the long hall, and plodded behind my quick steps. "Well, we'll get you printed and into the system."

"Never convicted." I grinned. "My record's clean as an old maid's wedding dress."

"I should know." He sighed and unlocked the door.

We entered a small room fitted with shelves filled with boxes of supplies and a lone metal table. I stood before the table while Will pressed my fingers in ink and rolled them onto a card sectioned for each finger and thumb.

When finished, he squirted goop into my hand and handed me a paper towel.

"Thanks, Uncle Will."

"Now mail that card to the Georgia Bureau of Investigation address and they'll do your background clearance. Piece of cake." He leaned against the metal table, while I worked the ink off my fingers. "When are you starting?"

"Today, hopefully. If I can catch the drama teacher."

"GBI won't have your background check done today, girl. Does that school normally let folks work without the background check completed?"

"Dunno." I focused on wiping my fingers. "And let's assume they're making an exception since it's just an after school deal for a short time. Maybe you could write me a note, stating I'm an upstanding citizen. Just in case."

"I don't like this, Cherrilyn. We should have done a scan of your prints instead of a roll if they wanted them this fast." Will tossed my paper towel in the trash. "Come down to my office for a moment."

I dragged my feet behind him. Now I was going to get the school in trouble over a little fudging of the rules. If Uncle Will complained, they wouldn't hire me on.

We entered Will's wood paneled office and I flopped into a chair before his desk. "You know, Uncle Will, this whole working without a background check is probably just a mix-up. The principal's secretary passed away, and I just came at a bad time."

Will sat back in his chair, steepled his hands on his belly, and eyed me. The chair gasped as his weight rocked back. "Passed away? Who was that?"

"Maranda Pringle. Did you hear about it?"

"Oh, right. Didn't come through our department." He paused. "They took her to Line Creek Hospital for an autopsy. Had breakfast with Harry McMillan this morning. He got the call over our ham and eggs."

Harry McMillan had been elected county coroner in a special election last Tuesday. Uncle Will had kept mum on his feelings about Harry. Will was a good politician and Harry was an outsider to Forks County having just moved to Halo thirty years ago.

"Why an autopsy?" I asked.

"Didn't say and I didn't ask."

"That's odd. She wasn't old or anything. I tell you what, one of the parents sure didn't like her bedside manner with the students."

Will rubbed his chin. "How so?"

"Said Miss Pringle was mean to the kids. And questioned her morals. But then again, Mrs. Hargraves also said Miss Pringle was incredibly efficient and saved the school from a PR disaster."

"What PR disaster?"

"Some incident that involved cyberbullying leading to a teenage suicide."

Will leaned forward, dropping his arms to the desk. "I remember that. There was evidence of bullying in all sorts of ways. Texts, emails, social networking sites. Line Creek police confiscated computer chips. The school shut down Internet service and didn't allow phones for the rest of the year."

"Writing on bathroom walls is a lost art." I shook my head, remembering days gone by. "Do they even fight in the parking lots anymore? Or pass notes? What's become of this generation?"

"Feeling your age?"

"Twenty-six is young." I kicked the chair leg with the back of my boot heel. "I've got plenty of time to play the field before I worry about settling down."

"Sure, hon'." Will began shuffling through the stack of files on his desk. "Anything else I can do for you?"

For the past month, I had wanted to ask Uncle Will about my mother. She'd been gone about twenty years, and as far as I was concerned, we were better off without her. But recently, I had discovered my brother had stolen some snapshots from Shawna Branson, showing my mother with Shawna's father. I didn't know what to make of them. However, Uncle Will, like my Grandpa Ed, found the subject of my mother a mute point.

As in we didn't talk about her. At all. I suspected these photos were Shawna's sticking point in her campaign of ugliness toward me.

This past year, Shawna had acted the turkey buzzard to the carcass of my dying art career. She had hated me since the fifth grade county art competition when I caught her trying to pass off a traced drawing of Tupac as an original. When my tribute to the Atlanta Olympics won first place, Shawna set the sculptured torch on fire, claiming patriotic inspiration.

"What do you know about Billy Branson?" My mouth surprised my brain with a blab sneak attack. I sought for spin control. "You know, Shawna Branson's father? I'm having a hard time with Shawna lately and her mother was no help. I thought maybe Shawna's daddy..."

Will looked up from his files. "Billy Branson? He hasn't lived around here in twenty odd years. Don't see how he could help you with Shawna."

"So he left about the same time as Momma?"

Will's eyes narrowed. "Lots of people leave Halo, not just Christy Tucker and Billy Branson. Billy and Delia had an unhappy marriage because Billy couldn't make it as a pro or keep his hands off his female golf students. Everybody knows that. Sad but true."

"Why'd he leave Halo? His family is here."

"I expect John Branson Senior had something to do with that. His boys were wild. JB was tearing up the town about that time, too. It's not easy to be a Branson in Forks County. You'd like to think they sit pretty on their perch, but heavy is the head that wears the crown."

Will laid the folders on his desk, pinning them down with a thick forearm. "That goes for stepsons, too. You were pretty hard on Luke Harper when y'all were seeing each other."

"He didn't tell his parents we were dating." I lifted my chin. "He was embarrassed to be seen with me."

"Luke Harper likes his privacy because he's a Branson. And he cared about you enough that he didn't want to drag you into the Branson minefield until y'all were ready."

I opened my mouth, then closed it. "How do you know?"

"Believe me, I know about these things." Will picked up the top folder and opened it. "We done here?"

"Yes, sir." I pushed out of the chair. "Thank you."

"Anytime, baby girl." He didn't look up from his folder. "And another bit of advice. That Tara Mayfield would make a good Branson. Better her, than you, navigating those minefields. Your hurt will heal. Believe me there, too."

THREE

Before I could distill Uncle Will's sage wisdom into something I could swallow rather than gnaw, my edification in humility continued. I opened the door, muttering how I wished everyone could leave off the subject of Luke Harper and myself, and almost stepped on that very subject. He squatted below me, tying his shoe, and gazed up.

"Hey, if it isn't the sun." His hands dropped from his shoe, but he continued to stare up at me. The gray eyes lightened and full lips softened, almost forming a smile. "I wasn't expecting you."

God had an odd sense of humor when it came to my love life. The harder I set my resolve, the more temptation came my way.

Luke rose and my eyes traveled with his ascension, up the long pair of legs clad in starchy brown. A utility belt hung off lean hips, accentuating a flat stomach. I rooted my gaze on the walkie, clipped on his broad shoulders, to prevent myself from further ogling.

One of these days, I'd find myself desensitized from Luke's good looks. But for now, he still made my eyeballs spring from my head.

"What's the occasion?" He pushed a hand through his dark, curly hair.

"I had to get fingerprinted." I clenched the fingerprint cards, using the paper's smoothness to keep from remembering the past feel of his silky locks tangling in my fingers.

"You need anyone to frisk you? Better yet, do a strip search?" His slow smile caused two deep dimples to emerge.

A flurry of butterfly wings beat against the walls of my belly and my toes curled within my boots. If Miss Tamara caught us, she'd take one look at my expression and accuse me of squirrelish behavior. While I worried about Miss Tamara's squirrels, Luke's gaze trailed from the hem of my dress to dawdle on Bert and Ernie. I took a long, slow breath while his eyes finished their journey to meet my cornflower blues.

"Aren't you a little old for *Sesame Street*?" He smiled.

"I believe in life long learning."

"I could teach you a thing or two."

"I don't need that kind of education."

"Come with me to eat lunch." He paused and the smile faltered. "I miss you."

I hated the pained tone in his voice, like I was kicking him in the gut every time he saw me. "If we're going as friends, I could eat. Lickety Pig?"

"Sounds good. I've got to get out of here fast. Before you-know-who shows."

"Tara still won't leave you alone?"

"Somebody should study that girl's brain. We could use her homing instincts as a new kind of radar. She will not take no for an answer."

"Tara is very persistent. That's a good quality for working with prisoners and children."

"You always look for silver linings, don't you?" He opened the heavy lobby door, and I stumbled through. "That's a good quality, too. See you there, sugar."

I turned to tell Luke to cool it on the sugar stuff in front of Tamara, but the door had already closed. I glanced toward her bulletproof shield.

Tamara sat with her arms crossed, her eyebrows arched, and her lips pursed. I ducked my head and fast-walked through the lobby and into the parking lot before I heard more talk about the love life of squirrels.

* * *

Fifteen minutes later, Luke and I eyed each other over a sticky Formica table dressed with red plastic glasses of tea and paper baskets of pulled pork. East Carolina vinegar sauce and coleslaw covered his sandwich. Mine dripped with sweet red sauce and pickles. A basket of fried okra sat between the two. We reached for the okra at the same time, our fingers touching and skidding away.

Luke cleared his throat. "Did you talk to the principal of that school this morning?"

"No, he wasn't in." I popped a hot bite of okra into my mouth, sighing in ecstasy at the salt, crunch, and tang dissolving on my tongue. "It seems the principal's secretary, Maranda Pringle, died. Did you hear about that?"

Luke set down his sandwich. "I did not. Where does she live?"

I shrugged. "Must be Line Creek. The call didn't come through County. One of the mothers had some ugly things to say about Miss Pringle. Those stuck-up Aureate folks need to learn some manners, talking trash about a woman who just died."

"Sounds like you did some gossiping yourself."

I cut my eyes to my barbecue. "I just listened."

"Are you sure you're up to working at that fancy school? Can't say you handle yourself well around the high and mighty."

"It's temporary. Gives me a chance to do something in the community. And I'll get paid."

Luke raised his brows, but kept his mouth busy with his sandwich. Sauce dripped down his chin. I resisted the urge to wipe it off, deciding Luke and the Lickety Pig staff would get the wrong idea. I chewed and transferred my thoughts to a safer plane. According to my Tara timer, she'd appear within the next five minutes, and I needed to broach the subject of Luke's cousin and ex-girlfriend in private. It's just not kind to talk ugly about somebody in front of that person.

"Speaking of the school, that mother showed me some interesting photos posted on my Facebook page."

Luke's eyes glazed over. He reached for a handful of okra.

I waved a hand before his face. "Photos of you and Tara Mayfield posted by your cousin, Shawna Branson. Naming me the crazy ex-girlfriend for all the cyber world to see."

The okra dropped into a puddle of vinegar sauce next to his sandwich. "Step-cousin."

"Whatever. Shawna's been poking sticks at me all year and now she's found another way to prick my skin. With you and Tara Mayfield."

"I'm not seeing Tara anymore." He reached for my hand, but I slipped it into my lap. "Sugar, can I help it if she doesn't believe me? What am I supposed to do? I can't bring myself to get a restraining order put on Tara. I wouldn't want to do the paperwork when she breaks it."

"Throwing Tara in the pokey for following you around like a love-sick swan is your business. Shawna's using the relationship to needle me. And poor Tara is caught in the middle."

"Poor Tara? What about me?"

"You're a big boy. I've been the recipient of rumors and gossip for the past six months. I can't afford the bad press as the homewrecker who broke sweet, little Tara Mayfield's heart."

"I broke sweet, little Tara Mayfield's heart, not you." He pushed his basket aside. "Besides, she's the one who thought dating meant getting married. Don't know what gave her that idea."

"Because you never tell anybody what you think or feel, so she jumped to conclusions. You introduced her to your parents." Something he had never done with me. I gave him an extra glower for that thought.

"I had to go to a Branson wedding and Shawna was angling for me to take her. I was desperate, so I asked Tara."

"In Tara's world, a date to a wedding equals a promise ring."

He gaped at me, then tore another bite out of his barbecue. "I don't understand women."

"You'd understand us better if you'd talk to us. So you need to start by telling your step-cousin to stop egging Tara on."

"I say it's nobody's business who I'm seeing and who I'm not seeing."

And therein lied the problem. When you lived in a small town, people made it their business whether you wanted it or not.

Particularly when a Branson wanted to date a Ballard.

Because the universe found favor in pairing gossipers with gossipees, when the little bell hanging on the Lickety Pig door rang, I knew who would walk through that door. I cut my eyes from the okra to Luke's as a shaft of sunlight fell across our table. Tara Mayfield glided into the cafe. Pink Keds shod her size four Barbie doll feet and a rosebud print dress with matching sweater swathed her petite frame.

Sunlight lit her golden, always-smooth-never-frizzy locks, producing a halo that dazzled my eyes. Her tiny dancer body spun as her wide, china blue eyes took in the barbecue crowd. In response, the mainly male lunchers stopped chewing to take in the radiant, beautiful glow that Tara offered. Her eyes lit on our table and she skipped forward.

I glanced at the okra squeezed into camo-colored pulp in my fist, then slid my hand into my lap to wipe the mangled mess into the paper towel that served as my napkin.

"Hey Tara," Luke and I chimed.

I noticed his dimples did not crease and his eyes had lost their luster. I wanted to shake him. Why in the hell would you drop a girl like Tara Mayfield? If I were into that sort of thing, I would marry Tara Mayfield. She made Mary Poppins look like Lizzy Borden.

Except for the stalking, which I wouldn't put past Lizzy Borden.

"Luke and Cherry," she squealed. "I'm so glad to see you. How are y'all? I thought I'd find you here."

"What a surprise." I smirked. "Have a seat, Tara."

Luke's shoe nudged my ankle, but I couldn't help myself. I wanted to dress Tara up and braid her hair.

"What have you been doing?" I turned to grab the free chair behind me and scooted it around to face our table.

"I just finished some volunteer work at the women's shelter and thought I could meet Lukey for lunch. The guys at the station said he was headed here."

"Lukey? That is so adorable."

"I've got to go back to work." Luke shoved the rest of his sandwich in his mouth and grabbed a handful of okra.

"Really?" Tara's smile turned upside down and somewhere a fairy died. "Well, I hope the rest of your day goes well."

"Thanks," Luke said through a mouth full of okra as he hopped to his feet.

"I'll just eat with Cherry. You don't mind do you?" She turned her sorrowful eyes on me and my heart just about broke.

"Please do, Tara." My eyes narrowed at the man scrambling to get out the door.

He shook his head and I mouthed "chickenshit."

Tara laid a napkin in the chair abandoned by Luke and pulled out an antibacterial wipe from her purse to clean the table. "Mercy, what a sticky mess. I guess y'all ate here because it's so close to the Sheriff's Office."

"We ate here because Lickety makes some of the best barbecue in the county. That it just so happens to be near the Sheriff's Office, makes it handy."

"I don't eat barbecue, but maybe I'll get a salad." Tara smiled and waved at the cashier behind Lickety's counter. "Where's the waitress?"

"Lickety doesn't have salad unless you count coleslaw. They don't have waitresses, either. You have to order at the counter. Tara, it's like you didn't grow up around here. How do you not eat barbecue?" Tara fascinated me the way zoo animals did.

Her small shoulders lifted. "What have you been doing today, Cherry?"

"Visiting Peerless Day Academy. The drama teacher needs help with set designs."

"My brother goes to Peerless. They have such a beautiful campus. I wish I could have gone there, but daddy said it wasn't worth the money for me."

"Because you're a girl?"

"No, silly. Because they don't have football." Tara's trilling laugh caused the grizzled farmer behind her to break a smile.

"You played football?"

"Cherry." She laughed again, and I hunted the air for animated bluebirds. "I did competitive cheering. High school and college. What about you?"

"I worked and painted." And drank beer and ran around with boys, but those were extra-extracurriculars. "So what does your brother think about Peerless?"

"He doesn't like it, but it's either Peerless or military school. After that big to-do last year, my daddy almost pulled him out. And now that it's happening again, a lot of parents might do the same. Peerless could be in trouble."

"What to-do? What's going on?" At the thought of Peerless Day Academy in trouble, I saw my possible paycheck floating away. "What happened?"

Tara grabbed six napkins, spread them before her, then leaned an arm on the table. "I don't like to gossip."

"Of course you don't." I pushed aside my barbecue basket and plunked my elbows on the dirty table.

"I think the poor girl who killed herself—you know, Ellis?—was troubled anyway. She was from Ballantyne Estates. Sophomore. Same year as my brother, Laurence. At first it started with photos on PeerNotes and then they hounded her with anonymous texts. I heard something like that is happening at the school again."

"What's PeerNotes?"

"Peerless Academy's version of Facebook. Girls would post photos of shopping trips and parties where Ellis wasn't invited."

"Flippin' mean girls," I said.

Sounded like something Shawna Branson would have done if Facebook had been invented back in our high school days. "What is wrong with teenagers? They are so warped. Maybe I should rethink working at that school."

Tara grabbed my calloused hands between her soft, vanilla scented palms. "No, you should totally work there. That stage is incredible. A Disney star went to Peerless and his parents left the drama department a huge alumni gift. Some other kid ended up on Broadway, and another performed in a reality show. The drama students win all kinds of competitions."

"Drama competitions? What happened to putting on plays?"

"I want to help you. I can keep my eye on Laurence at the same time."

I pulled my hands from hers. It was one thing to eat lunch with Tara Mayfield. Her cuteness made it hard to remember she was stalking Luke. But having Tara stalk me while I worked was a whole 'nother thing.

"Listen, Tara. Thank you for wanting to help, but that's not such a good idea. Luke and I are friends. It makes it hard on him to have you always around."

"I'm glad to see him enjoying friends like you, Cherry. If Lukey's happy, I'm happy. Thank you."

Damn, Tara was good. I tossed my trash in the red plastic basket and stood up. "Nice to see you again."

"See you around, Cherry." She pulled a hand sanitizer bottle from her purse and began squirting it on her arms.

"I'm sure you will, Tara." Like whenever Luke happened to show up in my proximity.

I said goodbye to the kindest, most thoughtful crazy ex-girlfriend of all time. If Luke decided to file stalking charges, maybe they'd let Tara continue to bake pies in prison.

Tamara would like that.

FOUR

I left Tara to talk the Lickety Pig staff into making her a salad and hurried back to Peerless Day Academy. With Uncle Will's warning about the timeliness of work clearance, I wanted to get my paperwork turned in, speak to the drama teacher in person, and secure the job before their faculty meeting. I had a roommate now to help with some bills, but money was tight. My local art patrons had essentially disappeared after my last few scrapes, but Peerless parents could open a whole new market for me.

Zig-zagging back to the northwestern border of Forks County and Line Creek city limits, I drove through the stacked stone pillar gate just before the dismissal bell. Parents paid plenty for Peerless's acreage and bucolic landscaping that included a stable and jumping arena, tennis courts, nine-hole golf course, lacrosse fields, and a working garden with greenhouses.

And judging by the line of vehicles waiting to pull into Peerless Day, the parents also paid a lot of money burning gas.

I pulled around the car pickup line, passing a Bentley and a hybrid Lexus, and found one empty slot in the visitor's section. In a row filled with Porsche Cayennes and Acura MDXs, my poor Datsun P.O.S. stuck out like a pit bull at a poodle show. I grabbed my portfolio bag and drawing satchel and slid from the Datsun. As I walked toward the line of cars waiting before the front doors, the window on a Mercedes-Benz M Class rolled down.

"You're back." Pamela Hargraves dangled an arm out the window. A diamond tennis bracelet slid over her wrist and she shook it up her arm. "They're going to have a faculty meeting. After-school activities are suspended."

"Yes, ma'am." I stopped at her door. "I want to catch the drama teacher, Mr. Tinsley, before the meeting."

"Mr. Tinsley is a weasel. Watch out for him."

Either Pamela Hargraves ate a bowl of negativity for breakfast or she had a finger on the pulse of gossip in this school. "Why would you say that?"

"He counts on big wins in the state and national drama competitions to get alumni dollars for his productions. He's taught Disney kids, you know. If he doesn't think you're up to his standards, he'll air his grievances publicly. He's got a blog that has hundreds of readers. They like his brand of snark."

Holy shit. Did I really want this job?

"But if he likes you, guess who gets star billing on his blog and in the community?"

"He's got a voice in Line Creek?"

She wrinkled her nose. "Who cares about Line Creek? He's a board member on a number of art and culture committees in Aureate County and Atlanta."

Aureate's boundaries stretched into the North Georgia mountains. The mountains meant tourist towns. Tourist towns meant galleries and community cultural events.

"So if he liked my work, he'd recommend me as an artist in other towns? Maybe Atlanta?" I ran my hand over my portfolio bag.

Pamela nodded with a smirk. "Or sink your career faster than a solid gold anchor."

I chewed my lip. "And if he liked my work, folks in Forks County might notice, too."

"If that matters to you, then yes. But watch your back. And keep an eye on his blog. He'll leave a trail of backstabbing bread crumbs before he finishes you off for good."

"Thanks for the advice, ma'am."

"Good luck to you. Kadence is trying out for *Romeo and Juliet*. I'm running her to an extra voice lesson today." She waved and the tinted window zipped to the top of the door, hiding Pamela and her leather and wood grain interior.

I sighed and gazed at Peerless's castle-like facade, wondering if this venture was worth it.

A carillon rang from the stacked stone bell tower. As if cued to the Peerless schedule, my phone erupted with its own musical preference. The Spice Girls "Wannabe," my best friend Leah's ring tone. That song always made me smile. I still remembered the girl power dance moves Leah and I performed in the Halo Middle School cafeteria.

Strolling to the sidewalk, I jerked the phone from my satchel and plugged my free ear from the noise of cars and bells. "Hey, friend." I backed toward the side of the building as an avalanche of kids poured through the front doors. "What's going on?"

"Cherry, honey." Leah's sultry drawl could race drying paint and lose. "I've got some bad news about Peerless."

"If it's about the secretary dying, you're too late. I got that news after I sat in her office for twenty minutes without her appearing."

"I'm so sorry. My cousin, Faith, just called to tell me, and I remembered you had an interview today. It's so upsetting. Are you coming back to Halo, then?"

"Actually, I had to get my background check done and I'm going to drop it off before the faculty meeting."

"Faith is pretty upset."

"She's the chorus teacher, right? Must be hitting the faculty pretty hard." I sidestepped three young girls, their eyes and thumbs on their phones. "Can't say the parent I met was too upset over Maranda Pringle's death, though."

"I'm not sure Faith liked Miss Maranda much either, but a suicide does rock your world a bit."

"Suicide?" I jumped behind a trashcan as another group of teens glued to iPads threatened to barrel into me.

How could they run, read, talk, and type at the same time? That was serious multi-tasking.

"You didn't know? I guess they wouldn't spread that news around." Leah paused. "Faith said Miss Pringle had been drinking and took a bunch of pills."

"Was she depressed?"

"I don't know. I met her last week when I went to help Faith set up for her fall choral concert. Miss Pringle seemed distracted, but what school secretary wouldn't be? The office was crowded. I couldn't get anybody to show me the way to the chorus room, so I wandered lost in the maze of hallways until a sweet child finally pointed the way."

"Sounds like something was going on that day."

"Everyone was worked up," Leah agreed. "Faith was too busy with her concert to notice, though."

"I hope this drama teacher isn't going to be a pain. I just got word that he loves to make and break careers on his blog."

"Merciful heavens. Maybe you should rethink working for him."

"Don't worry, Leah," I said, more for my sake than hers. "I'm sure I've faced tougher critics than Terry Tinsley. Shawna Branson will make him look like banana pudding."

We said our goodbyes and I slid my phone back in my satchel. I looked up and locked eyes with a boy of about sixteen. With a mohawk of curly blond hair and his Peerless blazer inside out and backwards, he stood with his hands shoved in his Peerless gray trouser pockets. Which looked difficult as they hung off his nonexistent hips at a precariously low angle.

"Who are you?" He squinted behind red Wayfarer sunglasses.

"Who are you?" I countered. He looked familiar in a deja vu-ish way.

"I don't give out my name to strangers." He slid his glasses down, peered at me with brilliant blue eyes, then shoved them back up his nose.

"Me neither."

He nodded and ambled off with the back of his trouser cuffs dragging on the cement.

Mesmerized, I watched him before turning back toward the door. The tide of exiting teens had slowed to a trickle, and I decided to brave the gauntlet into the building. The sidewalk opened onto slate tiles surrounded by an inlaid stone mosaic making up the crest of the school. Passing through the open front doors, I waved to the security guard and headed across the wide foyer to the front office.

Behind that set of glass doors, faculty members and students huddled in clumps, heads bent and whispering. I strode to the counter and flagged a nearby student to call Mr. Tinsley. A row of chairs lined the two glass walls near the door. I dropped into a chair near a group of girls, their school jackets and ties tossed into a pile on the chair next to me. The girls all wore the same gray and blue plaid pleated skirt hiked to mid-thigh and white blouse unbuttoned to expose their clavicle. All had straight hair falling midway down their backs. All spoke in chirps and squeals. I counted thirteen OMGs in the first thirty second interval.

Gradually my hearing tuned to their teen girl decibel and I gathered they were talking about a message that had gone around the school.

"I couldn't believe it. How did they know about Preston? You think someone, like, ratted him out?" said a dark haired teen.

"I know, right? Probably the drama department," said a blonde. "It's so uncool."

I eyed the third girl, only differentiated by a slight wave in her dark hair and beautiful mocha skin.

"You think Preston knows?" she asked.

"Of course he knows," said the brunette.

"Everybody knows now," said the blonde.

"Not everyone knew about Ellis," said the girl with the wave.

"True," said Brunette.

As I watched the girls, the name Ellis clicked into place. The sophomore who had committed suicide from cyberbullying the previous year. Curiosity got the better of me. I leaned into their group. "Excuse me," I said. "Did y'all know Ellis?"

I received three eyebrow raises and crossed arm hip pops, which I took as a why-are-you-talking-to-us move.

"Just curious," I said. "I understand last year they shut down your Internet and didn't allow phones."

"That was so uncool," said the blonde. "And stupid. You don't need Wi-Fi if you have 4G or whatever. And we don't need phones if we have tablets or whatever. And PeerNotes is a joke anyway."

"So Miss Pringle's plan didn't work?"

The brunette lifted her lip. "Of course not. But it made the parents feel like the school was doing something."

"They better not do it again," said the ebony haired beauty. "I mean it's not like the school secretary would kill herself over some stupid texts like Ellis."

"You think they'll take away our phones?" The brunette dropped her cool stance and twisted a lock of hair around her finger.

"Was Miss Pringle cyberbullied?" I guessed the news of Pringle committing suicide had already made it into the Peerless grapevine. Probably by electronic memo, judging by all the devices. "I heard she was kind of mean."

"Yeah, really mean," said the brunette.

"Miss Pringle got a ghost text, too," said the third girl.

"What's a ghost text?" This conversation made my head spin.

"You know, when you get a text and it's not from a phone and like a random name. Ghost text," said the blonde. "You can tell someone what you really think of them and it's totally anonymous."

How do you get a text that's not from a phone?

I jumped, hearing my name.

"The artist Cherry Tucker," the droning voice called.

I turned and witnessed a balding, goateed man with glasses sweep into the room in a long, black cape. With one arm held out and the other drawing the cape to his chin, he called my name again, this time adding a long, mocking laugh.

What in the hell was going on at this school?

Five

"Mr. Tinsley?" I guessed, figuring the whole dramatic bit fit the stereotype.

"'Seal my fate tonight.'" He moved forward, the velvet cape billowing as his hands swept toward me and retreated to cover his face. "'I hate to have to cut the fun short, but the joke's wearing thin.'"

My eyebrows landed somewhere near my hairline. I glanced around the office. The groups had stopped chatting to watch the performance. No one looked particularly shocked or confused. I didn't even detect any eyeball rolls, whereas this little stunt deemed eyeball-rolling worthy material. However, I was from a less genteel background. My brother probably gave wedgies to a Mr. Tinsley-type in high school.

"'Let the audience in.'" He extended his arm to acknowledge the faculty and students glued to his performance.

I had dealt with some divas in art school, but I felt a bit lost among this theater crowd.

"'Let my opera begin!'" Holding the cape out, he stopped in front of me and finished with a round of maniacal laughter. Followed by an enthusiastic applause by the office audience.

I waited for the producer of the reality show to walk out with the camera crew.

No producer or camera crew appeared.

Pulling off the cape, Tinsley folded it over one arm, then bowed. "Pardon me, Miss Tucker. A parent just handed me this to add to our costume collection, and I found myself carried away by this vehicle of creativity disguised as a cloak."

I suppressed my confusion. "Mr. Tinsley, I came by hoping to catch you before the faculty meeting. I have already turned in my background check."

"Your 'can do' spirit is duly noted and appreciated." Tinsley pulled a folded envelope from his pocket, handed it to me, and pointed toward the doors. "Shall we walk?"

Glancing at the envelope, I noted that it was check sized and peeked. With a gasp at the zeros, my mercenary heart blessed the Disney parents of Peerless for their generosity and shoved the check into my satchel. We left the office, walked through the half-moon shaped foyer and toward the first of a series of long halls spoking off the main lobby.

"This is the arts hall." Tinsley pointed toward the first sets of double doors that lined both sides of the corridor. "The chorus and band rooms. They both feature state-of-the-art recording studios."

"Nice." I wondered how these students handled the depravity of university life after leaving Peerless. College must feel like a mission trip to some impoverished nation.

We proceeded at a fast clip down the football field length hall.

"The dance studios." He waved at another set of doors, then to the double doors on the opposite side. "The art classrooms."

"Wait," I said. "Can I see the art studios?"

"If we must," he sighed, plodding toward the entrance. We entered an anteroom lined with more doors. "The sculpture lab is on the far right. Computer animation and graphic design over there. Drawing and painting in the middle. I believe there's also some kind of press in one. And something for textiles."

I peered through each of the narrow windows set inside the doors. "These are nicer than some of my classrooms at SCAD."

"Did you attend college in Savannah or Atlanta? I know a few faculty members in Atlanta."

"Savannah." I backed away from the last window as a tall, thin woman with a short crop of salt and pepper spied my gawk.

The door swung open. The tall woman stepped into the vestibule, crossed her arms over her chambray tunic, and fixed a cold, death-ray glare on Tinsley. "I told you to stay out of the art wing."

Tinsley shrugged. "Calm down, Camille. I was just showing your facilities to the art director for the new production."

She set her cool, hazel eyes on me. "The art rooms are not available for outsiders. Don't even think about using my supplies."

"I hadn't thought about it, ma'am," I said, disappointed to start on the wrong foot with a fellow artist. "I figured the theater department had their own stuff."

"They have plenty of 'stuff.'" She whirled around, slamming the door behind her.

"Well," said Tinsley, ushering me back into the arts hall. "I certainly lose to Dr. Vail on dramatic outbursts today."

I reminded myself of the zeros on the check and kept my mouth shut.

At the end of the hall, the double doors had been draped with red satin swag. A gold, sparkling lettered sign, entitled "Tinsley Town," hung next to the door. Like the art wing, these double doors led to a room with more doors. This area had been painted green and crammed with a table and beanbag chairs. Students were draped across and over the seating, all with various devices in hand. One mop-topped boy lay on the long table, viewing an electronic tablet held above his face while he popped goldfish crackers into his mouth.

"Ignore the denizens," said Tinsley, readopting his grandiose voice that included the wide arm sweep.

I did my best to ignore as I tripped over gangly teens, making our way to his office entrance, complete with another gold, sparkly sign.

The office had the wood and leather vibe that reminded me of my friend Max Avtaikin's office. I wandered behind a full length mirror standing before floor to ceiling bookshelves. With my back to Tinsley, I scanned the shelves holding stacks of both bound paper and hard cover scripts, various knickknacks that I took to be props, and framed theater programs. I felt surprised to find no personal photos of him, his family, or the students. The room appeared as staged as his gimmicky caped character.

"Have a seat." Tinsley pointed toward a chair before his mahogany desk. "Would you like some coffee? I always need a stimulant this time of day."

I thanked him, glad he had dropped his booming affectation and wild gesturing. Dropping into the chair, I watched as he gathered coffee materials from a credenza. Without his audience, his posture slumped and his facial features relaxed, exposing a fine network of lines around his eyes. Doling out ground coffee into a press, he added hot water from an electric tea kettle, then massaged his goatee, waiting for the coffee to steep.

Four minutes later, I held a delicate china cup and no fix on the real Mr. Tinsley. "Good cup of joe. Thank you."

He gave a small bow. "The extra effort is worth it, don't you think? I feel the same way about my little theater projects."

I had a feeling his theater projects weren't little.

Circling the desk, he sank into a leather office chair cranked to its fullest height. Either that or someone had sawed the legs off my chair and his desk.

He beamed at me from his perch. "Let me explain why I want to take you on as art director, even with your limited qualifications."

I masked the gust of air I blew out as a cough.

"I do nothing halfway and I always do my research." He leaned forward, pressing the tips of his fingers on the desk. "You, Cherry Tucker, have been in the local press several times in the past six months. Stories reporting you consorting with malefactors and pursuing criminals."

"Those reports are highly exaggerated. The *Halo Herald* lacks real news, so anything printed leans toward sensationalism."

"No matter." He waved his pinky ring. "My point is this. Your combination of visionary artworks and courage under fire has piqued my interest. Your friendship with Max Avtaikin as well. I suppose you have heard of these references on *Tinsley Talks*?"

"*Tinsley Talks*?"

"My small blog where I have referred to the surprisingly fresh talent emerging from the murky depths of the humble burg called Halo. But now you understand why I called on your assistance?"

"Not really."

"It's simple." He sighed. "First, my production of *Romeo and Juliet* will not be of the gauche amateurish melodrama usually portrayed in high schools. I'm thinking a musical comedy version. Like a *Glee* meets *Avatar*. Except underwater. The Capulets are blue humanoid sea creatures and the Montagues are the aquanauts. In retro-scuba dress."

I tried to remember to blink. "Retro-scuba dress?"

He stroked his goatee. "You are right, of course. Difficult for dance numbers. I may have to rethink that. Anyway, you can see why I need an unconventional artist for the groundbreaking scenery. I can't rent what I want for this production. It needs to be original. I want the Tiny Tony."

"Tiny Tony?"

"High school theater version of the Tony. The pinnacle of awards."

My intelligence seemed to diminish the more time I spent in this school. Maybe I needed to get out of my humble burg more often.

"Second," he said, "your name is often linked to Max Avtaikin. I would like his support."

"If you mean you want him to help fund your theater, I'm telling you up front, I can't persuade Mr. Max to do anything. He's got a foreign view of things that I don't understand."

"You can introduce us. Invite him to the production. He'll be impressed." Tinsley left his chair and began to pace. "Tell him the contribution is tax deductible."

I couldn't promise anything on Max's behalf, so I figured it safe to keep my mouth shut.

Tinsley stood facing the bookshelves with his hands clasped behind him, head bowed. "The third reason has to do with your vigilante spirit. Your willingness to disregard rational thought and safety in the face of danger."

"Excuse me for saying so, sir, but I use rational thought. And I've been schooled in safety by my uncle, the sheriff. I'm not a vigilante. I just have the wrong place, wrong time kind of luck and a strong sense of justice."

"Call it what you will."

"I'll call it stepping up to the plate and doing the right thing."

Tinsley turned to face me, his dark eyes somber. "Then I need you to do the right thing by me."

"By painting your alien underwater scenery?"

"By protecting me. I think someone's going to kill me."

Were all art patrons this crazy or just the ones who wanted to hire me?

SIX

I rehinged my jaw and spun in my seat so Tinsley couldn't catch site of my reaction. That reality show crew must be hiding. Someone's going to jump out and surprise me, I thought. No way is this guy for real.

No one jumped out to surprise me.

I sought a different explanation. And prayed it didn't result in finding out Tinsley was off his meds. Painting underwater alien scenery sounded fun. Protecting a crazy man from paranoid delusions, not so much.

"Mr. Tinsley, why do you think someone is trying to kill you?"

He left the bookshelf to do another circuit of the room, plodding the soft carpet with his hands behind his back and glasses pointing toward the ceiling. "Metaphorically trying to kill me. Kill my career. Which is the essence of me. However, my physical body might join the metaphorical if I am left in ruin."

I squeezed the bridge of my nose between my thumb and index. Didn't help to stop my head from spinning. "Sir, what do you mean?"

"They've been torturing me the past two weeks. The evil texter. Why do you think I chose that particular scene in the office? Beneath the bowels of this school, some sinister fiend is at work on his computer cum pipe organ. I am his Carlotta."

My face must have expressed my what-in-the-hell-are-you-talking-about thoughts.

"Have you never seen the *Phantom of the Opera*?"

When I shook my head, he waved off my ignorance. "No matter. This is the second year in a row that our school has been besieged by a social media hit man. Or woman. Last year, it affected a few students and an unpopular teacher. This year more of the faculty and staff have taken the brunt."

"What do the messages say? Can't they be traced?"

"Not yet." Tinsley stopped in front of the mirror to watch himself stroke his goatee. "It is my belief that Maranda Pringle was a victim of poisonous messages hinting at her illicit doings. The police have confiscated her computer and all her electronic equipment."

"No shit?" I fell back in my chair. "I mean, really? So she was cyberbullied. I'll be damned. She didn't sound the type."

"You see the seriousness of the situation. I heard she took her life last Friday night and lay in her apartment all weekend. They didn't find her body until this morning when Cleveland stopped by, hoping to give her a ride to school. Pathetic."

He glanced over his shoulder. "I mean Cleveland wanting to take her to school, not that Maranda was dead. Cleveland was constantly hounding Maranda like a lovesick basset hound."

"So you've been a victim of this texter, too." I ignored his digs at the principal. "That's why you're worried about the messages killing your career."

I knew exactly how that felt as Shawna Branson had tried some of that poison on me. I wondered what skeletons the texter had dug from Tinsley's closet. But, like in my case, even an innocent mistake could be twisted to appear ugly.

Tinsley gave up the distressed pacer affectation and collapsed back into his chair. "The texts," he moaned. "The texts are torturing us all. Maranda's must have been a doozy."

My heart went out to Tinsley and the other Peerless teachers. No matter how odd Tinsley acted, he didn't deserve this stress.

And no matter how mean or immoral Maranda Pringle had been in her life, she didn't deserve to be driven to suicide by a vicious prankster.

"So the police have been notified?" I made a quick mental note to question Uncle Will and Luke again.

"The police hadn't been notified about the texts. The administration took it as some cruel prank and told us to ignore them. But with Maranda's death, the police are now involved."

"Good." I nodded. "The cops'll trace the bugger."

"But these things take time." Tinsley leaned forward. "I need you now."

"I don't understand what you want me to do. I don't know anything about electronics. I'm a classical artist. I didn't even take a Photoshop class in school. I use my hands for art, not a mouse."

Tinsley steepled his hands before his mouth once again, practicing the full dramatic pause. "You can observe."

"Observe what?"

"As an artist, I trust you have strong visual instincts. The perpetrator is obviously someone jealous of my success. You're also an outsider without preconceived ideas about the students, staff, or parents. You have experience with felons."

"I wouldn't call it 'experience with felons.'"

"Miss Tucker, you are the perfect person to find the phantom texter." He opened a desk drawer and fished out another envelope. Smoothing the paper on his desk blotter, he pushed it toward me. "I'll add a personal check. To express my gratitude."

My eyes drew from the envelope to Tinsley's face, this time looking past the smug set of his lips to the dark bags beneath his eyes, the grooved lines, and the weariness he hid behind the theatrical bullshit. He felt hunted.

A voice from an overhead speaker announced the faculty meeting in five minutes and ordered all students and non-staff to leave the premises.

"Hell, I'll do it. I don't like bullies. Particularly ones who hide behind a screen to take potshots at their victims." I fingered the check and pushed to my feet.

He made a little bow. "Thank you. Auditions are Wednesday, but we'll start work on the show tomorrow. I'll see you have your clearance. I'll speak to Cleveland after the faculty meeting. He's amenable to my needs."

"I look forward to working on the scenery. But there's no guarantee I can help you find your phantom texter." My wallet cried as I slid the envelope across the desk toward him. "Hold on to this. If I figure this deal out, you can still thank me. A starving artist appreciates any dollar she can make, but I don't take money unless I earn it."

SeVen

As Max's name had come up in my conversation with Tinsley, I figured he deserved to know that Tinsley had set his funding sites on the Bear's wealth. A month ago, Max had blown out his knee. Since that time he never left his house, making him easy to track down. Once again, I hopped into the Datsun, cranked her windows down, and cut on her engine, pointing her grill toward Halo. Outside my hometown, Max lived on his own mini estate, dressed in the antebellum garb of Corinthian pillars, upper and lower verandas, and a modern cooling and heating system.

You could tell by his name, but Maksim Avtaikin a.k.a. the Bear, was not born and raised wrapped in Stars and Bars bunting. He found his way to the land of low property tax and high temperatures by way of Eastern Europe and a love for the history of the War Between the States. He also had a love for gambling, particularly the illegal kind, which got him into a spot of trouble in the past. The trouble mainly caused by yours truly. But we were past all that now.

For the most part.

I drove through his gate and up the drive to park near his Civil War cannon, part of the Bear's Ol' Rebel collection. Hopping out of the truck, I took the porch stairs two at a time and rang the bell. After a beat or two, the door opened and I was greeted by my sister, Casey.

Her long, brown hair hung in loose waves down her back and her thin lips quirked into a smile. She drew an arm back, welcoming me into the house that was not hers. "I thought you already had your sick visit with Mr. Max today. Are you into masochism now?"

I gave her a hug and took a second to take in her outfit. Black leggings, boots, and a black tee under a black leather lace-up vest. "No, but maybe Nik is. You got a whip that goes with this ensemble?"

"My husband doesn't need a whip from me. He gets enough from Mr. Max." She shut the door to lean against it. "I appreciate Max letting us stay here in exchange for helping him through his recovery, but man, is he crabby. I don't know how much more we can take."

I feared that meant Casey and Nik moving back in with me. And I already had a roommate. "Let me see what I can do. As patients go, grown men are worse than children. How's Nik's job search going?"

"Cody's trying to get him on at JB's dealership garage. Nik has an interview at a service station in Line Creek today. Actually it's good you're here. I've got to get ready for work. I'll leave the babysitting to you."

She waved at the stairway curling toward the second level and clomped her boots across the marble foyer. "Mr. Max's still in his bedroom. I've got a plate for him in the fridge. He wouldn't take it earlier."

"Thanks." I watched her open the door to the basement and disappear down the stairs, heading to the pool house where she and Nik now squatted. Nik shared the same motherland as Max, but Nik had immigrated to the land of opportunity with less money in his pockets. After a bout of indentured servitude to his immigration lawyer, he had met Casey and they eloped a few days later. He obtained his green card when Casey swapped the Tucker name for Ivanov. Now she supported him on her salary of tips from Red's County Line Tap. These were the kinds of relationships that coursed through the Tucker bloodline.

And folks wondered why I hadn't settled down yet.

I crossed the foyer, through a familiar route to the kitchen in the back of the house. The granite and stainless gleamed under Casey's care, although the espresso machine had been shoved aside for her set of cast iron-ware. I found a bowl of ham and beans in the fridge and a hunk of cornbread wrapped in plastic on the granite countertop. I popped the ham and beans into a microwave that cost more than my entire set of kitchen appliances. After another poke through the fridge, I emerged with a glass of tea and found a tray to carry the lot to the invalid.

The salt and savory aroma of the ham and beans had my stomach crying all the way up the grand staircase and down the hall to Max's bedroom suite. I knocked on the outer door, adjusted the tray, and popped into the little sitting alcove.

I glanced up at the portrait I had painted of the deceased Dustin Branson, hanging on the wall above a small loveseat. I'd gotten lucky that the Bear admired the work because in hindsight the composition had been a teensy creepy. Max had known Dustin in life and now had a daily view of the hooligan in death. Max said he liked the brushwork and perspective, but I think he used "Dustin" as a reminder of his past transgressions. I wanted to believe that anyway.

I knocked on the Bear's bedroom door and heard his grunt of welcome. With the tray balanced against my hip, I pushed open the door and blinked into the gloomy interior. The ham and beans aroma mixed with the scents of wood polish, leather, and the spicy sandalwood of Max's cologne.

"I've got you some dinner," I called.

"I don't want this food," said the growl from the far corner of the room. "You eat it. I hear your noisy stomach from here."

I found the overhead light and found him sitting at a small desk by a window, his focus on a laptop screen. Swaddled in a black robe and gray sweatpants, the big man hunkered at the edge of his armchair in order to lean over the tiny desk.

One long, heavy leg lay immobilized in a brace and propped on a footstool with pillows.

"You sure are living up to your nickname today. Stop being such a baby. Casey shows her love with food. Many people with knee surgery have a better attitude."

"I'd have better attitudes if your sister would leave me alone. I have the work to do." Shifting in his chair, Max angled his head back toward me. "I eat her food, I'll get fat from sitting all day. Please, eat."

I crossed the room and slid the tray on a dresser. "Have you been doing your physical therapy? You need to get out of the house. If you're not steady enough on your crutches, use the wheelchair."

The look he gave me almost put me off the ham and beans. I broke off a hunk of cornbread and offered it to him. He shook his head, and I sank my teeth into the moist, salty sweet bread.

"You are missing somethin' special," I mumbled between bites of cornbread. "When you're sick you want familiar comfort food."

"I am not sick. I am frustrated with the lack of mobility. And I don't want anyone to see me like this. The Bear can not appear weak." Max pushed a hand through the thick, brown hair that nearly brushed the collar of his robe. A lock flopped over his forehead, hiding the small scar above his left eyebrow. "Weren't you just here? Why are you bothering me again?"

"I'm just checking on you because that's what friends do when one is sick. Or frustrated." I licked the spoon, then dove it into the bowl for a bigger taste. "And I need to deliver a message."

"What is this message? Who gave it to you?" He leaned back in the chair and folded his arms over his chest. The small chair creaked in pain.

"It is from the drama teacher at Peerless Day Academy, Mr. Tinsley. He has his sights set on your coffers. Although from the look of the school, they already have plenty of money." I ate another spoonful of beans and considered Tinsley's request. "Anyway, he wanted me to ask you. I've asked you."

"I need more information. If he wants the charitable contribution, my accountant must investigate to be certain we can get the tax credits. I must be careful of the audit."

I shrugged. "He has a blog. Does that help? *Tinsley Talks*. Can you pull it up on your laptop? I want to check it out."

"Unless he publicizes his accounts, this blog doesn't help me. But for you, I will examine it." Max watched me lick the spoon. "Why are you involved with the drama teacher?"

"I'm not involved. I'm going to do some art work for his production." I paused to grin. "And he wants me to hunt down a heinous texter who is harassing the faculty." I explained Mr. Tinsley's worries and the death of Maranda Pringle.

"Blackmail?" Max's eyes sparked and he straightened in the chair.

"You get a little too excited at the mention of blackmail for my tastes," I said. "It just sounds like plain ol' bullying to me. I hate bullies and will be glad to ferret this one out."

"You also like to involve yourself in the suspicious business that is not yours. There must be purpose to the bullying. An exertion over the weak to prove strength. For power or money. Maybe revenge. Or in spite, due to envy or resentment. Perhaps it is a student who is the bully."

I dropped my spoon in the empty bowl and propped my hip against his dresser. "You seem to know an awful lot about bullies. Have you been the bully or the bullied?"

"Where I am from you are surrounded by the bullies. You must stand up to them or find yourself paying the extortion. It is not just annoying harassment. It is dangerous and sometimes deadly."

"No wonder you like it here in America."

"You will need my help." Max drug his leg off the stool, pushed out of his small chair, and grabbed the back to steady himself. "For weeks you have been smothering me with your friendship. I seek the balance in your need to aid me with my disability."

"Smothering? I think your English is off. You mean supporting." I wrinkled my nose. "You refuse to leave the house. How are you planning on helping me?"

Max released the chair and balanced on one leg. "I know you, Artist. You will do your best in hunting this verbal assassin, but your methods will be instinctual and reactive. You need guidance."

I narrowed my eyes. "That sounded vaguely insulting. And if I need guidance, I'll get help from Uncle Will or the Line Creek police. They're already investigating Maranda Pringle's death as suspicious."

"Bah, police." The Bear waved a hand, sending his balance to the braced leg. He grabbed for the chair, but the slight frame slipped under his weight. Max followed, slamming into the soft carpet with a low moan.

"Are you okay?" I fell to my knees beside him. "This is why you need me checking in on you. What would happen if I wasn't here? Maybe you need one of those emergency call bracelets."

"Stop treating me like I am the elderly infirm. I am not even middle-aged." Max opened his glacier blue eyes and exposed his pain. "Just help me up. Please."

The bedroom door slammed against the wall. "Hey, boss. I heard a loud noise," called Nik. His footsteps padded into the room and stopped. "What's happening? What did you do, Cherry?"

"I did nothing. Max fell." I glanced over my shoulder at the newest member of my family. "Get over here and help me. The Bear's too heavy for me to lift."

Nik strode to Max's prone body, then squatted beneath one brawny shoulder and pushed. I grabbed Max's other hand and pulled. Sweat broke across the Bear's brow, and I internalized my wince at the thought of his pain. Once Max had his good leg balanced, he wobbled, then sunk onto the footstool to glare at the floor.

"Cherry, you stop bothering my boss. He needs to work on his business." Nik folded his arms and rocked back on his heels.

I whirled toward Max. "Why is he calling you boss? Do you have something going on in your basement? Even with me checking on you every day?" I referred to the Vegas themed casino room where the Bear played house banker for groups of Atlanta tycoons for a nominally outrageous fee.

All illegal, of course.

The Bear held up a hand. "Don't worry yourself. Nik needed a job. I hired him to help me with my many legitimate businesses."

"I don't want my family mixed up with any dirty business. Not even Nik."

"You are not to worry about me," said Nik.

"You are my family now," I said. "That's what we do. You may not like it much, but you'll learn."

"Nikolai." Max jutted his chin to the door. "Out."

Nik glanced from Max to me. "Sure, boss. You want me to remove Cherry from your premises?"

Max studied me for a long moment. "No. She needs my help. We are going to talk about her new position and read the blog of Tinsley."

It looked like I would receive the Bear's advice whether I wanted it or not. More than likely, the Bear looked for a challenge to break the boredom of his infirmary.

But it felt a teeny bit like payback. I rolled my eyes at him just in case.

EIGHT

Tinsley Talks made no sense to me or to the Bear, as neither of us were schooled in the world of high school theater. However, the gist I understood made me worried for Tinsley. Without "dropping names," he slapped or hugged folks with a mixed bag of snark and praise. Which, ironically, sounded like cyberbullying to me. Max agreed that this sort of public whipping could come back to bite Tinsley in his theatrical hiney, perhaps in the form of the anonymous texter. I had promised to watch over said hiney, but hoped to talk Tinsley into reforming his blog. And hoped to see my name, thinly disguised or otherwise, out of it.

Put off by *Tinsley Talks*, Max seemed intent on spending his evening researching Tinsley. Or as Max called him, "the peevish little critic." I left the Bear to it. As it was Monday night and I had nothing to do, I headed to Red's County Line Tap, my home away from home, conveniently located a few blocks from my actual home.

I pushed through the foyer doors and into the alley shaped room that served chicken fingers to Halo's families and beer to everyone else. A small stage sat at one end where my roommate Todd's drum set rested during the week. Flatscreen TVs, softball trophies, and the mirrored wall behind the wooden bar provided the old roadhouse's decoration. Gossip provided most of the entertainment.

Red's auburn-self manned the long bar. My sister supposedly worked the room with a tray and a server's pad, although worked was a term best used loosely. The chatter of the Braves coming from flatscreens and the heavy strum of Southern Rock covered the sounds of the few families eating. I scanned the restaurant and didn't see Casey, but did spot Todd and Leah at the bar. I waved and sauntered over to grab a nearby stool.

I eyed the odd pairing as I said my hellos. Leah had the dark sensualness of a Jazz Age singer, although her personality ran more to Gospel. Todd McIntosh's blond-gold mane, wide Cerulean eyes, and winsome smile disguised a sharp cunning used on the poker tables. Leah hid her soft, bodacious curves in a tent of colorful cotton/rayon blend. Whereas Todd's tight t-shirt and cargo shorts emphasized the solid, packed muscle he formed by lifting boxes for a living. Together their appearance on stage in the band Sticks made for a yin and yang that pleased both the men and women of Forks County.

Except for Leah's mother, who would only be pleased by the plagues of the Second Coming, particularly when they smited all the bad seeds like me.

After giving Todd a quick hug, I hopped on a stool next to Leah. Todd pushed his beer down the bar and switched stools, placing me between my friends.

As he shifted onto his seat, the slot machine cherries permanently inked on his calf flashed into view. Those cherries marked him as another ghost-of-ex's-past. I slid my gaze off the tattoo and toward Leah. As she wasn't six three and a hard body, my eyes felt much safer there.

"Hey Cherry," said Red. He wiped the scarred bar top before I could lower my elbows. "You want a draft?"

"Why not? I start work at Peerless Day Academy tomorrow. I have a feeling they're going to keep me busy. Order me up a pimento burger and sweet potato fries, please."

The freckles and hazel eyes stretched with his grin. "Glad to hear you got a teaching job."

"She's not teaching, Red." Leah shook her head, causing a cascade of dark spirals to fall across her shoulder. "Cherry's doing art work for the drama department. They've got a big production of *Romeo and Juliet* this winter."

"That's nice." Red pushed a frosty mug toward me, which I accepted graciously. And a little greedily, I'll admit.

"So I guess your meeting went well." Todd drummed his hands on the bar top.

I stretched my hand over Todd's to stop the drumming. "Get this, y'all. This teacher, Terry Tinsley, is rewriting *Romeo and Juliet* as some alien musical. And he's hiring me to figure out who's behind all the cyberbullying at the school."

Leah and Red exchanged a long glance.

"What?" I darted looks. "What's with the crickets?"

"Hon', why does the teacher want your help with cyberbullying? Isn't that something for the police?" Leah toyed with the straw in her Dr Pepper, keeping her eyes off me.

"Sure it is, particularly since Miss Pringle, the principal's secretary, killed herself because of it."

"No shit?" Red blanched.

"Mr. Tinsley is worried about his rep. Someone is dragging skeletons out of the faculty's closets via text. He thinks while I work as art director for the theater, I have a good chance to observe as an outsider and find who's sending the texts."

"This is the same guy who wants *Romeo and Juliet* as aliens?" Red leaned a beefy arm on the bar. "I dunno, hon'. Sounds to me like you should stick with the art work. You don't need some teenager with a spleen full of hate spreading rumors about you, too. You've already dealt with that."

"Which is exactly why I want to help Mr. Tinsley." I was glad I didn't tell them about his *Phantom of the Opera* obsession. Tinsley's explanation for hiring me had sounded saner coming from his lips than mine. And I thought he sounded nuts.

"How is Mr. Max?" Leah asked, using her role as diplomatic subject changer. "Is his knee recovering?"

"Not as fast as he'd like. But Max wants to help me investigate Tinsley's anonymous texter. I think he's bored."

"I'll help you, baby," said Todd. "I love doing that stuff with you. Especially when you interrogate witnesses."

"Is interrogating witnesses the same as drinking beer and gossiping?" Red chuckled.

I hesitated before answering.

In the past, I had enjoyed Todd's enthusiastic participation in my amateur investigations. However, now Todd also enthusiastically participated in my daily living, and I didn't know if I should encourage his involvement in my new job as well.

We had made the transition from dating to a Vegas wedding, to exes, and on to friends and roommates within a ten month period. That's a lot of transitioning. And I got the feeling Todd might like to transition back to our original stage. I liked the friends and roommates stage. Much less scary than the Vegas wedding stage.

Although that stage had been pretty short.

I decided to try one of Leah's tactics and change the subject. "Nik's working for Max. But he didn't tell Casey."

Red slapped the bar with his rag. "Nik married her for a green card, I just know it. Poor Casey."

"Nik's not a bad guy. He loves Casey." I cast a quick glance toward the kitchen where Casey loitered to escape her tables. In my haste to cover my tracks, I had broken the unwritten rule of badmouthing family.

"Maybe Mr. Max wants a personal mechanic for his vehicle collection," said Leah, who never had these backpedalling problems because she had been raised right.

"Then he should hire Cody," said Todd.

I swung my gaze where it stopped on Todd's beatific features. "Why would Max hire my brother? Cody has a job."

Todd found interest in his beer glass.

"Don't even tell me he lost his job."

Leah patted my arm. "Cherry, you need to start talking to your brother again. It's not right for y'all to be on the outs like this."

"Cody's pushed me over the line this time."

"What'd he do?" Red reached to replace Todd's empty beer mug.

I shook my head, unable to spill. That dang family rule still applied. And it would mean explaining the photos which were one peek away from spewing a Pandora's Box worth of crap against my family's name. I needed to keep that lid on until I had a plan.

"You're holding back on us tonight," said Red. "That's no fair."

"Would you like to discuss the social media hit Shawna Branson has placed on me? She's trying to stir up issues between me and Luke Harper that I've put to bed."

"I thought you weren't sleeping in that particular bed." Red squinted at me.

"She's not." Todd tapped a quick staccato against his fresh mug. "But Harper doesn't seem to get it. I wish that guy'd leave Cherry alone."

"I can handle myself, thank you kindly."

"I thought Luke was with little Tara Mayfield," said Leah. "I love that girl. She helped me organize the children's choir last Christmas."

"He broke up with her," I said. "But she's hanging on for dear life. Sweet as pecan pie, though."

"You're not over him," said Red. "That's why Luke keeps coming back. He thinks there's more to plunder."

"Jiminy Christmas, Red. Plunder? I'm not pirate's booty." I shot Todd a look before he remarked on the word booty. "Luke and I have history. That's hard to shake off."

"Why don't you leave that history in the past?" Red gave me a hard stare. He played the protective brother better than my actual brother. "Every time he crooks his finger you run back. Besides, he's a Branson and that family's no better than pirates. They only care about power and money. JB actually used the words 'little people of Halo' the other day. And he wasn't talking about folks your size, Cherry."

"I'm not running to Luke. We're walking toward friendship. And his mother married a Branson. That doesn't make Luke one."

"That's true," said Leah. "You shouldn't judge the Bransons so harshly, Red."

For some reason, that statement did not make me feel better. But the sight of Casey carrying in my pimento burger and fries did. I pulled in a deep whiff of cheesy burger and deep fried, thin cut sweet potatoes sprinkled with brown sugar and tried to forget about crazy drama teachers, Cody's pilfering, and Branson pirates.

Before I could take a bite of ambrosial ground sirloin spread with tangy pimento and a slice of tomato, I heard the chirping voice of the Tara bird clamoring at someone. And where Tara roamed, certainly one Luke Harper must be in the vicinity. My eyes left the sesame seed bun to drift to the mirror directly across the bar and locked onto the flinty gaze of the man I once loved.

Maybe still did.

But shouldn't.

Dammit. I dropped the burger on the plate. For the love of pimento, when was fate going to give me a break?

I swung around on my stool to face him and instead, came face to face with Tara Mayfield.

"Cherry!" Her adorableness had not lost its punch with the passage of the day. "I spoke to my brother about the school play. Laurence's going to join the set crew to help you so he can get drama credits."

She squealed, hopped, and clapped like I had made some sort of touchdown on her behalf. I glanced at Leah to see what she thought of the high-pitched screeching, but Leah wore the smile she reserved for babies and surgeons who cured cancer. Todd, on the other hand, had the glazed-over expression that men reserved for the Dallas Cowboy Cheerleaders. I swallowed an eye roll and turned back to Miss Wonderful.

"Great," I said. "I'll be glad to meet him."

"I'm coming to the practices, too."

I disguised my "oh, shit" as a half-hearted "awesome."

"Did you hear about poor Miss Pringle?"

"Sure enough. That news was all over the school." I glanced at Luke. Like a gunslinger, he sat with his back to the wall, scanning the room while sipping a beer. At my turn, his eyes zipped back to mine. I adjusted my position to block him with Tara's head. Which didn't work because I had finally found someone with my height limitations. "Did you chat with Luke about Miss Pringle?"

"Talk about someone's self-inflicted death with Luke? He hears enough of that nasty stuff at work. Why would he want to talk about it when he's off the clock?"

I laughed, then realized she was serious. "Tara, you might learn some interesting tidbit he picked up at the station. Aren't you curious?"

She shook her head.

"Well, I'm sure as hell curious." I hopped from my stool, then grabbed my burger. "Why don't you speak to Leah about shoes or feeding the homeless or something?"

I wound around the tables, bumping into a family with multiple high chaired offspring, and slid my plate onto the table across from Luke. He had a basket of wings sitting untouched before him. "Mind if I take a seat?"

He pushed the chair out with his foot. "Please do. I came here hoping to see you anyway."

"And your girl, Tara, trailed along right behind you." I winked. "Say friend, here's something. That school secretary who died. She committed suicide. They found her today, but the drama teacher said she killed herself last Friday. I just wondered if you'd heard anything more. The drama teacher's all in a tizzy about this cyberbullying thing that's going on at their school again. This time it's the teachers being targeted, not the students."

Luke dropped his hand to the table. "I didn't know. Do the Line Creek police think the cyberbullying and the secretary's suicide are related?"

"Dunno. I'm just going by Mr. Tinsley's report, but he seems as reliable as an old Pinto. He did say that Miss Pringle received an insidious text. And sounds like Miss Pringle closeted a lot of secrets."

"What about Tinsley? Does he have any secrets?"

I snorted. "He must have some big ones. He's going to pay me to figure out who the mysterious texter is. Tinsley's worried the texts are going to ruin his career and he'll lose the Tiny Tony."

"Tiny Tony?" Luke shoved his wings to the side. "Never mind. What do you mean he's going to pay you to find the texter?"

If I had been drinking whiskey, my grin would've sparked a fire. "Tinsley has been following my local crime exploits as well as my art career. He thinks I'm observant and brave and willing to risk myself to help others."

"Sugar." Luke leaned across the table to take my hands, but I slipped them into my lap. His hand remained open, his arm stretched across the table. "This texting business sounds like a hot mess. You don't want to get mixed up in this."

"Tinsley needs my help. Besides, I'm already working on his set design." I folded my arms. "It's not dangerous. I'll talk to the kids and teachers. Keep my eye out for anything suspicious. I'm an outsider, so I might notice something they don't."

Luke slumped in his chair. "Just do me the favor of keeping me informed? At the very least, you might hear something the police aren't privy to. You could help out their investigation."

"I'm getting more offers of help today than I want. But I'd be happy to assist Line Creek with their investigation."

Excitement pulsed through my veins. Finally, Luke had conceded that I could help with an investigation. My head felt ready to explode with pride.

"I'd be glad to report to you," I said.

He gave me a nod and a smile, but the cool gray eyes seemed somber. And no dimples in sight.

I picked up my burger, but eyed his wings. "You're not eating?"

Luke's cheeks colored. "Not very hungry."

"Can I have a wing?" My stomach roared in agreement, causing the two-year-old twins behind us to start bawling.

"Help yourself." He pushed the basket toward me. "Shouldn't have ordered them."

"Something wrong?" I snagged a fat drummie.

He gave me an exasperated look and sipped his beer. "How does Todd do it?"

"Do what?"

"Live with you, hang around you. And not feel like crap."

I sighed and licked the hot sauce dripping off my fingers. "I'm sorry. Todd and I were friends before we started dating. But it hasn't always been easy for us either. We're in a good place now."

Luke picked up a fry and pointed toward the bar. "He's not looking too happy with you right now. You got that boy on a leash?"

I turned around in my chair. With his back against the bar, Todd leaned with crossed arms, watching our meal. I gave him a what-the-hell look. He tossed one back.

Shocked, I dropped the wing. Todd was my easy-going buddy. My sidekick. My pal. My Labrador retriever of ex-boyfriends. I glanced back at Luke.

His mouth twisted in a wry smile. "It's not as easy as you think."

"Come on, Luke. Give friendship a chance. Todd's just ticked because he thinks you've been an asshole to me. He's probably worried we're getting back together."

"Don't let everyone else dictate what happens with us." Luke glanced back at Todd, then dropped his gaze to his lap. "Do you think I've been an asshole? Is that why you won't give us a chance?"

"I'm giving you a chance at friendship." My hands trembled picking up my burger. I set it down. My stomach felt queasy, my eyes hot, and my head hurt.

"I don't want to talk about this anymore." I hopped from my seat and in my haste, banged my hip on the corner of the table. A tear slipped out, and I stamped my foot at my wussy reaction. "Dammit."

"Cherry, please." Luke snagged my hand. "I'll try harder. Call me tomorrow and let me know what's going on at the school."

"Fine." I brushed the tear from my cheek. "I'll give you a report on my investigation."

"It's not an—" Luke stopped and squeezed my hand. "Sure sugar, give me your report. We should meet. Some place where we can get away from everyone else."

I stared at my hand resting in his and pulled it free to cross over Bert and Ernie. "Maybe we should just meet here."

Luke tried to smile. "I'm sorry for being such a shit."

"Try being nicer to Tara," I said. "She's good people."

"I know." Luke blew out a sigh. "Too good for the likes of me."

NINE

I had left Red's troubled and full of doubt, feelings I didn't want to ferment. I drove the few blocks to my ninety-year-old Georgia bungalow, parked under the crammed carport, and slunk into my bedroom. After living in my Great-Gam's decrepit house by myself for five years, Todd's presence in the only other bedroom sometimes taxed my patience. Tonight was one of those nights. I wanted my big sister, who dished man-wisdom better than she observed it. But Casey was too busy shacking up with her new husband to pay much attention to my romantic trials and tribulations.

Besides, she was in the anti-Luke camp and I didn't want to encourage those sentiments. I crawled under my quilt and stared up at my painting of *Snug the Coonhound* until sleep found me.

The day dawned brighter and I chalked my isolation to bad pimento and hormones. I normally enjoyed sipping coffee and watching a half-nekkid Todd scramble to get to his day job, but I wanted to maintain the peace sleep had brought. I stayed in my room, piecing together an art director ensemble. I had finally settled on a white shift dress I had once painted with color blocks and black lines, Mondrian style. Later, I had found out Yves Saint Laurent had the same idea back in the '60s.

I was classic retro on accident. Peerless would dig it.

"I like that dress, baby."

I looked up from my bed to find Todd leaning in my doorway, watching me pull on my left boot. His uniform shirt, shorts, and steel-toed boots all had the same dismal shade of burnt sienna. However, they did make his cherries tattoo pop.

"Thanks, hon'," I said and grabbed my other red cowboy boot.

"Cherry, are you okay?" Todd plodded into my bedroom and sank onto the bed next to me. "You took off last night and I wasn't even sure if you were home except you left all the lights on."

"I'm doing all right." I smiled and patted his leg. "Going to my first day of school."

He ducked his tow head like a sheepish kid. "I'm sorry about last night. I got riled up seeing Luke pulling you in and stringing you along. And his girlfriend, Tara, is so sweet. I talked to her a bit. She's going to watch Sticks play this weekend."

"That's nice." I wrapped my arm around his brawny shoulder and squeezed. "Tara's not going out with Luke, though. She's just stalking him. But hey, she's single if you're interested. Doesn't take break-ups too well, though."

"I'm not interested." His blue eyes flicked toward me then away. "You know, she's not the only one who doesn't take break-ups well."

"You talking about me?"

"I'm talking about Cody, actually. You need to talk to your brother, baby. I don't know what's got you so ticked, but he's feeling it mighty bad."

"Fine. I'll see him. I need to swing by the farm anyway."

The unfortunate consequence of kicking my brother out of my house was having him move back to my Grandpa's farm. It didn't please Grandpa. Nor Grandpa's woman, Pearl, who felt we grandchildren had taken enough handouts from Ed Ballard. Nor Cody, who liked the in-town bachelor pad he had created in my house for a few weeks.

Nor me, who enjoyed Pearl's cooking and had just begun to enjoy her friendship when I had stopped visiting the farm to avoid Cody.

"I miss hanging out with Cody," Todd ventured. "He spends all his time in your Grandpa's barn working on his cars. He's not even interested in tailgating this fall. Something's real wrong if you don't care about football."

"You made your point." I shoved my other foot into the right boot and realized I had them backwards. I pulled the boots off and started again. "I'll talk to him. But I'm not promising anything. That boy is stubborn."

"No more than you, baby." Todd gave me a dimple-popping grin before the slight could strike home. He eased back onto his elbows, watching me hop to my correct feet and stride to my dresser to hunt for accessories.

"We're doing good as friends, aren't we?" My mirrored gaze left my image to seek Todd's. "And roommates?"

"You're about the best friend I've ever had. And you don't even play poker. As far as roommates go, as long as you don't try to cook and paint at the same time, we do just fine. We could keep on doing this forever as far as I'm concerned." He saluted me, rose from the bed, and walked out the door.

I squinted back at my reflection. Forever was a long time. I needed to figure out my messes before Todd and I began accidentally swapping dentures and realized we were too late.

Too late for what, I wasn't sure.

The farm had been my home from age five to eighteen, when I left for art school in Savannah. When I returned to Halo, Great Gam's in-town bungalow stood empty and I had eagerly set up residence with a lot of palmetto bugs and faulty plumbing in exchange for tax payments and my own studio. However, I still had made daily trips to the farm to see my family. And eat. When my siblings moved out and Grandpa had taken up with Pearl, my trips to the farm came less regular.

Grandma Jo had passed away to cancer more than ten years ago, but we grandkids had a hard time letting her go and Pearl in. Maybe it would be easier if Pearl were more like Grandma Jo, filling our bellies and minds with love and goodness. Instead,

Grandpa's new flame turned out to be as stubborn and cantankerous as himself. And less eager to feed us.

Maybe Pearl reminded him of his goats. Also stubborn and cantankerous.

I pulled the Datsun into the farm drive and scoped the yard for the other reason I had slowed my visits. One particular goat named Tater. A gigantic white billy complete with horns, long beard, and a wicked tenacity to take on any bridge-dwelling troll without fear. Or a pickup truck. Particularly certain yellow Datsuns with goat-head shaped dings in her sides.

However, Tater's days of playing chicken with my truck should be long gone. If I didn't want to let that rotten goat ram my truck before, I really didn't want to take the chance now. He limped on three good legs and a shot up fourth after saving my life in the same incident that also hobbled Max. That day had not gone well for neither men nor goats and now guilt shackled me to both creatures.

Sorry was not something I liked to feel for goats. Nor the Bear. Although, I had attuned to Max's condition better than Tater's.

The farm lane appeared clear to the split where I'd follow the right fork toward the house. A big Bradford pear and oak tree usually shaded the brick ranch from my view, but the pear had lost most of its leaves. A slash of white appeared behind the oak's thick trunk, but disappeared as the goat lurched in a jerky gallop past the tree. I slowed the truck and rolled down the window, calling out to Tater. Woodsmoke from some distant farm scented my cab. Beneath my tires, gravel and acorns popped and crunched, masking the trap-trap-trapping of goat hooves. Spying Grandpa's spindly form near the back fence, I waved. A sickening thud sounded from the side of the Datsun. The truck rocked. I jerked the shifter into park as my foot jammed the brake.

"Shit," I yelled, scrambling from my seat. I had finally done it. I had run over that damn goat.

Leaving the door swinging, I circled the truck but saw nothing but a deep crease in the passenger door. I dropped to my knees and peered under the truck. No dead goat. I rose and faced the laughing bray of the amber-eyed hellion. Through my passenger window.

"How did you do that?" I jerked on the handle, but the door wouldn't budge. "You. Get out of my truck. What have you done to my door?"

I checked the pop-up lock, but it was up. After pulling on the handle twenty times, I walked around the truck and attempted to grab Tater's horns to pull him out of the truck.

Which didn't work.

I abandoned the truck and the goat to join Grandpa at the back fence. He hung a hand through the barbed wire, feeding carrots to a new kid. The sable pipsqueak made quick work of the carrot and abandoned Grandpa to ram his soft brown head against my knees. I reached through to give him a pat and then yanked my hand back when he decided my fingers might taste better than a carrot.

"In his condition, Tater shouldn't be allowed to wander the yard." I told Grandpa after a quick peck on his grizzled cheek. "I almost hit him with my truck. Now my passenger side door won't open."

"Looked to me like he got you first," said Grandpa. "I can't have him in the back forty right now. He's gotten himself in a bit of a spot."

"What happened?"

"Can't keep him with the other bucks, because they give him a hard time."

"Because of his gimp? Do they laugh and call him names? Never let poor Tater play in any four-legged goat games?"

Grandpa shot me a side glance that cut off my joke. "Seems his bad leg gave him an extra shot of testosterone. He fights all the time. So I put him with the does, which is about the dumbest idea I've ever had."

"Uh oh."

"Pearl's ticked. She won't cook for me. I've been eating sandwiches and canned soup the past week."

"Well, that shoots my meal plan to hell. Let me see if I can talk to her," I said.

Something like a smile crossed Grandpa's face, and he pulled a couple carrots from his pocket, offering me one. "Thank you, hon'."

I shoved the carrot into my pocket. "Grandpa, is Cody here? I need to talk to him."

Grandpa shook his head and spat an end of a carrot in the direction of the barns. "I haven't seen him nor your sister in quite a while."

"I'll send Casey over to visit. She's chock full of wedded bliss."

"I suppose." He sighed. "At least, when you married that idiot, you fixed it straight away. Glad you're not seeing that cop no more neither. I know Will Thompson likes that boy, but I'd rather you not associate with him."

I avoided looking at Grandpa by squatting to pet the kid. "Why's that? Because Luke Harper broke my heart at one point?"

"Naw, that's going to happen. Because his momma's married to a Branson. We stay clear of them folks. When they get ticked, they're meaner than vipers. With your mouth, you're likely to step on toes in that house and get yourself in all kinds of trouble."

"Thanks for that vote of confidence." I rose, dusting my hands of dirt and goat spittle. "Luke's mother may be married to JB, but Luke's no Branson."

"Don't matter. He ain't gonna turn his back on his momma, no matter who she's married to."

With those words of wisdom ringing in my ears, I headed to the house. Inside the sunny yellow kitchen, I found Pearl wiping out cupboards. The house hadn't been this clean since Grandma Jo was alive.

"Pearl, you need to forgive Grandpa." I walked to the sink to wash my hands of goat schmeg.

Pearl carried the stack of dishes to the old rattan table. The spikes in her short, iron gray hair drooped and the goat tattoo emblazoning her left breast sagged more than usual. She adjusted her black Harley tank and folded her arms over her ample chest.

"I am a forgiving person. But now that we're in a family way, he needs to make clear his intentions."

I whipped around, flinging water with my turn. My eyes ached from their head-pop. I'd never scrub my brain clean of the images her statement produced. "Oh my stars. Are you sure? Aren't you kind of, you know, old?"

"Well, I never." Two bright spots burned in Pearl's cheeks. "Who are you calling old? I've got some good, long years left in me."

"I'm just talking statistically."

"Statistically, you're about to get run out of this house." She narrowed her eyes.

"Have you seen a doctor?"

"Why would I need to see a doctor?"

I paused, then retraced our recent conversation. "What did you mean by family way?"

"That damn Saanen, Tater. My best doe was in heat. I wanted her with a full-bred Sable. I expect some compensation."

I sagged against the sink. "Thank the Lord."

"Why are you so pleased with that coupling?"

"Never mind." Although relieved not to think of Grandpa and Pearl, I grimaced at the thought of Tater-Snickerdoodle spawn. Tater annoyed me. Snickerdoodle scared the crap out of me. "Hey Pearl, do you know where Cody is living?"

Pearl sank onto a kitchen chair. "No, I don't. I'm worried about that brother of yours. Something's bothering him. Does he have girl troubles?"

"I don't think so." Unless you counted my mother as a girl. "Has Grandpa told you much of our family history? Like what happened to my momma?"

"Ed isn't much of a talker, you know that." Pearl waved me over to the table, and I dropped into a chair across from her. "I know he and Josie Ballard raised you Tucker kids after your momma left. I thought she went back to Missouri. Isn't that where your daddy was from?"

"Yes." I leaned my elbows on the table. "But he didn't have much family back there. I can't think of a reason for her to go back to Missouri."

"It's too bad Christy Tucker turned out to be so shameless. Just don't go thinking any of that rubbed off. Y'all are Ed and Jo's kids as much as hers."

"Nurture over nature, huh?" I said. "I'm having major man problems. I fear my apples are falling near that tree."

Pearl hopped from her chair and returned with two glasses of tea and a plate of cookies. "Now, you tell me all about it. Is it that big oaf you're living with? Won't marry you? Rumors going around about you living in sin?"

"No ma'am," I said, reaching for a cookie. "Todd is just my roommate. Two separate rooms. And we were married for a minute. So that's not a problem."

"Your definition of problem and mine seem to be a little different."

I almost asked her if this wasn't a pot and kettle situation, but I didn't want to know if she was truly shacking up with Grandpa. I still hadn't recovered from the pregnancy scare. "It's Luke Harper. I'm trying my best to keep him as a friend, but he's pushing for more. And I want him to push, which is the problem. I don't think I've gotten over him well enough."

"If you both want to see each other, let him push. I didn't listen to my friends when Ed started sniffing around my door."

Another image I wished had never crossed my brain. I shoved the plate of cookies away. "So you think I should ignore the wishes of my family and the flak from the town?"

"If you really love each other, you'll find a way to rise above it all." Pearl snagged a cookie. "Or you can move away together. I say, go for it."

"My brother threatened to kill him just because Luke's a Branson. Ever since Shawna started her personal attacks on my business a few months back, Cody's been anti-Branson." Not to mention the pictures Cody found, which I wasn't going to mention.

"Well, then maybe it's not such a hot idea." Pearl dusted her hands of cookie and finished off her tea. "Thanks for stopping by, Cherry. Just talking to you, I feel better about the whole Tater and

Snickerdoodle situation. I'll get her through this gestation and hook her up with a proper Sable next go around."

Unfortunately, I didn't feel any better about my situation. But, if the chat had smoothed things over for Grandpa, some purpose was served.

On my way out the door, I snatched the rest of the cookies as a consolation prize. And as a bribe to move Tater from my truck.

TEN

I arrived at Peerless in time for their crazy lunch schedule that started somewhere around ten thirty and ended around one o'clock. As the Datsun and I pulled into the parking lot, my eyes stuck on the Line Creek patrol car decorating the fire lane. My brain buzzed with an adrenaline rush that juiced me into a tingling mess of nerves. I felt like a beagle who had caught a scent, straining at the leash to charge forward.

I'd make a terrible cop. Absolutely no control over my excitement for crime busting. They'd never promote me beyond meter maid. And Halo had no meters.

The Peerless front office buzzed with activity, but I didn't spot any boys in blue. While I signed myself in, students in gray and blue plaid paraded in and out of the open space, making me wonder if anyone populated the classrooms. I had hoped for Pamela Hargraves and her loose tongue, but another parent checked me in. This mother also had questionably pert breasts, but blonde hair. She gazed at me from behind the counter separating reception from the office hub.

"Which classroom are you visiting?" Her voice had a harsh drawl, not true Georgian. "I'll call for a student to accompany you."

"Theater department, ma'am. Mr. Tinsley's class."

Her lip injection made it difficult to scowl but Tinsley's name caused a mild tremor in her botoxed features.

Using the tips of her gelled French manicure, she tapped a few keys on the phone, and held the receiver away from her ear.

"Tinsley," she spit out the Tin and swallowed the sley. "You have a visitor."

Dropping the receiver into its cradle, she blinked at me. "Lucky you."

"You're not a Tinsley fan."

Her eyes cut to the gaggle of students wandering the office. "Not really."

My heart leapt at the immediate opportunity to explore Terry Tinsley's detractors. I would kick investigation butt at this rate. "Any reason why? It's my first time working for him. I've heard he can get pretty vicious on his blog. I'd appreciate any advice."

"I don't read *Tinsley Talks*." Her nose scrunched up, straining her forehead muscles. She dropped the scrunch. "He's a little egomaniac. You know that much, right? If you don't suck up to him, he'll cut you."

"Cut you with a sharp object or cut you from something?" I leaned on the desk, dangling her opportunity for a story.

"The stage." She glanced around the office. "My Audra is very talented. We came to this school just for the drama department. At age five she had her first part in *The King and I*. You'd think Tinsley would appreciate her experience. But she refuses to kiss his butt and become one of his psychopaths."

"I think you mean sycophants." I smiled.

"Tomato-tomato." The mother rolled her eyes. "Tinsley accepts fifteen students into his advanced acting class and those students get all the best roles. Guess what number Audra landed?"

I didn't want to guess. "Not in the top fifteen?"

"Sixteen. Audra's agent is shocked. Shocked."

"She has an agent?"

"Of course she has an agent. He says Tinsley is a total nudge. If Tinsley didn't bring in so much money for the school, they'd get rid of him. I'd like to get rid of him, that's for sure."

My brain shelved that statement into a motives-by-crazy-parents category. I wondered if Audra's mother knew how to ghost text. "I thought Tinsley was admired in the theater world."

"They're all actors. Who knows what any of them really thinks?" The mother's gaze swept over me. "By the way, are you helping with auditions? Audra's trying out for Juliet tomorrow night."

"I'm the art director. I have nothing to do with the play itself. Other than the art."

"Just in case, it's Audra Paulson. Paulson like Paul and son."

I stuck my hand out, and she gripped it like she was noodling a catfish. "Nice to meet you, Mrs. Paulson."

"Oh, I'm not Mrs. Paulson. That's Audra's stepmother. I'm Danielle Dobbs."

I felt a tap on my shoulder. I whipped around and found the kid with the inside out coat and curly mohawk retracting his tapping finger into his pocket.

"Are you my ride?" I asked.

"Are you Miss Tucker?" When I nodded, he pivoted and trudged toward the door with his hands shoved in his pockets.

"Laurence Mayfield, put your coat on right," called Danielle Dobbs.

I glanced back at Danielle, who had cast her slitty eye look toward Laurence. I guessed Laurence was on her "non-fan" list, too. I hurried to catch up with him. My boots skidded across the polished lobby floor, and I called for him to slow down.

"Hey Laurence, are you Tara's brother? She told me you were going to work on the set with me."

Laurence didn't slow, but amped his steady trudge down the hall.

I scooted to catch him. "Do you have a hearing impairment, son? I asked you a question."

He shoved his fists deeper into his pockets and turned up the speed on his walk.

Jogging beside him, sweat broke on the back of my neck. "Can you slow down? I'm not used to this much physical exertion."

Yanking a hand from his pocket, he pointed toward the end of the hall. "You see that set of doors with the curtains and gold sign?

That's where you're headed. Don't feel like you've got to keep up. I've got stuff to do."

He motored down the hall, leaving me in front of the art wing doors. I stuck a hand on the wall, leaned over, and tried to catch my breath. I really needed to start working out.

The art door swung open and Camille Vail poked her head out. "What's with the shouting? What's going on?"

I shot up and straightened my dress. "Sorry ma'am." I darted a look down the hall, but Laurence had disappeared into the theater department. I'd been busted without my accomplice. Felt like school all over again.

"Keep it down. I have students trying to focus." Dr. Vail squinted at me. She wore another floaty smock dress. Probably handwoven from flax or bamboo. She took her artsy look seriously, but when you had a PhD in Visual Arts, you couldn't afford not to take yourself seriously. You can't jack around with that much in student loans and not look like you have something to show for it.

"You're the new art director for *Romeo and Juliet*," she accused.

"Yes, ma'am." I rubbed one boot against the ankle of the other, wishing she'd let me go.

"Excuse me, ma'am." A man called from behind Dr. Vail. His dark buzz rose above her tight cap of curls. "You're blocking the doorway."

Dr. Vail moved to the side to allow the middle-aged man carrying a computer hard drive to pass. Despite his sports coat, I recognized the buzz cut and bearing as police officer material and guessed this was one of Line Creek's finest.

"Are you a student?" he asked me. "You don't have a uniform. Where's your visitor's pass?"

I patted my chest, realizing I forgot to wear a visitor's lanyard. Dangit. No hall pass. Busted twice in a matter of minutes. "I forgot to put it on. I'm helping Mr. Tinsley."

The officer jutted his square jaw toward the lobby. "Better follow me to the front office and get your badge."

I smiled, then noticed Dr. Vail's scowl. "Sorry, ma'am."

She glared at me, then glided through the art doors.

I traipsed down the hall, glad the officer didn't keep a similar pace to Laurence Mayfield. "My name's Cherry Tucker. Are you with Line Creek PD? Actually, my granddaddy's good friend is Sheriff Will Thompson. You know him?"

The officer smiled. "Sure, I know Thompson. Tell him Detective Daniel Herrera said hey."

"I sure will. Looks like you're confiscating some evidence. Is this in relation to the Maranda Pringle suicide?"

Detective Herrera pivoted and stopped in front of me. "What do you know about Maranda Pringle?"

"Nothing, really," I said. "I just started here yesterday and found out same as everyone else. I'm going to do art work for Mr. Tinsley and he's worried about the texts going around."

"Is he now?" Herrera's face remained impassive, but I was tuned to cop behavior. I'd just put Tinsley on a person of interest list. "Why's that?"

"He didn't say, but seems it's common knowledge that Miss Pringle got a revealing text that might've pushed her over the edge."

"Be careful with rumors," said Herrera. "They often turn out not to be true."

"Yes, sir. But what about in Pringle's case? Did she get a text? Maybe if it was known her suicide had nothing to do with the text attack, everyone will feel better."

"Nice try." Herrera smiled. "I'll tell you this. Pringle was a troubled woman. And don't worry about the text prankster. Probably some kid with his own issues."

"Are you Line Creek boys using a code name for the anonymous texter?" I grinned. "I've heard some creative codes used by the Sheriff's Department."

"If it was code, what would be the point in telling you?" Herrera chuckled and shifted the computer.

"Mr. Tinsley calls him the Phantom, after the *Phantom of the Opera*. There's some connection, but I've never seen the play."

Herrera smiled. "I like that. The Phantom Texter. Don't spread it around, though. The kids will probably think it sounds cool and a mess of copycats will start."

"Yes, sir." I saluted him. "Speaking of copycats, you think there's any connection to the Ellis Madsen suicide last year?"

Herrera's smile flipped to a scowl. "No, I don't think there's a connection. That was a case of cyberbullying and a teen whose parents didn't check her computer or phone to see what was going on in her life. These parents are too concerned with respecting their kids' privacy and not enough for their safety."

"Pretty bad, was it?"

He looked past me. The lines around his eyes and mouth tightened and lengthened. "No one stood up for Ellis Madsen. She felt completely alone in those attacks. Her friends abandoned her, fearing they'd get made fun of, too. Assholes, every one of them."

"So, Miss Pringle's text was completely different?"

He lost the far-off, pained gaze and settled his sharp, brown eyes on me. "Are you this nosy with Sheriff Thompson's cases?"

I laughed. "Pretty much. But I figure there must be something to this Phantom Texter or you wouldn't be confiscating computer equipment."

"Didn't say this had anything to do with anything. Maybe I like to carry around computers for kicks." He hoisted the hard drive to his hip and pointed to the office. "Go get your building pass, hon'."

"See you around, Detective Herrera."

He smiled and trudged toward the front doors.

Herrera worried about copycats and called the Phantom a prankster. But he didn't deny that Pringle had gotten a message from the Phantom. I needed to know how many other faculty members had gotten texts, too.

When I had finally stumbled through the theater wing doors with the proper identification hanging around my neck, I found Laurence lying on a bean bag, reading a book. He didn't look up from the book, but pointed toward the far left set of doors. I pushed through and found myself in yet another hall of doors. Some had gold stars. Some were marked for the girls and boys facilities. Others were labeled for props and costumes. All locked. Which I knew because I'm snoopy.

Someone should have drawn me a map. Or Laurence should have been more obliging. If he was indeed Tara Mayfield's brother, Tara must have hoarded all the helpful genes in that family.

And why wasn't Laurence in class? As I pondered the differences between my own and a Peerless education, I found the back entrance to the stage.

Hearing voices, I followed them until I encountered Tinsley holding class. With the cape draped around him, he sat cross-legged on a table, in cool teacher mode. Below him, the students adopted his cross-legged stance on the floor of the stage, gazing up at the Dali Lama of Theater.

He descended from his table to introduce me with grand, sweeping gestures that put Vanna White to shame. "Ms. Tucker will design our set and assist our set technicians in creating our underwater alien planet of Verona."

I smiled and waved. The students flicked an unimpressed gaze on me, then switched to adoration for Tinsley.

"The back drop's been delivered. Primed, flameproofed, and ready to paint." He pointed to draped fabric attached to a thick metal rod spanning the back of the stage. The drop had been suspended by wire from ceiling rigs, but lowered to my approximate height, puddling the extra length of fabric on the floor. "However, I've been thinking that we should also use periaktoi. I've eight prisms constructed from our production of *Lysistrata*. I feel Shakespeare would approve of our Greek scene device."

The students nodded.

I felt as sharp as a bowl of Jell-O. "Do you paint these periaktoi? I don't know what they are. Sounds like some kind of dinosaur."

Two students rolled their eyes and one snickered.

"But if I can paint them, I'll figure it out." I eyeballed the snickerer.

"Of course." Tinsley waved a hand at a group of tall, flat sided pillars. "They are placed together to create a backdrop. Each one rotates for three easily interchangeable scenes. You just need to paint over them."

"I can do that." I walked over to the prisms and pushed on one. Moving on wheels, it turned to reveal two more painted sides. "Painting these will be faster than building a set."

"Excellent. We will have some side sets, but I also have the stairs and balcony pieces from previous plays."

I strode to examine the backdrop, moving around a caged lightbulb hanging from an upright stand with a heavy, ornate base. "Is this a prop?"

The students sucked in their breath, and Tinsley calmed them with a gesture.

"You have much to learn about the stage and we look forward to teaching you, don't we, darlings? That, my dear Miss Tucker, is our ghost light. We use it to light the stage when the theater is blackened," Tinsley said.

"Ghost light?"

"One of our many superstitions. We always leave a light on for our theater ghosts, who detest the dark. And it prevents us from tripping backstage. See, fantastical and practical, just as theater should be." Tinsley stroked his beard and rocked back on his heels. "Now my puppets, we have visualized our concept of Verona as a beautiful water world divided between the antagonism of two houses. Capulets to be represented in blues and the Montagues in greens."

Eager to have the limelight off my ignorance, I pulled a sketchbook from my messenger bag, noted the colors, then moved to sit with the students.

"Mr. Tinsley, I don't understand this setting." A slight girl with straight blonde tresses stood and pushed her glasses up her nose. "Two ruling houses at war in an underwater planet doesn't make sense. There would be no family loyalty in a water world. The species only instinct would be survival."

"Tell that to Aquaman." I leaned toward a nearby student. "How does she know this stuff?"

"Skylar is our valedictorian," she whispered. "She's brilliant."

"What is Skylar doing in the theater program? Shouldn't she be hanging in a science lab?"

"You can't be serious." The girl curled her lip. "We have one of the best drama programs in the country. If you want to hang with the burnouts, go check out the art wing."

"Hey now," I said. "Artists aren't burnouts. We just think on a different level than other people."

"That's because you're all on drugs. Go take another hit off your bong, burnout."

"That's Miss Tucker to you, missy." I lowered one eyebrow, but thought about the hard drive Detective Herrera carried from the art wing. "So, is there a major drug problem among the art students?"

Little Miss Priss rolled her eyes at me. "Considering Preston King runs fine arts, what do you think?"

"Who is Preston King? A teacher?"

Priss scoffed and turned her back on me to listen to the continuing discussion between Skylar and Tinsley.

"Skylar, use these excellent questions in building the characters' motivations." Tinsley broke off his speech, frozen for a moment, then dug a hand into his pocket.

Around me, the students jolted upright from their cross-legged droops.

Hands wandered into pockets and purses, and a number of phones slid under legs, into palms, and beneath notebooks.

"It's settled," Tinsley announced, shoving his phone back in his pocket. "Verona WAS," he zinged a look toward Skylar, "a technologically advanced civilization and now covered in water."

"But how did the Capulets develop gills?" Skylar spoke before she raised her hand.

"They live in a bubble." Tinsley said. "Class is over early."

Skylar nodded, then bolted toward the side of the stage followed by other students, their eyes on barely concealed devices.

Tinsley waited until they left, untied the cape, and let it drop to the floor. He stared into the large auditorium, seeming to forget I remained on the stage with him.

"Did you get another text?" I asked. "Looked like an all-points-bulletin hit the airwaves at the same time."

Fishing his phone from his pocket, he drew it toward his face and touched the small screen. Shuddering, he shoved it back in his pocket. "Not a text. A PeerNotes communique. Or as you said, an all-points-bulletin. Announcements through PeerNotes are designed to pop up before and after school unless it's an emergency. Someone broke those rules."

"Can a student make these announcements?"

"I suppose if they had the password."

"What'd it say?"

Tinsley took a deep breath. "'Don't cry for me, Peerless. The truth is I never left you. All through my wild days, my mad existence, I kept my promise. Don't keep your distance.'"

"What does that mean?"

Tinsley whirled around to face me. "It's the chorus from 'Don't Cry for Me, Argentina.'"

"Sounds pretty creepy."

"You don't understand," said Tinsley. "That song is from the musical, *Evita*. Which we performed last year. I lost the Tiny Tony on that production."

"Why?"

"Because my lead died shortly before competition finals. Ellis Madsen was my Evita."

Eleven

"I need to see all your texts," I said, crossing my arms over my color blocks. "I don't care about your dirty laundry. If you want my help, I've got to know what the texter is texting."

Tinsley shoved his hands in his pockets. "I can paraphrase for you, but I'd rather not give the details. The specifics are unnecessary."

"Have the police seen your texts?"

He shook his head. "If they have a warrant, I'll have to show them, I suppose."

"A warrant?" Whatever he was hiding, it must be good. "This last message seems to be aimed at you. Has anyone else been targeted or just you and Maranda Pringle?"

He scuffed his shoe along the floor. "Oh, I'd say none of the faculty are safe from attack. Some of us just make bigger targets."

A bell rang, officially ending class.

"If the phantom's a student, they sure don't like you and they didn't like Miss Pringle," I said. "If we know the other teachers under fire, then we might be able to check student schedules and see if there's some kind of connection."

"It wouldn't be any of my students." Tinsley walked to the table placed in the middle of the stage and began to shuffle through photocopies.

"Even Skylar?"

He studied me over his shoulder. "Skylar's pigheaded but harmless. I encourage my students to ask questions. I'd start with

Dr. Vail's students. There's a real prejudice against my theater darlings in fine arts."

Of course, I'd have to play the heavy in the one department where I could have fit in. "It might not be a student, you know."

He splayed his hands on the table and his shoulders drooped. "Yes, I have thought it could be a staff member. Someone jealous of my success. Like Dr. Vail. But I'm not the only faculty member targeted, so it doesn't make much sense."

"I was thinking of a parent."

He turned, clutching the sheaf of photocopies. "Why would a parent do this? They pay an exorbitant fee to send their children here. The messaging disrupts classes, as you saw today. What would they gain?"

"I'd say they got rid of the mean witch Miss Pringle, maybe just not the way they intended. Now they're fixing to get you to quit. Just because someone is a parent, it doesn't make them nice or even sane." My thoughts drifted to my own mother, dumping her fatherless kids so she could run off with the milkman. Who just might be Billy Branson. My stomach squeezed and churned. Did that make Shawna my step-sister?

"No." Tinsley shook his head. "The parents are my biggest supporters."

"You aren't as popular as you think. Neither was Miss Pringle."

Tinsley turned back to his table and photocopies.

"Listen, Halo High was a Division A team, but we kicked country ass and made it to the state championship playoffs. And lost. Pissed off the tight end's daddy so much, he started a private campaign to get rid of the coach. Scooted around to all the Saturday night card games, church groups, and the golf course, sowing his little seeds of discontent. Rumors started floating around about the coach and a cheerleader."

Tinsley kept his back to me. "I suppose the coach was fired?"

"Actually the cheerleader's daddy shot the coach in the parking lot of the post office. In the foot. The coach was laid up for the next season, and the cheerleader's daddy arrested."

Tinsley's shoulders bowed. "I savvy your meaning."

"You really should show me your texts. Might give a clue that points to whether it's a student or an adult."

He shook his head. "I've erased them. By the way, have you spoken to Mr. Avtaikin, yet? I'm looking at costume rental. You wouldn't believe the price on retro-aquanaut suits."

Students began to file onto the stage for the next class. Tinsley's shoulders pulled back, his chin lifted, and voice brightened. Turning around, the Professor of Theater was reborn. Greeting his minions, he swooped to center stage to recapture the fallen cape.

I decided to skip class.

Not much changes in eight years.

I lost myself behind the stage and eventually found my way back to the lounge Tinsley had created in the drama vestibule. Why students needed more areas to hang out was beyond me, but hanging out suited my purposes very well. I wanted students' opinions on the messaging. Laurence snoozed on a bean bag chair, but a girl and boy sat across a table, sharing a notebook and googly eyes.

For a moment, I watched the mating ritual of the young teens. Darting glances, fidgety hands, and rigid spines, making an awkward lean toward each other. As they appeared about to combust, they seemed distracted enough to shoot some helpful information my way. I tossed my satchel on the table and pulled out my drawing pad. Tinsley had given me the dimensions of the stage and some basic set pieces. I could accomplish two tasks at once.

The students looked both relieved and annoyed to have me plop down next to them.

"Are you in *Romeo and Juliet*?" I asked. "My name's Cherry Tucker. I'm helping with the set design."

"We don't know yet," said the girl. "I'm Hayden Pendleton. I'm in Advanced, so I'm sure we'll be working with you some." She had pretty hazel eyes and stick straight auburn tresses. Peerless must sell straight irons with their tuition.

"I'm Layton Slater." He had a sweet face and a brown mop top, popular with the boys in the school. His hands played with the notebook, itching to touch Hayden, whose long fingers lay about an inch away.

I opened my sketch book and flipped to a blank page. "Y'all have any ideas about the underwater alien set? I'm fixing to brainstorm."

"Not really," said Hayden, darting a look at Layton. "Fish?" She giggled, then covered it up by running a hand through her hair.

"Fish make perfect sense," said Layton, staring at Hayden. A smile twitched his lips. The boy had it bad.

I needed them to focus. "I suppose, y'all got the PeerNotes announcement with the line from that musical."

They snapped out of their flirting. "*Evita*," said Layton. "I played Ché last year."

"You were so good as Ché," said Hayden. "Really, really good. Super fantastic." The brilliant pink coloring her cheeks made her appear touched with scarlet fever.

Layton's hands slid closer to brush against Hayden's fingertips. "Yeah? You really think so? I don't know. Maybe Josh would have been better."

I whacked my pencil against the table, drawing their attention back to me. "Do you think someone's trying to get at Mr. Tinsley? Or did the message mean something else?"

Hayden blinked. "Because the message was from *Evita*?"

Layton patted her hand. "He took Ellis's death pretty hard. Remember how upset he was? The announcement probably brought it all back to him." Layton stretched across the table to stroke Hayden's forearm. "But he'll be okay."

I slapped my pencil against Layton's wrist, causing them to turn and look at me. "Sorry. Pencil slipped. So I guess Tinsley was pretty close to Ellis, then? Or did he feel guilty about her death?"

"Ellis loved Mr. Tinsley." Hayden crossed her arms.

"I heard that when Ellis was bullied, no one stood up for her. Not even her friends. That's why she killed herself. She felt alone."

Layton reddened. "The rumors were pretty vicious. Anybody who got involved with Ellis was pulled in. We were worried about her, but she wasn't exactly popular either."

"Ellis was super talented, but a lot of students felt a senior should have gotten that role." Hayden's gaze dropped to her lap and her fingers flicked through her hair. "Ellis was really good, but she wasn't even a drama kid."

"So they bullied her because they were jealous?" I asked.

"If we had won the Tiny Tony with Ellis performing, she could have landed a big time agent. And Ellis wasn't even interested in a career. Just think of her resume with the lead in *Evita*."

"Her career? Wasn't she a sophomore?" I squeezed the bridge of my nose. "Good Lord. High school's changed a lot since my day."

"Yeah, I heard they didn't even have computers back then," said Hayden. "How did you do any research?"

"We had computers," I snapped and sketched a computer monitor on my pad with a pencil. "Hey, I saw a cop carrying a hard drive out of the art rooms. Do you know what that's about?"

Layton and Hayden straightened in their chairs. "No," they chimed. Then giggled.

They pulled phones from their pockets and began to type. Layton looked up and caught Hayden's eye. She giggled, then looked back at her phone, her thumbs flying over the keyboard.

"Are you texting each other or somebody else?" I asked.

"Just a minute," said Layton. He touched his screen and hopped into another app, then began scrolling through the screen using his thumb.

"What are you looking at?" I moved onto my knees to see over his shoulder.

"PeerNotes."

"Does it say anything about me in there?"

Hayden gave me an "as-if" look. "No. We're reading posts about the art department. Someone reported the cops coming in.

They don't know why they took the hard drive. It's from the design lab. And everyone knows Preston does his graphics on it."

"Preston King? Did they confiscate computers in other classrooms?" If they did, it might be related to Miss Pringle's death.

Hayden and Layton began tapping the keyboards with their thumbs. Then giggled again.

I pushed on Layton's arm to see his phone. "What are you writing?"

"Nothing," said Layton, scooting his phone into his lap.

"We should get to class," said Hayden.

"Exactly," I said. "Why aren't you in class? What's the deal with all these students wandering around, not in class?"

"Whatever," said Hayden. She stood and before she could take her books, Layton slid them in his arms. Bumping hips, they glided through the double doors and into the arts hall.

I glanced at my sketchpad. I had a fish and a computer. Not an award winning set design. Or even a good composition.

"They don't know much," said a voice from the floor.

I peered over the table at Laurence. "And why aren't you in class? What kind of school lets you sit in a bean bag all day?"

"Independent study," he said. "But I'm not allowed to leave the campus."

"Shouldn't you be independently studying instead of napping?"

"What do you care?" Laurence blinked at the ceiling and stretched. "As long as my grades are good, they leave me alone."

"Who?"

"Everybody." He pushed himself to standing and walked to the table. "You better watch yourself. Kids like Layton and Hayden won't pick up on your questions, but others will."

"Other students?"

"Not just students." His smile gave me the jitters. "Something wicked this way comes to Peerless."

"I'm kind of a literal person," I said. "Can you spell it out for me since you know so much?"

He shook his head. "It doesn't really interest me."

"Doesn't interest you?" What was with Tara's brother? Why didn't he have the eager-beaver Mayfield genes? "Would it interest you to speak to the police? I could arrange it."

"The police interest me even less. But it makes no difference to me."

"I need to know which teachers are targeted by anonymous texting."

"Some might tell you, most won't." He snatched his jacket from the table, shrugged it on inside-out, and shoved his hands in his pockets.

"Why don't you tell me?"

"It's not my business," he said and ambled from the lounge. "Peace."

"I don't get this school," I said to my fish drawing. "It's too hard."

TWELVE

I abandoned my student questioning to try an adult-oriented approach. I strode toward the office with my visitor lanyard slapping my belly. The office hummed with activity.

Flashing my badge to the parent volunteer, I moved around the long counter. An office assistant's desk sat in the back, and I honed in on the young woman typing on the computer. She had neither straight hair nor artificial body parts. I breathed a sigh. She was my people.

I glanced at the name plate on her desk. Amber Tipton. "Hey, Miss Amber. How are you?"

She looked up from her computer, searched my face, then my visitor's pass. "Can I help you?"

"Cherry Tucker. I'm Mr. Tinsley's art director for his new play." I dropped in the chair next to her desk. "Are you busy?"

"I'm always busy," she said. "Especially now that I'm the only administrative assistant."

"Miss Pringle's death must be hard on you. I heard someone sent Miss Pringle some horrible texts before her death. Mercy, that's awful," I prompted. "You didn't get one, did you?"

Amber slitted a glance toward me. "You think I'm letting anyone here have my cell phone number? The administration has my home phone and that's it. The only creepy texts I get are booty calls from my ex."

"I hear you there," I said. "Poor Miss Pringle. Did many other staff get messaged like Maranda?"

"I've heard a few teachers talk about it. Most think it's a kid with an axe to grind."

"Any idea who's doing it?"

"Like I have time to think about that," said Amber. "I barely have time to breathe this week."

I glanced at the girls leaning against the counter, snapping selfies. "You must be overwhelmed. Aren't Miss Pringle's student assistants helping out?"

Amber shot them a dark look. "Not really. But she didn't have them do anything useful anyway. And I don't have time to train them."

"What do you need doing? I'm sure there's something easy they can manage. I'll explain it to them."

Her eyes lit up.

After a quick explanation of Miss Pringle's filing system, I soon found my arms loaded with folders. My line of office ducks followed me into Miss Pringle's office and listened while I explained the concept of the alphabet. A bell rang and the students took off before a single file entered the cabinet.

I chewed my lip and glanced at my watch, wondering if anyone would notice if I skipped last period. Then realized I was alone in Miss Pringle's office. I left the stack of files and the open cabinet drawers to study her desk.

Pringle's hard drive tower had been dismantled. No photos or personal effects other than a horoscope-of-the-day calendar sat on her desk. I dropped into her chair and pulled open the wide, top drawer used for holding pens, paperclips, and dust bunnies. Finding her computer password taped under her pen caddy, I wrote that handy piece of information on the underside of my arm. The other drawers had stationary, procedural files, and boring memos about tornados, bomb threats, and fire drills. I shut the drawers, disappointed.

Relaxing my head against the back of her office chair, I wondered why the police took hard drives and computer chips for a "prankster" that might not have anything to do with Pringle's suicide. Anytime there's an unnatural death the police are called in. But if a suicide had been confirmed, the investigation would be dropped. Unless the death was still considered suspicious.

I tapped my fingers on the leather chair arms and tipped the chair back. Uncle Will wouldn't tell me diddly about an open investigation, even another department's. But Luke might play ball, seeing as how he was in a let-me-make-it-up-to-you-baby kind of mood these days.

My eyes slid closed as I contemplated the strategy of asking Luke to reveal police business. I jerked awake at the call of my name.

Assistant Principal Cooke stood before the desk.

My face burned, and I hopped from the chair.

Busted again.

"Sorry." I rushed over my words. "I was helping Miss Amber and just waiting on the next group of student office workers to show them how to file."

Brenda Cooke narrowed her eyes into a well-honed principal glare. "I thought you were assisting Mr. Tinsley, not helping in the front office."

"Yes, that, too." I smiled wide and patted my chartreuse messenger bag. "We had our brainstorm session, and I was just picturing an underwater alien Verona."

"Why do I keep finding you in Miss Pringle's office?"

"I don't know, ma'am. Bad luck, I guess."

She glanced at the desk and back to me.

I pressed the scribbling on my arm against my dress.

"Don't let it happen again," she said.

Crap, I thought as I trotted out of the office.

This investigation work was trickier than I thought. I walked back to Amber's desk. "Hey Amber, those students took off before they put away the files and Ms. Cooke just kicked me out of Pringle's office."

Amber blew out a sigh. "Figures. They better hire somebody soon or I'm fixing to quit. Ms. Cooke keeps handing me things to do. I can barely keep up with the front office as it is. I didn't even get lunch."

"Good luck," I said. "If I get extra minutes tomorrow, I'll try to help."

"Thanks." She turned back to her computer.

"Cherry." The squeal came from the visitors' area.

I recognized the voice by the headache it caused. In a pink knit dress and matching Keds, Tara Mayfield bounced on a chair before the windows.

If Tara had a tail, the school foyer would catch site of it wagging.

"Did you come to pick up your brother?" I asked.

"Sort of." She popped from her seat to skip to the counter. "I thought you needed help with your sets?"

"Rome wasn't built in a day, Tara," I said, sounding very art directory. "We just had our first meeting to brainstorm ideas. Auditions aren't until tomorrow. I won't start painting until later this week."

"Oh." Her pout caused a rainbow to vanish. "Darn it."

"Watch your language." I winked. "We're in a school."

Twenty shades of magenta scorched her cheeks.

"By the way," I said, feeling bad about my teasing. "What's the deal with your brother?"

"Is Laurence giving you a hard time? I am so sorry. He's a little different." Tara pressed her hands together and bowed her head. "I am at a loss at what to do with him. A loss."

"What do you mean? He's a teenager. You let him grow up." Of course, I was at a loss of what to do with my brother, too. But Cody had stolen from my nemesis and declared war on the stepfamily of my ex-boyfriend, stirring a pot of god-awful crap that would hit a fan aimed at me. Laurence was no Cody. "Laurence wasn't bothering me. I just don't understand him."

"I don't understand him, either," said Tara. "Why doesn't he want to get involved?"

"In what?"

"In anything! He spends all his time in his room reading. He doesn't talk to anyone. I don't think he has any friends. I'm so worried about him."

Tara's agony over her brother jabbed my heart with empathetic needles. "Listen, I'll keep my eye on him while I'm here. When we start the actual building of the set, feel free to help."

"Thank you, Cherry." Tara catapulted across the counter to hug my neck.

The edge of the counter dug into my stomach. I gently shoved her to the ground. "I'll see you around. I should go work on my sketches."

"Of course," she chirped. "By the way, Lukey was much nicer to me today. Whatever you said to him last night must have helped."

I contained my grimace and fled the school. I wasn't sure if Lukey would appreciate that thought or not.

On my way home from Peerless, I buzzed my Uncle Will's number. He picked up on the second ring. Expecting to leave a voicemail, I slipped my flip phone between my shoulder and chin and stumbled through a greeting. "Detective Herrera from Line Creek says to tell you hello."

"That's nice," said Will, "anything else?"

"Did the coroner officially call Maranda Pringle's death a suicide yet?"

"Get in here," said Will.

Dammit, I thought and hung up. Letting the phone fall into my lap, I drove the extra twenty minutes to the Sheriff's Office. I parked and walked into the building, holding a palm up before Tamara could open her surly mouth.

Eyeing my metacarpal stop sign, she folded her arms over her chest. The black G's on her red fingernails stood out against her firm biceps. "You are one hot mess, Cherry Tucker. What have you gotten yourself into this time?"

"Nothing, ma'am," I said, striding to the doorway to the back rooms.

"Sheriff calls you in for a talking-to, it ain't nothing."

"Please just buzz me through." I stared at the door. "I don't need an escort."

"You need a life escort, that's what you need, Cherry Tucker."

At her buzz, I yanked on the door and walked down the hall to Uncle Will's office. I knocked, heard Will's call to enter, and toddled through. Uncle Will sat behind his desk, his hands folded over his BBQ-bulged belly. Deputy Luke Harper sat in one of the two chairs before his desk. At my entrance, their conversation halted, and Luke turned in his seat.

Pasting on my best customer service smile, I strode forward. Unlike Maranda Pringle's desk, Uncle Will's held family photos including one of my siblings and I at my graduation from SCAD. First and only in my family to go to college. And they still wished I had gone to a school with football.

"Hello, gentleman. What can I do you for?" I nodded to each in turn.

"Have a seat, hon'," said Will. "Deputy Harper tells me you're doing a little investigative work at the Peerless Day Academy."

"Yes, sir." My mind churned, reexamining my time spent at Peerless and what constituted as interference in police business. Other than going through Pringle's desk, I didn't think I had done anything untoward. And no one knew about that, except maybe Assistant Principal Brenda Cooke.

Oh, crap, I thought. Did Cooke call Uncle Will? I hated it when the principal called home to tattle.

"I can explain." I slid back in the chair, letting my boots dangle.

"Explain what?" Luke glanced at Will.

"Am I in trouble?" I kept my eyes on Uncle Will. Could he ground me from going to Peerless?

"That depends on what you've done." Will drew the words out. "Let's hear it."

I recognized that tone from my childhood. That particular phrase used to force me into confession, but I had savvied to that lesson by the time I was fifteen. I straightened my spine and smoothed my Mondrian dress.

"Besides meeting with the theater class to determine what set to design, not much. But while I was there, a strange announcement went over the PeerNotes wavelengths to everyone in the school."

"Their social media website?" Uncle Will rocked back in his chair. "Was Detective Herrera there when the message went out?"

"What did the announcement say?" asked Luke.

I crossed my legs, eager to report what I'd learned. They hadn't called me in to holler at me.

The Sheriff's Office wanted to know what was going on in the school.

"Some lines from last year's musical." I explained the lyrics and how they implicated Tinsley and Ellis Madsen. "I believe Detective Herrera had already left. He confiscated a hard drive from the art rooms and I don't know what else. Didn't anybody from the school tell Line Creek PD about the weird PeerNotes announcement?"

Will rubbed his thick neck. "I'll call and ask them in a minute. You say Herrera confiscated a hard drive?"

"You think it was something to do with the Pringle case, sir?" asked Luke.

"That's what I wondered." I bounced in my seat.

"Maybe they were checking computer histories in relation to the Pringle case and something on the art computer sent up a red flag." Luke raised his brows at Will.

"Well," said Will, "there's probable cause for the Pringle case. Wouldn't need a warrant if the principal gave permission for a search."

"I have yet to meet Principal Cleveland," I said. "Haven't even glimpsed him."

"Who's running the show over there?" asked Luke.

"The assistant principal, Brenda Cooke, keeps catching me…" I paused to give my brain a chance to shut my mouth. "The assistant principal is always around."

The room fell silent except for the popping tick of the overhead clock as both men fell into a meditative stupor. I gave them a minute to collect their thoughts, but I was never one for long bouts of cogitation.

"So why am I here?" I said.

"We're interested in this Pringle case," said Will.

"And why's that?"

More silence. I studied each man, then focused on Will. "Did the county coroner call it a suicide?"

"Yes, but I am troubled," he said.

"Is Line Creek police troubled?"

"Not as much as I," Will admitted. "I don't like this text messaging business. Especially when they had the cyberbullying issue last year."

"Herrera said last year was completely different."

"Yes and no," said Will.

"That's helpful. So, if the suspicious death has been called a suicide, Line Creek is done investigating. But you disagree with the county coroner. Which means you could make this political."

"I suppose that sums it up."

I turned to Luke. "And why are you here?"

"Curiosity." He wore his hooded cop look, but I sensed a grin somewhere underneath.

"You usually zing me for that." I narrowed my eyes. "Y'all want to know what I've heard, don't you?"

"It's Line Creek's investigation," said Will. "Like Luke said, we're curious. And Luke told me the drama teacher wants your help with this texting business. We figured you'd have your ear to the ground."

A smile curled around my cheeks. "So, you're looking for inside information? You could deputize me."

"No," said Will.

"You don't have to be so quick on the draw."

"More like we should keep an eye on you." Will tapped a finger on his desk. "Someone's stirring up trouble at Peerless. I'm just not sure if it's a student getting his kicks from upsetting teachers or something more malicious. I don't believe they're dangerous, but these things can get out of hand quickly."

"Tinsley's shook up, that's for sure," I said. "Here's something. The art department might have a drug problem."

"Students or teachers?" asked Luke.

"I'm not sure," I said. "My source implicated the whole department."

"Who was your source?" asked Will.

"A student."

"Well, that may be the answer to the confiscated hard drive. Some idiot could be using the school's computers to organize their dealing." Will waved his hand. "What else do you have?"

"Your turn," I said. "Did Miss Pringle leave a suicide note?"

Will stared at his hands. "Yes and no."

"What is with the yeses and noes?"

"The note was typed. Printed from a computer." Will shook his head. "Didn't bother Coroner McMillan, but I didn't like it."

"The note or that fact that it was printed?"

"Both."

I kicked my boots against the chair legs. "What about the text messages she got? What did they say?"

"She deleted the messages, but Line Creek sent the phone to the GBI lab for analysis." Will leaned forward on his desk. "So, I bet you've heard a lot of scuttle about Pringle. What do you think the texts say?"

"I'm guessing they refer to her love life," I said. "A parent hinted she had an affair with the principal. Even Tinsley called Cleveland a lovesick basset hound or some such name. And maybe she slept with a coach and some fathers. I saw her picture. Maranda Pringle's a looker. But I can't see how any of that would cause her to commit suicide."

"Unless one of the affairs caused her a lot of guilt for another reason," said Will.

"Like?"

"A student who died."

"Holy shit." My eyes widened. "Pringle was involved with Ellis Madsen's father? So both Pringle and Tinsley are pointed out for Ellis's death?"

"How would Tinsley be involved in her death?" asked Luke.

"He gave her the lead in *Evita*, which may have prompted the bullying attack. Lots of jealousy hangs over that theater program," I said. "But I'm having a hard time reading anyone at this school. They're not my people."

"Let us know if you hear anything else," said Will. "If you have anything substantial, I'll tell Detective Herrera."

"Will do." I rose from my chair. "Set building doesn't start until after auditions, but I'm fixing to go back to school tomorrow anyway."

"Just a minute." Will pointed at the chair and I sank back onto the seat. "Harper, I need to talk to Cherry about some personal business."

My eyebrows hit my temples. Did Miss Tamara squeal to Uncle Will about me acting like a squirrel?

"Yes, sir." Luke stood, then placed a hand on my shoulder. "Let's continue our talk about this Peerless business. Red's at six tomorrow night?"

"All right." I watched Luke stroll out of the room and turned to Uncle Will. "I swear I'm not running around Luke's tree. I'm just reporting in on the Phantom Texter case."

"What tree?" Uncle Will's brows dropped. "You do not have a case. You're observing an event while you're working on something else."

"Yes, sir. Although if someone's paying me to do investigative work, I believe case is an appropriate term."

Will shot me a look that bespoke of an inappropriate term.

"Is that the personal business you wanted to talk about?"

"No." Will dipped forward in his chair. "It's about your brother. Something's going on with that boy."

"Cody's twenty-one. His brain isn't fully formed, that's what's wrong with him."

"Deputy Caruthers picked him up last night."

"Dammit. What'd he do? DUI?"

"Not exactly. Caruthers was patrolling Fetlock Meadows subdivision and found your brother sleeping in his car. Cody had been drinking earlier, though."

"Fetlock Meadows? Cody doesn't know anybody in Fetlock Meadows." Fetlock Meadows had been built around a golf course outside Halo. Not quite as posh as Ballantyne, but Halo's high and mighty needed a place for their own McMansions close to their ancestral digs.

Uncle Will ran a hand over his salt and pepper buzz. "He was parked outside JB Branson's house."

"What in the hell was he doing there?" I said, followed by a silent "Oh, shit." This might have something to do with the photos. But why JB's house? Except Luke bunked there with his mom and stepdad while waiting to get his own place. Was Cody serious about his threat against Luke?

Uncle Will saw the cuss words crossing my mind. "What's wrong with Cody?"

"I don't know. I'll talk to him."

"See that you do. Ed says y'all haven't been around the farm much. And I know you skipped Sunday dinner, which isn't like you." Will massaged his chin. "What's going on with you Tucker kids? Are you and Cody not happy with Casey's new husband?"

I chewed my cheek, wondering how long I could cover for Cody. And I didn't want to upset Casey.

"Takes some getting used to is all," I finally said. "But I have been going over to Max Avtaikin's house to eat."

"Figured as much. Your belly's always followed Casey's cooking. Just don't let it hurt Pearl's feelings. She's a good woman and good for Ed."

"Yes, sir. I actually made nice with her this morning." I jumped off my seat and hot footed it out of his office before he questioned me on why Cody might stalk the Bransons.

This was the problem with small towns. You spend so much time tripping over everyone's feet, after a while you can't remember where you were supposed to be stepping.

THIRTEEN

With the PeerNotes announcement implicating Tinsley and with Vail's ominous threats, I wanted to know what Max had learned about the illustrious director. I also needed to see if my sister had any idea why my brother had lost his ever-loving mind. I kick-started my Datsun into drive and aimed her east back toward Halo.

My sister answered Max's door again. Today she wore a pair of cutoffs most likely illegal in some states and a tube top covered by a black mesh t-shirt. A hole in the mesh exposed her belly button ring, which caught the light pouring from the second story chandelier. The ring beamed a tiny blue dot on the marble floor like a white trash laser pointer.

"Did you come here for dinner again?" she asked.

"What are you making?"

"Nothing special. Greens and chicken fried steak. Maybe I'll whip up some taters."

My stomach showed it's appreciation, and the door on the far right of the foyer flew open. Nik poked his head out. "What is that noise? Casey, you are okay?"

She popped a hip in his direction, throwing the belly ring laser light toward the far wall. "It's just Cherry. She's staying for dinner."

"My greatest hope is to have the dinner alone with my wife." Nik glared at me.

"Get a real job and your own house, and you can make it happen." My smile showed my teeth. "This is America, land of opportunity. Where dreams come true."

"This is not my meaning."

"Oh, I got your meaning," I said. "I want to talk to you, Nik Ivanov. Casey, have you heard from our brother?"

"Nope. I always assume no news is good news. It's been a peaceable honeymoon this way." The blue dot aimed toward the back of the house at her turn. "You're on dish duty tonight."

I waited for her to leave, hating the thought of killing her peace. "Is Max in there?" I pointed to the open study door.

"No." Nik shook his head. "He is still in bedroom as usual."

"Good," I said, walking through the doorway. "We need to chat. About my sister. And what you're doing for the Bear."

Nik made a sound of protest, but followed me in, shutting the heavy wooden door. The room still had the essence of Max's spicy cologne mixed with the other manly scents of wood oil and leather. And musty Old Rebel junk. Max stored most of his Confederate States memorabilia in this room. I avoided the cases of antiques and plopped into a plump, leather armchair in front of the carved marble fireplace.

"I'm kind of surprised Max lets you in here," I said. "He's pretty protective of his Civil War souvenirs."

"Boss is trusting me with many things," said Nik. He took the other leather chair, letting his arms fall across the back. "So is my wife. Casey is your sister, but she is my wife. Do not interfere."

"You are lying to her. That makes it my business." I narrowed my eyes. "She thinks you're applying at local garages to be a mechanic. What are you doing, Nik?"

He crossed his arms. "I can make more money working for Avtaikin. And he is helping us very much, so I want to help him. In truth, I need good job and a house for my wife."

"I thought you liked working on cars."

"I do, but I really like my old job as chauffeur. I want to own limousine company some day. I need much money for this. Boss says he can help me."

"What's Max having you do for him?" My stomach made an unsettled turn. "It's important that I know."

Nik shook his head. "Boss said I shouldn't tell you any information about the business."

The hairs on my neck rose. "And why the hell not?"

Nik shrugged. "He says it's game you play with him. And it's none of your business."

I collapsed back in the chair and stared at the coffered ceiling. "It's not a game if either of you land in prison."

"For what are we landing in prison?"

"I don't know, but Max has come too close for comfort on several occasions. And I don't want my sister spending her best childbearing years in the conjugal visit trailer."

Nik jumped to his feet in order to wave his arms more effectively. "You are ridiculous. You know this? I have done nothing wrong."

The door to the study banged against its hinges. I glanced over my shoulder and saw the Bear leaning on his crutches. His mouth twitched, as if it wanted to smile but couldn't in mixed company.

"Boss." Nik hopped from his seat and scurried to the door. "You are using the crutches. It is wonderful to see you moving about. Cherry is just leaving. She came to visit her sister."

"I heard the shouting. I assumed Miss Tucker visits." Max waved aside Nik's help and hobbled into the study. "I will speak to her. Alone."

Nik shot me a now-you're-going-to-get-it look, which I ignored. Having a new brother was not much different than having an old brother.

The door shut behind Nik, and Max crutched his way to his desk. He eased into a smile and into his big chair, then opened a drawer on his desk to prop his leg. Unbuttoning the top three buttons on his white dress shirt, he crooked a finger. "Artist, why are you locked up with Nik in my study?"

I hopped from the chair, but stopped in front of his desk. "What is it this time? Black market goods you're importing from the

Commies and selling here? Guns? Vodka? Those little stacking dolls?"

"Commies? You have no idea what I do, do you?" Max smiled. "Good. Let us keep it this way."

"We're friends. I should know what you do for a living."

"You have caught us. Nik helps me supply the church with gaming equipment for their casino night. Not so exciting, eh?" His raised eyebrow mocked me, but he dropped it to sigh. "This obsession you have with finding my illegal activity needs to stop. You say we are friends? Then I need to trust you. And you need to trust me."

I toed his desk with my boot. "I'm glad to hear you're putting Nik to legitimate use. That's a relief. He needs to tell my sister his plans, though."

"I agree." Max nodded, then turned to his computer to flick on the monitor. "Now, are you done interrogating me? Perhaps I can move on to a more useful passage of time."

"Actually, I'm here to interrogate you on another point." I dropped into a chair before his desk. "Have you learned anything about Tinsley?"

"His background is transparent to a point. Not much of his personal life is available outside his theater credits. What news about your anonymous bully?"

"Nothing really. It could be a jealous parent, a disgruntled student, or a spiteful teacher. I've detected hostile feelings toward both Pringle and Tinsley. Getting into Tinsley's advanced drama class is very competitive. Although the texts may point toward the loss of a star sophomore last year." I explained Ellis's suicide.

"Ah, so perhaps the motive is revenge."

"Perhaps. I wonder if anyone else finds Tinsley's choice in a play about suicidal teens in poor taste after what happened to Ellis last year. But maybe that's why he's making *Romeo and Juliet* into a musical comedy. With aliens living in a bubble."

Max's gaze flickered from his computer. "You are not selling me on making the contribution to this drama school."

"It's not a drama school. It's a school with a big drama department."

"I mean school with much drama. Did you not say that many parents threatened to remove their children last year because of this cyberbully?"

"Yes, that's true. You think the Phantom Texter is trying to get the school shut down?"

"Perhaps." Max shrugged. "If I paid the exorbitant tuition and had to deal with this mess, I would remove my children from this school."

I contemplated Max with children, but couldn't form a mental picture beyond the three bears and their porridge.

"Perhaps the bully just loves the anarchy."

"That could be. If someone wanted to shut down Peerless, I'd think they'd be more public with their accusations. But if the Phantom Texter does intend to ruin the school's reputation, I hope he's the one publicly outed. Playing with emotional blackmail which led to someone's suicide is heinous. I want to take this viper down." I raised my fist for a dramatic shake.

Max turned from the computer screen to watch me. His brows pulled together. "What have you done to your arm?"

I dropped my arms, twisting them back and forth to examine them, and spotted the mark. "It's not a bruise. I wrote Miss Pringle's computer password on my arm."

Max's brows lifted. "And what did you plan to do with Miss Pringle's computer password?"

"The police took her computer, but I figure the school staff must be linked in a system. Her account could already be wiped out, but could we check? I want to see if she had gotten any emails from the Phantom."

"I find it ironic that you worry about my legalities, yet you feel no remorse in your own illicit acts."

"My illicit acts are for the betterment of society."

Max rolled his eyes. "Well then, let us break into Miss Pringle's account. For the betterment of society."

I scooted to Max's side as he pulled up the school website. Ignoring the parent information, Max hunted the home page until he found the employee links and clicked onto the staff intranet site.

"All staff has the same type of email address," I said. "Their first and last name separated with a period at Peerless dot net."

Max typed, while I read the code off my arm. He smiled at the computer. "I think this information may also be helpful for my accountant."

"You're going to use Maranda Pringle's password to help you decide whether to contribute to the school or not?"

His gaze slid from the computer screen to me. "Why not? I always do the thorough investigation before writing the checks. Even before I bought your painting."

My eyes narrowed. "You investigated me?"

"Of course. You are an investment."

"I'm an investment?"

"Your art." He waved his hand toward the computer. "Please finish your checking of the Pringle emails."

I turned to the computer, my mouth itching to question him on his Cherry Tucker probe while my brain ordered me to focus on the task at hand. "Looks like Miss Pringle was not one to allow emails to loiter in the inbox. Most of these are flagged to-do types."

"You expect her to keep incriminating emails? Look in her deleted or sent messages."

I clicked on the deleted messages. "Nothing. Let me try sent messages." I tapped the mouse. "Bingo. She forgot to clear this cache."

"You realize the police can search these folders?"

"I know, unless they've dropped the investigation." I scrolled through the messages. "Lots of correspondence between her and Principal Cleveland. Her replies to Cleveland are very businesslike. Whereas his are of the lovesick basset hound type."

"Please explain. I do not know this saying."

"I'll give you an example. 'Maranda,'" I read, "'Please send Brenda Cooke the first quarter billings statements. By the way, I saw you at Little Verona's with Coach Newcomb. Dinner in public? I thought that wasn't your style. Is this to get back at me? Rick.'"

"Is this billings statement he speaks of attached to the email?"

I spun to face Max. "Stop thinking about their financial reports. This was probably the kind of stuff the texter used against Miss Pringle."

"Why should revealing her love affairs drive her to suicide?"

"Don't say love affairs. It gives me the willies. Americans don't say love affairs."

"How do you express the adult relationship, then?" He arched an eyebrow.

"You buy me a beer, look at the door, and I follow you home. Everybody sees it and boom, we're in a relationship. And if you deny it, they'll think I'm loose."

"Loose?"

"With the morals. And the shedding of the clothes." I turned back to the computer to scroll through more of Pringle's sent box. "I should tell Luke about this email."

"The policeman?"

"The deputy. He's also helping me on the case." I faced Max, scooting my hip onto the edge of his desk.

His expression appeared relaxed, but the earlier smile had faded from his eyes. "Is this at your insistence or the policeman's?"

"His insistence. But it works for me. I want us to be friends."

"Friends with man your family finds unworthy of your attention?"

"That's a nice way to put it, but yep. If Luke becomes my friend, then maybe they'll see differently. And stop trying to draw lines in the sand between his family and ours."

Max took my hand and gave it a pat. "You are the idealist in all circumstances, Artist. This is a good thing. But not everyone views the world as you do. And your problems arise when you do not attempt to understand this."

"Friendship's not idealistic. Everyone else has lost their senses."

"Exactly my point." With a smirk, Max tipped his chair back and rested his hands behind his head. "You are so besotted with your own ethical code, you have not the ability to see the other perspective. But perhaps your instincts are right and you can bridge whatever gaps are between your families. 'But go wisely and slow. Your speed will cause you to stumble.'"

"Obviously, this is some kind of compliment I'm too besotted to understand." I shoved off the desk. "Tell my sister we'll talk later. I need to work on my set sketches."

Maybe friendship wasn't the key. But I didn't feel like discussing those intimacies with Max.

The sweet sorrow of parting from Luke might be more than I could take.

FOURTEEN

Because it was a school night, I stayed out of bars and did my homework. However, my mind was not on designing an Atlantis alien home for the doomed romance of singing sub-aquatics. It remained on the inevitability of my own doomed romance. Like the aqua-Romeo, Luke clung to hope, making his advances hard to resist.

Maybe I needed a trident.

The following day, I began with a visit to JB Branson's dealership garage. It seemed Cody's last public appearance included a rendition of "Take This Job and Shove It," without the musical accompaniment. After suffering a long monologue by Cody's boss, who decided to spend his saved Cody harangue on me, I felt anxious to return to school and focus on rooting out the malevolent phantom messenger.

Much more fun than getting yelled at by my brother's boss. Or even drawing bubble homes for fish-men.

Pointing the Datsun northwest once again, I encouraged my reluctant starter to enjoy the autumn splendor of the tree lined drive dappled in yellow ochres, oxide-red lakes, and cadmium yellow oranges. The air smelled of fresh cut hay and fallen pine needles. Claude Monet may have had *Autumn in Argenteuil*, but I had "Fall in Forks County."

We chugged at a pace just faster than a cotton picker, but the beautiful day matched my mood. The way I saw it, the sheriff had given me further permission to stick my nose in other people's business. And I meant to do it. I wanted a list of teachers who had received messages from our phantom texter. And to see if the texts also intimated a relationship to Ellis Madsen.

Arriving late, I found a spot in the back-forty, then hoofed my way into the castle-like edifice. No parent manned the front desk, so I snagged a visitor lanyard and waved at Amber, still buried in folders. Behind Amber, the office buzzed with chatting teachers, waiting in a long queue that snaked around the corner to the back offices. I aimed myself in that direction, figuring the heart of the beast lay in the copy room.

"Hey," I said to the first group of teachers I encountered. "How are y'all? What's new?"

The khaki and polo clad group peered at me, recognizing a stranger in their midst. I should have bought khakis instead of educational themed wear. My "I Like Big Books" t-shirt dress didn't seem to impress them. And I had spent half the night Be-Dazzling the book covers.

"Who are you subbing for?" asked an older female with dark hair. She grasped a Peerless Academy coffee mug in one hand while her arm clutched copies to her chest. "You can leave the teacher's mail in their box. Lock their grade book in their desk, though. We've had a rash of grade book burglaries."

"Instead of using your attendance book, you should enter the grades immediately in your computer," said her bespectacled and mustached colleague. "Then the students couldn't fiddle with their grade."

"If you think a computer will stop them, you're wrong," an older woman in a Peerless polo replied. "At least a record book is somewhat alien to them. If a keyboard or touchscreen isn't attached, most of them won't recognize the item."

All three laughed. The fourth teacher, seeing movement in the copier line, darted away.

"What do you think of PeerNotes?" I asked. "That announcement yesterday interrupted the class I attended. Did you get another one today?"

"Not today, thank God. Yesterday was bad enough," grumbled Coffee Mug. "They should never have reinstituted PeerNotes after what happened last year."

"Because it was used to harass Ellis Madsen?" I prodded. "Did the bullies also text like they are now?"

"Poor Ellis might have been texted," said Peerless Polo. "But I understood most of the bullying had been done on PeerNotes, which was why Maranda suggested shutting it down."

"What's going on now?" asked Glasses with Mustache.

"Really, Frank?" said Coffee Mug. "Maranda supposedly received some upsetting texts. I heard she had some issues with depression, too."

"I didn't know, Debby," said Frank. "It's hard to believe someone like Maranda had issues with depression."

Debby arched an eyebrow. "Even femme fatales get the blues."

"Did any of you receive similar texts?" The little detective in my head rubbed her hands together in glee. These teachers were a hotbed of information.

Frank blinked behind his glasses, which I took as a no. Debby shook her head, and Peerless Polo spotted a free copier and shot into the copy room.

My little detective pouted. I fixed on one last question before I lost them to copying. "Who do you think sent Maranda those texts? The same person who put the announcement on PeerNotes yesterday?"

Frank's forehead creased. Frank was no help in matters of school gossip. I turned to Debby.

"It's hard for me to believe a student would say something so hurtful to Maranda. They'd have to know her personally, although enough rumors fly around here." Debby hugged her copies. "As for the PeerNotes announcement, I have no idea. Hacking into PeerNotes' push notifications is a hobby for a lot of students."

Frank nodded. "Blasted PeerNotes. I wish they'd go back to doing the announcements the old-fashioned way. Blaring them from speakers. At least that interruption can't be hacked."

"Yes it can, Frank," said Debby. "Remember when Preston King fixed his iPod to the sound system and played *Weird Science* during finals?"

"That kid." Frank shook his head. "If his parents hadn't donated so much to Peerless, he'd of gotten kicked out by now."

"Preston King sounds like a troublemaker," I said. "You think he's the one sending these texts and messages on PeerNotes?"

"No idea," smirked Debby, "but Dr. Vail might know."

I sighed. Of course, Dr. Vail. She already hated me.

Nothing is ever easy.

The arts hall vibrated with after school giddiness. Students from the advanced drama class hung around the open theater doors. A bun brigade in tights clustered near the dance studio. Instrument wielding band kids spoke with another group who periodically broke into a cappella riffs.

At that moment, I fell in love with the arts hall.

If only I had been born to wealthy, activity-minded parents, I would have found my niche much earlier in life. Maybe a more profitable career, too.

Near the open doors of the fine arts wing, another bunch slouched on the floor, checking their phones. This selection of students wore knit hats featuring animal faces. I recognized their stained fingers and dirty uniforms as byproducts of the art world and scooted toward my younger peers.

"Hey," I said. "Y'all working on some after-school projects?"

They looked up at me with incurious expressions. Three caps—a panda, monkey, and goldfish—bobbed back to stare at me as well.

"Is one of you Preston King?"

In the middle of the pack, a girl with the panda hat shook her head. "I think he's in trouble," she said. "He left school early."

"For doing the PeerNotes announcement yesterday?" Excitement kicked my voice an octave higher. If so, mystery solved. Preston King could be the Phantom.

"No," said Panda. "I think it had to do with what he was making on Adobe Illustrated."

Dangit. Mystery not solved. Although now I had a possible reason for the confiscated hard drive. "What was he doing with that software?"

Panda looked at Monkey. Monkey looked at Goldfish.

Why couldn't the art department be as brilliant as the theater? Just didn't seem fair. Remembering the drama students' scoff about the art department's use of bongs, I squinted at the trio. "You want to show me your eyes?"

All three dropped their heads. Their respective animal faces stared at my boots. Except the goldfish, whose binocular eyes pointed sideways.

I sighed. "Is Dr. Vail in?"

The animal hats bobbed, noses still pointed at the floor.

In the art vestibule, more students milled around, chatting. The studio doors stood open revealing projects in various mediums and stages of completion. I wandered through the classrooms, enjoying the sight of young artists intent on their works. Picture windows looking out onto a hallway brought more light, although artificial, into the rooms. In the sculpture lab, three students worked the loom using textured wool. I watched them for a few minutes before moving on to a long table where a student applied glaze to a group of clay pots. Behind them a large, top loading kiln stood open, baking the room.

"Is that kiln electric?" I asked.

"Yes. Much safer and holds an even temperature. I trust Tinsley doesn't have you making ceramic pieces for his play?" Dr. Vail approached the potter. "Very nice, Beatrice. That pot should fire well."

Beatrice beamed up at Dr. Vail.

"What are you doing in here?" Dr. Vail folded her arms, her sharp hazel eyes on mine.

"Actually I wanted to speak to you," I said. "It's about these texts some of the faculty are getting. And Preston King—"

"Out," she ordered, flinging her hand toward the door. "And stay out of my department."

"I don't mean any disrespect, ma'am," I said. "I'm just trying to learn—"

Vail grabbed my arm and pulled me toward the door. Around us, the students stopped their work to watch. Those lingering in the vestibule cleared a path for Vail.

"I warned you," she said. "Tinsley may pay you to spy, but you're not getting anything on me or my students. Tell your arrogant leader to keep me and mine out of his snippy blog and we'll leave him alone."

With a final push and a slam of the outer doors, I found myself standing in the hallway. High pitched chattering raced through the corridor. A moment later, a cloud of drama students enveloped me.

"We just heard what happened on PeerNotes," said red-headed Hayden, swinging an arm around my neck and forcing me toward the theater.

"Don't feel bad about Dr. Vail," cooed Kadence, tucking her arm through my right elbow. "She's just awful to us. Some teachers are like that."

"Prejudiced against our success," said Layton. "She hates anyone associated with the theater."

"Doesn't help that Mr. Tinsley rants about her in his blog," said Skylar.

"Shut it, Skylar," said Kadence. "If he's reporting what goes on at our school and happens to mention the art students have gotten out of hand, that's Vail's problem."

"That kind of reporting may become his problem," I said. "Vail's more than hostile. This feud sounds like an all-out departmental war."

With Vail's lieutenant, Preston King, as a known instigator.

FIFTEEN

I hung with the drama students, reveling in their youthful enthusiasm. They couldn't help me put together a list of teachers harassed by text messages, but they did give me pointers for my set sketches. Heralding the actual auditions, parents began to show, changing the teen enthusiasm into an outpouring of dramatic anxiety. When parents began to quiz me about their budding stars as the next alien Capulet and fish loving Montague, my enthusiasm also flipped to anxiety.

I got the hell out of there. The only thing scarier than stage parents are pageant circuit parents. They all reminded me of Shawna Branson's mother.

Although I had plenty of time to meet Luke for our six o'clock case report meeting at Red's, I still ran thirty minutes late. I had changed from my Big Books dress into a pair of viridian jeans and an "I Do My Own Stunts" t-shirt, and now a long CSX train separated me from Red's County Line Tap. As it clattered over the crossing, the freight train blasted its horn, jeering at my tardiness. I rested my forehead on my steering wheel and concentrated on the fear-mongering at Peerless. Would more texts or PeerNotes announcements come out this week? Who would be next?

And why?

I lifted my head as the last train car clattered past me. The flashing red crossing light cut off, the gate lifted, and the Datsun jerked over the tracks. We turned into Red's gravel lot, well populated for a Wednesday night. Among the dozen or so vehicles,

I recognized Luke's black, jacked-up Raptor pickup, Todd's red Civic hatchback, and my brother's 1979 buttercream Malibu.

I parked next to the Malibu, hopping from the Datsun to peer into the gloomy interior of the coupe. A gym bag, hot rod magazines, and assorted fast food trash decorated the red vinyl seats. Could mean Cody was living in his car. Could just point to Cody's lifestyle.

"What are you doing?" Cody called.

I spun away from his window and crunched across the parking lot to meet my brother's approach. His beard had a wooly appearance that meant he had given up trimming. The shaggy, dishwater blond mane touched his shoulders and his Braves cap had been pulled so low, darkness shrouded his eyes.

"Cody, what are you playing at?" I said. "I heard you got picked up last night."

"Evening, sis." He touched his hat and bumped my shoulder, pushing past me.

"You need to talk to me. Is this about the photos? They don't mean anything."

"Tell that to Shawna Branson."

I watched him leave, his rangy swagger reminding me of my Grandpa Ed and someone I didn't know. Not my daddy, whom I didn't remember and who had already been buried by the time Cody was born. I place a hand on my chest and flipped the hurt toward anger.

"You best watch yourself," I called.

He swung into his seat without a backward glance and slammed the door, making the car rock. Gravel sprayed as the Malibu reversed, then roared out of the lot.

"Jackass." I kicked a stray rock then trudged toward Red's. Catching some movement near the front door, my head lifted and my eyes met Luke's.

"What was that about?" he asked.

"That was the friendliest exchange I've had with Cody in about a month. We're making progress."

"Progress from what?"

Seeing as how Cody's issues would bring up the Branson name and Luke was Branson by stepchild default, I decided to continue my position on holding the line. "Dunno. I'll deal with him later. Sorry I'm late."

"Are you okay?" He stood with his hands on his hips and his head tilted down. The Coors sign gleaming through the glass door backlit Luke in a red glow. Between the Coors light and the overhead light beaming overhead, I couldn't make out his expression.

"Just dandy," I said. "I've got two brothers now that I've a mind to exchange for a couple new sisters. But you must know how that feels."

"I don't think I ever wished to exchange my stepbrother for a sister. I just wished for him to disappear. And then he did."

My shoulders slumped. Luke had lost his troublemaking stepbrother six months earlier. Dustin lost his life due to his thuggery ways, but the family still hadn't recovered from the shocking loss.

"Sorry. I love my brother. And I'm on the way to loving Nik. Although I liked him more before he was related to me. I'd never wish for them to disappear. But damn, if Cody's not acting like a first class donkey's behind."

"Sorry to hear it." Luke hooked an arm around my neck and pulled me toward his chest.

I fought off tears of frustration and let my head rest near his shoulder for a moment too long, then stepped back.

"Thanks, friend." I jammed my hands into my jeans' pockets. "I needed that hug. Have you been waiting long?"

"I got here early to chat with Red and then came out to wait for you. I thought we could drive to Line Creek and visit the Locked and Loaded."

"Where? Why?" I squinted at him then glanced over my shoulder at the parking lot. Spying a lime green Volkswagen Bug, I pursed my lips. "Are you hiding from Tara?"

"No." Luke crossed his arms and rolled his eyes. "She won't leave me alone."

"Why don't you give her a chance?" I said, although it pained me to mention it. "We're trying to take a break and be friends, remember? Let things cool off."

"I told you I don't want to see anybody else. Who are you seeing?" he said. "Not McIntosh."

"Lord, no. That would complicate our roommate status something terrible."

A whooshing sound marked the opening of Red's inner vestibule door.

Luke jumped to the side of the building. Holding a finger to his lips, he flattened himself against the wall. Half a second later, Tara pushed open the door and held it while she glanced around the parking lot.

"Hey, Tara." I waved and tried not to stare at Luke plastered against the corrugated metal building. The open door blocked him, but as the door was glass, it didn't make an effective hiding tool.

"Have you seen Lukey?" she chirped.

"I've seen him today," I said honestly. "What are you doing?"

"Luke was here earlier," she said, standing on her toes to peer around me. "Then he said he had to go. But I just had a feeling he was out here. There's his truck, by golly."

I rocked back on my heels. "A feeling that he was out here, huh? Maybe you got me mixed up with Luke. I just arrived."

Her little nose scrunched as she puzzled that idea. "Maybe. Did you find out who got the parts in *Romeo and Juliet*?"

"No, I'll find out tomorrow. Auditions are tonight."

"Okay then." Tara pouted, causing a star to fall from its orbit. "Aren't you coming in? Todd's waiting on you."

"Todd's always waiting on me," I said. "You know, you should keep him company. That'd be good for him. Help him write some new lyrics because his rhyming abilities are limited."

"Sure thing." She grinned and the moon's silver orb broke from behind cloud cover. "But why aren't you coming in?"

The girl was relentless. "I just saw my brother Cody in the parking lot. He ticked me off. I'm not good company at the moment."

"Cody's been sitting at the bar a long time. He wouldn't talk to me. Told me to leave him alone in a real ugly way when I said hello."

"Don't take it personally. Cody's been a real shit to everyone lately." I colored at my language choice before the fair gem. "Sorry, I've got a mouth. So, you go on in and I'll see you later?"

"Okey dokey. See you, Cherry." Tara leaned forward to hug me, giving me a glimpse of Luke cowering behind the door. "If you see Luke, I really think he needs a hug. He just has that look about him."

"Right." I drew out the word and closed the door behind her. I waited for the whoosh of the inner door closing and looked at Luke. "You're such a chicken."

He grinned and held out his arms. "How about that hug I need?"

"You don't need a hug. You need a kick in the pants."

"Actually, I need something else." The grin turned saucy. "But that can wait. Let's go to the L and L." He pushed off the wall and grabbed my elbow. "We'll drop your truck at home and take mine to Line Creek."

"Why the Locked and Loaded?" I asked.

"Because that's where the Line Creek cops hang out. I figured you'd want to talk to Detective Herrera again."

Locked and Loaded had the corner tavern appearance I had encountered in Savannah but didn't see much in middle Georgia where blue laws shaped the infrastructure. The strip mall habitat did not make up for the seediness of the blacked out window and signage featuring a down-the-barrel-view of a Smith and Wesson .45 revolver. On a bench before the window, a moldy Jack-o-lantern with a jagged tooth smile livened the scene.

I glanced at the Jack-o-lantern and then at Luke. "I've a feeling Locked and Loaded's Halloween party was not for kids."

"You'd think right." Luke smiled and grabbed the metal handle on the door. "L and L makes their own witch's brew and it's not for the weak."

"Sounds like fun." My grin froze as I scanned the dim interior. Conversation hushed and eyes shifted toward us from the dozen tables crowding the small room. A bar lined the wall near the door, where heads turned to take in the newcomers. The flatscreens on the walls featured sports news. Classic rock blared from hidden speakers. The bar shelves brimmed with economy bottles of liquor. This was a bar that didn't pretend to be anything other than a bar.

And it was filled with cops. Mostly in plainclothes, but I recognized the restless movements, shifty eyes, and need for privacy. Either cops or a room full of bank robbers.

"Do you think L and L has food?" I whispered. My stomach kicked in at that thought, and three men sitting near the door tightened their hands on their drinks and squinted at us.

Luke rested his hand on my shoulder. "Sheriff Thompson would kill me if he knew I brought you here."

"He won't find out," I said, but doubted my words. "I'm glad you did. This place is cool."

"Herrera's sitting in the back," Luke murmured.

We threaded through the tables to the far corner where Herrera sat next to a female officer. I didn't see any squad cars in the parking lot, but the other officer still wore her uniform blues.

"Hey." I winked at Herrera. "Fancy meeting you here."

He didn't wink back, but looked from me to Luke. "Do I know you?"

Luke stuck out his hand. "Deputy Luke Harper, sir. With Forks County Sheriff."

Herrera shot a sidelong glance at his friend then waved a hand at the bartender. "What are y'all doing in the L and L?"

"Visiting you." I stuck out my hand to the other cop. "Cherry Tucker. Are you Herrera's partner?"

"Officer Amelia Wells." Smooth, brown hair had been pulled back in a ponytail and freckles dusted her pert nose. Her handshake felt like a vise clamp.

"Mind if we sit?" I took the chair facing the wall, noticing no one else in the room sat with their back to the door. Luke took the chair to my right, next to Herrera. "I've got questions about Maranda Pringle."

"Why?" asked Wells. "She's not a relative. Or a friend."

"How do you know?"

"Because her parents are dead, she has no siblings, and her friends were all male. Except one gal, Olivia Hughes. And you said your name is Cherry Tucker." Wells smirked. "What kind of name is Cherry? Sounds like a prostitute."

"I am not a prostitute," I said, crossing my arms over my "Stunts" t-shirt. "I'm not even very good at dating."

The corners of Herrera's mouth rose. "That so? What're you doing with this one?"

"Luke and I are friends." I accepted the pint glass of beer handed to me by a stony faced waiter. "We've known each other a long time."

"Cherry's interested in the Pringle suicide because of what's going on at the school," said Luke, hurrying past our personal information. "An unofficial announcement went out on PeerNotes yesterday. Obscurely implicating the drama teacher she's working for."

"Do you know if other faculty have been targeted?" I asked.

"If they have, it's been private and they're keeping quiet about it." Herrera glanced at Wells. "The messages that popped up last year with the teen suicide were done from a generic email. It was traced to the school library."

"So that's the ghost texting some girls mentioned." I sipped my beer.

"Probably," explained Wells. "All you do is type the phone number, at, and the carrier's messaging service. And since most kids at Peerless use iPhones, that makes figuring the carrier easy."

"You think the Phantom is doing the same thing again?"

"It's easy enough to do," said Wells. "Could be a copycat, although it doesn't make sense if the target is teachers."

"Damn PeerNotes," said Herrera. "They should have shut that thing down permanently."

"Easier to monitor, Daniel," said Wells. "If it wasn't PeerNotes, the kids would use some other social media. What am I saying? They do use other kinds. It's impossible to keep up."

"I need to get on PeerNotes," I said.

"PeerNotes uses push notifications for big announcements," said Wells. "That's how the announcement buzzes their phones. Mostly PeerNotes is just a bunch of news about school events, activities, homework updates, and then all the socializing between students."

"So what about Pringle? Did you find anything about the private texts she received from the Phantom?" I asked.

Herrera leaned back in his chair. "Her phone's at GBI. Low on their list since it's a suicide."

"My Uncle Will isn't comfortable with her suicide. Why?"

Herrera shrugged. "We found bupropion in her medicine cabinet. Zyban. Bupropion's an antidepressant."

"Zyban's used to kick a nicotine habit," said Luke. "Doesn't mean she was depressed."

"I looked up the side effects and Zyban can cause anxiety and insomnia. Neighbors said she kept to herself," said Wells. "Sometimes had late night visitors, but they were quiet."

"Why do you think she committed suicide?" I said.

"I don't know," said Herrera. "She's educated. Degree in business, minor in accounting. Good job. Nice house. But grew up in foster care. And didn't make the wisest choices in her social life. That points to some issues. She liked to go to Little Verona's restaurant and hang out in the bar. That's where her buddy Olivia worked."

"That's the restaurant where Principal Cleveland saw her with Coach Newcomb," I said.

Herrera narrowed his eyes. "Where'd you hear that?"

My cheeks heated, and I slapped a hand over the scrubbed out scribble on my arm. "Around."

"It's also where Dan Madsen, Ellis's father, met her," said Wells.

"Have y'all looked at monitoring PeerNotes?" asked Luke.

Herrera shrugged. "It's a suicide. We've got other cases and until we get the analysis back, there's not much more we can do."

The conversation died as both men and Amelia Wells exchanged some sort of silent police dialogue, then planted their faces in their beer mugs.

I wasn't ready to give up. "Do you think someone's hot about Ellis Madsen's suicide and pointing fingers at Peerless?"

Wells slammed her empty mug on the table. "Why would they do it now? What would be the point? Ellis Madsen died last year. If someone wanted to point fingers they should have done it a year ago."

Herrera patted Wells' sleeve. "This is nothing to do with Ellis. Just some jackass who thinks it's funny to compare the two suicides."

"That's how you see it?" I asked.

"Yep." Herrera tipped his beer back.

"What about the text Maranda Pringle received before her death?"

Herrera set the mug on the table. "That's conjecture at this point since we don't have evidence of a private text message. But we do know she was on medication, had no family or friends, and had issues with men. I don't think the district attorney will be interested in prosecuting a nasty text even if it might have pushed her to suicide."

"Mr. Tinsley," I began and stopped at the look Herrera set on me.

"Mr. Tinsley seems to be as full of shit as everyone else at that stuck-up school." He looked at Luke. "Are we done? The coroner has ruled it a suicide. Peerless is a bunch of asshole kids and asshole parents with money to burn and too much time on their hands. You'd think they'd feel some remorse after poor Ellis Madsen, but no. I've got too much to do to waste my time looking at their inane conversations on PeerNotes."

"Come on, Cherry." Luke stood up from the table and drew a twenty from his wallet. "Herrera, Wells. Thanks for your time. The beers are on me."

"Wait." I hooked my ankles around the legs of the chair. "What did the suicide note say? It bothered my Uncle Will."

"It said 'I'm sorry, but I can't do this anymore.'" Wells folded her arms and leaned back. "Printed off her home printer. From her home computer."

"If Uncle Will's bothered by the note, there must be something there." I jumped from my chair and, forgetting about the position of my feet, fell across the table. My elbow knocked into my beer, spilling a pool of suds across the table. Luke grabbed my elbow and hauled me to my feet before the beer soaked through my t-shirt. Beer splashed onto Wells' uniform and rained onto her pants. She hopped to her feet, shaking off her wet hands.

"You idiot," she seethed.

"It was an accident," said Luke. "She tripped."

"Here," said Herrera, handing Wells some drink napkins.

She threw them back on the table. "What in the hell am I supposed to do with those? I'm soaked."

"I'm sorry," I said, "I'll get you a bar rag."

"Get her out of here, Harper," said Herrera.

I turned toward the bar and almost smacked into the chest of a beefy, young officer at the next table. His partner had also risen and stood with crossed arms, watching our scene. I made a slow pivot of the room and saw that all eyes, once again, were on me.

The big officer stared down at me. "I heard you say your name was Cherry Tucker. I remember your name from the paper. You like to get off on messing around with police investigations?" His eyes flicked from me to Luke.

"Excuse me?" I said.

A hand clamped onto my shoulder. "She's not messing around, Pettit. Cherry's with me."

"Your badge bunny, Harper?" Pettit's eyes took a long trip over my jeans and Stunt top. "I figured you for a higher brand of beer goggles. Or are you screwing someone else's fiancé now?"

Oh shit, I thought and ducked as Luke's fist swung over my head and cracked into Pettit's jaw. Luke pushed me away and leapt into Pettit's tackle. The room erupted into hoots and calls. Tables were shoved out of the way with a speed and accuracy that seemed choreographed.

Twenty seconds later, I was squirming under Herrera's arm as he hauled me toward the door. "I can't leave Luke in there."

"Sure you can," said Herrera. "This has been building for some time. Badges only." He shoved me out the door and locked it behind me.

"Badges only, my ass. Who am I gonna call to break up this fight?" I pounded on the door to no effect and then ran to the blacked out window, searching for some crack to peer through. They had painted that sucker well.

I collapsed onto the bench next to the moldy Jack-o-lantern, folding my arms around my knees. Ten minutes later, I heard the chunk of the lock turning in the door. Scrambling to my feet, I grabbed the door handle and yanked. Luke staggered over the threshold, holding to his cheek a bar napkin spilling ice. His t-shirt collar had been ripped and his jeans were soaked with beer.

"Oh my Lord." I ducked under his shoulder to support him. "What in the hell was that?"

He smiled and a drool of blood oozed out the corner of his thickening lip. "Fun."

SIXTEEN

"I should take you home." I had jacked up Luke's seat and perched on the edge to see the road over the Raptor's dash. "You look like a hot mess."

"I'm fine." Luke winced as he reapplied the ice to his lip. "We should go to Little Verona's and see if that Olivia is working. Maybe she'll know if Pringle actually got a text or not."

"I guess I've shown up places looking worse." I grabbed the keys, ready to feel the power of four hundred and eleven horses when my phone whistled the theme from *The Good, The Bad, and The Ugly*.

I left the truck in park and reached into my satchel. Glancing at the familiar but unrecognizable phone number, I answered with a tentative, "Hello?"

"Miss Tucker," said Tinsley. "Are you out and about, perchance?"

"Perchance I am, Mr. Tinsley. What can I do for you?" I raised my brows at Luke.

He tossed the ice out the window and slid closer.

"I'm still at the theater, finishing up my audition notes so I can post the roles on PeerNotes tonight." Tinsley paused. "I received another message. About the auditions."

"Do you want me to come to Peerless?"

"It would be of great comfort if you would," said Tinsley. "The auditions are public knowledge, but the Phantom suggested I am watched."

"You need to show me the message. Don't delete it. The police may be able to trace it."

"I understand."

His low, sorrowful voice affected a slight English accent. Which made me wonder if he really understood or if he enjoyed the limelight.

Didn't matter. I was on the Phantom like white on rice.

I hung up and scooted to face Luke. "Can't go to Little Verona's now. I've been called to school. I'll drive us back so I can get my truck."

"That's way out of your way. I'll just go with you." He hung an arm on the back of the seat.

I squinted in the dusky light. "You're getting a shiner. Who's Pettit anyway? Don't tell me you were just defending my honor. I know better. Y'all have history."

"Anthony Pettit is a jackass. Has been since high school. The badge did not improve upon his personality." Luke tugged on my ponytail. "What's going on with Tinsley? He got another text?"

I ignored the tug, flipped to face the steering wheel, and started his truck. "That he did. He sounded scared."

"A grown man's calling you in to protect him?"

"He feels persecuted. And my alleged dealings with criminals make me look bigger than I am." I smirked. "Anyway, you didn't answer my question. Who's Pettit?"

Luke crossed his arms over his chest. "Nobody important enough to talk about. I'm fine, how about I drive?"

"No point in switching now." I smiled and revved his engine. "I've wanted to drive this bad boy for some time."

"Just be careful with her."

"Her? No way is this truck female." I floored the accelerator, taking advantage of riding with a cop.

"Sure, she is." Luke stroked a hand over the center console. "She's pretty."

"Your Raptor's all jacked up on knobby tires. How is that pretty?"

"Pretty to me." Luke settled into the bucket seat, but fixed his eyes on me. "That's what counts. Some guys like the long lines of a sports car or the shape of a bigger truck, but I think she's pretty. The Raptor's got a fire in her belly I like."

I felt a warm tingle creep from my toes, slide up my legs, and send a flush up the back of my neck.

"Sometimes she's temperamental, but I know just how to get her going. Especially when she's cold. I just ease onto the gas. Fill her belly, you know? Get her to purr."

I clamped a hand over my stomach and felt heat burning through my t-shirt.

Luke folded his arms behind his head and gazed at the windshield. "Then I lay on the accelerator, get her motor cranking, and floor it. She just comes alive beneath me. Sometimes she bucks, but then smooths out and we just tear up the highway. Pistons pumping and burning up her fuel."

I swiped at the perspiration accumulating at the nape of my neck.

"Her seats are real soft, too. Just love to ease into these seats, although sometimes I've got to adjust myself to get the right fit. But when I do, she's so comfortable. I've slept in them often enough."

Grabbing the collar of my shirt, I flapped it away from my chest. I leaned forward to adjust the vents. "How about some air?"

Luke pushed my hand away. "Keep it on ten and two, sugar. Let me fiddle with the buttons. I know what to do."

I gripped the steering wheel, trying to focus on the road before me. A blast of cool air dowsed my body and I sighed.

"See?" Luke's voice sniggered. "I know how to get you feeling just right."

Luke and I waited for Tinsley behind the school by the back theater entrance. Beneath the harvest moon, the castle-like exterior of the school cast shadows better made for a gothic horror movie. I waited for a murder of crows to flap across the sky and a dude in a hockey mask and hatchet to round the side of the building. I shivered and hugged my arms against my chest.

"Are you cold?" asked Luke, rubbing his hands together. "You want me to warm you up?"

I thought about his truck and shook my head. A little cool off was exactly what I needed. "I hope Tinsley kept this text. Why does he have to be so secretive with me when he wants my help?"

"He must be embarrassed. Or guilty."

The metal door shifted, then heaved open. Tinsley blocked it with his body, giving off an odor of stale coffee and sweat. He had rolled up his sleeves, and wisps of his thinning hair stood as if electrified.

Even his bald dome had lost its shine. Every time I suspected Tinsley of over-dramatizing, he did something that made me feel sorry for him.

I greeted him and introduced Luke as a friend. Revealing Luke as police might cause Tinsley to assume a new character, and I'd rather Luke see the real Tinsley. Or as close to real as Tinsley could get.

Tinsley gave Luke's ripped shirt and shiner a long look, but stepped to the side to let us in. "Thank you for coming."

We followed him down a short corridor and passed through another door into the long hall that ran behind the stage. I really needed a map for this place. Or a sherpa.

"What's going on?" I asked.

"It's been a long, stressful night as auditions usually are," said Tinsley.

"Do the kids give you a hard time?"

"The students know where they stand with me." Tinsley held open another door. The green room with the bean bag chairs. "The parents, however, do not always agree with my decisions."

Luke glanced around the drama lounge before following us into Tinsley's office. "Let's see this text."

"It wasn't a text. A message on PeerNotes. Our Phantom did not seem satisfied to keep this private." Tinsley walked behind his desk, tapped his mouse, and turned his computer monitor to face us. "Evidence to humiliate me, I suppose."

Luke and I approached the desk and bent to look at the monitor. At the top of the screen, "PeerNotes" written in large, cursive script overlaid a misty photo of the exterior of Peerless Day Academy. Beneath the heading, short posts fed on to the screen in a slow, continuous stream. Some content had photos or videos attached, while others only had text. Tinsley paged down and clicked on a post. The screen changed to bring up the message in full view.

A series of blurry photos showed Tinsley sitting at a table with a large coffee, an even larger binder, and a pile of papers. Some of the photos showed him examining what looked like glossy head shots. Another photo showed him massaging his scalp while he scowled at the mess of papers. The final photo showed him dumping the paper into a trash can. The caption read, "Then I defy you, stars."

"It's a quote from *Romeo and Juliet*," said Tinsley.

"That's not so bad," I said. "Looks like someone with sour grapes about your choice in cast."

"These were taken after the auditions were finished and everyone had gone home," he said. "That's what makes me nervous. I was alone in the theater. That table was on the stage."

"What happens if you click on the person posting?" I snagged the mouse and clicked. The screen changed, showing the PeerNotes header again. Below, lay an empty information box. Instead of a name, someone had listed the alphabet.

Luke clicked back to the photos. "Does your auditorium have a balcony? They would have needed an aerial view to take these."

Tinsley nodded. "The theater has a balcony."

"Let's go take a look." Luke turned to me.

"Wait," I said. "Mr. Tinsley, did you get a text as well?"

His fingers played along the edge of his desk. "Just the PeerNotes notification. I told you the Phantom suggested I was watched."

"You have to tell me what the texts said."

"She's right." Luke folded his arms and cast Tinsley his cop stare. "If the Line Creek police do get involved in this texting issue, they can confiscate your phone and pull up the deleted messages anyway."

I secretly smiled and slipped the "she's right" into a pocket to save for a metaphorical rainy day.

Tinsley gusted a long sigh. "The texts accuse me of using theater funds for personal expenses."

"Is that true?" I asked.

"Of course it's untrue." Tinsley gripped his desk. "The IRS may have nosed around my receipts a few times, but they never found anything in their audits."

I glanced at Luke. His flinty eyes could have drilled holes into Tinsley's forehead.

"Let me see the texts anyway." I put an extra lump of sugar in my smile. "It's not the messages that interest me as much as how they're written. There might be some clues."

"I will give in, Miss Tucker. 'A stage where every man must play a part, And mine a sad one,'" Tinsley quoted and dug the phone from his pants pocket. Tapping on the screen, he entered a code, then pressed to retrieve his text messages.

Again with the weird quotes. I took the phone from his hand. "Thank you."

Tinsley bowed.

"I meant for the phone."

I held the small screen near my face, and Luke edged in next to me, circling his arm about my waist to get a better look. I ignored the fingers that hooked onto my belt loop and allowed him to peer over my shoulder. The woodsy scent of his cologne enveloped me as Luke reached around my shoulder to widen the message on the screen. I ordered my nose to shut off from the cologne sniffing and my brain to focus on Tinsley.

"'While the theater feeds your appetite, you feed theirs,'" I read. "'If Peerless lost its idol, wouldn't they worship the next fool who feeds them pizza and compliments? You're buying love. How long can you go on acting without real accolades? Soon everyone will see you as the fraud you really are.'"

"It's vaguely threatening," said Luke. "Does the 'they' referred to mean the students?"

"I believe so." Tinsley collapsed into his chair. "Although the idol could refer to the Tiny Tony."

I ran my finger over the screen, hunting for more messages and found none. "This seems to be more about you bribing the students than using theater funds on yourself."

"It's all interpretation, I suppose." Tinsley tapped his fingers on the desk. "Now that you've viewed that message, any clues?"

"I need to think about it," I said. "We'll check out the theater while I think."

Tinsley tossed his keys on the desk. "I'll wait here. I'm in no mood to approach the stage."

Luke released my hip to grab the keys. "Let's go."

I rubbed my hip of the scorch marks left by his hand and followed Luke out the door. Glancing back, I noted Tinsley had swiveled the computer screen toward his side of the desk. He began pounding on the keys.

I needed to know more about the man who had hired me to chase down a phantom. A phantom that put him and his theater in the spotlight.

SEVENTEEN

We made our way through the hall of doors until we reached what I thought was a side entrance into the theater.

Using a master key, Luke unlocked the door, and we entered the dark auditorium. On the stage, the ghost light's caged, single bulb lit the table and chair Tinsley had used for auditions. In the theater, red exit signs burned above the doors, but didn't provide enough illumination to do anything other than cast an eerie glow on the doors themselves.

"I guess we should have asked about the lights," I said, stepping back and bumping into Luke.

"Hold still," he said and a moment later a pen light flashed on the floor. "If I had to guess, we'll find the light switches near the auditorium entrance or in a sound booth."

"Sound booth?" I blindly reached for Luke's hand and focused on the small beam of light. "Look at you with your theater jargon."

"I ran the sound and light board for extra credit in high school a few times." He tugged my hand and I followed him up the path between rows of seats. "Used to sneak girls in the booth and we'd fool around during the plays."

"How educational."

I felt his smile. "I learned plenty." He gave another tug to bring me closer to his side. "I could tutor you."

"Thanks, but I've got a job to do. And friends don't make out in sound booths when they're hunting for phantom texters."

"Now, that's a shame. I could use more friends like that."

I needed to move to a safer subject. "What did you make of the Phantom's accusations against Tinsley? I still don't think Tinsley's telling me everything."

"More than likely, Tinsley did use his theater funds inappropriately and someone found out. And it probably wasn't spent on buying pizza for the students."

"Unless he was buying especially for Ellis Madsen," I said. "There was that *Evita* announcement."

"Or the Phantom is just tossing balls in the air and one came close to hitting Tinsley. I don't think that idol message had anything to do with misuse of funds."

We had reached the apex of the theater. Luke shone his pen light on the door to the sound booth and then on the walls next to the double doors leading to the auditorium's lobby. "No switches here. I'll look in the booth."

I tried the double doors. They gave at my push, and I peered out. "There's a window, so I can see. I'll look for a light switch out here."

"Holler if you find one. You might need a key for it." Luke fumbled with the key ring, trying different keys in the doorknob of the booth.

I left him to relive memories of high school necking sessions and walked into the theater lobby. Pale moonlight shone through a large window, painting a silver square on the dark carpet below. Two single doors set at the far corners, I assumed, led to the balcony. Enough diffused lighting allowed me to see an absence of light switches.

The lobby entrance opened onto a school hallway. This hall was lit with inset fluorescent panels, and I could make out the front foyer and office in the distance.

I realized I had not traversed this spoke in the Peerless labyrinth, which must run parallel to the arts hall. I glanced back at the theater doors and decided to leave Luke to find the lights. It would be impossible to see anything in the balcony without some overhead illumination.

I scooted down the hall, searching for lighted classrooms, curious to see if anyone else worked late. Perhaps the Phantom had holed himself up in one of the rooms, waiting for Tinsley to respond to the audition photos on PeerNotes. Or on *Tinsley Talks*, as I suspected.

I stopped a few yards down the hall. A large picture window had been inset, and I realized no doors, but windows aligned both sides of the hall, all dark save one. Parents walk this hall on their pilgrimage to the auditorium, I thought. Views into the students' lives. Watching their children through glass.

Very *Planet of the Apes.*

I moved to the next window. By the glow of an electronic panel, I could make out the nearby shape of a bulky machine. Closing my eyes, I imagined the other side of the hall and knew these were the art studios. Smart for Peerless to give the parents a window onto another creative process while they made their way to the theater for plays and whatnot. Much more interesting than a history classroom.

The next window glowed in stark contrast to the others. I crept with my back against the cinderblocks and peered around the side. Easels had been set in a circle around a central dais made from a plywood box, holding a table draped in a white cloth topped with a cow's skull. Still lifes. I smiled, remembering the number of charcoal cow skulls I had drawn as a student. Then noticed movement in the closest corner.

Not quite able to see, I squatted and waddled below the window to peep up. The teacher's desk sat diagonally in the corner, a good spot to hide from the constant surveillance of the picture window. I could see the side of a computer monitor and stacks of books and papers. I hunker-walked toward the opposite corner and peeped up again. This time, Dr. Vail's profile appeared, bent toward the computer screen.

She appeared to be typing or scrolling and stopped. Her hand rose to the screen, then flew to cover her mouth. With slumped shoulders and a hand clamped over her lips, Camille Vail sat, fixated on the computer screen. I squinted to make out the website, but from the side I could only see the glow of illuminated pixels.

Slamming her hand on the desk, Dr. Vail bumped a haphazard stack of piled papers, starting an avalanche. Drawings slopped onto the floor. With eyes and mouth drawn tight, she glared at the fallen pieces. Grabbing a piece of pottery on her desk, she chucked it at the far wall. The object smashed against a chalkboard and rained on the carpet.

"That's what I call ticked off," I whispered, dropping below the window. "Who peed in her grits? Tinsley?"

I wanted to see her computer screen, but the angle worked against me. My peripheral caught more movement. Across the hall, a light flickered in a window. I stiffened. The tiny light bobbed inside the dark room, went out, then flashed again. Someone besides Luke had a flashlight and were doing their best to hide it from the window. Which classrooms were in the next hall?

More importantly, could the flashlight holder see me hiding in the hallway?

I peeked above the art window. Dr. Vail paced before the chalkboard. I dropped to the floor and scuttled the length of the window, my eyes on the opposite wall where the penlight cut on and off. A door creaked, and I froze.

"Cherry? Where are you?" called Luke. "I turned the lights on in the theater."

The penlight cut off. I flattened against the wall and inched toward my full five foot and a half inch.

"Cherry?" Luke strode to the entrance of the hall, located my position, and halted.

With my eyes on the dark window, I held a finger to my lips, but the flashlight had been doused. A sliver of light appeared as the classroom door cracked. A figure blocked the light and the classroom fell into darkness.

"Come on," I called over my shoulder and took off down the hallway. I glanced in the drawing classroom as I passed and noticed Camille Vail no longer paced. The room was empty.

My boots rang on the tile floor. Behind me, I heard Luke's boots echoing mine. Except faster and heavier.

He caught me in three seconds, pounding the floor next to me. "Why exactly are we jogging down the hall?"

"We're not jogging, we're running. Someone was poking about in the classrooms in the next hall. With a flashlight. They just left and I'm going to catch them."

Luke's long legs hit warp drive and he shot off, reaching the school foyer and rounding left. He disappeared while I still chugged up the middle hall. Panting, I skidded to a stop in the half moon foyer. Lights shone in the back of the administration office. I spun left and noted the sign above the next hall. Math and Sciences.

My least favorite hall.

I jogged forward and stopped. The dim florescent panels revealed an empty corridor that ended in another double set of doors. Where was Luke? Like the arts hall, this area didn't have windows, only sets of doors. I backed into the foyer. The next wing held Language Arts and Social Sciences, and the following had been marked for Consumer Science, Business and Computer Science, and Physical Education.

I wasn't crazy about any of those fields, either. And those halls were as deserted as the math and science area.

I slipped back to the science hall, jiggling door handles as I reached them. Midway down the corridor, I discovered another passageway connecting math and science to the other academic halls. I hesitated, wondering if Luke had followed this arc or if he had continued down the science hall.

I was going to get so lost.

Boots tramped somewhere in the distance. Luke still navigated the byzantine school, searching for the flashlight carrier. I decided to continue my course of trying doorknobs, until I reached the locked double doors at the end. The cafeteria. Another hall sprigged right here as well.

Peerless Academy was one big wagon wheel with some additional arcs crossing the spokes. Although it felt more like the game board from Clue. Phantom Flashlight must have taken the secret passageway from the conservatory to the lounge.

I closed my eyes and listened. Footsteps rang somewhere nearby. I jogged back up the science wing, turned the corner of the connector hallway and smacked into Luke.

He grabbed me by the shoulders and peeled me off his body, steadying me on my feet.

"Did you see anybody?" he asked.

"No, not a soul."

"There are a couple custodians vacuuming and dusting the library. They didn't see anyone either." He ran a hand through his short, dark curls. "Are you sure you saw somebody?"

"Sure as I could in the dark. I don't think the bogeyman uses a penlight to search through a desk, which is what I guess they were doing."

Luke jiggled the ring of keys. "You think you can figure which classroom it was?"

I paced down the hall and chose a door on the right, the classrooms facing the windowed hall. The nameplate next to the door named the room "Chemistry."

Luke unlocked the door with his master key and paused.

"Should we turn on the lights?" I felt for a switch on the wall.

"That's what I was wondering. I don't think anyone's around, but if the lurker is still about, they might see us through those damn windows."

"So will Dr. Vail." I pointed to her lighted window across the hall. "Let's continue with the skulking. I'd rather not anyone know I'm in a science room. I have a reputation to protect."

"I don't think anyone would believe you spend much time studying chemistry. Maybe biology." He nudged my hip with his leg. "Get it? The birds and the bees."

"Hilarious. I meant I don't want anyone in the school to know I'm looking for the Phantom." I glared toward his murky shape. "Are you done playing around? I'm on the track of a maniacal slanderer."

"Maniacal slanderer? I don't remember that term from the Police Academy."

"You don't treat this any more seriously than Herrera, do you?" I said.

"Sugar." Luke leaned against the jamb. "I'm here, aren't I?"

"I'm still not sure why. But let's see what our flashlight lurker searched for. They were somewhere close to the window, near the far right corner."

I moved with my hands out, stumbling past long counters and bumping into stools. Luke flicked on his pen light, guiding us to the corner. Buried beneath notebooks and stacks of paper, we found the teacher's desk. Luke glided the small light over the papers. I moved around the desk to block the light from the window.

"I don't see much other than kids' homework." Luke laid a hand on the hard drive tower. "Feels cold. They didn't boot up the computer. See if the desk drawer is open."

Having Luke's help was more beneficial than I realized. However, I didn't need to explode his ego with that comment and kept it to myself.

I pulled on the front middle drawer. It lurched open. Luke handed me the penlight, and I shined it on a mess of pens, paperclips, pencil shavings, and other educational flotsam and jetsam. Finding the end of a lanyard, I yanked on it and a Peerless name badge flew out.

"I guess we're monkeying around in Scott Fisher's desk." I shined the penlight on the badge's tiny picture. "Kind of cute for a science teacher."

"Stop ogling Scott Fisher," said Luke. "Let's hurry this up."

"Wasn't an ogle. More of an admiration." I replaced the lanyard and tried another drawer.

"One thing's for sure," I said. "Scott Fisher isn't up for any Cleanest Desk awards. I just found half of a mushy banana."

"Leave the banana."

I opened the bottom drawer. "Here's his secret stash of mini candy bars. Scott Fisher has a sweet tooth."

"Don't even think about it," warned Luke. "What else is in the drawer? Look for something out of place."

I flashed the pen light around the drawer, afraid to find another moldy banana. A manila envelope lay beneath the bag of candy. I lifted the candy and ran the light over the envelope. It didn't have the markings of dirt or wear as the rest of the desk clutter.

"I'd say this qualifies as one of these things is not like the other." I grabbed the envelope and stuck the penlight under my chin, shafting the light toward my bellybutton.

"Are you trying to spotlight your boobs?" Luke chuckled.

"Not getting any hasn't improved your sense of humor, that's for sure," I snapped. "You think this was what Mr. Flashlight was looking for? Should I peek inside this envelope?"

"You peek. I can't tamper with potential evidence."

A sheaf of papers slid out of the unsealed envelope and into my hand. I flipped through the three sheets.

Each contained a single screen shot of a text message bubble.

Eighteen

"Well, this answers one of my questions." I smiled. "The Phantom has sent Scott Fisher messages, too. That's three faculty members, so I'm going to guess there's more."

Luke circled the desk to stand next to me, pulling the flashlight from under my chin to shine a light on the paper. "Those are screen shots. That was smart. Must have sent the picture to his computer and printed them out."

"Can my phone do that?" I asked.

"Your phone doesn't do anything."

"I think it can text, I just don't pay for the plan. It's only five years old."

"Sugar, technologically speaking, a five-year-old phone is the equivalent of a dinosaur."

I scowled. "I'm going to read Scott Fisher's texts now. You stand back so you're not accused of tampering with evidence."

Luke stepped closer, pressing against my back. "I'll just hold the flashlight for you. That's what friends do."

"Feels to me like your flashlight is in the wrong place." I squinted at the wavering light highlighting the first text box and read aloud, "'Your private lessons aren't so private.' This is dated two weeks ago."

"Who's it from?" Luke's breath dusted my cheek.

"A bunch of random letters and numbers. Scott Fisher answered, 'Who is this? What are you talking about?'"

"Maybe Mr. Fisher isn't giving private lessons and the Phantom is just guessing," said Luke.

"Could be." I flipped to the next sheet. "'I saw what you did.' Fisher didn't bother to answer. The last one said, 'I know about you and your special student.'"

"These texts sound different than the ones Tinsley received."

"Each message was ghosted. Just a bunch of random characters."

Luke flashed the penlight on the desk. "You better get that envelope back in his drawer. We still need to check out the balcony."

I slid the papers back in the envelope, replaced them under the bag of candy, and shut the drawer.

"If these are the kinds of messages the faculty are getting, I can see why they're not telling anyone. What's the purpose of sending these nasty texts?"

"Sounds to me like someone's getting off on upsetting the staff," said Luke.

"Is it illegal?"

"If they can be proven as cyberstalking. The fact that no one will report them to the police tells me they don't feel suitably harassed to fear for their safety. Other than Tinsley."

"And Tinsley refuses to go to the police."

"Then, not much can be done about it. You can't convince Herrera of cyberstalking unless he has some evidence to go on."

I skidded a glance toward the desk drawer.

"And the evidence can't be stolen," added Luke.

"Dammit."

With our thoughts quiet and our senses alert for more stalkers, we left Scott Fisher's room to return to the auditorium. And discovered the left side balcony door opened without assistance from the master key.

Luke pulled open the door and squatted to examine the lock. "Looks like someone stuck a wad of gum in the jamb so the door wouldn't close all the way."

"So a kid probably took those pictures of Tinsley?" I shoved my finger into the lock hole and picked at the hardened square of gum. "Hubba Bubba by the looks of it."

Luke rose from his squat. "I bet kids use the balcony for secret hookups. That's what I would have done."

I rolled my eyes. "Did you learn anything in high school besides sex ed?"

After a fruitless search of the balcony and a few misguided turns, we wound our way back to the drama lounge. Tinsley's office door stood open, making the hollering-fest inside all the more apparent. With Luke trailing behind me, I hurried forward and halted just before entering. Camille Vail leaned over Tinsley's desk, waving her arms and pointing fingers. Tinsley slunk in his chair. While his body displayed apathy, his face had hardened under her onslaught.

I pulled in a breath, but before I could charge into the office, a hand settled on my shoulder and yanked me back. I flicked a what-the-hey glance at Luke, but he lifted a finger to his lips and pulled me to the side of the door.

Grandma Jo might have had issues with eavesdropping, but if a cop encourages me, who am I to contradict him? I hugged the wall next to Luke, hoping for something juicy.

"I know you're behind this." Dr. Vail hadn't stopped her rant. "Don't think I can't read between the lines. Your blog minions may love you, but I can see right through your bullshit."

"Camille." Tinsley's voice held a mocking blend of compassion, pity, and annoyance. "I am sorry you're so upset, but you're being a tad overzealous."

"Am I? We'll see what Cleveland says."

"Don't bother Principal Cleveland with this. You know how distraught he is over Maranda's death. I don't expect him back to school this week."

"Convenient for you, isn't it? Then I'll just take this to Brenda. She might be interested in what I've learned about your expenditures." Her voice grew louder.

Luke and I slipped off the wall to pose near the table.

With her tunic billowing, Dr. Vail stalked out of Tinsley's office. She whipped around to ply us with a hardened look, then slammed out the drama lounge door.

"Well, hell." I glanced at Luke. "If the woman didn't hate me before, she does now."

He nodded his head toward Tinsley's office. "Let's see if we can get Tinsley to talk while he's still shook up."

"I bet you always play bad cop when you're interrogating suspects."

"You want a demonstration of my good cop skills after this?" A dimple popped in his cheek, and I mentally slapped my hormones back in place.

"Does Uncle Will approve of you searching personal property without a warrant and eavesdropping while hitting on his niece?"

"I'd prefer you not tell him," said Luke. "Particularly the hitting on his niece part."

"Then cool your jets, son." I pivoted on my boot heel and marched into Tinsley's office.

Tinsley jerked his head up and straightened at our entrance. Luke strode to his desk, tossed the keys on it, and retreated to stand with his back against the bookshelf. I parked myself across the desk from Tinsley. With his jacked up chair, we could look each other in the eye.

"We didn't find anything in the balcony," I said. "What's going on between you and Dr. Vail?"

He rolled his eyes and began gathering papers into a neat stack. "An old rivalry. She's jealous of the popularity of the theater department. Unfortunately, the art students have a bad reputation and it reflects on her. Rightly so. They need a strong leader to reign them in."

"You mentioned this in your blog, didn't you?" I accused.

"Perhaps, but I only speak in generalities. I never use names. Besides, it's supposed to be funny." He pushed out of his chair and lifted his briefcase to the desk, keeping his gaze from mine.

I folded my arms over my chest. "You know, that kind of stuff will come back to bite you in the butt."

Bent over the desk, Tinsley peered at me over his glasses. "I'm not distressed over Camille. She's harmless."

"You don't think Dr. Vail could be the one sending these messages? Or one of her students?"

Tinsley straightened and laughed.

"My dear, that's why Dr. Vail is so irate. She's received texts, too, and believes I wrote them."

"What did they say?" Luke edged forward.

"I daresay it referred to something about her relationship to her notorious students, judging by the ferocity of her complaint."

"Like covering up their drug use?"

"Something like that."

"Do you think she'll show the texts to the police?"

He shook his head. "She'll do what she always does and complain to the principal. And Cleveland will look at the revenue I bring in versus her expenses in the art department and tell her to ignore me."

I glanced at Luke and wondered if this was why he wanted to talk to Tinsley "still shook up." Tinsley's personality had grown cold.

"Don't fret about Camille. Have you spoken to Mr. Avtaikin about contributing? How are the sketches for the set design coming along?"

"I've spoken. And I finished several designs for each setting."

"Already?" Tinsley gasped. "I didn't expect you to work this fast. If you finish so quickly, how can you watch the school?"

"I don't do anything slow, Mr. Tinsley. That includes finding the Phantom." I delivered a stiff smile. "I expect that's why you hired me. I'll bring in the drawings tomorrow."

"Very good," said Tinsley. "I'll see you tomorrow."

"By the way, do you know Scott Fisher?"

Tinsley's features blanked out for a moment. "I believe he teaches science? Why?"

"His name popped up recently. Just curious if you'd heard of him. Or if something about him had appeared on PeerNotes recently?"

Tinsley shook his head. "I'm sorry. I don't recall anything about him."

"Just wondering. One more question, besides you and Dr. Vail, who else would be at school this late?"

Tinsley shrugged. "I've been in the theater or my office since dismissal. Any of the faculty involved in extracurriculars could stay late."

"We'll see ourselves out," I said. "Don't worry about those photos. I'll keep my eye on the balcony while we work on the set. In the meantime, you better get someone to fix the lock to the balcony door."

Tinsley bowed his head. "I am in debt to your service."

"Just be careful with your blog." I backed toward the door with Luke strolling behind me. "You might have pissed off more than just Dr. Vail."

Maranda Pringle, Dr. Vail, Scott Fisher, Tinsley. Seemed the Phantom had several axes to grind.

With Tinsley's assistance, we exited through the theater's outside door, but stopped on the edge of the parking lot to survey the school and remaining vehicles. Two Prius, a Lexus, a newer model Dodge Ram pickup, a couple battered sedans, an old pickup, and a paneled van remained.

"If I were going to judge folks by their vehicles," I folded my arms over my chest as a night breeze brushed over my skin, "I'd say that grouping of tired transit parked in the handicapped spaces belongs to the night cleaning crew."

Luke nodded. "And I'd say one of the Prius belongs to Tinsley. Or maybe the Lexus."

"So the green Prius, I'd guess is Dr. Vail's. That is if she's still here. That leaves the Ram and one other car."

"I can run their plates," said Luke.

"That'd be pretty cool if you did. One of them might be our flashlight stalker."

"Or not," said Luke. "There were more vehicles here when we arrived. They might have taken off. Or if it was a kid, they might have ridden here on a bike."

"I'm not so sure if Peerless has the kind of students who ride bikes. Maybe a golf cart. Or a Bentley." I rubbed the gooseflesh on my arms. "You're being awful helpful."

Luke rocked back on his boot heels. "I don't want you to think I'm a total dick. And I do want to make it up to you."

"And it helps that this isn't your case."

"This isn't a case at all." Luke grinned. "But yeah, it helps a lot, sugar. You've given me a couple ulcers in the past, but this here has been fun."

"Are we friends now, Luke?" I swung my gaze up. And found myself centered within dusky gray eyes staring back at me.

"We're trying, sugar," he whispered. "But it's real hard when you look at me that way."

Shit. He was looking at me that way, too.

Thoughts of Tara, family feuds, and squirrels fled my brain. A rush of heat invaded every cell in my body like the rumbling of a volcano ready to erupt. I felt barely cognizant of strolling up to Luke, my hand reaching to brush his bruised cheek, and he capturing my hand to place his lips against my palm.

I pulled in a breath as his lips feathered from my palm to my wrist, and down my arm to the crook of my elbow. His eyes met mine and I caught the wicked glint of steel that doused me in more fire, until I couldn't breathe. I realized I held my breath and let it out in one long rush as Luke hitched me against his body. His hard planes met my soft, slight curves. His lips fell over mine and set to plunder and invade my mouth.

I was the defenseless village to his barbarian horde. And I had thrown open the village gates to give a welcome party. One of my hands curled to fist his ripped t-shirt and the other tangled into his luscious, soft curls. Luke's hands slid lower to hike me harder against his body.

"Lord, I missed you." Luke's mouth fled my lips to anoint my neck with pledges and promises of what he'd like to do to the rest of my body. His hands slipped beneath my thighs, hoisted me up, and he began to carry me across the parking lot to his truck.

I wrapped my legs around his torso, closed my eyes, and tried not to think about anything other than Luke's lips. And tongue. And hands.

Oh my Lord, his hands.

This was wrong. Wrong, wrong, wrong. My family was going to kill me. The town was going to scorn me. Tara would die of heartache.

My body told my brain to shut the hell up and just enjoy myself for once.

When my back bumped the side of his truck, Luke fumbled in his pocket for the keys. "Put me down, Luke."

"Sure, baby." He slid a kiss against my cheek and lowered me to the ground. "Just give me a second."

I shook my head. "No, we're not ready for this."

"I beg to differ. That felt like we're both pretty ready." Luke forced a smile, but his eyes had tightened. "Don't do this to us, Cherry."

"Look where we are, Luke. We're in a school parking lot. It's no different than when we were kids. We haven't grown up at all."

He leaned forward, fitting his forehead against mine. "You've grown a little. You want me to show you where?"

I glared up at him. "You're not helping."

His grin popped a dimple, but his eyes remained sad. "I'm trying, sugar. I really am."

"It's not just you. I'm just as guilty." I grabbed his hands and squeezed. "I can't do this to Tara."

"Tara? Tara is crazy. She created a whole relationship that never existed in her head." Luke dropped my hands to grasp my shoulders. "Baby, what about us?"

"I don't want to be with you just for our relationship to blow up in our faces again. You're gasoline and I'm the match."

His hands slid up and down my arms. "We just need to figure out how to keep that match from sparking. We can do it. I can't get you out of my system, Cherry. Believe me, I have tried."

"We have to work at this friendship and get to a place of stability first. Where our friends and family accept us, too," I said, wondering when I started channeling Red's TV psychology speak.

"Hell." Luke stomped away from me to kick a tire. "Why does everything have to be so complicated? I just want to be with you."

I slumped against his truck. "We just need some time. I don't know about our families, but Tara will eventually get over you. And then the town will forget about it, too."

"And when do you see that happening?"

"Well, considering Halo's a small town with a long memory..."

"Screw that." Luke pivoted, took two steps, and captured my face between his hands. His palms cupped my cheeks and one thumb stroked my bottom lip. "I'm not letting a small minded town and a psychotic woman get between us."

"I don't think Tara's so much psychotic as very determined. She took her cheer team to All State finals four years in a row. Even when she had a broken ankle her junior year."

"Listen, Cherry. I am going to explode here in a second. You make me nuts, but I'm crazy for you. Just shut that brain off for a minute and let me kiss you until we're all better."

"Okay," said the drunk-in-love idiot girl. I tipped my face toward his, but a flash of movement caught my attention.

Damn my excellent peripheral vision.

Before Luke could lower his head, I had turned mine. Hopping on my toes, I leaned against his arm to see around his broad shoulders.

"Baby?" I said. "Why'd you think there's someone running away from the school like their tail's on fire?"

NINETEEN

Luke jerked his head from mine, spun around, and trained his eyes in the direction of my point. In the distance, a teen sprinted toward a far corner of the parking lot, where a forested area grew as part of the "naturalizing" of the Peerless landscape.

"Looks like he came from behind the school."

"I'll get him and meet you back there," Luke called over his shoulder, charging after the student.

I galloped onto the sidewalk. A moment later I heard the distant sound of an engine firing, but didn't bother slowing to check. Rounding the corner of the auditorium, I passed the back theater door and continued down the sidewalk, cursing Peerless's architect for choosing to spread out the structure instead of building something more compact.

I skirted another corner and saw the fenced in dumpsters that marked the cafeteria area. The land behind Peerless sloped here toward a set of greenhouses. Behind the greenhouses lay the stadium and field house.

Acting on instinct, I cut left and followed the sidewalk toward the greenhouse and stadium. I had spent some time behind the bleachers at Halo High and knew if kids were sneaking around the school, they'd likely hide back there.

I aimed for the stadium, but behind the greenhouse, voices rose from a small garden bordered in privet shrubs and gated with an arbor covered in a vine with yellowing leaves. I halted, eased close to the bushes, and covered my mouth with my hand to disguise my heavy panting. Inside, garbled voices giggled and whispered.

"Did you hear that? I heard footsteps," called a female voice. "Is it Ellis?"

"That's messed up, man," said a boy's voice, reminding me of Shaggy from *Scooby-Do*. "Ghosts can't make footsteps. They don't have feet."

"What do you mean they don't have feet?"

Daphne, I thought. She sounded like a red head.

"Like they float, man," said Shaggy.

"Shut up," said a third kid, his voice already deepened. Obviously Fred. "It's the shrooms, not Ellis that's making you hear things."

"I don't think the shrooms are working," said another girl. Probably poor Velma who went along with this lark to impress Fred. "I want to see Ellis."

"Preston said it takes time," said Fred. "Anyway, if we see Ellis, it'll be a hallucination."

"No way, man," said Shaggy. "The shrooms'll just help us connect with the spiritual world. It's a full moon and we're close to the anniversary of her death. If we call on Ellis, she'll have to show."

"Well, she better hurry it up because I have early equestrian practice," said Daphne.

"For idiot's sake," I thought, rising from my crouch beside the bushes. Somehow, these kids had gotten magic mushrooms and were using them for a seance. Poor Ellis. Not even allowed to rest in peace. I couldn't see over the hedge, but the voices sounded low to the ground. I imagined the four kids sitting cross-legged in a circle, probably holding hands or some such foolery.

I smirked. This might be fun. And hopefully educational for both me and these dumb kids. Served them right to get stoned on a school night.

"Who are you seeking?" I whispered through the hedge and added a moan.

The giggling and rustling cut off.

After a few long seconds, Daphne's shaky voice called out, "Ellis Madsen."

"Why?" I whispered.

"She was our friend." Fred's deep voice rose at the end.

"Liars. Her friends would have saved her life."

Daphne shrieked and Velma began crying. Sounds of scrambling made it evident the kids readied to bolt.

"Stay where you are." I narrowed my eyes, wishing I could see through the hedge. "Ellis wants to know who's bullying Peerless now."

"I don't know," sobbed Daphne.

"Is someone trying to blame the teachers for her death?"

"Maybe," Velma wailed.

Behind me, I heard the heavy slap of boots running on concrete.

I sped up my questioning. "Which teachers besides Miss Pringle and Mr. Tinsley have gotten texts?"

"What do you mean?" called Fred. "Shouldn't a ghost know these things?"

"Ellis wants to know," I hedged, not quite knowing how the spirit realm worked. "She hasn't gotten full access to earth events yet."

"Who is this?" Fred's voice steadied.

"A real friend of Ellis," I said. "Or an illusion caused by the intake of psychedelic drugs."

"Dude, we're having a mass hallucination," said Shaggy. "I told you this would be trippy."

"I don't feel anything," said Fred. "Someone's messing with us."

"Like, a ghost dude," said Shaggy.

"Shut up, Shaggy," I said in my best scary ghost voice. "Or I'll haunt you every time you take a hit. Ellis wants to know who's texting the teachers at Peerless."

"We don't know," gasped Velma. "We didn't do it."

"Who did? Who did this to Ellis?" I stood on my toes and tried to peer over the hedge.

"Some senior theater students, but they're gone now. We were all afraid of them."

"Which seniors?"

A hand landed on my shoulder. I screamed and fell into the privet. Through the hedge, four more voices joined mine in screaming and shrieking. Our voices wrapped together in one long howl and four bodies shot through the arbor, cutting left, away from the sidewalk and up the grassy slope toward the cafeteria.

Luke hauled me out of the hedge, brushing off bits of leaf and twig. "What in the hell were you doing?"

"Tricking those idiots into giving me some information." I rubbed my scratched face. "Can you not sneak up on me like that?"

Luke ducked around the side of the hedge and under the arbor. I followed, noting a small sign naming the garden in memory of Ellis.

The small garden had a stone bench at one end and a raised flower bed of dying roses along the hedge walls. A statue of a girl reading sat amongst the roses.

"This is nice," I said, "but all this school needs is one more place where students can hide."

In the center, Luke knelt on the grass next to four abandoned backpacks. He poked at a bag of Doritos and unscrewed a water bottle for a sniff. "What were they doing?"

"Taking hallucinogenic mushrooms and trying to contact Ellis Madsen's spirit. Something about the full moon." I opened a backpack and glanced at the folders and papers inside.

Luke grabbed a stick from beneath the hedge, lifted the backpack, and used the stick to drag a baggy from beneath the pack. "I'd say this is in plain view. What about you?"

The baggie had several pieces of dried mushrooms inside. "You calling it in?"

"Yep. I couldn't catch that kid. Took off on an ATV through the woods. Maybe he was the one sneaking around the school."

"Or it's a student named Preston who sold them the shrooms. I heard them say his name."

"We'll tell Line Creek PD. What exactly were you doing?"

"Pretending I was a ghost," I said. "Hopefully, I scared them straight."

I gave my statement to Detective Herrera while Officer Wells searched the backpacks for the owners' names. They didn't find my *Scooby-Do* monikers helpful. Nor my ghostly interrogation method. Tired of their eyeball rolling and with nothing left to do, I called Todd for a ride. Luke planned to stay to offer Herrera his unwanted assistance. I left them in the garden with one last longing glance toward Luke.

Then told myself the drug bust interruption of what could have become a bust for lewd behavior was for my own good. My guardian angel had girded my loins with Scooby snacks without me knowing.

Todd's red Civic squealed into the parking lot with a quick donut spin flourish. From the sidewalk, I waited out his inner high school boy who couldn't resist a mostly empty school lot, then hopped into the passenger seat with a thank you.

"What's going on, baby?" he asked. "I thought you were coming to Red's tonight."

"It's been an exciting night." I grinned. "First, I experienced a cop bar and witnessed a fight. Then, I got to skulk a dark school for a mysterious intruder. And witness another fight. Last, I pranked some kids who thought they were high on shrooms. The officers said the mushrooms in question looked like plain ol' shitake."

"Cool," said Todd. "I wish you'd taken me. I'd love to prank some kids."

"What have you been doing?"

"Hanging out at Red's with Tara Mayfield."

"Oh, Lord," I said. "That may have been my fault. Sorry."

"No problem. Tara said she wanted to help me with my lyrics.

But I don't know her well enough for something so personal as lyric writing, so I figured I should get to know her first."

If only Todd would put that kind of consideration into everyday living.

"What's going on with all these fights?" he asked.

"One was between Tinsley and the art teacher, Camille Vail. She tore into him like a free catfish dinner at the VFW. Tinsley doesn't think she's a threat, but I'm not so sure. And she may think Tinsley's the texter."

"Who do you think is doing all this texting?"

"It's hard to tell. Luke thinks the Phantom may be throwing punches in the dark, just to stir up trouble. It almost seems like the messages are meant to relate to the teen suicide last year. Maybe the Phantom is driving someone to confess their sins. Like Maranda Pringle who had an affair with the girl's father."

I grasped the arm rest as Todd used the open student lot for one last donut. He cut the wheel hard to the right and gunned his car toward the exit.

"You've been with Luke Harper tonight?" Todd glanced at me as we skidded down Peerless's long drive. "Your sister's likely to scalp you."

My cheeks heated. "Purely investigative work. He got me into the Locked and Loaded so I could talk to a Line Creek officer. Then I got a call from Tinsley to go to the school, so he brought me here."

"Just investigative help. That's a relief." Todd kept his eyes on the dark lane. "Your family would have a fit. And remember what Red said about you choosing self-destructive relationships?"

"First of all, Luke's just a step-Branson," I said. "And second of all, the self-destructive relationships would include you."

"Not the way I see it." Todd grinned. "You called off our marriage because it wouldn't self-destruct. Red said it was your way of sabotaging your own happiness. Because you're emotionally stunted from your past family trauma."

"Dammit, Todd. I keep telling you Red can't apply every episode of Dr. Phil to my life. And I annulled our marriage because you were more fixated on the Vegas poker tables than our honeymoon. That's a red flag if there ever was one."

We had reached the Peerless gates. Todd downshifted and careened onto the county highway. "Who was in the other fight?"

I studied the dark landscape from my passenger window and far from Todd's accusing eyes. "Luke and Anthony Pettit, a Line Creek officer at the Locked and Loaded. Pettit made an ungentlemanly remark about me and Luke socked him. They have some history from high school."

Todd stomped on the clutch and pounded through the gears.

"Go on and say it." I turned from the window to look at Todd. "But you know I'm trying to stay friends with Luke."

"Funny thing, baby," said Todd. "Tara and I talked a lot tonight."

"And?"

Was Todd sweet on Tara? I felt a thrill of excitement mixed with a pang of jealousy.

I reminded myself I couldn't keep everyone corralled in Cherryland and firmed myself on Todd's happiness. Even if it meant never ridding myself of Tara. Lord help me.

"Isn't Anthony Pettit Tara's ex-fiance?" Todd continued.

"What?" I rubbed my temples. "Are you sure? Maybe Tara's just into cops."

"She said Pettit introduced her to Luke."

"Oh shit," I mumbled. "Luke went out with Tara knowing it would piss off Pettit?"

"Tara said she was engaged to Pettit. They started going out in high school. He played football for Line Creek. She was a cheerleader. Pettit had cheated on her and she had forgiven him, but when she met Luke, she broke it off officially with Pettit. You know what I mean?"

I leaned my head back on the seat and stared at the dark ceiling. "Yep, I know what you mean."

Looked like the *Scooby-Do* kids had unwittingly saved my virtue. And for all his explanations about Tara, Luke hadn't mentioned settling a score. How very high school of him. He was well and truly a Branson.

And damn my lack of fortitude when it came to that man. Men. I rubbed an aching spot on my chest and glanced at my roommate, wondering if Red was right about me sabotaging happiness. Everyone said I looked for trouble. Whereas I had always thought the Tucker name had been attached to a trouble homing device.

Which led to another, "oh, crap" thought. "Todd, did you ever see Cody again tonight?"

"Earlier at Red's, but not later." He glanced at me. "You haven't talked to him yet?"

"I tried at Red's, but he blew me off. He was picked up in front of JB Branson's house Monday night, passed out in his car."

"You want to drive by the Branson's?"

"Thank you, hon'. I'd hate to think what kind of excrement might start flying if Luke catches Cody stalking his momma's house."

TWENTY

Cody and his Malibu didn't materialize in our drive around Fetlock Meadows, the subdivision for Halo's one percent. Todd and I made it home without further comment on my heart's failings to kick the step-Branson to the curb.

The next morning, I rose after Todd had left for work and donned a skull print pyramid top. After a quick hot glue job on a ribbon of skull beads to the hem of my flared jeans, I pulled on my boots and headed out the door.

It felt like a skull-crusher kind of day.

When I arrived at the Peerless office, it appeared someone had ordered a delivery of bedlam with a side of insanity. Pamela Hargraves manned the counter, answering phone calls and registering visitors. Behind her, the office girls ran around like uniformed, headless chickens, carrying papers and folders under their wings. A parent sat at Amber's desk, looking close to tears. Assistant Principal Brenda Cooke stood in the middle of the room, catching students as they passed, glancing at the items in their arms, and pointing them in a different direction. She wore another expensive suit and her pumps had a familiar designer emblem, but her blonde bob had not been fully squashed of cowlicks and the knot of her snazzy scarf had been loosened like the groom's tie midway through a wedding reception.

I stood at the counter, watching disorder reign with Max's warning of Phantom-induced anarchy sailing around my brain. "What's going on, Miss Pamela?"

She grimaced. "Amber, the school secretary, quit. Ms. Cooke's fixing to get a sub to catch up on the office work. In the meantime, she's trying to organize Mrs. Overmeyer's students into doing actual work and they're not taking to it. They can't even figure out how to file the attendance sheets."

"Ugh," I said. "Amber seemed pretty fed up with trying to handle both the front and back office stuff."

Pamela shrugged. "Cooke is going to have an aneurism if she doesn't get some help. I don't know why she doesn't make Cleveland come back to school. He must realize how pathetic he looks, taking grief time for Pringle's funeral."

"At least someone's mourning her. Miss Pringle doesn't have any family."

"Really?" Pamela leaned closer until I could see the swirls of her foundation powder. Her heavy perfume smelled of roses dipped in patchouli. "The funeral is Monday. I heard Dan Madsen, Ellis's father, might show."

"I thought he didn't live around here."

"He and his wife moved away after Ellis died, but they split soon after. Between the death of her child and his infidelity, Bethany Madsen kicked him out. I believe he got a job in Atlanta, but I don't know where he's living."

I leaned away, taking a breath of fresh non-patchouli-rose air, and thought about Dan Madsen's move. "When did he move back? Recently?"

Pamela shrugged, wafting another blast of perfume toward me. "I just heard with the news of Pringle's funeral."

"Where does his wife live?"

Pamela squinted. "North Carolina? Tennessee? I'm not sure. They lived on the other side of Ballantyne, and Kadence wasn't friends with Ellis, so I didn't keep up with the Madsens."

"Was anybody friends with Ellis?" I muttered, then directed my thoughts to Pamela. "Besides Mr. Tinsley, were there any other staff who would have known Ellis well? Maybe an adult who might have seen the signs of her impending suicide and didn't do anything? Or gave her a hard time? Anything that could have been related to her death?"

Pamela tried to arch a brow. "Why?"

"Just wondering. The more I learn about Ellis, the worse I feel about her death."

And perhaps that teacher might be next on the Phantom's list, but kept that thought to myself.

"I didn't really know her," said Pamela. "Ellis was a sophomore, so she would have taken chemistry, English, World History, and pre-Calc that year. Probably a foreign language and a couple electives."

"What about art?"

"Generally, art and drama don't overlap. The drama kids might take chorus, maybe dance, and don't have room for other electives."

"What do the art kids take?"

"More art. And chemistry." She chuckled.

"What do you mean by that?"

"It's well known that one of the art seniors deals drugs. I heard he uses the print shop. You know, designs graphics for sheets of acid tabs?"

What an entrepreneur. "Does he sell magic mushrooms, too?"

Pamela turned up her nose. "Entirely possible. I told Kadence to stay away from the art rooms."

Preston King. Vail's favorite student.

Behind Pamela, the noise grew. With the skill of a good cat wrangler, Ms. Cooke herded the office girls to another room. A good time, I thought, to do some scrounging without ol' Eagle Eye Cooke around. "Who handles student schedules?"

"The guidance counselors are in charge of schedules. But you can look them up on any of the office computers."

"Thank you, Miss Pamela." I grabbed my visitor badge and scooted around the counter. At Amber Tipton's desk, I waved to the parent. "Hey there. You look like you need a break. Why don't I take over for a minute?"

At her enthusiastic nod, the mother's sleek ponytail bounced against her velour hoodie. She bent to snatch her Coach bag, giving me a glimpse of a butt-full of rhinestones spelling "Juicy."

"Thank you, I didn't expect to have to do this kind of work," said the mother.

"Of course you didn't," I replied. "You don't pay twenty thousand a year to do office work."

"I know." She laid a hand on her extra firm breasts. "I'm supposed to go to the spa this morning. I'm not even dressed."

"You go get yourself a Diet Coke and I'll sit here until the temp comes in."

Her extra-white teeth gleamed. "Thank you, sweetie."

"No problem." I dropped into her chair and switched on Amber's monitor. The guest password had been sticky-noted to the front of the computer. I logged in, then stared at the screen before randomly clicking on an icon. A spreadsheet of names and numbers appeared, blinked at me, then disappeared.

"Computers hate me as much as I hate them," I muttered. Clicking again, a different screen showed a blank form. Panicking, I hit the escape button.

"Cherry!" squealed an all too familiar voice. "I'm here to help!"

I felt the blood drain from my head and a nerve began to hammer near my eye. Turning in my chair, I spied Tara bouncing before the visitor sign-in log. Two seconds later, she skipped to Amber's desk. Today she had kept the pink Keds, but swapped the dress for navy skinny capris and a pink and navy print blouse.

Tara got an A for prep school attire. I glanced at my skull top and jeans. D+. Although I hoped the skull beads were good for some kind of extra credit.

"I'm volunteering to sub for Miss Amber," she shrieked. I waited for her herkie jump, but it never came. "We get to spend the day together!"

"Great." I winced. "Do you know how to work Miss Amber's computer?"

"Let me try!"

"Tara, you've got to stop shouting. This is a school."

Her cheeks flared to match the color of her brilliant pink shirt. "I'm so sorry. I'm just excited."

"I know you are," I said, feeling abashed. "Just show me how to look up a student's schedule. Please."

She leaned over my shoulder, smelling of sunshine and orange blossoms. How could Luke break this bundle of joy's heart just to get back at some old high school rival? I felt like pulling Tara in my lap and stroking her hair, but even Tara would find that unnerving.

Good Lord, Tara was turning me into Lennie from *Of Mice and Men*.

"Which student schedule do you need?" she chirped.

"Preston King. I need to talk to that boy."

Tara clicked and clicked again. A moment later, a paper chugged from the printer. "Anything else?"

"Does this computer have last year's schedules? I want to look at Ellis Madsen's classes."

"Oh," breathed Tara. "Let's see. I think she had some classes with Laurence. Maybe her transcripts?"

Tara was such a trusting soul. I would have questioned myself, but then like a barnyard cat, I leaned toward suspicion in most matters.

A moment later, another sheet shot from the printer.

"Can I help you with another schedule?" Her smile caused the pixels to spontaneously vibrate on the computer screen.

"Is there anything you can't do, Tara?"

She tapped her chin, thinking. Her smile plummeted. "I can't get Lukey to love me."

My heart nosedived, and I grasped Tara's hands. "Luke Harper is a piece of dirt. You don't deserve him. So is Anthony Pettit. I heard about him. You need to find a better man."

"How can you say that? Luke's your friend. He's wonderful. Kind and caring. Patient. Loyal. Handsome."

"No, you are describing a well bred golden retriever. Or my roommate, Todd McIntosh."

Her smile brightened. "Todd is very sweet. I enjoyed talking to him last night."

"Good. Luke is bad news. Forget about him." My lecture done, I moved on to a less personal topic. One that didn't involve memories of me snogging Luke in the school parking lot. "Now, show me how to access Miss Amber's email."

"Cherry, isn't that wrong?"

Dang this girl's ethics. She doesn't question me wanting a dead girl's transcripts, but does question a peek at someone's private correspondence? "What if a parent has emailed Miss Amber about something important?"

"You're right." Her cheeks brightened again. "What was I thinking?"

"I don't know." Hopefully she wasn't thinking about any financial reports from the principal that I could forward to Max.

She clicked on the email box. "It's not password protected."

"That's not too smart on Miss Amber's part. But good for us." My eyes sped over the lines of text. "While I look over her email for important messages, why don't you get busy filing Miss Amber's folders?"

Tara toddled off with an armload of folders, while I scanned Amber's email, filled with forwarded recipes and jokes of the day. I paged through a half-dozen online ads and found a string of PeerNotes updates. I left those to search the previous day's emails. No messages from Cleveland. Clicking on her sent mail, I found several Amber had sent to Cleveland. Including one marked "Urgent." I clicked.

"Mr. Cleveland," Amber had written, "I'm trying to catch up on Maranda's work and have found several items that she question marked for you. Should I send them on to Brenda?"

She hadn't attached anything to the email. In Amber's dictionary, urgent must mean vague. I clicked back to the inbox and began to scan her PeerNotes messages. An earlier email listed an announcement of new photos loaded onto the site. I clicked and a new screen popped up. I recognized the PeerNotes header and eagerly paged past the photos of Tinsley tossing student audition sheets in the garbage. The day's cafeteria meals (Chicken biscuits. This school had everything.). Lacrosse team news. Solo auditions for the choral Christmas concert. Finally, "Peerless Memorial Garden: Drug Bust or Ghost Bust?"

I clicked.

"Four drama students abandoned their backpacks and a baggie of porcini after witnessing the apparition of E.M. who now haunts this school in revenge for the students who bullied her. Police came to investigate and didn't find evidence of drugs or ghosts. Nice going drama geeks, you losers."

I rolled my eyes and clicked on the comment box. "Shitake not porcini," I typed. "And people who sell drugs, fake or not, are bigger losers than the ones who take them."

Three seconds later, the computer pinged and twenty responses to my message appeared. Most with creative uses of the word shitake. Realizing I had used Miss Amber's login, I tried to delete the message and instead reposted it.

I stuck my tongue out at the computer and moved on.

"Is Ellis Madsen haunting the teachers with ghost texts?" read the next post. I clicked and scanned. Most of the comments belittled the poster, who responded with greater creativity than those liking the word shitake.

However, one student comment made my mind hum. "Then shouldn't she be haunting last year's senior drama students instead of Mr. Tinsley? He made her Evita. They made her die."

The response to that comment knocked my eyebrows into my hairline.

"Did Tinsley notice what the seniors were doing to her? If not, why? If so, why didn't he stop them?" Dr. Vail didn't disguise her comment.

Her war with Tinsley was available for all the students to see. Not very professional of Dr. Vail. But maybe her conflict with Tinsley went beyond departmental jealousies. Maybe she knew Ellis and felt Tinsley had done her an injustice.

I snagged the two schedules from the printer cache and glanced at Preston King's. He had four academic courses and three art classes. I scanned Ellis's schedule from the previous year. Five academics, two-dimensional design, and basic drawing with Dr. Vail. No drama. How did she get the part of Evita?

I needed to talk to Dr. Vail. But how could I get her to talk to me when she thought I sided with Tinsley?

A fresh wave of chattering accompanied by violent shushing made me slip from Miss Amber's seat and steal back to the counter. Ms. Cooke, followed by her gang of office chicks, strode into the reception area.

Cooke had her finger on the pulse of the school. Useful, except she didn't seem to like me. Probably picked up on the anti-authority vibe I had cultivated during my school days. I followed her toward the back offices and stopped in her doorway.

Ms. Cooke had a handful of letters and tossed them on the desk before looking at me.

"Did Miss Amber quit?" I asked, using the first segue that came to mind.

"Amber's not here today," she answered by way of non-answer. "Can I help you? I'm very busy."

"Some teachers feel they are being cyberstalked. Tinsley is one of them. That's a crime. Have you made them aware that they can report it to the police?"

"The police learned about the messages during their investigation into Miss Pringle's death," she said. "But I'd rather not have any more negative publicity for Peerless. Especially if it's just a prank. If we ignore the texts, they'll eventually stop. The parents get agitated with too much controversy."

"Are you getting texts, too?"

"That is not your concern." Cooke's brow furrowed. "I heard you found the students in the garden last night. You shouldn't be roaming the grounds."

"I wasn't roaming. We saw a kid running from that direction," I said. "Were your texts like the ones Miss Pringle received?"

"No." Ms. Cooke firmed her lips. "Miss Pringle's loss is devastating, and this week is a terrible burden for Peerless. We'll get through it by staying on our respective tasks. I suggest you respect our loss and do the same by focusing on set design and not on harmful gossip."

She walked forward, forcing me to back out of her office, and shut the door. I stared at the closed door, wondering what kind of text Cooke had received. Must have been a humdinger.

Pringle. Tinsley. Vail. Fisher. Cooke. If only these adults would set aside their pride and admit they were being bullied.

And where the hell was Principal Cleveland?

TWENTY-ONE

Troubled by the news that Ellis's father was back in town and Cleveland missing, I slipped into the school foyer, snuck out my cell phone, and called Detective Herrera.

He didn't sound pleased to meet my request, but promised to check on Cleveland. His interest piqued when I mentioned Dan Madsen's return to the area.

"I'll be at the funeral on Monday," said Herrera. "If Madsen shows, I'll talk to him. Unfortunately, I got to know him because of Ellis's death."

"Do you think Dan Madsen's the kind of guy who'd badger the teachers with these texts?"

Herrera didn't speak for a long ten seconds. "People do all kinds of stupid, crazy stuff you'd never think possible of them. But if Madsen wanted to point fingers, I wouldn't think he'd blame the teachers. He should be pointing them at Ellis's friends and the kids who did it. Madsen and his wife should have been checking Ellis's texts and social media messages. They could have seen what was happening and gotten her help."

"What if I could convince one of these teachers to report the cyberstalking?"

"Until it's reported, there's not much we can do on this end."

"Thanks, Detective Herrera."

He paused again. "Hey, we got the tox screen back on Maranda Pringle. A cocktail of alcohol, atomoxetine, and benzodiazepine. One benzo was Xanax. We found an empty Xanax bottle. No label.

Probably bought it off someone. The other benzo was lorazepam. Probably Ativan, used for insomnia. Easy enough to get."

"Wait, I thought she was taking Zyban. Why wouldn't she try to OD on that?"

"She only had a few pills left of Zyban in the bottle. Maybe she thought it wasn't enough. There was a trace of it in her system, though. That and birth control pills."

"What's the other drug you mentioned?"

"Strattera."

"The ADHD medicine? Did she have ADHD?"

Another long pause. Long enough for me to circle the Peerless foyer two times. "She did not have a prescription for Strattera."

Cops. "So where did she get it?"

"We're looking into it."

"And you still believe Pringle committed suicide? You don't find that suspicious?"

"Suicide is a suspicious death, but yes, I think it's suicide. The Strattera combined with alcohol would make her sleepy. Add in the Xanax and Ativan and she would have fallen asleep and not woken up."

"And the coroner?"

"Now wonders where she got the Strattera."

I smiled. "Thanks for the info. I know it pained you to give it to me."

"If you can convince a teacher to report the cyberstalking, I'd be happy to investigate it."

"I'm on it," I said and hung up. A teacher passing through the lobby frowned at me. I shoved my phone into my satchel. The kids needed to teach me their skills on sneaking devices.

A bell rang and the halls flooded with students. Caught in the tidal wave of bodies, I swam toward the arts hall, then paddled toward the fine arts wing.

In the small entryway between classrooms, I found myself crushed between exiting and entering students and allowed them to pull me into the nearest classroom. A young woman looked up from

Dr. Vail's corner desk, while the new class of students took their place at the easels.

I squeezed past the easels to the desk and smiled at the young teacher. "Hey, I'm Cherry Tucker. Is Dr. Vail around?"

"Sorry, she's out today. I'm another art teacher, just filling in. Can I help you?"

"Will Dr. Vail be back tomorrow?"

"I'm not sure. Today was unplanned, but she had some concerns over the arts budget and wanted some time to go over the numbers before getting out of town this weekend. She's showing student work in a festival in Berea, Kentucky."

A good excuse for Vail to check out Tinsley's accounting like she had threatened. "While I've got you here, have you been getting odd texts?"

"Like books? They made pop-ups in three-D design a few weeks ago."

"Never mind." I leaned closer. "Did Dr. Vail mention feeling cyberstalked? Some other teachers are having that problem."

She leaned away, then flicked a glance at my visitor badge. "Who are you again?"

"Cherry Tucker. Fellow artist and new set designer. I need to speak to one of your senior students anyway." I glanced at Preston's schedule. "He has sculpture right now."

Sticking her hands on her hips, the sub leveled me with a dark gaze. "You can't talk to our students. I'm going to call the office if you don't leave."

Crap. I didn't want Cooke involved. "Can you tell Preston I'm looking for him?"

"No. Out." She pointed at the door.

I turned around.

Fifteen students watched us from their easels. Trudging toward the door, I stopped by a student who had made a sketch of my encounter with the teacher.

I grabbed his pencil and adjusted his skewed perspective. "I'm bigger than the teacher because I'm closer to you," I explained.

"You made her look like Godzilla." I added scales and sharp teeth to the sub's image to make my point.

"F-off," said the kid, snatching back his pencil. "You're not my teacher."

"Good luck in college with that attitude." I wormed my way toward the door and into the art vestibule. I peeked in the other doors until I spied students gathered around a working lathe. Sculpture class.

These Peerless teachers were brave. A lathe seemed like an expensive lawsuit waiting to happen.

I hauled open the door and stepped inside the classroom. Three students glanced up, peering at me through thick goggles. The fourth slipped a chisel off the block of wood rotating on the lathe. He shut off the machine, pulled off his goggles, and glanced up.

Not a student. A young, male teacher in a flannel shirt and Carhartt utility pants. He had clipped his teacher badge to his shoulder, near his round cheeks and bright, green eyes.

"Did we forget to put the attendance folder out again?" asked Mr. Cute.

I glanced at the door and didn't see a folder. "Yes."

Tossing his goggles at one of the kids, Mr. Cute strode to his desk. He searched through the mess, then looked back at me. "I don't see it. Are you sure? Anyway, Preston King is the only one out today."

Dangit. I was two for three already. Scott Fisher was last on my list. "Thanks. Do you know why he's absent?"

Mr. Cute shook his head. "Nope. Sorry."

I left them to their sharp instruments, headed back to the main hall, and turned west toward the theater doors. With class in session, I would need to hunt down Fisher after hours. Which gave me time to speak to Tinsley.

In the drama department, Tinsley conducted class on stage again. He organized the students into small groups. "Experience an ice cream cone," he ordered them and waved me over.

I walked past the groups of melting ice cream cones and pretended it seemed normal.

"Let's examine your sketches, shall we?" said Tinsley in his over loud, I'm-the-theater voice.

I pulled my sketchbook from my satchel and flipped to the pages I had worked up in colored pencil. I had chosen a palette of blues and greens from viridian to ultramarine. Instead of fish populating the underwater alien world, I had drawn sea monkeys.

"Fantastic," said Tinsley. "I wonder if we could get readymade costumes like these creatures? Brilliant adaptation of my ideas, Miss Tucker."

My theatrical contribution to *Romeo and Juliet* was sea monkeys.

I walked to the lowered backdrop. "I've never painted anything this big. I'm looking forward to it."

Tinsley scooted closer to me. "And how goes the other front?" he whispered. "Any news on our phantom?"

"I'm working on it, but I keep uncovering other oddities. You heard about us catching your drama students in the memorial garden last night?"

"An unfortunate incident. I spoke to them this morning. Thankfully, my students are not versed in drug culture and were taken for saps by a nefarious miscreant who trades in the vile stuff."

"Preston King? He's not in school today."

Tinsley darted a look toward his students and scooted closer. "Camille lets him get away with murder."

"Murder?"

"I am prone to exaggeration. She covers for him."

"Dr. Vail's out today, too."

"Really? How odd." Tinsley rubbed his beard. "Something I said? No matter."

"Do you know Preston King well? Does he sell other drugs besides fake shrooms?"

"There are all manner of rumors, but he's never been caught. Unfortunately, these children have money and much freedom.

Where there's money and freedom, they find all sorts of negative ways to recreate."

"How about prescription drugs? ADHD meds? Does Preston sell drugs like that?"

Tinsley shrugged. "It would not surprise me in the least. That particular student has placed a pall over our fair school. Do you believe Preston King is the Phantom?"

"Not sure about that." I turned to gaze at Tinsley's supposed angelic students, wondering if Maranda Pringle would have bought Strattera from Preston.

If proven, it could jerk a knot in the drug peddling tail at Peerless. But I was not hired to bust drug dealers. Tinsley wanted the Phantom.

"Listen, I've been talking to the cops. You and the other teachers need to report your texts as cyberstalking. Prosecute this guy for real."

"This is why I am paying you, so I don't have to involve the police. Peerless doesn't need the negative publicity. We shouldn't have to suffer the arrows and daggers of gossip when we're at competition. Not only could it skew the judges' opinion, it distracts the students from their work."

He turned toward his students. Their ice cream-selves having melted, they now played with their phones on the floor. "Rehearsal begins next period. The advanced choir is joining us to begin work on the musical."

"Sounds good. I want to speak with other teachers about the anonymous messaging. But if you have the materials, I may as well start painting now."

"I'll have your assigned assistant ready the paint for you. Whatever we don't have, I'll order." He approached the students and began to direct them into another activity.

I still didn't understand his reluctance to report to the police. Weren't the students already distracted from their work?

Why would drama judges care that some prankster had stalked Peerless? I hoped Max's investigation into Tinsley turned up the reason for his recalcitrance. Tinsley looked to beat both me and Tater the goat in stubbornness.

And that was saying something.

I wandered to a bathroom to change into painting gear. My usual wife beater and cut-offs felt inappropriate for public, particularly in a high school, so I had brought a pair of overalls and an old Tybee Island t-shirt featuring a Tybee turtle holding a Solo cup. My overalls' bib hid the Solo cup.

When I returned to the stage, the bell had rung, signaling the next class, and Laurence waited for me with a cart filled with buckets of the acrylic theater paint. Laurence also wore old jeans and a t-shirt. I had a feeling he volunteered for set painting just to get out of wearing his uniform.

"Ready to get your art on?" I grinned.

"I am ready to do the necessary steps to get my theater credits," said Laurence. "Your Tom Sawyer whitewashing attempts will not sway me to do more than that."

This was going to be a long two weeks of painting.

I explained the concept of crosshatching fat Xs on the hanging muslin to apply a base coat of cobalt blue turquoise. While he slapped Xs, I examined the rotating pillars and began to cover their three sides in a neutral base coat. Shoved together, one side of the pillars would show the Capulet's high-tech underwater alien home. Another side would portray a street scene. Instead of a medieval castle town, I would paint futuristic bubble homes for the singing sea monkeys. The last scene would be the Friar's monastery. As a spacey techno dance club.

I kept my opinions to myself since I knew diddly about theater.

While Laurence and I did the drudgery of base coats upstage, rehearsals began downstage. The chorus teacher, Leah's cousin Faith Bairburn, had brought in a group to huddle around a piano. They stumbled through a medley of pop songs Tinsley had pieced together for the musical numbers. The chosen Romeo, mop-topped

Layton, crooned "You're the First, the Last, My Everything" to Hayden, his giggly, red-headed Juliet.

I concentrated splitting my focus between Laurence's painting and the balcony, seeking any spying phantoms. When the next bell rang, I snagged Faith Bairburn before she could leave, introducing myself as Leah's friend. She had an upper girth to accommodate a powerful voice, but moved with the grace and rhythm of a dancer. All hidden beneath a floral tent of a dress. Seemed all the Bairburn's shopped in the same stores and with the same intent.

"Hey, Cherry." Faith offered me a cheery smile that also reminded me of Leah's, then hugged me. "I heard you're fixing to help Tinsley figure out who's sending all these horrible messages. Let me know what I can do to help."

"Have you received any?"

She hesitated. "Well, yes, but they were so ridiculous, I didn't even respond."

"Did you keep them? The police need to see one."

"No, honey. I delete trash. The message was so far-fetched. Something about seeing me dance in a stripper bar." She laughed. "Obviously, they don't know the Bairburns well."

The Bairburns could straighten rulers with their morals. Leah, the church choir director, was considered the black sheep. Only because she hung out with me and sang in Todd's band.

"Now that's just silly. I'm glad you weren't offended."

Her teeth shone white with her chuckle. "I was too busy laughing to be offended. If the rest of the staff were the same way, they'd probably quit getting texts, too. Unfortunately, maybe they have more to hide."

"Do you know if Ms. Cooke's gotten any texts?"

"When I told her about mine, she indicated she had gotten one, too. 'A ludicrous assumption,' Brenda had said."

"I thought as much. How about other teachers? Everyone's keeping quiet, and I have nothing to go on."

Faith pulled the sheet music to her ample chest and thought for a moment. "Tinsley's been the most vocal. He brought it up in the faculty meeting. The librarian received a message as silly as mine. She also deleted it."

"How about Miss Pringle? Does anyone know for sure if she received a text? Or what it said?"

"Oh, she got one all right." Faith shook her head. "That poor child. Found her crying in the staff bathroom. Something about an inappropriate relationship with a parent."

I studied Faith to see if she believed the truth of the text Maranda Pringle had received. She didn't. Just like Leah, she believed the best in people. I hugged Faith.

"Thanks, honey," she said. "I feel real bad about Maranda. Maybe I could have said something to her that would have snapped her out of whatever funk she had fallen in. Despair is the devil's instrument."

"Miss Faith, let me know if you hear about anyone else getting texts. And if you can convince them to go to the police, that would be a lot of help."

"I will, baby. Now I've got to get to class. If you don't sit on these students, they just squirm out the door, looking for trouble." She laughed and sauntered away, her hips rotating beneath the floral drapery.

I glanced around the empty theater, then squinted up into the dark balcony. Why discredit these teachers when they hadn't done anything? Or had they? Certainly not Miss Faith, but what about the Tinsleys, Vails, and Pringles who seemed to react to the messages?

Sometimes smoke does reveal fire.

It also bothered me that I couldn't get a good picture of Maranda Pringle. Was she a harlot or just misunderstood? Why did she leave such a boring suicide note?

Where had she gotten the ADHD medicine? And why take it and Xanax when she had a prescription for Zyban? I needed to learn more about Pringle.

Four people might have answers. Her friend Olivia who worked at Little Verona's. Grieving Principal Cleveland. Coach

Andy Newcomb, who according to Cleveland, had been recently stepping out with Miss Maranda.

And Dan Madsen.

Before leaving the school, I found Scott Fisher in his classroom. He wore a white lab coat and his short, brown hair had a tousled look, like he often ran his fingers through his hair.

The Expo marker smudges on his forehead provided further proof. I knocked, entered the classroom, and closed the door behind me.

Framed in the picture window, he looked up from his desk where he chewed on a pen and appeared to be sorting through a large stack of notebooks.

I scooted between the lab tables to his desk, considering ways to make him admit he'd been ghost texted. I decided on a kernel of truth approach, as I couldn't admit going through his desk and finding the printed out text messages.

"Hey, Mr. Fisher." I introduced myself as Tinsley's set director.

"So Tinsley's been hassled by this anonymous texter." I leaned over his desk, trying my best wheedling look. "I want him to go to the police, but he won't do it. I thought if other teachers were getting hassled and they went forward, maybe he would, too. It's considered cyberstalking."

Fisher stuck his pen behind his ear. "I'm sorry to hear he's having this problem."

"What about you? Are you having any problems?"

He fixed his gaze on a molecular model hanging behind my head. The pen slipped off his ear and fell to the floor. Fisher bent over to search for the pen under his desk. "I'm fine," he called from beneath his desk. "No problems."

I crossed my arms and waited for his head to reappear from beneath the desk. "Are you sure? It's not like the text messages have to be true to be considered stalking."

"No. No messages."

Narrowing my eyes, I fixed him with a hard stare. "Really? I thought I saw someone in your room last night. I was here after hours helping Tinsley after the auditions."

His brown eyes widened, causing the pupils to shrink to pencil nubs. "My grade book is missing."

"Someone stole your grade book?" I didn't have time for the Case of the Missing Grade Book. I also didn't have time for the Case of the Pervy Teacher, but I'd have to make the time. This guy was not going to admit he'd been accused of messing around with a student. If he had, I'd turn him in. And probably threaten to shoot him. Then, I might do just that if the student's parents didn't first. But if he was innocent and I turned him in, I could ruin his life.

Dammit. Why couldn't anyone be honest with me? I'd have to resort to lying. "Listen, Mr. Fisher. I've heard you've gotten texts. I'm close to the Sheriff's Office. We need to crack down on this cyberbullying thing and I'm going to give them a list of everyone who's been harassed." I paused to let him volunteer information.

He nodded, glanced at the notebook on his desk, and drew a big checkmark on the page with his wayward pen.

I felt ready to walk around his desk, grab the moldy banana, and smack him with it. "Let me put this to you another way. Are you fooling around with a student?"

The color drained from his face. The pen dropped from his hand and rolled off the desk. He made a move to bend over, but I held up a hand to stop him.

"Mr. Fisher, you are forcing me into a difficult position. There is no point in lying about the texts, unless you are guilty. And if you're guilty, I'm declaring a citizen's arrest and hauling your ass to jail."

"Why would you say that?" He spit the words out like he was choking and his face purpled. "It's a big misunderstanding."

My eyes narrowed and my chest heaved.

Behind me, the classroom door slammed open. "I'm going home with Chantelle."

Fisher gulped air and turned toward the door.

With my fists clenched at my side, I eased to face the student.

A young girl dressed in the Peerless uniform tossed a backpack on a lab table and looked up. "What's going on?" Her face scrunched tight. "Who're you?"

"Cherry Tucker," I said. "I'm working in the drama department."

"Right," she said. "I heard about you. What are you doing in here?"

I glanced at Fisher. The purple had faded to a carmine pink, and he had collapsed in his chair. "I'm wondering that about you. How do you know Mr. Fisher?"

She shrugged. "He's a teacher."

"That he is," I said. "Are you in his chemistry class?"

"Chloe," Fisher said. "She heard about the accusations. I told you it was a bad idea. We can't hide this anymore."

I tightened my fists and stepped around the desk to stand next to Fisher.

Chloe looked from Fisher to me, shaking her head. "No. You promised. Everyone will know. They'll treat me differently."

"I'm fixing to call the police in two seconds, Chloe," I ground out the words, willing my fist not to slam into Fisher's face in front of the girl. "You don't have to tell me anything, but you're going to have to talk to them. This is seriously wrong."

She blanched. "I didn't think..."

"She's my step-daughter," blurted Fisher. "Chloe doesn't want any of the students to know. It's innocent. Someone saw her getting into my car. The staff knows, just not the students."

I unclenched my fists, took a deep breath, and let it out slowly. "Okay then." I bit my lip so I wouldn't let out a string of curses in front of Chloe and took another deep breath before continuing. "Chloe, honey?"

"Yeah?" She stared daggers at Mr. Fisher, full of fifteen-year-old piss and vinegar.

"That'd be a yes, ma'am." My voice caused her to peel her gaze off Fisher and stick it on me.

Her eyes widened and voice shook. "Yes, ma'am."

"I almost got your stepdaddy in a crapload of trouble. Like lose his job and go to jail trouble. Is Mr. Fisher a nice guy? Does he treat you and your momma well?"

"Yes, ma'am." She found interest in her backpack strap and focused on winding it around her finger.

"I'm guessing you couldn't go to this school unless he was teaching here. Am I right?"

"Yes, ma'am."

"Then put on your big girl pants and own up to having such a nice stepdaddy. Someone out there is spreading ugly rumors. Rumors that can cause really bad things to happen. You want that to happen to him?"

"No, ma'am."

"Do you know who is spreading those rumors? Some kid having fun on his computer?"

"I don't know." Her cheeks flared. "Scott's cool. But his class is hard. Some students have pressured another teacher's kid to help them cheat. I don't want to deal with that, so I asked Scott not to tell anyone he's married to my mom."

I patted Fisher on the shoulder with a trembling hand. "Sorry about that, Mr. Fisher. I have a tendency to get overprotective in certain situations. No harm done."

He mopped his face with his hand. "Where did you hear about this?"

I stopped my trek toward the door and turned back to face him. "You got texts just like the other teachers, didn't you?"

"I figured it was Preston King, trying to blackmail me so I ignored them. He's flunking my class and won't graduate if he doesn't pass. After the nine weeks grade report, he threatened to do something to me. I told Ms. Cooke what had happened and showed her the texts. I assumed she took care of it."

I whirled away from Scott Fisher, pulled out my phone, and ran out the door.

TWENTY-TWO

I dialed Herrera as I scurried to the office. He must have learned my number, because he answered with a familiar, "What now?"

Too many people answered my calls like that.

"Rumor has it this Preston King is running a drug cartel at Peerless."

"We picked him up last night, but his parents lawyered up and got him out. We couldn't hold him on selling fake drugs, but I'm working on a warrant to search his room. His lawyer said it was a prank, but the kids who bought his mushrooms gave us all kinds of interesting information about Preston. They stole a grade book in exchange for the mushrooms."

"It was probably Scott Fisher's grade book. I hope you get something on Preston. But it's really hard to tell rumors from fact at this school and all my intel on Preston King is gossip. Do you think he could be our phantom texter?"

"I checked his phone. No texts to any teachers."

"He would probably email the texts from his computer. That's what the kids say."

"The warrant will cover his computer and other equipment. We'll find out if he did."

I hung up and hooked a right into the office.

Tara hopped from her seat behind Amber's desk. "Cherry, I haven't seen you all day. How are you?"

"Fine, thanks." I walked past her. "How're you?"

"Wonderful. It's so busy in the office, but I'm very glad to help." She scurried to match my stride. "Did you see Laurence today? Is he assisting you? Are you going to work on the set after school today? Do you need any help?"

"Yes. Yes. No. No. Listen Tara, I need to talk to Ms. Cooke. I'll see you later."

"Okey dokey, Cherry. If you see Lukey, please tell him I've been thinking about him."

I considered telling Tara what I knew about Luke and Pettit, but figured it would do more harm than good. Besides, I had more important business. Like going to the principal's office again. I knocked on Ms. Cooke's door and entered at her command.

She looked up from her computer. "Yes?"

"What if Preston King is the one cyberbullying the teachers?"

"And that would be none of your business. I am not going to discuss a student with you."

I blew out my breath and turned toward the door.

"Miss Tucker." She spoke with her clipped principal tones.

I turned back.

"You have no right to deal with any of my students. Your clearance checks out, and I'll allow you to paint the set, but that's it. I don't want you here during school hours. You are only allowed at Peerless under Tinsley's direct supervision and only in the theater during the scheduled rehearsal time. Is that understood?"

"Yes, ma'am." I scraped my beaded cuff along the ground and knocked off a skull.

"You're dismissed." She turned back to her computer.

I stalked from her office, held up my hand to stop Tara's mouth from running, and stormed out of the building. After-school rehearsal wasn't scheduled until tomorrow.

I'd been suspended from school. If Grandpa found out, he'd kick my can for sure.

If I had a better vehicle I would have burned rubber out of the school parking lot, but the Datsun didn't burn anything but oil, so I had to content myself with puttering back to town. I never got a chance to eat in the Peerless cafeteria, so I pondered the best place to fill my stomach and work out my current troubles. I headed southeast into Line Creek, swung by Lickety Pig, and pulled into the Sheriff's Office smelling of barbecue. Grasping paper bags and cups of tea in both hands, I backed through the glass door and dumped a bag in front of the shielded reception window.

Tamara arched a brow. "Is that for me?"

"Yes, ma'am," I said. "And I've got one for Uncle Will. Is he around?"

Tamara slid an arm through the window's hole and snagged the bag. She tossed her braided pony tail back, causing a frenzied clicking from the red, white, and black beads. "You bringing anyone else barbecue?"

"No, ma'am. Just myself. I thought I'd eat lunch with Uncle Will."

Her deep ochre eyes studied me. "I thought you were working at that school."

Dammit, how did Tamara sense I had gotten expelled? "It's an after-school gig. Set painting."

"Stay out of trouble." She pushed the buzzer.

"Yes, ma'am." I scurried to the door, yanked it open, and sped up the hall. Just before I knocked on Uncle Will's door, the entrance to the junior officers' room opened, and Luke poked his head out.

"Thought I saw you on the monitor," he said. "Is that for me, sugar?"

I steeled my loins and thinned my lips. "No. I am visiting my Uncle Will."

He sauntered over, his uniform hugging his lean frame and causing a frenzy of hormones to ping pong inside my body. "How are you today?"

I tipped my chin up. "Just fine and you?"

"Feels a little cold in here." Luke faked a shiver and tucked a stray hair behind my ear. "Are you mad I didn't take you home last night? I wanted to take you home." He winked.

"Ha." I clenched the barbecue bag and styrofoam tea cups and used my shoulder to untuck the hair. "Actually, I was glad Todd picked me up. I got to hear about his conversation with Tara. She told Todd all about her prior engagement to Anthony Pettit."

"Oh." Luke's swagger dipped into now-I've-done-it realm.

"Nice work, Harper. You broke Tara's heart just to get back at Pettit. Hope you taught Pettit a good lesson." I backed toward Will's door. "I sure learned one."

"Hear me out." Luke snatched the Lickety Pig bag from my hand. "I wasn't trying to use Tara. Pettit is an asshole. Everyone knew he was getting some on the side. When I saw Tara at Red's, I felt sorry for her and asked her to dance. I didn't tell her to break up with Pettit. I didn't tell her anything."

"You asked her to a wedding."

"I needed a date and she's nice. And I thought you were with Todd McIntosh." His voice softened. "I'd rather have taken you."

"You can't take me to a Branson wedding, Luke. You can't even bring me to the house without causing a fracas." I felt my eyes tear up, and I kicked the wall with the heel of my boot. "Our family history is too ugly."

And about to get uglier. Damn Bransons. And Cody.

"They're not my family, sugar. I meant what I said about not letting them get between us." He pushed the Lickety Pig bag back into my hand. "What's going on at school today? Everyone talking about the kids we caught in the garden?"

I nodded, glad to be on the safer topic of suicide and stalking. "Dr. Vail and Cleveland weren't at school today. And Dan Madsen's back in town, which I find a little too convenient."

"See if any of them will meet you at Little Verona's. Maybe you'll get a reaction from Pringle's friend."

The door next to my elbow swung back and Uncle Will's bounty filled the opening. "There you are, hon'. Tamara said you brought me lunch. Kind of late for lunch, but just pleased as punch to have you think of me. And then I wondered if you'd changed your mind."

"Just got sidetracked," I said, handing Will the bag.

"Come in and share my repast." He nodded at Luke and guided me into the room. "Talking about the Peerless case, were you? I heard about the fake drug bust last night."

Luke stepped into the doorway. "Turned out to be a prank, but the kid in question might actually deal."

I followed Will to his desk, plopped into a chair, and scooted sideways to face both men. "Herrera is trying to get a warrant. They're going to check Preston King's computer to see if he's also sending the texts."

"Deputy Harper, you got some place to be?" Will paused from unwrapping his sandwich to glance at Luke. "I don't believe your orders include chatting with my niece."

"Yes, sir." Luke spun on his heel and shut the door.

I turned back to face Will. "Herrera told me about Pringle's tox screen. Why would she take ADHD meds when she had antidepressants available?"

"Perhaps the young drug dealer will have information about that. Kids will try any kind of drug, and ADHD meds are easy enough for them to get and sell. Strattera is not something an adult would normally seek out for getting high, though. From what I understand, it's non-stimulatory. Not like Adderall."

"So if Maranda Pringle wanted to commit suicide, Strattera makes sense."

"I suppose." Will sighed and took a bite out of his sandwich.

"I wish the GBI would hurry up and decrypt her phone to check for those deleted texts. Herrera and Luke think the Phantom is just some kid causing mayhem. Poison pen stuff without really knowing if the insinuations are true. I think certain texts may be deliberate. Possibly blaming certain folks for Ellis Madsen's death last year."

The clock on the wall clicked off seconds. Will chewed his barbecue, and I unwrapped my sandwich, both of us consumed by our thoughts. "Of course, some texts seem to have nothing to do with Ellis or anything at all." I sighed. "I don't get it. I need more information, but maybe Luke's right about the Phantom's scatter-shot approach."

"You're spending some time with Harper on this." Will eyed me over his sandwich. "Remember what I told you? Are you taking my advice seriously?"

"Of course," I said. "I take catching the perp who's bullying teachers very seriously. One woman may have lost her life to him. That's pretty sobering."

Will swallowed and coughed. "You're not catching any perps, honey, that's Herrera's job. You're just solving a puzzle."

"Right." I smiled like I meant it.

"Anyway, that's not what I'm talking about. You're not fooling around with Harper when I told you to leave him alone?"

"What if he doesn't want to leave me alone?"

"Then I'll get a restraining order, although I'd rather not since he's a good officer and it would reflect badly on my department."

I rolled my eyes. "I understand."

"Have you talked to Cody?"

"I can't find him to talk to him. I saw him for about two seconds and he took off before we could have words."

"What is going on with that boy?"

"I don't know." The barbecue stuck in my throat and I took a long sip of tea.

Will's forehead produced new wrinkles. "Did he and JB Branson get into a scuffle at the dealership? Is that why Cody quit?"

I kept my lips busy with the tea straw.

"Damn, I bet Cody mouthed off to JB and got fired. Now Cody's mad and looking to get even with the boss." Will shook his head. "Y'all are too stubborn for your own good, you know that?"

"I know," I muttered.

"I can't waste my man power on a family issue," Will said. "You've got to find your brother. Before Cody does something really stupid and one of my deputies ends up arresting him."

I'd add it to my to-do list.

TWENTY-THREE

By Friday afternoon, I still hadn't found Cody. I also couldn't get Principal Cleveland to answer his door or Dan Madsen to return my calls.

According to Little Verona's restaurant, Miss Pringle's friend, Olivia, had taken bereavement time to argue the details of Maranda's funeral with Principal Cleveland, which made me more curious to speak to both parties. Coach Newcomb's golf team had left for a state tournament. And I avoided Luke for fear of loin-girding slippage.

My detecting skills had fallen lower than a snake's belly in a wagon rut.

That left me with my original job in the theater. Happy to meet my newly assigned set design crew, I taught them how to wrap newspaper strips around chicken wire to create paper mâché bubbles to suspend from wires for the techno-underwater Capulet versus Montague dance-off scene. I backed away from the flinging wet newspaper, checked on Laurence's balcony project, and lost myself in stippling cinnabar green over cobalt green turquoise to add depth to my backdrop.

I declared a Coke break for my industrious little set designers. From the auditorium seats, they hunkered over their devices, while I watched a group of young Capulets attempt hip hop steps while singing "Vengeance is Mine" by Alice Cooper. As they did the Dougie, a pile of phones flashed and buzzed on the corner of the stage. The dancers' gazes flew to their stack of devices. Around me, students began to shoot looks at their friends, murmur and type, their thumbs flying over their keyboards.

I leaned over my seat and tapped Laurence on the shoulder. "What's going on? Another message go out over PeerNotes?"

He glanced up from his iPad. "I find Kierkegaard far more fascinating."

"Okay Einstein, you can go back to Kierkewhatsit in a minute. Dial up PeerNotes on that thing and tell me what's going on."

Laurence offered me a lengthy sigh filled with sixteen years of pent-up exasperation.

A Tara screech interrupted Laurence's screen tapping. He slunk in his seat, his head disappearing from view. I turned in my chair. Tara ran down the aisle toward the stage. She hustled pretty well for someone my size, further proving I had greater issues with running than short legs.

"Cherry, I need to talk to you." Tara's squawk carried through the auditorium. Her cheerleading voice made an effective megaphone. "It's an emergency."

From his table on the stage, Tinsley tore his gaze off the dancers and held a hand to stop the scene. The dancing Capulets sped to the side of the stage and snatched their devices.

I hopped to my feet and scooted toward the aisle where Tara had parked her pink Keds.

"Tara," I whispered. "You're freaking everyone out. Keep it down." When had I become the one to tell other people to shut up? Times were a changing.

"Cherry." Tara brought her voice down, but couldn't suspend the tremor. Her pale face had blanched geisha white except for two rose madder spots on her cheeks. "The police are in the front office again."

"Hold on a minute." I shimmied down the aisle to where Laurence still hunkered on the floor. "Laurence, what did the message on PeerNotes say?"

"'A plague on both your houses. They have made worms' meat of me,'" he whispered.

"Hey brother." Tara hopped and waved. "How are you? What are you doing on the floor? You can't make friends from down there. Why aren't you up on the stage?"

I ignored Tara and fixed on Laurence. "What does this worms' meat thingy mean?"

Laurence glared up at me. "It's Mercutio's line, genius. Aren't you paying attention to the play? Mercutio's blaming both the Capulets and Montagues for his death."

I glanced up at the stage. Tinsley paced and spoke on the phone, leaving the dance teacher and Faith huddled together. Abandoning Laurence to the floor, I scooted down the aisle toward Tara, grabbed her arm, and marched her to the empty theater hallway.

"Tell me now," I said. "Who died? Cleveland? Is that why he's missed school this week?"

She shook her head, tears brimming in her eyes. "The police found Amber Tipton."

"Suicide?"

"My stars, no. She was shot in a home invasion. The police are in the office now."

"Dammit," I said. "Get Laurence and go home. Let Cooke handle the police. You're just a sub, and it's Friday afternoon. You don't need to stay. They'll probably cancel practice now anyway."

"What are you going to do?" She took a folded tissue from her pocket and dabbed under her eyes, careful of her mascara.

"I'm going up to the office and see what I can find out." I glanced at my clothes. I had changed into my overalls and Tybee Island top to paint. "I'll grab my bag and say a word to Tinsley first."

Leaving Tara in the hall, I sped back to the stage.

Tinsley had collapsed into a folding chair, while the other teachers gave instructions to the students on clean-up and dismissal procedures.

I ambled to Tinsley and laid a hand on his shoulder. "Are you okay? I guess you heard about Amber."

He used both hands to massage his temples. "The world is not a safe place and evidently Line Creek township is included. But it seems rather coincidental, does it not?"

"Seems kind of strange to me, too," I said. "And the message on PeerNotes appeared pretty quickly."

"And damning toward me. A quote from my current production?" Tinsley's hands shook as he rested them on the table. "Why me? This phantom besieges me, causing self-doubt and guilt."

"Guilt?"

His face turned ashen. "I have not always lived an exemplary life."

"What did you do?" I whispered.

He collapsed his head into his hands. Before I could get his answer, Faith approached to circle her arms around Tinsley's bowed shoulders. "You go on, honey," she said to me, sinking in the chair next to Tinsley. "I'll stay with Terry. This is quite a shock to us all. Poor soul. So much has happened this week."

Faith shook her head and patted Tinsley. "There now, baby. Let's pull ourselves together and take care of the children. Then we'll talk."

Tinsley lifted his head, his eyes wet and mouth drawn. "Thank you, Faith."

I narrowed my eyes, trying to gauge his reaction. Was Tinsley consumed by grief or guilt? The man played so many different parts, he seemed impossible to read.

In the administration area, Cooke and Herrera had closeted themselves in her office. I spied Officer Wells speaking to a counselor and waited until she was done to approach. Wells still wore the cute pony tail and freckled, pert nose, but this time her uniform did not reek of beer.

"Officer Wells." I stopped short before the copy machine room. The look she delivered did not speak of "nice to see you again." It screamed "I would rather punch you in the throat than talk to you."

Having grown up with those kinds of looks, they no longer bothered me. But I apologized twenty more times, then offered to pay her dry cleaning bill.

"Forget about it," she said. "What are you doing here?"

"I have an after-school job working for the drama teacher, remember? I heard about Amber. Armed robbery? Any witnesses?"

"No witnesses. She lived alone. Several items are missing."

"Find a weapon?"

She answered that question with silence. I tried a new approach. "On PeerNotes, another alphabet user posted an announcement about Amber's death with a *Romeo and Juliet* reference. That's the play the drama department is doing."

"We got the call on Tipton this morning. Neighbor found her. You asked Herrera to check on Dan Madsen and Principal Cleveland?" Her fingers drummed against her thigh. "You're getting your nose right up in this business, aren't you?"

"I have found this school reeks like a dried-up pond."

Her brows drew together.

"Fishy," I said.

"What else have you noticed?"

"Pringle, Dr. Vail, and Tinsley all had a relationship to Ellis Madsen one way or another. Cleveland and Cooke, too, if you consider their position in the school. I'm not so sure about Amber Tipton."

"I still don't see why anyone would wait this long to blame the faculty."

"Do you really think Amber was killed in a robbery? Don't you think it's awful convenient that two school secretaries died within a week of each other?"

Wells flicked her sharp gaze over me, then walked away. "Call us if you hear anything more."

"What about Principal Cleveland? Did you talk to him?"

As I spoke, Herrera strode from Cooke's office. Cooke stepped out behind him, and before I could slip around the side of the copy room, she spied me. Narrowing her eyes, she crossed her arms and began tapping her Christian Dior pump.

Dammit, busted by the principal again. I was going to get kicked out of this school for good. Fortunately, we had the weekend. I'd spend it hunting off school property and out of her hair. Might as well start with the newest victim.

With Amber Tipton's house covered in crime tape and her neighbors tired of speaking to cops, I learned nothing more than an unfortunate early morning break-in had cost Amber a brand new laptop, her grandmother's jewelry, and her life. As Amber's neighborhood featured year round Christmas lights, herds of stray cats, and old bath fixtures used for ashtrays, her neighbors seemed neither surprised nor alarmed by the burglary. The general consensus seemed a contempt toward Amber for having something worth murdering.

Most pointed their finger toward her no-account ex-boyfriend. Disgusted, I climbed back into the Datsun and called Luke to see if he had any more information. He didn't, which discouraged me further.

"You need a new phone," said Luke. "We could try sexting."

"I'm put off by any electronic messaging at this point." I watched Amber's neighbor climb into his Mercury Tracer, flip me the finger, and drive off. "And friends don't sext."

"Are we back to that?" He sighed. "Sugar, you can't let the town run our lives."

"Your boss is now telling me to stay away from you."

"Damn." He fell silent for a moment. "You know this just makes me want you more."

"I know." I cut on the Datsun's ignition, flipped on her lights, and revved her engine.

"Are you going to Red's? It's Friday night."

"Everyone will be at Red's. Sticks is playing. But I'm in no mood for a party."

"How about a party for two?" At my long pause, he continued. "It's not your fault Amber Tipton died, sugar. Burglaries do happen and that area of Line Creek keeps the patrol officers busy."

"An odd coincidence if you ask me. Peerless is now out of secretaries. Makes me fear for Tara, who is subbing."

Luke drew in his breath. While he dwelled on that horrible thought, I tore out of Amber's beaten-down neighborhood and angled east toward Halo. Which meant leaving a fart-cloud of burnt oil while I gunned my pickup to a shimmying twenty-two miles per hour.

"Let the police handle Tipton's homicide," said Luke. "I'll call in a possible link between Pringle and Tipton's positions at school and these deaths. Don't worry. Line Creek will put a lot of man-power into solving this crime. "

Which meant less man power on examining the suspicious texts at Peerless Day Academy.

TWENTY-FOUR

My brother proved stealthier than a fox on a hen house run. With no rehearsals and a wait on leads, I spent another day of fruitless searching for Cody and his Malibu. I suspected he had driven his miserable self out of town. I had never been a group project kind of person, but this week my friends had taught me the value of their assistance. Now I realized I couldn't handle Cody's mess on my own either. It was time to spill the truth to Casey. Our family's closeted skeletons had thrust Cody into Interventionland.

Red would be pleased. His favorite daytime episodes always featured a riotous intervention. Usually divulging some god-awful, white trash-styled family secret.

The Tucker kids would make for good ratings.

The drive to Max's faux plantation spoke of all things autumnal in Georgia. Sunshine, accumulations of pine straw, and a crispness in the air due more to a lack of humidity than an actual chill. I barely acknowledged the beautiful weather with my mind on dead school secretaries, a brother gone commando, and a heart longing for forbidden step-Branson fruit.

Parking in front of the big house, I hopped the steps, and rang the bell. This time, Max answered. On crutches. He frowned at my truck peeing oil on his drive.

"Good to see you moving around," I said. "I'm glad you've taken my advice and stopped moping in your bedroom."

"I do not mope. And I am mobile of my own accord. Not because of your badgering."

"You just keep telling yourself that." I held the door to his study, waited until he had lowered himself into his desk chair, then paced toward his kitchen.

Casey sat on a bar stool at the granite island, leafing through a tabloid with a cup of coffee and a smile.

"Where's the hubby?" I strode past her to the coffee maker. "Can't this thing make a latte? I could go for a latte."

Casey sat up and narrowed her eyes. "Have you heard from Shawna Branson lately?"

"No." I set my empty coffee cup on the counter. "Why?"

"Her mother's house was broken into yesterday. But nothing was missing. Except a family photo."

"Damn. That's in Line Creek. That might have been Cody."

"Cody? He was sore pissed at Shawna for her treatment of you, but I don't understand why he'd break into Delia Branson's house. I thought it might have been you."

"About that." I abandoned the coffee and leaned against the counter across from Casey. "I haven't wanted to bother you in your newly wedded state. But Cody had snapshots of Shawna's daddy with Momma. I found them. Cody had somehow stolen them from Shawna and that's what started the feud."

"What in the hell," said Casey. "How dare you keep this from me. I have a right to know what's going on."

"Something has messed with Cody's head. He's acting like a total ass. Won't talk to me about how he got the pictures or why he's holding on to them. Now he's hiding from me."

"What do you think the photos mean?"

"They don't mean anything." I studied my nails. "Who knows when they were taken? Could have been after Daddy died and Momma moved back here. I figure with Billy Branson's reputation, he and Momma got involved. Probably why she was shunned by the town, although no one will come out and lay blame on a Branson."

Casey shoved her coffee away.

"Figures. The Bransons could get away with sneaking around, but we Tuckers sure can't. And it explains why Grandpa and Uncle

Will won't talk about it. They're ashamed, too. So you think that's why she took off?"

"I think that's what Cody's wondering. Particularly since Billy Branson left around the same time. And Cody wasn't born here."

"Hell," said Casey. "That's some real messed up shit. Poor Cody. But why's he blaming the Bransons for this? Grandpa and Grandma Jo should have told us the truth."

"Told us what? That Cody might be a Branson? I'll tell you what that would have done. Cody would be seen as some bastard kid to a stuck-up family who wouldn't acknowledge him." My eyes smarted. I bit my cheek rather than admit any tears. "All that crap we took in school about Momma? A hundred times worse if they thought Momma stole Shawna's daddy and shipped their baby back to the farm."

"Or what if the Bransons took Cody in?" asked Casey.

"Or what if they had refused? You think Shawna's snotty mother would have raised her husband's bastard? Or would JB Branson have raised Cody alongside his own demon spawn, Dustin? Don't forget JB was wild then, too. That was before he married Luke's mother."

Casey laid her head on the cool granite. "I hate the Bransons."

"This was not all their fault," I reminded her. "Grandpa and Uncle Will kept their mouths shut to save us from looking more trashy than our mother already made us. I say they did us a favor."

Casey poked her chin up. "What are we going to do?"

"About Cody? We need to find him. Todd and I have been looking every night, and I searched all day. I think seeing those photos has unscrewed Cody's head clean off."

"Maybe Cody's right. We have never perpetrated ugliness toward the Bransons, yet they have rubbed our Momma's disgrace in our face for years. And here it may be the fault of Billy Branson."

"Takes two to tango." I swallowed my bitterness wishing it were sweetened coffee instead.

Casey sucked in her breath. "What if our Momma is like you and can't see the clear light of day through her heart-shaped, rose-colored glasses? You're constantly falling in love with the wrong men. Maybe Billy seduced her and forced her to give up baby Cody. Maybe Billy's got Momma holed up in some sex slave organization."

"That makes no sense, Casey. Billy Branson is probably running a golf course in Texas. And our mother is probably married to some Bubba in Missouri and too humiliated to show her face here."

I shoved away from the counter. "You read too many tabloids. And I can see just fine. I'm sorry about all this. Let me know if you find Cody."

I left Casey, wishing I had kept my mouth shut, and trailed back toward Max's study. I knocked and entered, dragging my feet to plop into a chair before his desk.

He looked up from his computer and raised his brows along with the little scar. "This mood does not suit you."

I crossed a leg to play with the threads hanging around the ankle of my jeans. "Did your hometown ever have historic family vendettas?"

"Like the Hatfield McCoy?" he said. "Of course. We have much longer history than United States. Long histories always have the family feuds. But in my country, the feud is often political. Result is arrest or assassination."

"Well, I guess it could always be worse," I said. "Although I fear my brother has gone commando in a vendetta against the Bransons. Which could lead to his arrest. Idiot."

Max steepled his hands beneath his chin. "I can send Nik to find him. The Slavic people are very good hunters."

I chewed my lip. "Seeing as Nik's family, I guess that'd be all right. Don't want to get outsiders mixed up in this."

"Anything else I can do for you?"

I gave him a sharp glance, not liking his innuendo. "This isn't just for me, now. If you're going to invest in Nik's limo company, you don't want his name sullied with Cody's poor judgement."

"Of course, Artist. I wouldn't want to help you unless it concerned me."

"Exactly what I thought." I nodded, figuring sarcasm didn't translate.

"By the way, I have looked at the Peerless finances. There are some discrepancies in their accounting. Have you heard about this at the school?"

"There's been rumors that Tinsley is misusing theater funds." I slid forward. "What kind of discrepancies?"

"My accountant pointed out some irregularities in the bookkeeping I sent to him. Of course, these are the reports I took from Miss Pringle's email. I can not bring this forward to anyone officially."

"Wouldn't want to do anything above board."

"It is not attractive when you make that face, Artist."

I rearranged my expression into a smile. "You could send those financial reports to the Line Creek police anonymously."

"They would trace them to me and wonder how I obtained them. Besides, you said they have Pringle's computer. They have access to the same information."

"But I bet they didn't look at the reports."

"That's their problem."

"You and your distrust of authority." I sighed. "Bear, it's everybody's problem if we can't find the Phantom."

"Not really, Artist." Max hoisted his leg onto an open desk drawer and eased back in his chair. "If the Phantom seeks to discredit the school, any financial issues should come to light."

"I don't think the Phantom wants to discredit the school. The other school secretary was killed. In a home invasion."

"You are suspicious of this robbery. You believe the Phantom murdered this secretary?"

"Maybe Amber knew something." I slapped my thigh. "But what would Amber Tipton know that would put her in danger? She wasn't like the other Peerless folks. She was more removed from Ellis Madsen's death than anyone else."

"However, the secretaries hear many things. People talk around them without thinking."

"True. Amber probably heard all kinds of stuff about teachers and students. And parents."

Max leaned forward. "Please be careful. Don't trust anyone."

"At least the police are investigating Amber's murder," I said. "That leaves the other teachers who were texted and Maranda Pringle's suicide for me. And I'm having a real hard time believing she killed herself."

TWENTY-FIVE

After a tense Sunday dinner at the farm featuring Cody's noticeably empty chair, I called Luke to update him on my progress. Dan Madsen still wouldn't answer my calls, but I fixed on trapping him at Maranda's funeral. Cleveland remained elusive. Dr. Vail had left town for the weekend. However, I had arranged to meet Coach Newcomb and Maranda's friend, Olivia, at Little Verona's that night.

"That's considered an accomplishment," Luke whispered. We had snuck from our respective dinner tables to our respective bathrooms to talk. "You've managed to track down two witnesses."

"If that's progress, I never want to be a cop," I murmured.

"Glad to hear it. You have no patience for this business. And you're too reckless." He stifled a laugh at my protest. "Speaking of reckless, I know sexting is out of the question. But considering our locations, how about some good ol' fashioned phone sex—"

I smacked the flusher and held the phone over the toilet. "You're breaking up," I called. "Gotta go."

Little Verona's, located in another Line Creek strip mall, was one of the few restaurants in Forks County that didn't feature barbecue or fried chicken on their menu.

With tasty Italian food and an extensive wine list, Little Verona's served appetites for the Atlanta-commuting carpetbaggers who missed their northern cuisine. And for us locals who sometimes wished for Alfredo sauce on our basic mac and cheese.

In the dim bar, I set aside memories of Little Verona dates-with-Todd-gone-by and searched for Coach Andy Newcomb. Tall wooden booths separated the bar from the rest of the restaurant. Crimson and gold wallpaper, potted palms, and an old-fashioned brass bar gave the room a warm, cozy feeling. I spotted a sun weathered, lean guy in a windbreaker and coach's pants sitting at the bar. A beer and a bowl of soup sat before him, but he focused on the football game appearing on a small flatscreen hung above the old-timey, brass cash register.

A wooden bar stool separated Coach Newcomb from Deputy Luke Harper. I chewed my lip, not realizing I had also invited Luke to Little Verona's. He wore boots, jeans, and a flannel shirt and also had a beer and bowl of soup. Before the empty stool sat a third bowl of soup. And a breadbasket rested between our soup bowls.

I scrambled to the bar quicker than Goldilocks upon spying that third bowl of porridge.

Luke hopped from his stool at my approach. He grinned at the denim miniskirt I had studded with pumpkin buttons and paired with a fuzzy orange sweater decorated for autumn. I found velcro an easy way to attach the die-cut felt leaves to fuzz.

"Very festive," he murmured, skimming a long look over my bare legs shod in worn, brown boots. While helping me shimmy off my denim jacket, two ochre leaves caught and fluttered to the floor.

"Thank you." I gave Luke a quick smile and then inhaled a deep breath over the bowl of minestrone. The savory blend of tomato, oregano, and basil shocked my stomach into roaring its thanks. Causing the hostess to hurry around the corner and search the bar for the stray wood chipper.

"I appreciate the dinner," I murmured, tipping my head toward his. "But this isn't a date. I'm here to get the skinny on Maranda Pringle."

His hand slid down my back, tapping down a stray leaf before flying off. "I'm not interfering. Just here to enjoy the scenery. Although, I'm hoping to get a bowl of something else later."

I actually blushed. Clearing my throat, I hopped onto the bar stool and introduced myself to Coach Newcomb. "Hope your golf tournament went well."

"We've got a couple talented girls." He swallowed the remnants of his beer. "I don't really understand why you wanted to meet me."

"I heard you knew Maranda Pringle pretty well. I'm really sorry about her death. Amber Tipton's, too."

"Yep, a real shame."

"Can you tell me about Maranda?"

"Nope." Newcomb stared into his empty soup bowl. "You heard wrong. I met Maranda here a few times after work, but as athletic director, I'm pretty busy in the evenings. We had a couple of drinks together. That's about it."

"She and some of the other faculty members were sent insinuating text messages. Have you gotten any?"

He shrugged. "I get so many messages from parents, I don't really pay attention. They're always ready to fire me for something."

"Do you know anything about Maranda's messages?"

He shook his head, circled a hunk of breadstick in the soup residue, and shoved it into his mouth.

I felt my blood pressure tick upwards with each of his blasé non-answers. Newcomb dated a woman who was now dead. How could he be so insensitive?

"How did you feel when Cleveland accused you of stepping out with Maranda on him?" It was a long shot but worth it to see the closed-mouth coach almost choke on his breadstick. "Was she going to cost you your job? Or did she blow you off just like she did Cleveland? I bet that pissed you off."

I felt Luke's hand graze my arm. I shook it off.

Coach Newcomb swung his gaze off his soup bowl to face me. "What do you know about it?"

"I know your school has suffered an odd amount of death in the past year. And this woman you supposedly didn't know? Your boss harassed her about seeing you."

He pointed a finger in my face. "You don't know anything. I'm under a lot of pressure. Our great leader Cleveland kisses the parents' asses while chewing out mine. He was looney for Maranda, but he's also looney for trophies and anything else he could use to impress the parents."

I swiped the finger away. "You don't bring home trophies? The theater program does."

"The Lacrosse team is young. We've got some good golfers and tennis players, but Cleveland and the parents want big team sports. Those programs take a long time to build."

"You can't explain that to the parents and Cleveland?"

"They don't want to hear it." He pulled out his wallet, threw a twenty on the bar, and slid off his stool. "Look, I met Maranda here a couple times. She was a sexy, gorgeous woman and smart. No idea why she wanted to work at Peerless. But we weren't dating."

He began walking away, then stopped. "Killing herself? A real waste."

I watched him leave, then turned to Luke.

He leaned against the bar, eyes on the retreating coach. "I don't like that guy."

"You don't like most people," I said. "But I didn't like him either. Not a very winning attitude."

"Nope."

"I got angry."

"It worked. You provoked him into telling you something about Cleveland." Luke clasped my shoulder. "Doing good, Watson. Let's see what this Olivia says. Wonder what she thinks about Coach Newcomb."

"I hope she's friendlier." I flagged the bartender to snag Olivia for me, bent over my bowl, and shoveled in the cooling soup. "Delicious."

Luke leaned an elbow on the bar. "You're very determined to catch this phantom."

"I am." I pushed away my bowl and faced him. "At first, I felt sorry for Tinsley. The idea of a faceless bully just ticked me off. Now

I think there's some deeper level of malice going on at Peerless. Two deaths in a week? I don't really understand the Peerless kids and parents, but I'll be damned if I let this sonofabitch get away with ruining their school."

"You shouldn't let it bother you so much." Luke toyed with his spoon. "You get so wrapped up in helping other people that you forget to worry about yourself."

I laid my hand over his. "Is that why you would get so steamed with me?"

Luke dropped the spoon and slipped his hand in mine. He remained quiet for a beat while he studied our hands, stroking his thumb over my wrist. Looking up, he unnerved me with the intensity of his cool gray gaze. "Every time you charge into a dangerous situation, I worry I'm going to lose you. And dammit, you do it too often."

"I can't help it, Luke. Some things are worth fighting for."

"I just wish you'd rely on me to do more of your fighting."

"I don't like to rely on people."

"You say that, but you do call on your crew. How many times has Todd McIntosh accompanied you on these escapades? Hell, you've even asked Max Avtaikin for help. And they all encourage you. That's what I don't get. If they love you, they should want to keep you safe."

Sirens rang in my head at the "L" word. I slipped my hands from his and gripped my stomach. The minestrone soup had somehow developed claws and battled with my innards for ownership.

"They care about me." My voice sounded hoarse. "They just know me well enough to let me go my own way."

"I know you better." Luke's eyes darkened from pewter to charcoal. "Enough to know that you won't stop, even if it means putting yourself on the line. That's why you scare the shit out of me."

"I've got to use the facilities." I slipped from my stool, clutching my stomach, and hurried out of the bar. What if he used the L word again and I upchucked all over his snug-fitting jeans? I didn't think I could bear that humiliation. If someone pukes after you tell them the L word, it's most likely a deal breaker.

What in the hell was wrong with me? Why would the L word make me want to vomit? I needed another session with Red.

As I passed through the dining room, I heard a recognizable giggle followed by an all-too familiar snort. I dropped my hand from my belly clutch and spun toward the wooden booths lining the far wall. Tara spotted me and began bouncing in her seat and waving. Her dinner companion, the all-too familiar snorter, did not bounce nor wave.

At the sight of me, Shawna Branson straightened from her slouch, causing the snakeskin print of her dress to ripple, then stretch across her curves, like a python sensing her next meal. She tossed her long, red locks over one shoulder and commenced to give me the stink eye. Her combination of snarl and scowl caused my seized innards to shift toward a different kind of bellyache. But an ache in which my stomach had become accustomed. It accompanied a gritting of the teeth and a curling of the fist.

Shawna was my shot of medicinal whiskey. God bless her.

I stalked to their booth. "Haven't seen you in a while, Shawna. Although I know you've been active on social media lately."

Her blue-green eyes glittered. "I've been feeling a bit puny since the Halloween party, so I've stayed home. Just a little cold. I guess you saw the adorable photos I posted of Tara and Luke."

Tara's face fell at the mention.

I dug my fingernails into my palms to keep from slugging Shawna. "Tara, how did y'all end up at Little Verona's tonight?" Maybe she had hidden some sort of GPS tracking device on Luke's truck.

"Sunday night is minestrone night," said Tara. "Unlimited soup and breadsticks. Isn't that why you're here?"

Part of me wanted to announce to Shawna that I was with her step-cousin in the bar, but the nicer part of me didn't want to make Tara feel bad. The nice part won out. "Sure, minestrone."

Tara was making me soft.

"Where are you sitting?" asked Tara. "Why don't you join us? Did you already eat?"

I hesitated long enough to watch Shawna's lip curl. "Thanks, but I already ate in the bar and was just heading to the ladies. Nice of you to ask, though. If only I had known y'all were here, I would have sat with you."

"I didn't realize you knew how to sit on anything but a bar stool, Cherry," said Shawna.

"Better a bar stool than a lap, I guess," I said.

"Too bad your momma didn't learn that lesson." Shawna arched a well plucked brow.

I took a deep breath and counted to ten.

"Didn't your sister marry some immigrant? How's that working out? Is she still supporting him by waiting tables, bless her heart?" Shawna scooted forward to fake a whisper to Tara. "He needed a green card."

Tara looked from Shawna to me. "Did y'all have a wedding this summer? I must have missed hearing about that. Where'd she get married?"

"They eloped," I muttered. "Panama City beach."

"And you and Todd McIntosh married in Vegas. Y'all have something against church weddings?" Shawna hooted. "And isn't your Grandpa shacking up with some goat farmer?"

"Grandpa and Pearl are just good friends."

If only my eyes were laser beams. Shawna's head would have exploded by now.

"You and Todd were married?" Tara's eyes had doubled in size. She looked like an anime character.

"That's old news," said Shawna. "Todd McIntosh dumped her the next day. One of those 'whatever happens in Vegas' deals."

"I was not dumped. We annulled the marriage before the honeymoon began. Shawna wouldn't know the truth if it bit her in the ass." I slapped my mouth, hating to upset Tara more than she already was. "I mean, her butt. Hiney. Derriere."

Judging by Shawna's triumphant smile, the only ass was the one just speaking.

"Anyway," I continued, "gotta go. I need to speak to a server."

"About time you got a real job." Shawna waved the empty bread basket. "You want to give us a refill while you fill out the application? I promise to tip real well."

"I'd like to give you a couple tips," I said. "The first has to do with snakeskin prints. When you swallow your prey whole, a dress that tight will show it."

My touch for cheap shots seemed to have gone south. This issue with my mother and Shawna's father made me self-conscious. Or maybe it was Tara's influence. I did not enjoy self-awareness. The uninhibited life was much more fun.

Before Shawna could remark on my pumpkin attire on the way back from the bathroom, I scooted back to the bar. Our bowls had been cleared, and Luke chatted with a waitress with a love for liquid eyeliner and hair wax. Her dark hair stuck out in all directions in rigid waves and swoops. Piercings studded her entire ear, eyebrow, and nose, and tattoos peeked from the edges of her shirt sleeves and collar. I hurried to introduce myself to Olivia.

"I am so sorry about Maranda," I told her. "I don't like what's going on at the school. The faculty who received texts don't want to share the details. I can't even get a good answer on the kind of text sent to Maranda that would have caused her to do something so horrific."

"Thanks." Olivia's bright eyes dimmed for a moment. "I was just telling Luke here that Mandy received a couple texts. Just some bullshit about her sleeping around. I find it real hard to believe that Mandy would kill herself over that. I told the cops the same thing."

I glanced at Luke, but he wore his no-tell cop face.

"Why do you think she killed herself?" I asked Olivia.

She leaned against the bar, cupping a glass of soda. "I just can't believe she'd do it at all. Mandy was tough. We grew up in foster care together. She was smart, too. Really good with numbers. She could have done something more, but never pushed herself. The school paid pretty well, had good benefits, and easy hours. It was enough, she said."

"Don't take this the wrong way, hon'," I hesitated, "but did she, you know, get around? With men? She had a reputation."

Olivia shrugged. "Sure. But it wasn't a big deal to her and she never cared about reputation. It was just sex. You know how it is. You don't necessarily want to deal with some dude day after day. Most guys turn out to be assholes anyway."

I caught Luke's quick flinch from the corner of my eye, but refocused on Olivia. "But Rick Cleveland wanted more."

"That was real stupid on Mandy's part, but yeah. Rick would come to Little Verona's often enough, knowing she'd be here. Mandy got drunk one night. He finally got to take her home, but she kicked him out after she sobered up. Regretted it later."

"What about Coach Newcomb?"

"Newcomb didn't want anything from her other than sex. Mandy could handle the one-night stand much better than something long term."

Luke leaned forward. "If you don't think she committed suicide, what happened? They found a note."

"I don't know," said Olivia. "Hell, how do we even know it's a suicide note? It's not like she signed it or anything."

A very good point, I thought.

"Did anyone have a reason to push Maranda to suicide? The chorus teacher found her crying after a particular text about sleeping with a student's father. I thought maybe it pushed her over the edge."

"You think somebody made her want to kill herself? I hadn't thought about that. She started getting texts about two weeks before she died." Olivia twisted the glass back and forth, creating a pattern of water rings on the bar. "Rick Cleveland was so obnoxious. Still is. I could see him wanting her to feel bad about being with other guys, but I don't think he'd want her to die. He just, you know, wanted her. Mandy could make men come unglued. Probably because she wasn't that interested in them."

"Thanks, Olivia." I patted her arm. "I am real sorry about your friend. I hope if we figure out who's sending these anonymous texts, maybe we'll know what happened with Maranda."

"Yeah." Olivia's face fell, "but it doesn't do much for Mandy now, does it? She had a shitty life growing up and it sucks how badly it ended for her."

"Don't give up." A golf ball had lodged in my throat and I struggled to clear it out without tearing up. "Olivia, you need to find somebody to talk to."

"I've been hearing that all my life." Olivia gave me a half-hearted smile. "Don't worry. I've been through worse."

That did not make me feel better. In fact, I felt more determined than ever to root out the phantom poisoning the wireless waves with their evil little texts.

TWENTY-SIX

Olivia returned to her station and I ordered a fresh beer. "So Coach Newcomb was just another guy using Maranda Pringle," I said to Luke. "Principal Cleveland had obsession issues and Maranda was messed up. But maybe not the type to commit suicide. What do you think?"

"I think you should let Line Creek police focus on Maranda Pringle's suicide and you should focus on the other teachers who also got anonymous texts." Luke sounded grim. "Remember, that's what Tinsley hired you for. To find the texter, not the motive for a suicide. Don't let your feelings about Maranda take you down the wrong rabbit trail."

I sucked my beer and pondered his opinion. "Maybe you're right. I just feel so sorry for Maranda."

Luke rubbed my shoulder. "I know you do. What took you so long getting back from the restroom? Are you okay?"

"I ran into Tara and your cousin, Shawna. They're eating minestrone in the dining room."

Luke tipped his stool in his scramble off. "Why didn't you tell me earlier? Shit, how the hell did Tara know to come here?"

"Maybe you need to swap vehicles for something less obviously you." I hopped from my stool. "Listen, Shawna's still encouraging Tara to be with you. You need to go in there and tell Shawna to quit. It's making Tara feel even worse."

He froze, one hand reaching for his wallet, the other held up in protest.

"You want to prove something to me?" I crossed my arms over my orange fuzz. "This is how you do it."

He pursed his lips, then relaxed them. Tossing some bills on the bar, he strode into the restaurant.

Luke was putting me before his cousin. I sucked in a deep breath. A Tucker before a Branson. Somewhere a pig had grown wings. Or had been shot out of a cannon.

I followed at a safe distance, peering around the corner of the bar. His long legs made a quick crossing of the crowded restaurant. Stopping in front of their booth, he nodded to each woman, exchanged some quick pleasantries, then jerked his thumb toward the hall leading to the bathrooms and kitchen. Shawna rose, smoothing her python dress with practiced grace, and snagged his arm before he could march away. They strolled to the small hallway while Tara watched, her eyes dappled with curiosity and heartache.

I longed to console Tara, but felt it inappropriate considering the circumstances. After all, hadn't I stolen the Luke prize from Tara? My stomach cramped and I felt the result of my recent beer bubbling into heartburn.

Crap, I didn't reckon this well enough. Was I asking Luke to act the knight for me or for Tara? Someone needed to stop Shawna from nudging Tara toward Luke, for both their sakes. But what if Luke tells Shawna he wants to see me? After all our sneaking around, she would whip off my Miss Understood Snuggie and brand my backside with a hot iron A.

And don't tell me that A won't sizzle scarlet for a good long while.

I sprinted through the tables, bumping into chairs and sloshing soups. In the entrance to the hall, I stumble-halted my mad dash, yanked Shawna's hand off Luke's arm, and whipped around to face him. Thereby shoving Shawna into a potted palm.

By accident, of course.

Not that her holler would make anyone think so.

"What are you doing?" Luke leapt toward Shawna to help her out of the palm. "Are you nuts?"

"I've known you to be jealous, Cherry, but making another public spectacle?" Shawna's voice rose, causing the diners at neighboring tables to stop slurping their minestrone to watch. She grasped Luke's hand and leaned against him for support. "I think you broke my heel."

I grabbed Luke's free elbow, yanking him toward me. "Forget what I said. I don't want Shawna to know anything about me."

"Anything about you doing what?" Shawna clutched Luke's free arm, pulling him from my grasp, and leaned over to grab the offending shoe. Gifting him with a fair view of her snakeskin-stretched backside.

Talk about a spectacle.

"Making some pitiful attempt to win my cousin back in front of poor Tara?" She spoke from her bent-over position, like a center ready to hike a peep toe stiletto.

"No." I floundered, my eyes searching Luke's. This was worse than puking. What was I thinking? I turned to Shawna. "I'll pay for your shoe. I'm sorry about that."

"You can't afford to pay for these shoes," she sneered, rising with Luke's aid. "You probably don't even know the designer."

The kitchen doors swung open, and Olivia pushed through. "What's going on? Does somebody need help?" She glanced from me to Shawna's cling on Luke's arm.

Shawna held the broken heel out, exposing the red sole to the restaurant crowd. "This girl is causing a ruckus. She saw me with her ex-boyfriend, got jealous, and tried to start a fight. Look what she did to my shoe."

Olivia scanned Shawna then looked toward me. "Maybe we should get you out of here."

"Maybe." I agreed and cast my reddened face toward Luke. "I'm sorry."

His cop-cool face gave me no indication of how he felt, but he slipped an arm around Shawna's waist and began to help her limp back to the table. Always the gentleman. And once again leaving me to stare at him from my across-the-tracks point of view.

I cast a quick glance at Tara, who hadn't bothered to close her mouth during the spectacle. That poor girl. I jerked my eyes back to Olivia. "Can I sneak out through the kitchen?"

She gave me a half-smile. "Yeah, sure."

We bumped through the doors together and she pointed toward the delivery exit. "What was that about anyway? Crazy ex-girlfriend moment? Don't worry, we've all had them."

"Something like that." I shook my head. "You know, I try to rise above it all, but I always seem to get kicked back into the dirt."

"Mandy used to say things like that, too," said Olivia. "That woman with the shoe sounded like a real bitch. Don't let her get to you."

"Did Maranda have crazy ex-girlfriends after her, too?"

"Just one. An art teacher at that school. I'm not sure if she was an ex-girlfriend, though. She got mad at Mandy for seeing this businessman. Another bad choice on Mandy's part. He had a kid who went to the school."

"A child who was bullied and committed suicide. Very poor choice on Maranda's part." I grabbed Olivia's arm. "The art teacher who bothered Maranda. Camille Vail, right?"

"The name sounds familiar." Olivia stared at me through dark rimmed eyes. "Did the student find out about Mandy and her dad?"

"I don't know, but the school bully might think so."

I stopped in an all-night laundromat and found Dr. Vail's home address listed in the Line Creek phone directory. She owned one of the historic, turn-of-the-century homes that populated the blocks around the town square in Line Creek, one I recognized from a popular tour of homes during the holidays. In the dark, with only the moon and street lights to light the turreted house, the deep veranda appeared gloomy and the asymmetrical gables and eaves menacing. However, in the daylight, the Queen Anne house was a gorgeous deep violet with cadmium red-purple, blue, and green trim work. Hand-painted indigo rockers and flower boxes filled with yellow mums decorated the porch. Carefully tended flower beds mixed with annuals and perennials covered her tiny front lawn and side yards.

My dream house.

Wishing I could have met Dr. Vail under different circumstances, I opened the wooden screen and turned the antique door chime centered in the wooden door. The bell jangled on the other side of the door with a mechanical thrumming like my old bike bell, but louder. The effect fit the eerie mood, causing a prickle of goosebumps to rush up my spine. Inside the house, all remained quiet.

I waited a moment, then walked the porch, my boots clattering on the wood planking. The curtained windows gave no indication whether Camille Vail was still away on her weekend jaunt. However, it was a school night and a light gleamed somewhere within. I doubled back to the porch steps and glanced at the other houses lining her street. Most had television lights flickering through the shades and curtains. The damp smell of a doused wood fire hung in the air. The street was still except for the incessant barking of a nearby dog.

I proceeded to hop down the steps and follow the inset stone path that sprang from the sidewalk, through Dr. Vail's front garden, and toward the back fence. The dog's barking grew louder, and as I approached the fence, a large shape slammed against the gate.

"Hey boy," I crooned. "It's okay."

Maybe the boy was a girl, for she growled with a fierceness I reckoned came with sharp teeth and a large body.

Perhaps Dr. Vail had turned werewolf.

"I'm not perpetrating a break-in," I told the dog. "I just want to know if your momma is home."

The dog snarled and snapped, then began howling.

"Okay, I'm backing off." I gave up on sneaking in through the back door, unsure what I hoped to find anyway.

I followed the path around the side of the house and paused. Between the dog's barks, a creaking sounded from the veranda. I dropped behind a large azalea and squinted up into the murky porch. Some shadow wrapped in a long coat stood before the front door.

A Sunday night booty call?

I held my breath, waiting to see if they attempted to enter or had just exited. The figure crept from the front door to the far side of the porch, hugging the shadows. The cape billowed as a breeze shook the dark leaves of a nearby sweetgum.

Had Tinsley called on Vail in his opera cape? More importantly, was this house call made to further their argument? Maybe their departmental fight was an illicit romantic cover-up.

Preferring to picture a different scenario than Tinsley and Vail getting it on, I scrambled through the flower beds toward the front of the house. At the sidewalk, I flashed a look around the quiet street, then ran up the steps. I cut left toward the far side of the veranda where I had seen Tinsley disappear. Rounding the corner, the porch ended at another screened door, most likely the kitchen entrance, with a set of wooden stairs dropping to the garden below.

I peered over the porch rails into the yard, but didn't see Tinsley. The stone path from the steps led through Vail's well-tended side garden back toward the front sidewalk. The dog hadn't sounded off, so it wasn't likely Tinsley went round back. Evidently, he had cut through the neighboring yard, divided from Vail's by a small stand of ornamental trees. His vehicle must have been parked on another street.

But why? To keep the neighbors from talking when nary one peeped from a window? Or had he gone into the house through the kitchen? Maybe he had tried the front door and also found it bolted.

The screen door had been well oiled, for it swung out without a sound. I tried the brass knob on the kitchen door and it turned. Vail would get my compliments for a well maintained home. I hesitated before pushing the door open, wondering if probable cause could keep me from breaking and entering charges.

"Hello, Dr. Vail?" I called before stepping a boot over the threshold. "Anybody home?"

Behind the house, the dog stirred into a barking frenzy.

"Tinsley? I thought I saw you. I don't care about your hanky-panky. I need to talk to you both," I shouted into the still house. Faint light ringed the door on the other side of the kitchen.

"Beautiful cherry cabinets, Dr. Vail." I hoped my compliments would deter Dr. Vail from calling the police when she kicked me out of her house. I moved through the kitchen and pushed open the door to the dim hall. "Love this wainscoting. Nice color choice with the red walls and cinnabar green trim. I would have chosen it myself."

The hall led left toward what I guessed was a powder room and closets and right toward the front entryway. I found a wooden staircase with a different floral motif painted on each riser. Overhead light glowed from the second story and filtered down the stairs and into the hall.

"Boy, do I love what you did to these stairs." I eyeballed the staircase, following the flowers up to the empty second floor landing. "You up there, Dr. Vail? Did I wake you?"

I tread past the stairs and into the parlor, then rushed past the camelback couch to the marble fireplace. I gazed up at a work lit with a tiny brass lamp clipped to the top of the heavy gold frame. "Oh my Lord, is that an authentic Miro print?"

A bump against the outside wall startled me into turning away from the Miro. A part of my brain told my inner artist to stop appreciating the decorating and focus on the bumps in the night. Why in the hell did I enter this house in the first place? What kind of an idiot creeps into dark houses to view the artistic details? And what if I caught Tinsley and Vail doing the hot and heavy? What then, braniac?

That side of my brain probably needed to grow larger. I tiptoed from the piano back toward the hallway. As I crept past the staircase, my eyes cut right, following the hall as it circled the side of the stairs. On the other side of a small table, a curtained, French door stood open. Behind the table and in the open doorway lay a long bundle of cloth that I almost mistook for a partially rolled rug.

Except the rug had bare feet. One pointed up. The other had fallen to the side. Dark toenail paint stood out against the pale skin.

I shuddered and stopped my tiptoe walk, reaching for my cell phone shoved in the back pocket of my denim skirt. Dialing 9-1-1, I brought the phone to my ear and stepped around the tole table. Camille Vail's long, thin body lay sprawled on the floor, her loose tunic wound around her torso and arms, like she had twisted and fallen backward. Her head had rolled to one side. The piercing eyes were closed and her mouth hung open, but something seemed odd about the up facing ear. I shoved the phone between my shoulder and chin and dropped to my knees beside her.

"Dr. Vail." I nudged her shoulder, then felt for a pulse at her neck. Her throat felt cool, but not cold.

I couldn't find a pulse. My hand slid to the back of her neck. The side felt sticky, and in the gloom, I realized the dark wood beneath her head was damp with blood.

A sobbing gasp left my lips and hearing a voice in my ear, I jerked upright, dropping the phone on the floor. The acrid scent of blood and the more pungent odor of less desirable aromas overwhelmed me. The rise of minestrone and beer burned in my chest and little dots of light swam in my vision.

Outside, the dog howled and yapped.

Snap out of it, said the area of my brain which functioned under stress. Dr. Vail's hurt. She could still be alive. Find the wound. Beneath me, I could hear a tiny voice from my phone asking me if I was still there. "Dr. Camille Vail's unconscious and bleeding," I hollered at the phone, then announced the address. "She may still be alive. Send an ambulance."

"Dr. Vail, can you hear me?" I touched her face, examining the upturned ear and then noticed half of a dark, oval burn behind her ear that extended into the short, salt and pepper hair. "Lord have mercy, that's a gun shot wound."

I jerked back, my hands flying away from her body. The raised, black burn meant the muzzle had touched her head. "Not another suicide. What do I do?"

I ripped off my sweater, held my breath, and inched the folded cloth under the side of her head lying on the floor. Blood seeped into the orange cloth and darkened the velcro leaves that had fallen around Vail's head.

"This is not good. Hang on, Camille. Someone's coming."

Bending over Vail, I laid my head against her chest, listening for a heartbeat. As I contemplated the effectiveness of chest compressions, the room seemed to darken further. I brought my head up only to have it slam against Camille's chest.

"Tinsley?" I turned my head, seeking the intruder, and pushed up. A wallop against my back splayed me across Camille's legs.

"Holy hell," I mumbled.

A sharp, blinding pain cracked across the back of my skull. I tried to lift my hand, gave up, and sank into oblivion.

TWENTY-SEVEN

I recognized the Line Creek hospital ER room immediately, but not the man sitting in the chair next to me. He wore blue with his worry, whereas brown seemed a more familiar color match to that particular feeling. I blinked through my aching head, and gradually placed Herrera's name to his face.

"Oh shit." I sat up, then dropped back as my vision swam.

Herrera leaned forward and patted my hand. "Just hold on there. Probably shouldn't move. You've got a big bump on the back of your head."

"I can feel it." I stared at the ceiling. The base of my skull throbbed and my reckoning processor had siphoned to a trickle rather than my usual tsunami of thoughts. "What am I doing here?"

"You don't remember calling emergency services?"

I blinked up at the ceiling tiles. "Was I in an accident?"

"Hon', you called in a gun shot wound and we found you lying in the entryway of Camille Vail's foyer, knocked cold."

"What in the hell? How did that happen?" I squeezed my eyes shut, but the last I could recall was the look of distress crossing Tara's face as she knocked back a glass of Chianti.

Did someone slip a mickey in my minestrone? How did I end up in Camille Vail's foyer? Who was shot? I patted my head and felt gauze. Surely, a gunshot wound to the head would hurt more than this. "Was I shot?"

"No, walloped from behind. But I hoped you could tell me what happened." Herrera stood and stretched. "You've been talking gibberish for the past five hours with that concussion. Lots of 'I know you. Who are you?'"

"My head hurts like hell." I crawled into a sitting position. The room spun and I breathed through my mouth to make it stop. "What time is it?"

Herrera glanced at his watch. "Early."

I rested my head in my hands and tried to sift through the cobwebs shrouding my memory. "I went to Little Verona's to talk to Coach Newcomb and Maranda's friend, Olivia."

"What happened at Little Verona's?" Herrera flipped open a notebook.

"I shoved Shawna Branson into a palm," I mumbled. "She broke her shoe. Which I think is pretty expensive."

"Who is Shawna Branson?"

"A two-faced snark who wields cleavage as a weapon. She's not an artist, no matter what she claims. And she thinks I'm not good enough for her cousin."

"Step-cousin," spoke a rich baritone.

I tore my hands off my face, resulting in a seismic rumble in the back of my head.

Luke stood in the doorway, pushing an empty wheelchair. "Don't say anything more, Cherry."

Herrera glared at Luke. "This woman is a witness to a suspicious death. And overly involved in another death."

"I'm a witness to a suspicious death?" I sucked in a long breath. "Whose death?"

Luke moved the wheelchair next to the hospital bed and laid a hand on my shoulder. "Cherry is also an assault victim. Sugar, don't say anything just now."

"I can't remember what I'm not supposed to say." I looked from one man to the next and experienced a tilt-a-whirl without the carnival.

"I need to know why Cherry was in Camille Vail's house," said Herrera. "She'll remember soon. The effects of the concussion are wearing off."

"I'm taking her home," said Luke. "I already spoke to the hospital staff and got her discharged. Cherry needs to rest."

"She's under my custody. And she'll be more comfortable here than at the station."

"Holy crap." The men's sharp barks drilled into the shifting plates of my head quake. "Am I under arrest?"

"Cherry will make a report in the morning. You're not getting anything out of her now." Luke squeezed my shoulder. "And tomorrow, she's going to wait for a lawyer."

"Lawyer?" My voice shook.

"Give me a break, deputy. There's a woman dead with a potential witness." Herrera mopped his face, exposing his exhaustion. "Fine, take her home. But I'm coming to get her if she doesn't show at the Line Creek station tomorrow."

A nurse bustled into the room. The men remained mute as she checked my head, handed me a sheet of instructions, and helped me into the wheelchair. I looked at the hospital gown I wore with my denim skirt and boots.

"Where's my top?"

Luke looked at Herrera and back to me. "We'll talk about that later. Come on, hon'. Let's get you home."

Fearing more time spent with Herrera, I nodded, then regretted the action.

Luke wheeled me out of the small room, down a corridor, through a set of double doors, and past the line at the reception booth. Across the hall in the glassed-in waiting room, Todd, Casey, and Nik scooted off chairs and hurried to my side.

"I'm taking her home," Luke announced.

Evidently, my concussion produced auditory hallucinations. Or maybe our relationship had progressed beyond flirting and parking lot snogging during my blackout. I shifted to catch Luke's attention, but he was too busy freezing Casey with his don't-try-me-I'm-the-law stare.

Casey glared at him through raccoon eyes. "The hell you are. You've caused my sister enough trouble. Cherry needs to be with family. Bad enough they wouldn't let anyone but cops back there with her."

Todd's hands tapped against his jeans. "How're you feeling, baby?"

"My head hurts and I'm really confused. How long have y'all been here?"

"I contacted your sister after Sheriff Thompson called me," Luke clipped his words. "I wanted Casey to know what had happened, but told her it wasn't necessary to come to the hospital."

"My sister's been clubbed and possibly abducted, I have a right to be with her."

I rubbed the back of my neck. "Abducted?"

"We don't know you were abducted." Luke laid a hand on my shoulder. "Casey's speculating. When we need to keep Cherry calm."

I turned to look up at Luke. "You have got to tell me what you know. Right now."

"You made an emergency services call from Camille Vail's house, although the dispatcher couldn't hear you very well. Your phone was found under Vail's body. And your, uh, sweater. The police found you in another room, unconscious. Because of the position of your body and some smearing on the floor, it looked like you'd been dragged."

I felt the blood drain from my head and the pounding in my neck shot to the top of my skull.

"Camille Vail's body?"

"She died of a gunshot wound that appeared self-inflicted. The handgun was found next to her hand."

I pressed on my temples. "I don't understand. What was I doing in her house?"

"We don't know. But whoever knocked you out was interrupted from whatever they were planning to do." Luke squeezed my shoulder. "At least that's my belief. Your emergency services call brought the cruisers. It sounded like the perp left you and took off."

I shifted in the wheelchair to study my family. Nik held Casey, whose store-bought tan had turned a sickly shade of gray-green. Todd's leg tapping had gone to rapid-fire thrumming.

"Where's Cody?" I said. "Did anyone find Cody?"

Nik kissed Casey on the cheek before fixing his attention on me. "I will find him. You don't need to worry about your brother at such a time."

My thoughts traveled back to Little Verona's, my last memory. I glanced back at Luke. "Can you give us a minute? Let me speak to my family."

His hand trailed from my shoulder. "I'll be right back. Let me bring my truck around."

Casey's lips thinned, but waited to speak until Luke had passed through the sliding outside doors. "What are you doing with Bad News Branson?"

"He's not a Branson," I said. "He's Luke Harper and he's been helping me on this case."

"Looks to me like he's helping himself to more than a case," Casey spat. "But we'll deal with that later. Tell me what's going on. Why were you under police custody?"

I shook my head. "I don't know. Probably because they found me in Vail's house. I don't think I'm under arrest, but Luke told me not to say anything unless I have a lawyer."

"Girl, how are you going to afford a lawyer? What were you thinking?" Casey dropped to a squat and took my hands. "Little sister, what are we going to do with you? I didn't call Grandpa yet."

"Thank you. I'd rather he not hear about this, although it'll probably get out soon enough." I looked over Casey's shoulder to Nik. "Cody?"

Nik shook his head.

"I saw Shawna tonight," I said. "She's been home sick. You better add her apartment to your list of places to scout. I don't think Cody would try to get in while Shawna's at home, but if he stole the photos from her, there's a good chance he might try to look through Shawna's stuff again."

"Did Shawna say anything to you about the photos?"

"Not this time, but she was eating dinner with Tara Mayfield. She wouldn't want the publicity."

Casey nodded and flipped her hair over her shoulder to exchange a look with Nik.

I bit my lip. "But there was an altercation of sorts. I accidentally pushed Shawna into a plant and she broke her shoe. She thinks I'm trying to get back with Luke."

I heard Todd's quick intake of breath, and I cast my eyes to my lap.

"But you're not," said Casey. "Harper's just helping you on a case, right? Shawna's jumping to conclusions."

I studied my lap. "That's what it seems. I certainly don't want anyone to think Luke and I are together. It would break Tara Mayfield's heart and make the town angry when I'm already on the outs."

Todd dropped next to my wheelchair, running a hand along my arm. "Baby, don't worry about any of this. You need to rest your head. Maybe I should take you home."

"Todd, I am taking my wife to my boss's house, then will go to this Shawna's apartment to look for my wife's brother. Do you join me?" Nik jerked his head to the door. "The policeman is back."

I glanced over my shoulder. Luke strode through the ER doors, carrying a brown blanket. I turned my attention back to Todd. Almost hating myself, I willed Todd to join Nik and not make me choose between the two men. The wallop had knocked the fighting spirit from me.

Todd kissed my cheek and rose. "Sure, Nik. I'd be glad to join y'all."

"Thank you, hon'," I said, squeezing Todd's hand. "And thank you, Nik."

Nik gave me a weary Eastern European smile. "The family sticks together, eh? Blood matters. Remember this before you do the more stupid acts."

"Just find Cody," I muttered.

Casey rose, then bent toward my ear. "Nik's right. This stays in the family. But I say Todd McIntosh is as good as blood. You've always been able to count on him."

I flashed a look at Todd, who rocked back on his heels with his hands in his pocket.

He caught my look and offered me his easy Labrador retriever grin. "We'll take care of everything, baby. I'll check on you when I get home."

Luke wrapped the blanket around my shoulders. "Ready to go?"

I nodded, my head buzzing and banging with uncertainties. What was Cody doing and where was he hiding out? Why was I in Vail's house and what had happened to me? More importantly, what had happened to Vail? For some reason, the gun bothered me.

All I could recall beyond Little Verona's was something dark, flapping in a breeze.

Back at my house, Luke made me wait in the kitchen while he poked through the rooms, assumedly checking for perps who knocked girls on the head and abandoned them in suicide victims' homes. Befuddled, I stood at my back door with Luke's warm, brown blanket wrapped around my shoulders. Upon his return, Luke read over my head wound instruction sheet while I disappeared into the bathroom, shed the nasty hospital gown, and rewrapped my bare essentials in the fuzzy blanket. I stumbled back into my bedroom, where my quilt had been turned down and ibuprofen and water waited on my bed stand.

"This says you shouldn't sleep more than a few hours at a time," said Luke. His eyes flicked from the blanket and back to the instruction sheet.

"So in exchange for a big goose-egg and limited memory, I get no sleep and OTC drugs. Just great." I sighed, hugging the blanket around me. "Fine, I'll set the alarm. At least my head isn't hurting as much as it did."

"I'll set the timer on my watch," said Luke. "I'm staying, then I'll take you to the station tomorrow. I can sleep on your couch."

"So I am under police custody?"

"No." Luke laid the sheet on my nightstand and jammed his hands in his pockets. "I just want to take care of you. Is that all right?"

"Aren't you mad at me after what happened with your cousin?"

"Of all the things to remember." He scrubbed his curls, sending them into a disheveled frenzy.

I noticed my hair did not take well to clouts on the head nor hospital conditions whereas Luke's silky hair appeared even sexier at three a.m.

"No, I'm not mad at you about that," said Luke. "Bewildered would be a better word. You ask me to prove that I mean what I say, I go to do it, and you stop me. Now Shawna's going to make Tara a hotter mess and you appear even crazier than before."

I shifted the blanket and dropped onto the edge of the bed. "Sorry. I didn't want Tara to think I'm a home wrecker."

"Sugar." Luke dropped next to me and wrapped an arm around my waist. "You can't wreck where there's no home."

I leaned a head on his shoulder. "It's the appearance that matters. You never did understand that."

"I understand something now." Luke kissed the side of my head. "I am a miserable S.O.B. without you. And you scared the shit out of me once again. You have to stop doing that."

"How much trouble am I in?"

"They can get an approximate time of death from the body, but the police really need to know when you arrived. They don't know why you entered the house. Did you hear something, like a gun shot, and then enter? Or did Vail invite you in and something happened? Or were you planted there?"

"Planted? How would I be planted?" I sorted through the sludge in my brain, trying to imagine someone knocking me cold at Little Verona's and carrying me to Vail's house. "Why?"

"Evidently, your nosing around pissed someone off."

"Hell," I said. "I suspected Maranda didn't kill herself. Or maybe she did, but was driven by the phantom's message. Through blackmail? Guilt?"

Luke leaned his head against mine. "I want you to stop thinking about this. I'm sorry I brought it up. You need to rest. In the morning, we'll talk to Herrera. I want to hear what he thinks before you give him any details."

"Why?" Luke's eyes had gone smoky, making it harder for me to concentrate.

"At the least, you're a potential witness. At the most, a suspect. You have to be careful what you tell him."

A shudder wracked my body, and Luke pulled me against his chest. I tensed, but my body fought to relax into the security of his embrace. Traces of his aftershave scented his skin and his t-shirt felt like down beneath my cheek. "Why are you helping me? You're a police officer. You hate it when I get mixed up in these messes."

"Because I know you and Herrera doesn't. You're not nosing into these crimes because you're perpetrating them. You're nosing into these crimes because you're just nosy."

I giggled. Which felt odd, considering the circumstances. Enjoying the steady pressure of Luke's firm chest against my weary head, I allowed my arms to wrap around him. My blanket slipped from my shoulders. Luke reached for it, sliding his hands down my bare arms and pulling it back in place.

Most likely, we had just stepped onto that hell-bound road paved with good intentions. But my need for Luke bounded over my barriers of prudence and sound judgement. Of which, I had little. Heck, the man had offered to face down Shawna Branson for me. He was willing to stand up to our families. Why not me?

"How long do you think your family's going to stay mad at me?" He slid a kiss on top of my head, then slipped his hands under me. Before I could object, Luke lifted me onto the bed, ready to tuck me in.

"I don't know. You're a Branson to them, whether you like it or not."

"And you're last name is Tucker, not Ballard." Forcing his gaze off me, he pulled the quilt up, covering what his brown blanket didn't. "But I don't care about last names."

He reached for the chain on my bed light, and I placed my hand on his arm to stop him. "You don't care about last names at all? Not even preserving your daddy's name?"

"You mean making new Harpers?" He released the chain and rooted his gaze to mine.

Heat licked my cheeks, but I held to my question by nodding.

"All in due time, sugar," he whispered. "But I do like the practice."

My breath quickened and the heat dropped from my face to my toes, then flashed up my body to burn my neck. "I want you to stay."

"I'm not leaving." The solemn gray eyes didn't waver. "You've a head injury."

"It's not my head that's hurting right now."

"What about McIntosh?"

"He's out with Nik." I sat up and the blanket fell from my shoulders, leaving me in my tangerine bra. It had matched the fuzzy sweater I had somehow lost during the night.

Luke swallowed. "You're exhausted."

"I don't feel tired."

"You are wearing me down, sugar." His hoarse whisper made my toes curl.

"I mean to." I smiled, wondering if my inhibitors had been whacked. Evidently, hormones were a great pain reliever, because I no longer felt sore nor tired. Drunk on pheromones, I reasoned.

"Don't tempt me." He stood and pulled off his t-shirt, exposing his V-cut to *Snug the Coonhound* hanging above my bed.

I covered my heart with my hand, sure that Luke could hear it whumping as I took in his gloriousness. Taut, wiry muscle beneath sun-browned skin. I rolled on to my side and propped my head on my hand. He called to mind the ancient Greek idealized athlete or my favorite, Michelangelo's *David*. With chin and cheekbones hewn with God's own chisel and beautiful gray eyes that exposed Luke's emotions against his will.

I was in deep trouble. More than "need a lawyer" trouble. Probably "turn your back on your family" trouble. Definitely "lose my heart" trouble.

Where was that dizzying headache when I needed it?

"We're just sleeping. Until my timer goes off." He pointed toward his watch, unaware I was memorizing his form for a future sketch.

Luke's gaze swept from his watch to my curled position. His finger dropped from his watch to his side. Hitching a breath, he fumbled for his belt buckle. With his eyes on mine, he leaned over to pull off his boots and socks, then shimmied out of his jeans.

I sucked in a breath and held it.

He slipped into the bed and gathered me against his chest. Kissing my head, he reached for the pull chain, and cut the light. "You need sleep. Don't worry about tomorrow."

"What made you think I'm worried about tomorrow?" I looked up, trying to find his face in the dark.

"You're trying to distract yourself." He smoothed my hair and settled his chin on top of my head. "I know you. You're riling yourself up any way you can to keep your focus off what happened at Vail's. Just using me for my body." He chuckled.

"Can you blame me? I might be a murder suspect. And somewhere out there, an evil lurker is sending malicious texts, driving people to suicide. Or murder."

Luke stroked my cheek. "Do I need to distract you from thinking about this?"

"I was wondering. Do you think the texts were meant to make one person murder another?"

"I think you need distraction." I felt his body shift, then his breath against my face as his lips sought mine. A tongue flicked, a hand soothed, and I pressed against him wanting more.

"I think you're right."

TWENTY-EIGHT

The phone woke me. I shot to sitting, felt the earth shift beneath me, and grabbed my head to keep it from rolling off my neck. My eyeballs seemed to spin faster than a slot machine cranked by a blue hair on her annual pilgrimage to Mississippi. But the events of the night began sliding into place, my mind clearing out the concussed cobwebs. When the world stopped rocking, I released my head and found Luke slipping into his jeans, his phone stuck between his chin and shoulder.

Unless I had dreamed it, the same shoulder found above, below, and beside me at various times the night before.

Probably not recommended practice for a head injury.

I needed to purchase a football helmet.

"What's going on?" I croaked. "Time for me to turn myself in?"

Luke shook his head, patted my leg, and sank onto the bed, his attention on the phone and his socks. By his focus and indeterminate expression, I judged the call to be Forks County Sheriff business.

My foggy brain and wistful heart hadn't yet attuned toward regret or happiness. I'd need coffee to make that decision. I slipped out of the bedroom, checked for Todd's return, then stole into the bathroom. No sign of Todd, but I needed to hurry Luke's walk of shame before the clan showed and started gathering shotguns and pitchforks.

Back in the bedroom, Luke had pulled on his t-shirt and was gathering his belongings. I crossed my arms over my oversized

Talladega t-shirt and wished the bandage stuck to the back of my head didn't make my hair look worthy of scarecrow stuffing.

"Come over here and let me give you a proper good morning, sugar." Dimples popped in his cheeks to accommodate his warm smile. "But then again, maybe you shouldn't. This time I'll be the one distracted, and I've got to get to work."

I told my hormones to simmer down. Keeping my eyes off his dimples, I used the pain in my head and my exhaustion to throw some cold water over the fires he set blazing with that smile.

"I remember better now." Leaving off the good mornings, I headed straight for a cold shower topic. "I went to Camille Vail's house because Olivia told me Dr. Vail had gotten on Maranda about seeing Ellis Madsen's father. I wanted to talk to Dr. Vail."

Luke's dimples disappeared as his brows pinched. "Was she alive?"

"I don't know. She didn't answer the door. I went around to her back gate and thought I saw someone. It's kind of hazy." I closed my eyes. "I can't remember who I saw. But I did enter Dr. Vail's house. A door was unlocked. She had an original Miro print above her fireplace."

I opened my eyes.

Luke had smoothed the worry from his face, but his body had drawn taut. He hovered next to the dresser, one hand gripping his wallet.

"There was a piano and a hand painted staircase. And a body on the floor." I gulped and shivered. "Dr. Vail's. She was bleeding. I took off my top to try and stanch the bleeding, but I couldn't touch her wound. I should have done something more."

"Don't worry about that now. What else did you see?"

"I called 9-1-1, but dropped the phone. She had a burn mark behind her ear." I clapped a hand over my mouth. "Lord have mercy, she shot herself in the head."

In two steps, Luke pulled me into the safety of his arms. Pressing my head against his chest, he rubbed my back. "Did you see anyone in the room?"

"I think we were in a hallway. I was going to perform CPR. I can't remember anything else."

"I want you to see your Uncle Will first thing. Get your sister or somebody to take you. Tell the Sheriff everything you remember. Talk to him before Herrera. If I can, I'll meet you at Line Creek police." He kissed the top of my head. "I have to get. A deputy on call needs my help."

I nodded against his chest. There didn't seem to be a lot of good in this morning. Grandma Jo had tried to warn me about what happened to wanton women. Unfortunately, she hadn't mentioned head wounds, dead bodies, and police stations.

"Cherry, look at me." Luke used a finger to tip my chin up. "You have to be careful about what you say and what you do. Not only should you get out of this hunt for the texter, you should probably quit your theater gig."

"I'll call Tinsley later," I hedged. "But what about the lawyer? Am I going to need a lawyer?"

"Sheriff Thompson will advise you. I'm sorry, but I've got to go." He dropped a kiss on my lips. "Don't worry. It'll all work out. I'll find you." The dimples reappeared. "Besides we've got some unfinished business that should take place when you're not concussed."

Maybe I wasn't so wanton after all. I wanted to ask, "What about us? Would we work out?" But I had already stepped into my big girl panties and figured the two ship thing might have to do for now, considering Cody and Tara. And the fact that I wasn't about to stop my hunt for the texter or quit my theater gig.

And those were the kinds of facts that tended to cause a rift between Luke and I. Better we had our little moment before passing in the night.

Back to our separate sides of the tracks.

Ships continued to pass as Todd rolled in soon after Luke had rolled out. By that time I had showered and replaced the Talladega t-shirt with jeans, a tank, and a comfy orange and grape flannel shirt. I decided to remove last night from my mind and pretend the party under the sheets never happened. I had succumbed. I was weak. Achilles had a heel. Samson had his hair.

I had gray eyes and dimples.

I reckoned I'd just blame it on my concussion. A sore noggin had to be good for something.

At my kitchen table, I attempted to lighten the circles under my eyes with a pot of coffee and to jog my memory with a sketch pad. My roommate and husband-that-never-really-was appeared in my doorway, dragging a shot of early morning chill inside with his haggard expression. Crossing from the kitchen door, Todd snagged a cup and poured his own shot of caffeine before joining me at the table.

My guilt-ridden, enthusiastic greeting embarrassed myself.

"You alone, baby?" His drawl had gone cautious and edgy.

I blushed. "You see anyone else here?"

He slanted a look down the hall before burying his face in his coffee cup. The skin around his wide, cerulean eyes wore new creases and smudges.

"I'm guessing you didn't find Cody," I said. "Thank y'all for looking, though."

"I'm worried about Cody, too. He's like a brother to me." Todd slumped in his chair. "How's your head?"

"Still attached." I grimaced. "I'm gathering courage before heading to the Sheriff's Office." I gave him a scant report of what had happened.

"You think this teacher was murdered or committed suicide?"

"Two suicides? If it had been teens, there could be copycats, but not these adults. I don't know Dr. Vail, but every time I've seen her she's either on the verge of a hissy or royally pissed. Doesn't sound like a suicide victim to me. And the gun bothers me."

"Why?"

"My memory is still fuzzy to be sure, but I can't recall seeing a handgun. Luke said the police found one on her."

"Maybe you were too focused on other stuff. You did find her bleeding out."

"Maybe. Look at what I've drawn from memory." I flipped back a page in the sketch book. "I just doodled, hoping it would trigger something. I've got her lying between a table and a door. I don't know what room she's in, but I was able to sketch her position pretty well. I knew she didn't wear shoes."

"That's a good detail," said Todd.

"Thanks. And something about her clothes. All wrapped around her or twisted up. I can't remember. But she was fond of long tunics and leggings."

"Maybe the gun was underneath her clothes," said Todd.

"True." I tapped the sketch pad. "They found my phone under her body. But why would someone knock me out and drag me from her body if she had committed suicide? Unless I had interrupted them planting the gun."

"Maybe they thought you had hurt Dr. Vail, so they attacked you." Todd paused, tipping his head to the side. His forehead creased, reminding me of a confused puppy. "Then moved you?"

"Then why run when the police showed?"

"So they wouldn't get in trouble? Maybe they left you for the police to find."

"Which is something a teenager might do," I conceded. "Freak out, then run. They must have been hiding in the house."

"You think it was the same person texting everybody?"

"That I don't know. I'm ninety-nine percent positive Dr. Vail was murdered. Even with my faulty memory. But did the so-called prank texts cause Maranda to commit suicide or was she murdered? I want to know where Maranda got the ADHD meds. Maybe Preston King? I wish I could talk to that boy."

I sighed, pushing away the notebook to lay my aching head on the table. "Herrera brought Preston King in for selling the fake shrooms, but his parents got him a lawyer. Most likely he's untouchable."

"You think he's behind all this?"

"No idea. The idea of a kid so malicious that he'd drive somebody else to kill is so shudder inducing, I can't imagine it. Could you picture a seventeen-year-old evil genius? And an art student, for heaven's sake. I hope to God he's just a drug dealer."

"Baby, after what's happened, maybe you should leave it to the police."

My hair moved from my face and I blinked up at Todd reaching across the table. He looked like a pointer sighting a quail, quivery yet still. I sat up and patted his hand to let him know I'd be all right.

"The police are on the case. They're all over Dr. Vail's murder, which means a lot of focus on Amber's robbery homicide and Pringle's suspicious death." I sighed. "But I need to know who sent those text messages. I did not finish the job. What if my failure means someone else is going to get hurt?"

"What are you going to do?" asked Todd.

"Maranda Pringle, Vail, and Tinsley reacted badly to those texts. What if Tinsley is next? The PeerNotes messaging seems to focus on him."

That fear broke goosebumps under my flannel shirt. I shivered. "I'm supposed to be protecting Tinsley, and all I've done is suspect him. Mostly of being self-centered and snarky."

"Baby, you're taking it too hard. This Tinsley sounds like his brain's gone south."

"Gone south or not, I made a promise to him." I stared into my coffee cup and wondered if they served coffee in jail. Line Creek used the county lockup. I could probably get Tara to sneak me in some java with her Bible lessons.

"What's that?" Todd pointed to an area I had sketched on the side, separate from the body.

"I don't know," I said. "It keeps coming back to me. Just a dark image."

"Looks like a cape."

"A cape?" I squinted at the pad, then turned it upside down to view it from another angle. "Dangit, if you're not right."

"I like it when you say that." Todd grinned.

"I've gotta go." I hopped from my seat, leaving the sketch pad and coffee, and began hunting for my truck keys. "Aw hell, my truck must be part of a crime scene. And my phone."

"Should you be driving anyway? I'll give you a ride to the police station." Todd yawned. "I called in to work. Said I'd been at the hospital all night. Which is mostly true."

I laid a hand on his cheek. "You're sweet, but you need sleep. You look like you're going to fall into your coffee. I'll get someone else to take me."

"Okay." Todd kissed my hand, then yawned. "Good luck at the station."

"Thanks, hon'." I ruffled his hair. "You're a good friend. Sweet dreams."

"You keep my life exciting." He smiled. "When you move boxes for a living, you need some excitement. Especially since I gave up poker."

I gave him an extra hug for guilt. My kind of excitement would get a risk-taker like Todd in trouble. Therefore, I felt it best not to let on that I'd be stopping at Peerless before turning myself into the police. Tinsley had a cape. Either Tinsley was our evil genius or he was in a shitload of trouble.

Whichever, I had to keep my eye on the man.

TWENTY-NINE

A normal person found at a crime scene and thought to be a potential witness/suspect would immediately report to the police station. Lucky for Tinsley, I'm not a normal person. And lucky for me, my neighbor, Mr. Johnson, was headed to Line Creek. I made it to Peerless in time for third period.

After scooting through the parking lot, I found the front doors locked and pressed on the buzzer that alerted the office to guests. A bubble camera attached to the buzzer aligned with my forehead and a voice sounding like Pamela Hargraves gave a tentative, "Hello?"

"Miss Pamela? It's Cherry." I jumped so she could see me in the camera. "What gives? I can't get in."

"Hey Cherry, we're on lockdown. Ms. Cooke thought it prudent what with Dr. Vail's death, but we're trying not to make a big deal about it. I just have to buzz you in."

"I'm headed to the theater and I'm late. Any possibility you could send a student to meet me in the lobby with my pass?" I crossed my fingers, hoping I could avoid the office, Tara, and Ms. Cooke's eagle eye.

"I guess that'd be all right." Pamela paused. "I'll sign you in."

"Thank you." I hopped, hoping she could see my smile of thanks.

A buzzer sang and I slipped through the front door, reminding me of the Sheriff's Office. Tamara would not have let me through so easily, but Pamela was no Tamara.

Thank goodness.

A security guard leaned against a wall and nodded as I entered. I smiled back and strode toward the approaching office girl. Her long, straight hair swung as she skipped toward me. I grabbed the lanyard she handed me, hung it around my neck, and shot toward the arts wing.

At the fine arts double doors, I paused, wondering if Preston King attended school that day.

I hauled the door open and poked my head into the vestibule. Between the drawing and sculpture studio doors, a student leaned against the wall working magic on her smart phone. She jerked her head up at my entrance.

"I'm heading to the bathroom," she said, pointing in some vague direction.

"Of course you are, hon'," I said. "Must have gotten an important message to get you off track."

She had pale skin that easily turned an unfortunate mottled shade of Royal Purple Lake. "Well, there's the announcement about the lockdown on PeerNotes."

"I'm sure there's a lot of comments about that. What did Preston say?"

Royal Purple Lake flared into Madder Red Lake. "Preston says Peerless killed Dr. Vail. He's angry."

"And working on revenge?"

Madder Red Lake heated to Burgundy Wine Red. "Of course he is. Dr. Vail was the only teacher who cared about him. Preston's a brilliant artist and no one outside fine arts can see that."

"If he's a brilliant artist, someone will notice," I said, wondering if his brilliance ran toward evil. "What is Preston planning to do?"

"For college?"

"No." I tempered my nervous shout. "About Dr. Vail. What's his revenge strategy? Is he at school today? How angry is he?"

"He's suspended for the shroom thing. I don't know what he's going to do." The girl had gone vermillion and began edging toward the drawing studio door. "I need to get back to class."

I left her and ran toward the theater, agonizing between searching for the cape and checking on Tinsley. I banged through the double doors and into the drama lobby where Laurence reclined on a bean bag, reading. He lifted his head as I rushed past. I jiggled the handle to Tinsley's office door. Locked.

Of all the times to begin locking doors.

"Tinsley's on the stage," said Laurence, his eyes back on his book. "Are we painting now?"

"Laurence, does Mr. Tinsley have his cape today?"

"I don't know."

"I need to get in his office, could you get his keys for me?"

"Will this count toward my participation grade?"

"Good grief. Yes, I'll mark it toward your participation."

"Let me finish this page." Laurence held up a finger and continued to read.

I kicked the beanbag.

Sighing, he dogeared the page and rose.

"I'm aging here," I said, dancing before the locked door. "And you don't have to mention to Tinsley that I need to get in. Just say you need something from his office."

Laurence halted his turtle-like pace. "What would I ever need from Mr. Tinsley's office?"

"You need to read a play?" I guessed. "Something old and boring?"

"Aristophanes." Laurence nodded. "Got it. And why am I doing this for you?"

I waved him on. "So I won't tell Tara you're skipping class again. What are you missing? Phys Ed?"

He glared at me, then donned his inside-out coat and schlepped to the stage door. I paced the room. Approximating glacier melt speed, Laurence returned with the keys. He watched as I jimmied a master into the lock, shoved the keys in my pocket, and pushed open the door. Cutting the lights on, I darted to the coat stand in the corner. A trilby hat, windbreaker, and hooked cane hung from the brass arms.

"No cape." I rushed past Laurence to the desk. A sports coat draped the back of the desk chair. I poked around the drawers, under the desk, the coffee credenza, and the file cabinet. "No cape."

Now what?

"He's wearing it," said Laurence.

I turned toward the doorway where Laurence stood with his hands shoved in his pockets. "Why didn't you say so?"

I shot past Laurence, yelling over my shoulder to lock the door, and rushed to the stage. Either Tinsley was an absolute idiot for wearing the cape, incredibly ballsy, or didn't know it was evidence from a crime scene. I banked on ignorance.

Yanking open the stage door, I stumbled up the steps and bumped through tables of props, racks of costumes, and a collection of giant, paper maché bubbles. Pushing through the curtain, I found Tinsley sitting cross-legged on his table with the cape draped over his shoulders. He spoke to an invisible object sitting in the palm of his upraised hand. Beneath him, the students focused on the invisible object. At my bumble-halt, Tinsley's hand fell and the students' gaze followed the tumbling, invisible object to the floor.

"Yes?" Tinsley droned.

"I need your cape," I said. "And you might think about calling in a substitute today."

"Impossible," said Tinsley. "I can not be replaced."

"It's important."

"I literally can not be replaced, the sub list is full." He climbed from the table and strode toward me, pulling off the cape. "And why do you need my cape?"

I motioned for him to follow me offstage. Tinsley glanced over his shoulder at his students, eagerly watching our production. "Hamlet. Act five. Scene one. Get a partner and do the soliloquy, one as Hamlet and the other as Yorrick. Take turns so you can both hold Yorrick's head. I'll be right back."

"Did you leave this cape at school this weekend?" I said, bunching it in my arms.

"Of course," he said. "Why would I wear it home?"

"Because I think someone borrowed it to murder Dr. Vail."

Tinsley paled and grabbed the front of his shirt.

I snagged his arm as his knees buckled. "You're going to be okay. I'm on it."

"Someone is portraying me as a murderer? I thought Dr. Vail committed suicide."

"If that's the news, then the police haven't broadcast her suspicious death as homicide yet. That's why they're going to need this cape."

"And how do you know of the cape?" Tinsley's face remained white, but he raised his goatee and peered at me below his glasses.

"I saw someone who might have been wearing a cape. I can't remember the details, but the cape is burned in my mind."

"The noose tightens." Tinsley fingered his neck. "The Phantom looks to hang me for his own vile deeds."

"Maybe," I agreed. "But we still don't know the reason. What happened with you and the Tiny Tony?"

Tinsley's swagger disappeared, making his goatee droop. "A cauldron of lies. Did the rumor appear on PeerNotes?"

"No, I guessed." I eyed him. "And what exactly did the cauldron of lies say? It's too late to cover up. Spit out the truth so I can figure out this mess."

His body sagged, and Tinsley caught the edge of a prop table. "I was sure we would win the Tiny Tony for *Evita*. When Ellis died, I panicked. There might've been distribution of pecuniary funds used to sway the judges in a sympathetic light toward our cause."

"You tried to pay off the judges to win the Tiny Tony?"

Tinsley's goatee quivered. "The accusation stands. I felt desperate. There's a rivalry between theater departments and I had boasted on my blog and couldn't deliver."

"Of all the..." I stopped, thinking. "Did you happen to use school funds for this?"

Tinsley gripped the folding table, making it rattle. "I bring in school funds with my trophies. I add monetary value to this school.

Besides, after Ellis's death, Peerless Day Academy needed the morale boost that a Tiny Tony could provide. We would win for the sake of Ellis."

"Through cheating and embezzlement," I said. "Not a fair tribute to Ellis. Is this what Vail suspected? Is this why she hounded you?"

"The Phantom's curse has come to fruition," cried Tinsley. The prop table shook. The near side folding legs slipped and buckled, spilling props onto the floor. Tinsley's hands flew from the table, nabbed the cape from my arms, and fled toward the exit.

"Crap," I said, leaving the table, and darted after Tinsley. "That idiot is going to get himself killed."

THIRTY

In the drama vestibule, I found Laurence hovering in the doorway to Tinsley's office. "Did Mr. Tinsley come through here?" I asked.

"I know I was supposed to lock the office, but I really was looking for the Aristophanes' plays," said Laurence, sheepishly. "I heard someone slam a door, though."

"Which door? This school is nothing but doors and hallways." I stared at the line of drama doors and wished I had paid better attention when Casey and Grandma Jo had tuned into *The Price Is Right*. "Listen, Mr. Tinsley's not well. Can you go watch his class for him? I think they're studying *Hamlet*."

Laurence beamed and scrambled toward the stage entrance. I had just committed a class of freshmen to thirty minutes of tedious lecturing. By a sixteen-year-old.

Choosing the closest door, I poked my head into the long hall that ran behind the stage. No Tinsley. However, he knew the maze of Peerless and I didn't. He could have slipped into a bathroom, the theater, or a props room to hide his shame and fear. And I still had his keys.

I walked the hall, trying locked doors. After calling into the men's room and scaring a freshman boy, I found the auditorium door unlocked. On the stage, Laurence lectured the ninth graders on some indiscernible thematic point. Behind them, our turquoise blue backdrop screen had been lowered to puddle on the ground. I forced my attention back on the dark theater where Tinsley might hide and watch his students on his beloved stage.

My heart hurt from the shock of his admitted sin, but also in fear. Tinsley may want the Tiny Tony at any cost, but he was no murderer. The Phantom's moving finger had pointed out the faculty's indiscretions, but that malevolent accuser was the real culprit. If the Phantom was the murderer.

Tinsley really needed a sub today.

I rubbed the back of my neck, feeling the headache rear again. The theater appeared empty. I let my eyes trail over the shadowed seats while walking up the aisle and calling for Tinsley in the most reassuring voice I could muster. Reaching the top of the slope, I peered through the window of the sound and light booth and then pushed on the doors to the theater lobby. They swung open.

No one trolled the windowed hallway, so I tried the balcony doors. The far right door still had gum shoved in the strike plate and jerked open at my pull. I glanced around the dark balcony. No Tinsley. But I did shoo out two students caught neckin'.

Frustration rose within me as I jogged down the hallway toward the office, the last place I wanted to show my face. I glanced in the windows as I passed, catching glimpses of students vying for academic brilliance. In Scott Fisher's class, the students wore lab coats and fiddled with test tubes and beakers. In the drawing studio, Dr. Vail's students stood in a corner of the room, holding hands and hugging in consolation at their loss.

My heart twinged, and I amped my jog to a run. I tried the rear door to the office, near the copier room. Edging past Cooke's closed door, I stopped in the back of the open admin area. Tara still manned Amber's desk. Today she continued her preppy line in a brilliant pink oxford and paisley pink and viridian green skirt. Aware of my tank and jeans, I pulled the orange and grape flannel around me, then dropped my hands. Now was not the time to worry about fashion.

At my entrance, Tara's Luke-related sensor went off and she swiveled in her chair to face me. The look on her face shot a sizzle of fear through me. I had never seen Tara peeved. Her eyes narrowed into electric blue fire. Her perfectly coifed blonde ponytail seemed to thicken, like a cat rearing its back, ready to hiss.

The gaggle of office girls sensed trouble and took off to hide in the copy room. At the front counter, Pamela twisted in her seat. Her plumped lip smirked, sensing the upcoming battle.

"What are *you* doing here?" Tara spat. "Assistant Principal Cooke said you were only allowed in the school during extra-curricular hours."

"I had an emergency." I wondered if she could smell Luke on me at that distance. Maybe Tara had bloodhound in her DNA. "I'm looking for Tinsley. Did he come into the office?"

"He's speaking with Ms. Cooke." Tara raised her chin to better look down her nose at me.

I knew that look. She must have learned it from Shawna.

"I felt sorry for you Tuckers," Tara said without a hint of sorriness in her tone. "But the rumors about you seem to be true."

"I did not mean to push Shawna into a palm."

"You told me Luke was dirt. You have been trying to make me forget about him. And now I know why."

I looked to the ceiling for help. No hand of God reached through the roof to save me. All I saw was a half-burnt fluorescent bulb and some high-grade ceiling tile. Served my wanton-self right, I supposed.

With a heaved sigh, I drew my eyes back to Tara. "I'm sorry. I never meant for anything to happen. I just wanted his help on this case. I've been trying to get over him, too. But right now, I really need to find Tinsley."

"But what really boils my buttons," said Tara, ignoring my lame apology, "is what y'all are doing to the Bransons. Shawna is my true friend. She knew all along the game you were playing, while I tried very hard to look toward the positive in your nature."

This time I turned to the floor and the fine, high-tread carpet beneath my boots. I welcomed hell's fury in exchange for Tara's scorn. But no hole opened for me to jump into. I had disappointed the sweetest girl in the world. Who had drank from the pool of gray-eyes-and-dimples and received a dose of crazy for her trouble.

Been there. Done that. Lost my t-shirt.

My stomach hurt and my head hurt and I didn't want to let down Tara now that she was on a denunciatory roll, but it was time for bygones and the taking of Tinsley and his cape to the Line Creek police. "Tara, I am really sorry. Let's talk about this another time."

But Tara, who managed sharp words only once a year, could not stop. "And what your brother did just proves what a shameless family you really are."

"Hang on now." I marched to her desk, holding up my hand to stop her tide of accusations. "What did my brother do?"

"This morning? Shoved Shawna into his car at the Tru-Buy and took off with her? Everybody's talking about it. What kind of people are y'all? Some kind of sex maniacs?"

"Holy crap, of all the idiots." I spun on my boot heels, running toward Cooke's office. Without knocking, I flung the door open. Tinsley turned in his chair to gape at me. His blotchy face and spotted glasses gave evidence of his despair.

"I need Tinsley. Now," I hollered. "Or at least his cape."

Placing her hands on her desk, Cooke shoved out of her chair and pointed at the empty seat next to Tinsley. Her scarf fluttered and then fell back into position onto the lapels of her hand tailored, blue suit.

"You will sit."

"I can't sit. My brother's kidnapped Shawna Branson and Tinsley's cape is criminal evidence," I babbled. "Give me the cape and I'm running to the station with it."

Cooke's eyes widened. "Criminal evidence in what?"

"Dr. Vail's murder."

"You come with me young lady. And you," she pointed at Tinsley, "you stay right where you are."

I decided nabbing the cape and running was a better idea. But I hadn't counted on Cooke's quick hand. As I snagged the cape off Tinsley's lap, Cooke grasped my wrist in a tight fisted grip. My hand opened and the cape fell back in his lap.

"You," she announced, "are a trouble maker."

I nodded. "But not as much as my brother, so let's do this another time. I need to go. Tara's already bawled me out. I'll just carry that over to whatever you have to say."

"Oh, you're going to listen," said Cooke, dropping my wrist. "Did you know about Mr. Tinsley using school funds for bribing judges? There's money missing from our accounts."

"Theater funds," sobbed Tinsley. "I have not dipped into other reserves. Honestly."

"It was good you came clean, Mr. Tinsley. You'll feel better for it." I patted his shoulder and nodded at Cooke. "He finally told me. I knew he had done something. But he's harmless. Just caught up in Tiny Tony fever."

"You need to tell me what you know. Come with me." She snagged her phone off the desk, pushed a bottle of water toward Tinsley, and pointed me toward the door. "Leave the cape. Tinsley can take it to the police himself."

Tinsley moaned, burying his face in his hands. "Just as the Phantom predicted. I am doomed."

"You're not doomed," I whispered. "Just tell the truth without the drama. The police don't like theater. Your crime is white collar. Just make sure they get the cape so they can catch the true villain."

With her phone in hand, Cooke grabbed her Louis Vuitton purse and a long, navy trench coat from a hook on the back of the door.

"Wait," I said. "Where are we going?"

"After we talk, I need to do school business," she said. "Let's make this quick."

"You shouldn't leave the school. I'm worried Preston King is going to do something terrible. I need to talk to Detective Herrera."

"I won't be gone long and we're on lockdown. Don't worry about Preston." She turned toward Mr. Tinsley. "I want you to think carefully about what we discussed. Your classes will be covered. I've already shifted the subs."

Cooke nodded to me to exit the room and pulled the door shut behind us. Slinging her leather purse over one shoulder, she folded the Burberry coat over her arm, then called behind her. "Tara, I'm running to the bank in a bit. No visitors unless they're a parent picking up a child. And if a parent calls, all after-school activities have been canceled for Miss Pringle's funeral."

I slunk before Cooke, scuffing my boots along the carpet. "Ma'am, I promise I'll come back to school later and you can ream me out then. My brother needs my help. And I've a concussion. I really need to leave. My head is killing me."

"Is your brother an adult?" Her clipped tone could hammer nails.

"Yes, ma'am."

"Then he's sufficient to help himself. But let's stop in the nurse's office and see what we can do for your headache."

Before I could protest, she pushed open the door of a room across the hall. I heard her speaking to the nurse and she returned with a handful of pills and a bottle of water.

"These are for children so I doubled the amount." She poured a handful of tiny A-shaped pills into my palm.

I popped the little pills in my mouth and slugged the water.

"Give them a few minutes to take effect," she said. "Come with me."

She led me through the back door and into the passage running behind the office. Stopping before a closed, windowless door, she flipped through her large ring of keys. "Did you know I've been at Peerless since it opened twenty-five years ago?"

"No," I said, rubbing my neck. "Twenty-five years ago I was still in Missouri, wearing diapers. I don't know much about Peerless."

"I began as a counselor. Devoted my life to this school and its students for little reward other than knowing they are getting the best education I can provide. When I see potential, I guide the child toward honing their talent. I've produced scientists, executives, film stars, professional singers and dancers. And artists."

"I admire anyone who goes into teaching. Lord knows you don't do it for the pay." I bounced on my toes while she hunted for the key. "I am kind of expected at the Line Creek Police Department."

"You strike me as the type of student who didn't care for rules," she said. "I've known a lot of students in my time. I can judge them fairly quickly. Faculty, too. Although Tinsley surprised me."

"Surprised me, too," I said. "But I knew he was covering up something. Listen, what do you want to know? I'm in a rush."

"Everything you know about Tinsley. This will only take a moment." She held the key aloft, eyed the serial number, then unlocked the door. "I do not like my students agitated and since you have arrived, my school has been in an uproar. You have not followed my rules. I think you owe this explanation to me and to yourself."

"Myself?" I squinted. "I owe myself more than a talking-to. I've got a concussion. And I missed breakfast. I owe myself a trip to the Waffle House and a rest. But I'm not going to get it because there are people depending on me."

"There are people depending on me, too, Miss Tucker." Cooke's eyes blazed with condemnation. "Do you see anyone else working as hard as I do to protect these students?"

"No, ma'am." The hair rose on the back of my neck and my goose-egg thrummed.

"I have run this ship as second-in-command, for twenty years. I hired Cleveland. And Maranda Pringle. And Vail, Tinsley, and every other teacher in this building. I keep Peerless running smoothly. And I mean to continue to do so."

"Of course, ma'am," I said, wishing I had turned myself into the police like a normal person should.

THIRTY-ONE

"This room isn't in use." Cooke pushed wide the door. "Tinsley needs my office, and I don't want students overhearing us. I thought we could talk in here. I need to know more about what Tinsley's done and other goings-on you've noticed in my school. Before I talk to the police."

I breathed a sigh of relief at her explanation. Just like the other principals I had known, Cooke wanted to shove her authority in my face by forcing me to explain my behavior. Followed by a chewing of the posterior session for breaking said rules.

In the large, windowless room, dusty bookshelves lined the walls and divided the room into rows. Boxes, extra desks, and chairs had been stacked between the shelves. An old, plastic-lined cot rested against one shelf, probably used for naps by the janitorial staff. The air had a stale smell and bits of paper littered the floor. Cooke shut the door behind us and pointed toward the cot.

"This is where I hold my unofficial conferences, when a faculty or staff member doesn't want other teachers to know we're speaking," she explained.

"This looks like a large supply closet," I remarked.

"The book room." Cooke tossed her coat and purse on a desk, then smoothed her blonde bob. "In the summer, the textbooks are kept in here. Now, tell me what you know."

"The anonymous texting bothered Tinsley." I lowered myself onto the edge of the cot, hoping to get this over quickly. My head buzzed in anticipation, focused on Cody more than the Peerless issue. "Tinsley heard I had been involved in some criminal cases. Unofficially involved, of course. So he asked me to figure out who was sending the texts."

"And did you?" Cooke leaned against a desk and folded her arms against her suit jacket.

"After considering a perturbed parent or some kid wanting to prank, I thought it could be Dr. Vail." I blinked, trying to sort my muddled thoughts. "She had written some accusations against Tinsley on PeerNotes. Or it could be Preston King. He observed the bullying of Ellis Madsen, and I bet he's not beyond blackmail. Or possibly, Dan Madsen since a lot of the insinuations in the messages had to do with Ellis."

"I hadn't thought about that." Cooke's fingers tapped against her folded arms. "But thirteen faculty and staff received anonymous messages. With a variety of accusations."

"And most ignored them as ridiculous shots in the dark. The ones who reacted the most—Vail, Pringle, and Tinsley—all received messages relating to Ellis."

"Poor Ellis. I'm not even sure if she knew about her father. Very few did. I wish she had told me about the anonymous texts." Cooke stared at the shelf behind my shoulder, brooding. She had bitten off her lipstick and fine lines marked the skin beneath her eyes. Clearly, the ordeal had taken toll on the woman while she had done her best to keep Peerless running efficiently.

"What about you, Ms. Cooke? Was your message about Ellis Madsen?"

Her gaze swiveled back to my face. "No."

"What was your message about?"

"I don't even remember." She waved her hand. "But let's continue our discussion on Tinsley. Why is his cape criminal evidence?"

I yawned. "I saw someone wearing the cape outside Dr. Vail's last night."

"I see," she said. "Is that why the police are looking for you? They called the school."

"Dammit." I blinked. "Sorry. I really should go."

"Don't worry. The police don't know you're here. When they called I had no idea you were in the school," she said. "It seems you are in a lot of trouble. Found at a possible murder scene. You mentioned your brother. And Tara's unhappy with you. Tell me why."

"For some odd reason, Luke Harper loves me and not her," my words slurred. "Isn't that the damnedest thing you've ever heard?"

"Because you're not worth loving." Not a question, but a fact. "You lack the better qualities Tara has."

"That's an ugly way to put it. But yes, my mother abandoned me for Shawna's father. That's a pretty crappy way to start off in life. Red says I have self-worth issues." I wondered why my lips decided to spill all this sensitive information to a woman I hardly knew. My bottom slipped forward on the plastic lined cot and my head bumped against a book shelf. "Ouch. You're better than Red in getting to the heart of my problems."

"I've counseled students for twenty-five years. I told you I was good at summing people up. Don't you wish you could make the pain go away?"

"Dang right." I peered at her through foggy eyes. "But that Advil you gave me is working pretty well. Didn't even feel that bump to my head."

"Would you like more? Maybe you should rest before going to the police. You seem unable to speak properly." Reaching into her purse, she pulled out a vial of pills. "You must be sleepy."

"In a minute." I nodded. Or at least my brain sent the signal. My head flopped back.

"I'll just leave them with you." Cooke nudged the pills into my hand, closing my fingers around the bottle. "Your water bottle is in your other hand."

"By the way." I spoke with my head cranked back, watching her through half-closed eyes. My thoughts climbed through our conversation, landing on a passage. "How did you know thirteen of your staff received messages? Most haven't shared with anyone."

Cooke's cheeks brightened. "I'm obligated to know anything related to this school. Occasionally, I check the staff email accounts. I'd rather nip a scandal in the bud before it erupts."

"So you knew about the love triangle between Cleveland, Pringle, and Coach Newcomb?"

"That was obvious, although I wouldn't call it a triangle. I hadn't realized what an idiot Cleveland would become around someone like Maranda Pringle." She shook her head. "His wife left him a few years ago. That should have been a red flag."

"So Cleveland's ineffective?" I tried to lift my head, but couldn't manage the effort. Damn concussion. "But you keep him as principal? Does he know what's going on with the accounts?"

"The accounts? No." She laughed. "Cleveland likes the prestige of the school. His own private school background was great for PR. And the children like him. But he leaves the grunt work to me."

"The Bear said something's wrong with your finances," I mumbled and tried to watch her reaction. "Maranda sent Cleveland an email about it. So did Amber."

"A talking bear? You're not making any sense. Why don't you rest, dear? I'll be back later to check on you."

"I need to go." I told my brain to tell my body to move, but everything south of my neck had shut down. The water bottle slipped from my hand and rolled to the floor.

"Do you want my help?" Cooke asked. "Does your head still hurt?"

"I'm not sure," I mumbled. "I'm really tired."

"Here, dear. Let me help you." Cooke shook out a handful of pills, dropped them into my slack mouth, and poured water after them.

I moved the pills around with my tongue, shoving them into my cheeks. Water ran from my lips and dribbled over my chin.

Cooke massaged my neck with her scarf and wiped my face. "This will make you feel better. I promise."

"Just lie down." She pulled on my legs and my body slid, collapsing on the cot. Through slitted eyes, I watched her dust her hands and don her dark trench coat. One that when she turned, blew out behind her. Like a cape.

Dammit. The expletive cut through my drowsy thoughts as I tried to spit out the pills that were not Advil. Cooke made a good phantom. And an even better killer.

My tongue searched for the last pill, and I rolled it to the edge of my lips where it fell off my chin. Luke was going to kill me for coming back to the school, I thought, edging toward sleep.

If I weren't already dead first.

THIRTY-TWO

I woke to cramped muscles, a throbbing head, and a god-awful taste in my mouth. Whatever I lay on felt like a cold slab. In a dark room. One alarming thought, quicker than its sluggish cohorts, feared I had landed in a tomb.

Or, said a brighter thought, the cot in the Peerless book room.

My dim mind sorted through the last events. Panic over my missed police visit and Cody's kidnapping pushed my heart into my throat and cleared my head. How long had I slept? I held up my watch arm, bare as usual. Couldn't see in the dark anyway. I stretched my other limbs, checking my mobility. Tinsley's keys rubbed against my thigh.

She hadn't searched my pockets.

Maybe Cooke wasn't as wicked as I thought. Maybe she was just a very bad dispenser of medicines. What the hell had she given me? Fear washed out the remaining grogginess. And what about Tinsley? Was he still in the school or had he turned himself into the police?

Were we the next suicides? One victim of scandal and one broken heart?

Slinking off the cot, I stumbled forward in the dark, slammed into a desk, and found the door.

The handle wouldn't turn.

I felt along the wall, seeking the switch, and shut on the lights. I blinked as the fluorescent bulbs twitched, then flared overhead, illuminating the book room. I prayed the lock worked both ways, fumbled on the ring for the master key, and jammed it into the lock. The handle turned.

The darkened hall did not bode as a good sign. I shivered in the stillness, my thoughts flitting to *Twilight Zone* plots. Maybe it was the end of days and I had gotten my just desserts. Left in a school forever. My personal ring of hell.

Fear for Tinsley led me deeper into the school rather than toward escape. I headed toward the front lobby rotunda and its spoked hallways. The office or a hall? I hesitated, then chose the arts hall. I bounded forward with Tinsley's pocketed keys rubbing against my groin and my flannel shirt slapping my thighs. At the end of the passage, the double doors of the drama wing loomed like a shot from a horror movie. My chest heaved as I lurched toward the growing doors. Slamming to a stop, I yanked on the levers.

Unlocked. Which made me pause, but I hauled open a door anyway. Running through the bean bag strewn vestibule, I tried Tinsley's office first. Unlocked and empty.

"I don't like this," I said to Tinsley's mirror.

I spun out of his office and tried the stage door. Also unlocked. I stumbled up the steps, almost collided with the props table, and fell onto the wooden floor. My eyes began to adjust to the soft glow of the ghost light left on the stage. Hopping up, I felt along the table, letting my fingers bump along until they recognized a hammer someone had forgotten to put away. I smacked the metal head into the palm of my hand, then shook the ouch off my palm. Creeping forward, I pushed through the dark curtains. The caged ghost light cast an eerie glow on the stage. Darkness shrouded the theater.

I expected to find Tinsley left in some kind of macabre hara-kiri scene. Instead I found my turquoise backdrop raised and covered in graffiti. Well drawn graffiti, but graffiti nevertheless. A lanky boy of about eighteen tossed his can of spray paint to the stage floor and held up his hands. His frightened eyes cut my exclamation short. I realized I held a hammer above my bandaged head, like some wild stalker from a slasher movie.

"Who are you?" I said, then eyed the backdrop that featured a spray portrait trinity of Dr. Vail, Amber Tipton, and Maranda Pringle. He had written "R.I.P. Peerless" above their heads and "Rage, rage against the dying light" beneath. Reminiscent of the PeerNotes messages quoting *Evita* and *Romeo and Juliet*. Was this the phantom texter and not Cooke? I couldn't seem to hold a fixed idea in my brain. As soon as I thought I knew the culprit, the facts slipped from my fingers. But then why had Cooke drugged me? My perspective was skewed. Was the phantom and the killer not one in the same? Fear and frustration edged me toward anger.

"You are Preston King," I amended. "The art genius."

He bobbed his head, edging backward.

"Preston," I said, swinging my hammer. "Did you publish all those announcements on PeerNotes? The ones about Tinsley and Amber Tipton's death?"

His eyes on the hammer, he nodded and bumped into the director's table.

"Why?" I stalked toward him.

"I don't know," he said. "I thought it was funny?"

"Funny?" My voice rose. "You thought it was funny to harass the staff? That kind of funny is illegal. It's called cyber stalking. And this kind of funny is illegal, too." I pointed at the backdrop. "It's called vandalism."

"Dude, you don't know what it's like to go to this school." He pushed his hand through his sandy brown hair. "Dr. Vail was the only teacher who stood up for me."

"I don't know what it's like to go to this school." I slapped the hammer into the palm of my hand. "But I know what it's like to not fit in. That's a bullshit reason to scare adults."

"I wasn't trying to scare anybody. I'm just sick of all the fuss over *Romeo and Juliet* when the focus should be on real people." He had the effrontery to tear up. "Real people dying, like Dr. Vail. And I didn't like her, but nobody seemed to care about Miss Pringle. And Ellis." His voice broke and tears spilled over his cheeks. "The theater geeks' jealousy killed Ellis."

I pushed on, ignoring his tears. "What about the photos you took of Tinsley? That proves you're stalking him."

Preston wiped his face on his arm. "I was just trying to show the drama geeks what Mr. Tinsley really thinks of them. He only cares about his awards. I didn't mean it as stalking."

"You can tell that to the police, Preston. They have PeerNotes and the texting evidence. If it's not on your computer, they'll get it off the school computers."

"Everybody hacks into PeerNotes. They can't prove that. Just like they couldn't prove who was bullying Ellis." He rubbed his nose on his shoulder. "And I didn't text anybody."

"Liar. Thirteen teachers received anonymous texts." My words slowed. The PeerNotes announcements started last week with the outset of *Romeo and Juliet*. The anonymous texting began two weeks before Maranda Pringle's suicide, but none after her death. That I knew of. I eyed him. "You didn't send text messages to Pringle or Tinsley? Or Vail?"

Of course he wouldn't text Vail. She was Preston's champion. I had been examining the anonymous messaging all wrong.

"I'll be damned," I spoke to myself. "The texting is completely different than what's going on in PeerNotes. Two different cases of cyberbullying."

"Dude, I wasn't cyberbullying," Preston whined. "I meant it like art as social protest."

"Save your contemporary art thesis for college." I narrowed my eyes. "Did you sell Miss Pringle some ADHD meds?"

"No, dude. I would never sell to an adult. Besides, the school nurse has a cabinet full of that stuff. We have to keep our medications in there. Why would Miss Pringle buy it if she could easily take some?"

Or an administrator could easily steal some. "Are you alone? Is anyone else in the school?"

He shook his head. "They were on lockdown all day. Closed the campus as soon as school got out. Everyone cleared out quickly. I think most of the teachers were going to Miss Pringle's funeral."

"What time is it?"

"Around seven o'clock." He gave me a look that bespoke of crazy. "What are you doing here?"

"I was sleeping." I paused. "The funeral was at four. You need to get out of here and explain to the police what you have done."

I held up my hand to silence his protest. "Believe me, you'll be in much bigger trouble if you don't. They want whoever sent those texts. Those texts are what triggered the murders."

"Murders?"

"My gut was right. Pringle didn't kill herself. The texts were sent to make Pringle's murder look like suicide." Fear sluiced through me. "Preston, you need to get out of here now."

I didn't want to freak him out, but I had a feeling we weren't alone. Cooke would have attended the funeral, but after the falderal and casseroles, she'd come back for me. After the school had emptied.

Which was right about now.

THIRTY-THREE

Tinsley's keys didn't include disarming the security system to the theater's outside door. I kept my curses mental and my optimism visible. Surely somebody must have figured out I was missing. And would make the conclusion I had never left the school. Except they didn't know I had gone to school. And were too busy dealing with Cody's kidnapping attempt. I was going to kill that kid.

"How'd you get in here, anyway?" I asked Preston.

"I had a friend let me in before school got out. I hid until everyone left."

Damn. "Let's try the front doors," I replied with a smile I didn't feel. We maneuvered through the back stage maze to the arts hall. "You got a phone on you, by the way?"

"No." Preston focused his scowl on his Nikes. "My dad took it when I got in trouble for selling the shrooms. Where's your phone?"

"Mine is evidence from a crime scene." My face warmed.

Preston and I were a good match.

The front doors were also locked. Once again, the lights on the nearby security pad mocked us. Frustrated, I smacked the butt of the hammer into my palm, then held back a whimper.

"Since you hacked into PeerNotes, can you hack a security system?"

"Are you kidding me?" he gaped. "I'm not a criminal. A monkey can figure out how to send push notifications from PeerNotes."

"Let's go in the office and call somebody to let us out."

"What about the cleaning crew?" asked Preston.

"I have a feeling they were told not to come in tonight," I said, then smiled to make him feel better.

"Dude, can you stop smiling like that? You're freaking me out."

I dropped my fake smile and waved for him to follow me into the office. The front reception area appeared dark, but light glowed from the back office hall.

The location of Cooke's room.

My mouth stretched into that odd, nervy smile before I could stop it. I now freaked myself out. I used Tinsley's keys to unlock the glass doors and led Preston into the office. He leaned over the counter to grab the phone. While he left a message for his parents, I honed in on a soft jangle of metal coming from the back. My hand snatched the receiver from Preston. With a finger to my lips, I set the receiver back on the phone, then grabbed Preston and drug him below the counter.

A moment later, we fixed our attention on the scrape of the back door opening. Preston's eyes had rounded within their sockets. I leaned into his ear.

"Quick, before that person turns the corner and sees you, get out of the office and find some place to hide. I'm going to try the police. They can override the security system and let us out."

"Who's here?" asked Preston.

"I don't know, but don't trust anybody. Particularly Principal Cooke." I gave him a shove. "Just go."

Preston sped toward the glass doors and slipped out. I watched him shoot toward the arts hall. Behind me, I could hear the padding of feet on carpet and the shifting of a door. I crawled to the end of the counter and peeked around. A wall blocked my view to the back area, although I could see the edge of a door open in the hallway. Cooke's office door.

The door swung shut. I spun around and slammed my back against the high counter wall, the hammer still clenched in my hand. Squeezing my eyes shut, I listened to the footsteps tread into the front office, then stop.

I held my breath. The footsteps receded. I waited for the soft scrape of the back door opening, before peeking around the corner of the counter again. I couldn't let Cooke roam the school. I hated to think what she would do if she found Preston. And me missing from my book room slumber. And where was Tinsley?

I darted into the main office area, weighing losing sight of Cooke over taking the time to call the police. As I turned the corner to the back hall, the shrill ring of a phone jerked me to a stop. My heart pounded in my throat. I waited, gripping the hammer. The phone continued its clamor. Through the glass of the back office door, a dim shadow moved in the faint glow of the hall security lights. I dove left into the closest room and left the door cracked.

Then realized I had just hid myself in Cooke's office.

On the wall below the desk, the fuzzy arc of a small nightlight illuminated the basic contents of the room. The water bottle she had left Tinsley still sat on the desk. But no Tinsley. However, an IBM Business Phone blinked and buzzed, alerting the school stalker that the outside world needed attention.

I slipped behind the desk, too frazzled by the phone's obnoxious jangle to listen for any sound from the admin area.

Mid-ring the phone quit, the silence causing an echo ring between my ears. I took a deep breath, sinking to a squat on the floor between the desk and the wall. My ears picked up a muffled banging. Had Preston been caught?

I shot up from my squat, tuning my ears to the faint sounds, and reached for the phone on Cooke's desk. The distinctive snick of a closing door came from the reception area. I stilled, the receiver in one hand and my fingers dangling over the keypad. While I strained to hear footsteps, my digits danced a quick staccato over the emergency numbers. I slid to the floor, pulling the phone to the edge of the desk.

My short pants deafened the rustling in the front office. I clenched my jaw, forcing my breathing to slow. A muffled voice resonated from the phone. I couldn't risk a whisper. I had excellent hearing, but so could Cooke. A drawer scraped against its runners.

My right hand clenched the hammer. My left clamped the receiver against my belly, and I squeezed against the desk, peering around its side.

The crack in the door stood no bigger than a finger. I focused all my attention on that cool gray void. My thoughts flickered from Tinsley, to Cody and Shawna, and back to Preston, hiding somewhere in the school.

I had to stop Cooke. Fear was not an option.

The stirring of feet on carpet began again. Hurried tromping replaced the soft steps.

My belly vibrated from the voice's resonance on the phone. I pushed the receiver harder into my stomach, hoping the dispatcher would note the school's number and guess something was amiss. The glow in the doorway seemed to vibrate. I tensed, pushing onto the balls of my feet, and tightened my grip on the hammer.

The gray light winked out. Then reappeared.

Someone had passed by the office. I waited, counting off seconds. The dispatcher on the phone had stopped calling out, and I released the receiver, letting the cord dangle over the edge of the desk. Hopping from my crouch, I tiptoed to the door and widened the crack. After a pause, I opened the door and peeked out. To my right, was the corner of the wall leading to the front administration area. To my left, the back office door banged shut.

I closed Cooke's door behind me and ran for the back exit. Cracking the door, I heard the efficient Ms. Cooke marching down the corridor, her sneakers squeaking on the tile floor. She headed toward the book room, where she would find me missing. I danced, deliberating my next plan of action.

A shrill siren cut on, then stopped.

I whirled back inside the offices, wondering if Preston had tried to monkey with the security. A door banged and sneakers squeaked on tile. I flew down the rear office passage, rounded the bend into the main administration space, and dove beneath Amber's desk. Behind me, the back door opened and slammed shut. Peering out from under the desk, I watched Cooke hustle through the space toward the glass front doors. She had traded her pumps for sneakers, but had left on the blue pant suit. Her scarf fluttered behind her, marking the long strides of someone used to making quick trips through the large school.

As she rounded the counter, I crawled out from beneath the desk, clutching the hammer. If Preston had tried to leave, I needed to protect him. Keeping low, I squat-ran toward the counter, then peered around the side. Cooke had darted out the glass doors and crossed the half-moon foyer toward the front doors' security panel. I slipped into the reception area, pushed open the entrance, and saw Cooke zip down the arts hall. Her shoes squawked and scarf blew behind her.

She must have seen Preston. Had he tried the front doors and gotten caught? My heart battered my rib cage. I bolted across the foyer on my toes to keep my boot heels from echoing Cooke's squeak with a clack. Like everyone else, Cooke proved a better runner than me. She made quick work of the hall and popped through the theater doors before I had reached the art wing. I cursed my short legs and lack of lung capacity and hustled after her.

If she got an eyeball of Preston's art work, there's no telling what she'd do to that kid.

I swung through the theater doors and hesitated in the green beanbag lobby, eyeballing the closed doors before me. Would Preston hide somewhere in the backstage hall, on the stage, or in Tinsley's office? I took a chance on the stage, stole through the door, and up into the dim backstage. I hesitated on the top step, listening for Cooke and Preston. Stillness reigned.

Clutching my hammer, I moved forward, peering into the dim ghost lighting. And caught my hip on the props table. The table shuddered. As I reached to steady it, the collapsible leg slid center. Props clattered to the floor, hammering the wooden stage. Romeo's scuba tank rolled and struck the metal costume stand with another raucous clang.

I rubbed my hip, mentally cussed the weak table and Tinsley for using it, and waited for Cooke to show.

THIRTY-FOUR

Once the clamor had quieted, I moved in mouse-like jerks toward front stage, whispering Preston's name. I sidled up to the ghost light, hoping if he hid in the balcony or auditorium seats he'd spot me. A rustling of the heavy stage curtains sent me spinning toward stage left.

Cooke strode out from between the curtains. "What are you doing here? Put down that hammer." She glanced up at the backdrop and placed her hands on her hips, making me feel all of fifteen and caught in the art room after hours once again. "Did you do that to the backdrop? It's very inappropriate. That quote is not even Shakespeare. And definitely not from *Romeo and Juliet*."

"Of course I didn't vandalize my own work." I raised my hammer, shifting my stance. "I've been looking for you. I've called the police. It's time to turn yourself in."

"Turn myself in for what?" She dropped her hands and took a step closer. "You're the one trespassing on school property."

"I don't consider getting drugged and waking in a supply room trespassing." I glanced into the dark theater, wondering if Preston was still out there. Hopefully, he'd bolt. "You just didn't get your chance to get rid of my body like you did everyone else who found out about your embezzlement scheme. You've been dipping into school funds, haven't you? Probably for years, but finally been caught. Must be hard to be surrounded by the wealthy on a principal's salary. But you must have stolen a fat lot to need to cover with murder."

"Don't be ridiculous," she said. "Mr. Tinsley embezzled, not me. You and he are the ones in trouble. You were found on scene at Dr. Vail's house. You came to the school today to force Mr. Tinsley into his confession. I feared what you would do to me, so I just gave you a sedative to calm you down."

"Bullshit. You drugged me." My arm began to throb, but I stiffened it, keeping the hammer aloft. "And how would you know I was found at Dr. Vail's house?"

"You told me about your concussion, remember? You just woke from sedation and are mixed up. Now set down that hammer. You're scaring me."

"Where's Tinsley?" I did feel confused. And exhausted from all the skulking and running. Cooke didn't sound crazy. Her voice had that reasonable, coaxing tone used by nurses when they were explaining why you needed a shot. She gave me the heebies.

"Tinsley disappeared after you laid down for your nap. Tara said he left the school. I just came back to check on everything." She held up a hand. "The security panel said someone entered from the outside theater door. We're not safe. It could be Tinsley."

"I'm holding you here until the police arrive." But I doubted my words. My hands felt sweaty and dry. My arm drooped. I tried to raise it again, but my muscles felt like they were on fire. I needed a better plan than standing with a hammer raised over my head.

"You're confused. You're making assumptions again without knowing all the evidence. You've done it before."

She was right. I did it all the time. I frowned.

"We need to be careful." Cooke's voice hushed. "Tinsley may be hiding in the school."

"No way." Cooke had thought someone entered, but it may have been Preston exiting. The dumping of adrenaline left my thoughts cloudy. "Why would Tinsley confess his bribing scandal if he wanted to return to the school and attack us? And why make his own texts so damning if he's the culprit?"

"All the anonymous texts were damning," said Cooke. "It would throw off the police if his texts were, too."

"And who killed Vail? And Amber?"

"I don't know about Amber. Maybe it was just a robbery." Cooke shrugged, sliding her hands into her pockets. "But you're the one who saw Tinsley's cape. Camille knew he had stolen all that money. She spent her time off last week researching the accounts to prove it. Called me on Sunday to report it. Tinsley was always a Nervous Nelly. He suspected she knew and killed her."

"And Pringle?"

"Suicide." Cooke shook her blonde bob. "So sad those texts about Dan Madsen pushed her over the edge. If Tinsley is the culprit, they should add stalking charges to murder."

Her lies sounded so convincing. I pondered her theory for a moment and slowly moved toward her. "And why did you keep me in here?"

"I didn't keep you. I thought you needed a rest and you would leave when your nap finished."

"You have a reasonable explanation for everything, don't you?" I switched my hammer to my left hand and lowered my right, shaking the blood back into my fingers.

"What are you going to do?" Cooke's eyes remained on the hammer. "I thought we were waiting for the police."

"I don't trust you." I switched the hammer back to my right.

"I don't trust you either." Cooke pulled her hands from her pockets and took two long steps toward me.

Then shot me with a taser.

During the longest five seconds of my life, I felt unaware of anything but pain. My muscles fought the charge, seizing and snapping like pit bulls in a cage match.

I screamed like a girl, but couldn't muster the ability to stop myself from that humiliation. The pain cut off and I found myself panting on the floor of the stage, staring up at Cooke. She leaned over me, each knee planted on either side of my body, busily wrapping her scarf around my neck.

"Oh, hell no," I said, swinging my arm up and realizing too late I had dropped the hammer. Probably about the time my muscles seized and then turned to jelly.

Dodging my ineffectual slap, she jerked on the scarf, squeezing my neck. "Lucky for me, the school keeps a taser for emergencies. You're dangerous." Her eyes narrowed as she yanked the scarf. "This is self-defense."

I had hated those scarves for good reason.

I shoved my arms between hers, punching and slapping at her face. The silk noose tightened.

I began to gag.

Cooke grunted and her expression hardened. I grabbed at my throat, trying to curl my fingers beneath the scarf, but it wouldn't give. Cooke yanked harder. I hammered the floor with my feet and reached for her face, grappling for her eyes. Cooke twisted her head, elbowed me in the face, and pulled the scarf taut.

A door banged in the distance. I wanted to call out to Preston to run away and wait for the police, but I couldn't catch a breath to make any sound. Spots danced before my eyes and my lungs heaved. I bucked beneath her, writhing and punching, but the scarf continued to pull tighter.

Everything seemed to slow, but one thought hopped in my brain, jumping and screaming. It wanted me to give in. Which went against my nature. I had always fought, even for the pettiest and dumbest of reasons. Mostly for petty and dumb reasons.

But, said the thought, if Preston thinks it's too late to help you, he can still get away.

I collapsed beneath Cooke. My lungs and throat burned, worse than the short-lived taser pain. Cooke's grip on the scarf lessened, and I now fought my body not to gasp. I couldn't see for my eyes had rolled somewhere north, but heard very male shouting and Cooke's firm rebuttal.

I would have liked to yell at Preston to run. However, my body was too interested in oxygen to focus. The scarf still bound my neck, but Cooke's grip had relaxed. My swollen throat worked teeny gasps into my fiery lungs. Air trickled through and my head began to deflate.

I should probably thank Preston for that accomplishment. But I still wanted him to get.

As the oxygen began to replenish my starving body, I became more aware of the scuffle above me. The intruder pushed Cooke away and worked his fingers into the knot on my neck. As I filled my lungs, a body slammed on top of me, whooshing the air out like a fat kid on a leaky beach ball. The body had planked but rippling spasms coursed through the dead weight.

My rescuer had been tased. And felt too large to be Preston.

The spasms cut off and the body relaxed. I lifted my head and saw familiar dark curls spilling across my chest. Not Preston. Somehow, my Romeo had found me. Found me laid out near dead. And now his dead weight lay over me. Which felt horribly fitting for our stage setting.

Luke and Cherry, Act five, Scene three.

I lifted my head and tried to push Luke off. And felt my gut back up my throat as Cooke snatched the ghost light and swung the heavy, metal stand above us.

"Luke, move," I croaked and pulled my muscles tight, heaving us into a side roll.

The stand smashed into his right shoulder, missing his head. In it's metal cage, the lightbulb winked off and dimmed on. Luke cried out and rolled onto his stomach. His right arm flopped at an awkward angle.

Gasping, I scrambled to get off the floor. My eyes left Luke to search for a weapon. Where was his pistol? No gun in sight. My hammer had slid a few yards away. Cooke's Taser lay behind her. Useless.

Cooke grunted, lifting the stand with both hands. She boosted it to waist level, then adjusted her stance. The long, electric cord trailed behind her, pooling at her feet as she raised the heavy light.

"Stop." My voice wheezed.

"This is self defense," she repeated.

Diving over Luke, I scuttled toward Cooke.

"Get away from me," she screamed. She swung the ghost light above her shoulder, teetering backward before righting herself.

I reached for the cord, looped it around my hand, and yanked. Cooke's front foot lifted and back knee bent, fighting for balance. Pushing back in a squat, I jerked the cord taught. Unable to swing the clumsy weight and control her balance, Cooke stepped back, slipped, and fell. The heavy lamp crashed on top of her. Dropping the cord, I scrambled to my feet.

Amazingly, the lightbulb still remained intact. However, the ornate stand had slammed against the floor and one of its clawed feet had caught the side of her head. The wound trickled blood and Cooke appeared unconscious.

I turned away from Cooke and rushed to Luke. He lay on his stomach with his head turned, watching me. I winced at the blood soaking through the split seam near his neck and stopped him from trying to roll over. "Your shoulder looks bad," I rasped. "Stay where you are."

"Damn pain nearly knocked me out," he said. "I can't move my right arm. But how are you? Your throat? Is Cooke conscious?"

"I'll be okay. She's unconscious." I paused. "She would have bashed our heads in."

"Don't think about it. You moved fast on your feet and stopped her. My cell phone is in my pocket. Call it in. Tell them you have an officer down."

I slipped my hand in his pocket and pulled out his phone. "What about you? What can I do for you?"

"You've done enough." He tried to smile but couldn't. "My pistol's somewhere. I held it on her when she was choking you. Didn't stop her. I had to jerk her off and when I did, she friggin' tased me."

"I don't see your gun."

"Herrera should be here any minute." His eyes squeezed shut and opened. "You need to know something. My call this morning..."

"Cody." I stared at the phone.

"I had to bring him in. It took a while. And after booking him, I couldn't find you. Your family wouldn't give me the time of day, let alone your location. Herrera said you hadn't gone to the station and Sheriff Thompson hadn't seen you either. I went to Pringle's funeral and when you didn't show, I got nervous."

I looked up at the stage lights hanging above us. Adrenaline rushed from my body and a few tears squeezed out. "Good Lord, you arrested my brother."

"Cherry, I had to do it. Let's not talk about it now."

"How did you find me?" I croaked.

"At the funeral, I got a key and codes from Cleveland and spoke to Herrera about searching the school. He wanted to come with me, but wanted to speak to Dan Madsen first. The longer he took with Madsen, the more anxious I became. So, I just left. Called the school, pounded on the front doors. No one answered. Came in through the back door we used the other night."

"The theater exit."

"Yep. I searched the theater and had gone up through that windowed hallway when I heard what sounded like an elephant stampede on the stage. Knew it had to be you."

"You arrested my brother." I dropped my gaze from the lights to the floor. "Cody's confused. Something terrible's eating at him."

"He kidnapped Shawna. I don't care what's wrong with him."

"Kidnapping? That's a federal offense." Panic welled in my chest, giving me flashbacks of the choking.

"He didn't cross state lines. But he could get ten to life."

"Ten to life?" I dropped the phone to cover my mouth. I turned away from Luke. "Oh, shit."

"Sugar, I'm sorry. I was doing my job."

"It's not that." I whirled back to look at Luke. "Cooke's gone."

THIRTY-FIVE

I left Luke and my perilous emotions on the stage. After helping Luke up, I dialed 9-1-1, gave him the phone, and slipped away as he talked. I heard his shouts from the stage stairs, but didn't stop to argue, only hoped his shoulder would keep him from chasing me. I still didn't know where Preston hid, which now seemed as short-sighted as the rest of my failed detection plans. Pulling off the damnable scarf, I stumbled off the stage and into the green beanbag room. I gunned my oxygen deprived body toward the front doors.

It ticked me off that the whole sorry mess didn't have anything to do with Ellis Madsen. She had been used as a tawdry scandal to throw people off Pringle's murder as a guilty suicide. All because Cooke had been helping herself to Peerless's coffers and finally been caught by the social-misfit-cum-business-braniac Maranda Pringle. Then flagged again by the overworked Amber Tipton.

The shameful use of Ellis Madsen's death gave me renewed vigor. I had been tasked with finding the Peerless Phantom and found her.

Along with a bunch of other crap.

But it was time to put the Phantom to rights. I was not going to let her get away. I staggered down the arts hall, taking a quick detour into the fine arts wing, figuring Preston must have hid there. I hollered for Preston to go to the stage and assist Luke, then snagged a chisel from the lathe tool set.

Which wouldn't do me much good against a Smith & Wesson, if Cooke had taken Luke's gun. If only Peerless had been a military school, I could have raided their armory. Instead, I armed myself with art equipment.

I staggered from the studios and stumble-jogged toward the front doors. Outside, blue and red lights flashed. A team led by Herrera and Amelia Wells ran toward the front doors. I could hear the scream of an ambulance in the near distance. I glanced toward the office. Through the glass, I saw Cooke standing before the counter. With a hand on Preston's shoulder.

I lurched forward, chisel in hand, and slammed through the glass doors. At my approach, Cooke turned and screamed. Very effective with blood still dripping from the cut on her head.

"Get your hand off of him," I croaked, wielding the chisel.

"Dude, did you take that from the art room?" Preston blinked. "That's wicked sharp."

"I told you she's dangerous," said Cooke. "Let's go, Preston. Quickly. Out the back."

"The police are here," I said. "It's over. Let Preston go."

"Preston, to my office. We'll wait until I feel it's safe." Cooke glanced through the windowed wall. "Let us go, Miss Tucker."

"No way am I letting you take Preston to your office." I positioned myself near the end of the counter, holding the chisel before me.

Preston struggled beneath Cooke's grip. "I'll go. You two stay."

"No, she's armed," said Cooke, stepping behind Preston and pulling him toward the back wall. "Stay with me. I'll see you get home safely."

"Cherry?" called Herrera from behind the glass door. "Who's all with you?"

"Principal Cooke and a student, Preston King."

"Where's Officer Harper?"

"On the stage." Fixing my attention on Cooke's right hand, still in her suit pocket, I searched my brain for the police ten codes I had memorized in my youth. "Herrera, you've got a possible 10-32."

A person with a weapon. Or open alcohol. I always got those numbers confused, but hoped Herrera could figure it out.

"Get the hell out of the way, Cherry," yelled Herrera. "Immediately."

"The police can't shoot us through that glass, can they?" asked Preston.

"Don't be ridiculous," said Cooke. "The police aren't going to shoot us. They're here to capture Miss Tucker. Besides, that glass is fire and impact safety-rated. We buy the best products to keep you safe."

"I don't feel safe right now," mumbled Preston.

"That's because your principal is holding a gun on you," I said, gripping my chisel. "Keep cool, Preston."

"Officers," screamed Cooke. "Help me! This woman has threatened me and has a weapon. Just look at the wound on my head. And we need emergency services for the man on the stage. I thought he was going to hurt me."

"She poleaxed Luke with a lamp," I called over my shoulder.

Behind the door, I heard Herrera's rapid staccato, delivering orders to his crew.

"Cherry's dangerous," cried Cooke. "Apprehend her and I'll come out willingly. She has a concussion and has been creeping around the school. I had to tase her and she still wouldn't calm down. I fear for my life."

"Cherry, I mean it," yelled Herrera. "Get out or get down."

I moved forward, focused on Cooke. "You tried to drug me, strangle me, then bash my head in. And that doesn't even include last night's concussion."

"She's unstable," hollered Cooke, backing toward the wall and gripping Preston as a shield. "Tinsley confessed, didn't he? You have your culprit."

"Tinsley didn't hurt anyone." I stalked closer. "You sent those texts. And you murdered Maranda Pringle, Amber Tipton, and Camille Vail. Then you tried to murder me and Luke."

"Everyone calm down," called Herrera. "Stop where you are, Cherry."

"Help," cried Cooke. "She'll hurt us. That instrument is sharp."

"I'd like you to come out of the room one at a time," said Herrera. "No one's going to get hurt."

"Cherry first," said Cooke. "Then I'll go. I don't trust her."

"If you think I'm leaving you alone in here with Preston and a gun, you're crazy," I said.

"Look my hands are in the air," she said. "As soon as Cherry drops her weapon and leaves, I'll move."

I looked toward the glass door, knowing what would happen if we didn't leave this room willingly. Officers would enter the administration area through the back door, ready to take Cooke out. But she had positioned herself with enough coverage that only Preston would be in danger. Cooke was forcing my hand. She counted on me to do something. Did she think I would leave or stay?

Oh dear Lord, I thought. What do I do? Would she really come out peaceably? Or would she use Preston as a human shield? She must know of the evidence mounted against her now. Evidence she couldn't get rid of before the police arrived. Namely me and Luke.

I had my decision.

"Exit now, ladies," called Herrera, "Or we're coming in with our guns drawn to arrest you both for resisting."

"Let's go, Cherry." Cooke lowered her hands to her pockets and smiled at me. A winning smile. The smile of someone who had her story figured out, even on the fly. Who had years of counseling experience to learn how to manipulate people and the system.

Which pissed me off.

Warning bells sounded in my head, screaming at me to check my idiocy, but I couldn't stop myself. I dove at Preston, knocking him to the floor. My tackle left Cooke gripping the gun.

Pointed at my head.

But my body covered Preston's, and I felt good about that.

THIRTY-SIX

A moment later, Cooke realized a half-dozen weapons had been aimed at her from several different directions. I scooted Preston and I in a sandwiched, reverse army man crawl until I felt safe. Popping up, I pulled on Preston's trembling hands, until he had climbed to his size thirteen feet.

"Dude." His voice shook and his face had paled. "How are you not freaking out?"

"This is why I get paid the big bucks." I faked a smile for show. "Although Tinsley's checks will most likely bounce. However, I am ready-made for emergencies. I don't know why. Something's wrong with the safety part of my brain, I suppose. I am better at action than thinking."

"Which means you're an idiot," said Herrera. "And you just proved it."

"That is true," I agreed. "But you have apprehended your perp. 'All's well that ends well.'"

"You're coming to the station. You've caused me a shitload of paperwork." Herrera glared at me, then pushed us back to allow his officers to walk the handcuffed Cooke to a squad car. "And you just took about ten years off of my life."

"I know you want me at the station, but I need to check on Luke. And find out about my brother. He was arrested today. By Luke."

Herrera gritted his teeth and shook his head. "I'll cuff you now, if that's what it takes. Officer Harper is on his way to the hospital in an ambulance with a broken collarbone. He followed you down the hall. My officers had to hold him back to keep Harper from apprehending you himself."

My eyes rounded and fire licked my cheeks. "He saw me corner Cooke and tackle Preston?"

"And nearly get your head blown off with his own piece? That he did." Herrera fished out his handcuffs. "Put your hands together. Or I'll cuff them in the back."

"Really?" My voice shook. "You're arresting me?"

"I told you to get out of this room. You resisted my orders and obstructed Cooke's arrest."

"Damn," said Preston. "That's harsh."

"You're coming, too," Herrera said to Preston. "Trespassing and destruction of property."

"Dude," said Preston.

"Dude," I agreed. "That's harsh."

After my forced visit to Line Creek Police Department, I decided I missed Tamara's ferocity. At my familiar law enforcement establishment, my idiocy was only implied and not called out as an introduction. And where my friendly Sheriff's Office deputies often threatened obstruction, it turns out Line Creek doesn't joke around.

They really needed to lighten up.

Figuring my family had enough jail visits for one long day, I made my bail call to Max. I felt surprised when he posted in person the next morning. I guess it took the hope of seeing me in an orange jumpsuit to finally get him out of the house.

"Suspicion of obstruction, Artist?" The Bear hustled surprisingly well on crutches. I guessed he wasn't overly fond of police stations. "I had hoped to post bail for something more exciting."

"Herrera's just ticked that instead of one of his officers, I saved Preston," I said with more confidence than I felt. "I'm pretty sure they'll drop the charges."

"You're assumptions are always enlightening, Artist." Max paused to let me push open the outside doors. "You'll still owe me for the bail. But we'll talk about that at another time."

That statement distracted me from the further humiliation of walking out Line Creek Police Department's front doors and into the chilly morning sunshine. Talk about a walk of shame. The sight of Max's sporty Maserati didn't even cheer me up. With two arrests in one day, Cody and I had just shoved the Tucker name into white trash territory. As soon as the biddies got an eyeful of the *Halo Herald*'s local arrests column, our name equaled sheep dip. I'd have to convince Dot at the *Herald* to write an exclusive on my takedown of Assistant Principal Cooke to give my arrest a more positive spin.

Which would also make me look as trashy as a celebrity selling her baby's pictures to a tabloid.

We kept our thoughts quiet on the ride home. Mine on saving face for Grandpa. I imagined Max focused on how to squeeze blood out of a Cherry Tucker turnip. But after parking the electric blue Granturismo, Max cut the engine off and spoke his mind.

"As no one else is likely to say this, I congratulate you on finding your phantom."

"Thanks." I toyed with the seatbelt. "My successes always seem to be outweighed by my failures."

"You have failed because you prevented an innocent man from a homicide investigation? From saving a child in the hostage crisis? For proving a woman did not take her own life? And exposing the culprit who stole three innocent lives in order to cover her embezzlement?"

I unclicked my belt and straightened in my seat. "Thank you, Bear."

"You are most welcome." He grinned using his teeth. "I'm glad to hear your gratitude."

"Wait a minute." I reevaluated his tone. "Gratitude for what?"

"My success in the investigation. For uncovering the financial fraud. It was through my efforts you have caught Cooke." He leaned a large hand on my leather seat back. "Perhaps I should claim Tinsley's check as service."

"My ass."

I raised my chin and continued. "I got you that info. You thought the phantom was an anarchist when Cooke is the extreme opposite. A puppeteer control freak buying Louis Vuitton purses and Gucci scarves to use as mortal weapons. She loved the power of orchestrating the future careers of talented students. You could see it on her face when she talked about *her* famous alumni. Maybe she thought it would pay off someday, I don't know. But I think Cooke liked wielding authority over rich parents who want their child to become the next Disney star or whatever. She also liked controlling the faculty, pitting popular teachers, like Tinsley and Vail, against each other to keep herself at the top of the pyramid."

"Feel better? Guilt does not become you as much as umbrage." He laughed at my scowl. "What of the real principal?"

"Cleveland was only a figurehead. He just signed off on whatever Cooke told him. The danger happened when Pringle noticed. Remember that email where Cleveland asked Pringle to send the first quarter statements to Cooke? Pringle flagged the questionable accounts and sent them back to Cleveland. Those are the same emails Amber saw. Pringle didn't seem the type to rat, but she had Cleveland wrapped around her finger. I bet Cooke worried Pringle might blackmail her, or at least spell it out for Cleveland and let him deal with the embezzlement accusations."

"The art teacher, too?"

"Vail seemed pretty vindictive. She would have turned Cooke in just to upset the imbalance towards Tinsley." I shook my head. "Peerless had a lot of money pouring in and Cooke managed everything herself."

I pointed at the Bear. "You might have seen the discrepancies in their accounting, but I knew Pringle wasn't the type to commit suicide. Or Vail."

"All right. It is your win. Now, what about Tinsley? Will he continue in the theater?"

"While I was knocked out, Tinsley had turned himself in to the police. Although Cooke convinced him to confess to cover her own embezzlement, he did fudge his own accounts. And try to bribe a Tiny Tony judge. But Tinsley does win a lot of awards for Peerless. I guess Cleveland will decide if Tinsley can keep his job." I folded my arms. "I hope Cleveland can pull Peerless back on track. The parents will be scary angry."

"I imagine they will want the social media shut down again."

"Probably. Although that cat left the bag years ago." I sighed. "Kids are inventive. Cooke stole the anonymous texting idea from the students. They did it to Ellis Madsen the year before. Cooke just wanted the appearance of social bullying against the staff so Pringle's fake suicide would have a motive. That's why the texts stopped after Pringle died. There are too many ways and means to spread information. That's why I got the PeerNotes finger-pointing and texting rumors confused. Herrera firmly believes parents need to police their kids more. Schools can't be held responsible. Unless, of course, you have a sociopath running the institution."

"Maybe more brilliantly desperate than sociopathic," said Max. "And you? Do you have closure on this successful fiasco?"

I stole a look at my hands. "Have you heard how Luke Harper is doing?"

"One would think a bail call wouldn't include demanding her benefactor to visit police in hospital, but as you faced spending the night in jail, I gave in to your request. It appears your policeman will need surgery to fix some screw or the rod for healing of clavicle."

"That sounds terrible. Did you see anybody with him at the hospital?" I crossed my fingers for luck.

"His mother. And the bouncy blonde girl."

"Tara Mayfield. She'll drive him crazy." I sighed. "Or he'll realize girls like Tara Mayfield don't get his collarbone broken."

Max rolled his eyes.

"Collarbones heal. What kind of man should worry about injury when love is at stake? If he prefers the Tara Mayfield, he wants the boring life. And the boring life is not for you," Max said.

Maybe I should stick with Todd who craved an unboring life, I thought. I could guarantee him one.

I avoided the Bear's piercing winter stare by turning toward the view of my house. Casey's Firebird sat behind Todd's Civic. Pearl's Lariat had been parked in the grass. "I guess I should face the family inquisition. Bad enough I missed Cody's arraignment for the making of my own."

Max touched my arm. "Your brother pled innocent. He claims Shawna Branson went with him willingly, although they did argue in the Tru-Buy store parking lot. He wanted Shawna to have the DNA test. He offered some old family photos as an incentive for her to accompany him in his car."

I turned back to Max. "That's just wonderful. Cody's pleading blackmail instead of kidnapping? With photos he had originally stolen from Shawna. To prove that they're related? That idiot."

"He had the DNA kit in his car. It is evidence now, but if the results of the test can be relinquished, I would advise you to use this information to your advantage."

"You want me to steal evidence from the county Sheriff's Office to blackmail Shawna myself?" I picked up my jaw and thrust it forward. "Are you out of your ever-loving mind?"

"She would likely drop kidnapping charges. Charges that would give your brother a minimum ten year sentence."

"I just got out of the pokey myself, remember?" I opened the car door. The engine of an approaching vehicle caused me to glance down the street, but I turned back to Max. "I do thank you for your help. But I'll handle this Branson mess myself. Without any additional crimes to add to our count."

He gave me the two finger salute. "As you wish, Artist."

On the curb, I waited for his V8 engine to power the Maserati back to Max's less than humble abode. Then awaited the approach of the V8 of a jacked-up, Ford Raptor pickup.

Like the men driving them, similar engines but completely different vehicles.

At the Raptor's stop, I strolled around the grill to Luke's open window. "I thought you were having surgery?"

"Not yet." He popped his door, kicked it open, and stepped off the running board. His right arm lay in a sling. New lines and creases marred his chiseled features. He looked battle worn, but I feared I looked worse. "Come here, sugar."

I stepped into the space between his door and laid my head against his good shoulder. Luke pulled me tighter, and I drew in a long breath of the woodsy, pheromone-racing Eau de Luke before looking up.

"I guess things are worse between our families now," I said. "What with you arresting my brother."

"And your brother trying to kidnap my step-cousin." His voice told me he felt more regret than irritation. "And you trying to take out a woman holding my gun."

"I didn't try to take Cooke out, just the kid she was using as a shield." I circled an arm around his waist and rubbed my chin against the soft cloth of his t-shirt, wishing I could invite him into my home.

"It's always something with you." Luke kissed the top of my head, and rested his chin on the kiss. "Herrera could've handled it."

"I couldn't take that chance. I've heard enough stories about hostage situations gone bad. I saw the opportunity and took it."

"What are we going to do?" Sorrow pitched his baritone toward a tune I didn't want to hear. "We can't see each other unless we want to cause an all-out feud, which I can't imagine going well for your family. Folks around here will side up pretty quickly against y'all."

"I'm going to find a solution to the Tucker-Branson problem," I said, thinking of Max's advice. "And one that doesn't involve felonies. After that, I guess we'll see where our road takes us."

"I hope it takes us home."

I looked up into the cool gray eyes, wondering if he marked his words with longing or for longevity.

"I hope so, too."

READER'S DISCUSSION GUIDE

1. How do you feel about the increase in social media options? Do you think it's caused an increase in bullying? Have you ever seen cases of social bullying with adults?

2. How do you feel about Cherry getting back together with Luke? Who would you choose for Cherry?

3. What do you think about Cherry's relationship with Max? How do they compliment each other?

4. Were you surprised at the revelations about Cherry's mother? Where do you think that story line will lead?

5. Have you ever dealt with extreme office or departmental politics as seen at Peerless Day Academy? Did they involve people spreading rumors? How did you handle it or what do you wish you had done differently?

6. Were you ever in a high school play? What were your favorite memories?

7. Who's the zaniest character you've ever known? How about a drama queen or king? What's the funniest thing they got upset about?

8. What was your favorite scene from *Death in Perspective*? Who's your favorite character? Which character do you relate to the most?

9. How do you think Cody's arrest will effect the longer family story arc? What do you imagine will happen between Cherry and Shawna?

LARISSA REINHART

After teaching in the US and Japan, Larissa enjoys writing, particularly sassy female characters with a penchant for trouble. She lives near Atlanta with her family and Cairn Terrier, Biscuit. Visit her website or find her chatting on Facebook. *Death in Perspective* is the fourth book in the bestselling Cherry Tucker Mystery series.

PORTRAIT OF A DEAD GUY

Larissa Reinhart

A Cherry Tucker Mystery (#1)

In Halo, Georgia, folks know Cherry Tucker as big in mouth, small in stature, and able to sketch a portrait faster than buck-shot rips from a ten gauge -- but commissions are scarce. So when the well-heeled Branson family wants to memorialize their murdered son in a coffin portrait, Cherry scrambles to win their patronage from her small town rival.

As the clock ticks toward the deadline, Cherry faces more trouble than just a controversial subject. Between ex-boyfriends, her flaky family, an illegal gambling ring, and outwitting a killer on a spree, Cherry finds herself painted into a corner she'll be lucky to survive.

STILL LIFE IN BRUNSWICK STEW

Larissa Reinhart

A Cherry Tucker Mystery (#2)

Cherry Tucker's in a stew. Art commissions dried up after her nemesis became president of the County Arts Council. Desperate and broke, Cherry and her friend, Eloise, spend a sultry summer weekend hawking their art at the Sidewinder Annual Brunswick Stew Cook-Off. When a bad case of food poisoning breaks out and Eloise dies, the police brush off her death as accidental.

However, Cherry suspects someone spiked the stew and killed her friend. As Cherry calls on cook-off competitors, bitter rivals, and crooked judges, the police get steamed while the killer prepares to cook Cherry's goose.

Available at booksellers nationwide and online

Visit www.henerypress.com for details

Be sure to check out Cherry's novella adventure QUICK SKETCH (prequel to PORTRAIT) featured in

HEARTACHE MOTEL

Terri L. Austin, Larissa Reinhart, LynDee Walker

Filled with drag queens, Rock-a-Hula cocktails, and a vibrating velveteen bed, these novellas tell the tales of three amateur sleuths who spend their holidays at Elvis's beloved home.

DINERS KEEPERS, LOSERS WEEPERS by Terri L. Austin
When Rose heads to Graceland right before Christmas, she gets all shook up: the motel is a dump and an Elvis impersonator turns up dead. Will Rose be able to find the murderer and get home by Christmas day? It's now or never.

QUICK SKETCH by Larissa Reinhart
Cherry Tucker pops into Memphis to help a friend who's been hustled out of his savings, and quickly finds herself in a dangerous sting that could send her to the slammer or mark her as a pigeon from cons looking for an even bigger score.

DATELINE MEMPHIS by LynDee Walker
A quick stop at Graceland proves news breaks in the strangest places for crime reporter Nichelle Clarke. When the King's home gets locked down with Nichelle inside, she chases this headline into the national spotlight, and right into the thief's crosshairs.

Available at booksellers nationwide and online

Visit www.henerypress.com for details

Henery Press Mystery Books

And finally, before you go...
Here are a few other mysteries
you might enjoy:

DINERS, DIVES & DEAD ENDS

Terri L. Austin

A Rose Strickland Mystery (#1)

As a struggling waitress and part-time college student, Rose Strickland's life is stalled in the slow lane. But when her close friend, Axton, disappears, Rose suddenly finds herself serving up more than hot coffee and flapjacks. Now she's hashing it out with sexy bad guys and scrambling to find clues in a race to save Axton before his time runs out.

With her anime-loving bestie, her septuagenarian boss, and a pair of IT wise men along for the ride, Rose discovers political corruption, illegal gambling, and shady corporations. She's gone from zero to sixty and quickly learns when you're speeding down the fast lane, it's easy to crash and burn.

Available at booksellers nationwide and online

Visit www.henerypress.com for details

FRONT PAGE FATALITY

LynDee Walker

A Headlines in High Heels Mystery (#1)

Crime reporter Nichelle Clarke's days can flip from macabre to comical with a beep of her police scanner. Then an ordinary accident story turns extraordinary when evidence goes missing, a prosecutor vanishes, and a sexy Mafia boss shows up with the headline tip of a lifetime.

As Nichelle gets closer to the truth, her story gets more dangerous. Armed with a notebook, a hunch, and her favorite stilettos, Nichelle races to splash these shady dealings across the front page before this deadline becomes her last.

Available at booksellers nationwide and online

Visit www.henerypress.com for details

FIT TO BE DEAD

Nancy G. West

An Aggie Mundeen Mystery (#1)

Aggie Mundeen, single and pushing forty, fears nothing but middle age. When she moves from Chicago to San Antonio, she decides she better shape up before anybody discovers she writes the column, "Stay Young with Aggie." She takes Aspects of Aging at University of the Holy Trinity and plunges into exercise at Fit and Firm.

Rusty at flirting and mechanically inept, she irritates a slew of male exercisers, then stumbles into murder. She'd like to impress the attractive detective with her sleuthing skills. But when the killer comes after her, the health club evacuates semi-clad patrons, and the detective has to stall his investigation to save Aggie's derriere.

Available July 2014

Visit www.henerypress.com for details

In the mood for something fun?

Check out this lively chick lit romp
from the Henery Press Humor Collection

THE BREAKUP DOCTOR
Phoebe Fox

The Breakup Doctor Series (#1)

Call Brook Ogden a matchmaker-in-reverse. Let others bring
people together; Brook, licensed mental health counselor, picks up
the pieces after things come apart. When her own therapy practice
collapses, she maintains perfect control: landing on her feet with a
weekly advice-to-the-lovelorn column and a successful consulting
service as the Breakup Doctor: on call to help you shape up after
you breakup.

Then her relationship suddenly crumbles and Brook finds herself
engaging in almost every bad-breakup behavior she preaches
against. And worse, she starts a rebound relationship with the most
inappropriate of men: a dangerously sexy bartender with anger-
management issues—who also happens to be a former patient.

As her increasingly out-of-control behavior lands her at rock-
bottom, Brook realizes you can't always handle a messy breakup
neatly—and that sometimes you can't pull yourself together until
you let yourself fall apart.

Available at booksellers nationwide and online

Visit www.henerypress.com for details

CPSIA information can be obtained at www.ICGtesting.com
Printed in the USA
LVOW13s0002110814

398504LV00017B/436/P